Maple Lane

MAPLE LANE

MATTHEW MCCONKEY

BROKEN TRIBE PRESS

Maple Lane, Second Edition, 2025

Copyright © 2023 by Matthew McConkey

Originally published in 2023

Book cover art and design by Jacob Arms
Interior design formatting by Anissa Cosby

This book is a work of fiction. Any references to historical events, real people, or real places are used fictitiously. Other names, characters, places and events are products of the author's imagination, and any resemblance to actual events or places or persons, living or dead, is entirely coincidental.

ISBN: 978-1-965412-30-5

Published by Broken Tribe Press
Lawrence Landing Company
Raleigh, North Carolina 27609
USA, North America

Broken Tribe Press is a proud member of:

Independent Book Publishers Association
 and
Community of Literary Magazines and Presses

www.brokentribepress.com

BROKEN TRIBE PRESS

BOOKS BY MATTHEW MCCONKEY

Home Again
Scarecrows and Shadows
Maple Lane
Everything Fades in Time
Summerland

For Daniel…thanks for the thirty-years of conversations

"The Edge. There is no honest way to explain it because the only people who really know where it is are the ones who have gone over."

Hunter S. Thompson

Chapter 1

1

Bobby sat in the funeral home alone on a front-row pew two nights after his young son was killed. His wife, Dana, was off to the side talking to some random family members he had never seen before. Were they at their wedding a long time ago? Were they cousins? Long-lost relatives? He did not know and more importantly, did not care. Bobby stared off into space thinking about how unreal this all felt; how this has got to be a dream, no, a nightmare, of some kind; stuff like this was not supposed to happen, right? Not to kids; especially to kids. Kids should be off limits from death; should be a law. No parent should ever have to bury their children. It felt like it was against nature, against the natural order of things: birth, youth, adulthood, old age, and eventually death; that was the natural order of things, or at least how they ought to be. Not birth, youth, and death.

Bobby, Dana, and Freddy were living a modest life in their modest home in a modest neighborhood. They had been living there ever since Bobby had gotten his teaching job and Dana her job as an office manager at Blue Cross/Blue Shield. Then Freddy came. Bobby's family was young and growing. For a while, Bobby and Dana were trying for another baby, maybe a girl this time, God willing. But two miscarriages later, Dana was finished. Eventually, she and Bobby decided to forget all about another baby. The mental and emotional toll had frayed her. The decision for Freddy to be the only child was not an easy one by no means, but Bobby yielded to his wife. He understood. He didn't want her to undergo any more duress. He had seen it twice and agreed with her. At the end of the day, his wife's mental state and health were more important. Besides, they still had Freddy…until they didn't.

Bobby looked up at stared up at the open casket where his ten-year-old son was lying in repose and something struck him odd, downright scary. He thought for sure that he had seen Freddy's fingers gripping the edge of the casket from the inside as if he was trying to find purchase to raise himself. Bobby's eyes grew wide, and he looked around at all the people in the funeral home to see if they saw what he had seen. They were all too in-depth in their conversations to notice anything. Bobby turned his gaze back to the casket and the fingers were no longer on the edge of the casket from the inside. Too much stress, Bobby thought to himself. Get a grip,

Bobby. Hold it together here.

Bobby leaned back on the pew and blocked the talking out of his head from the mourners that came to pay their final respects. His eyes were locked on the casket up front. After a few minutes of nothing, Bobby ran his fingers through his black and gray hair and rose to his feet. He needed some fresh air. The funeral home was beginning to feel as if it was clinging to him like a wet tee shirt. Bobby walked alongside the pew and was about to walk down the aisle when he heard a whisper cut through all the talking. It was Freddy's voice. He could never misplace his son's voice…even a whisper. Bobby stopped mid-walk and slowly turned to look behind him…to look at his son's casket.

The fingers, the four of them, exposed themselves from the inside of the casket and found purchase again on the outside edge of the coffin. Bobby stood and looked around again to see if anyone was watching what was happening. They were not. Dana, who was in the closet in proximity to their dead son, had her back turned away from Freddy's casket talking to her mom and Aunt Brandi. Bobby looked around some more hoping that someone was watching what was going on. "Daaadddyyy," Freddy's voice called in a sinister tone. Bobby's heart fell into his stomach as he watched the fingers grip tighter and then a sight to behold as his dead son sat up just like Dracula from his coffin.

Freddy, dressed in his dark blue suit, was sitting upright in the casket looking straight ahead. He slowly turned to look at his dad who was a good thirty feet away down the aisle where rows of pews flanked him to his left and right. "Daaadddyyy," Freddy's voice again called just above a whisper this time. "Cooommmeee heeerrreee." Bobby began to walk towards Freddy on legs that were not his own, somehow being pulled in that direction against his will.

Before he was aware, he was standing before Freddy who was sitting upright. Bobby frantically looked around behind him and no one saw the macabre spectacle that was going on. Bobby turned his eyes back to Freddy. He was lying back down in the casket, hands neatly folded on his lower stomach just as before. A thin boyish smile was etched on his face with red pinkish lips; ten-year-old lips. Bobby stood there trying to figure out what had just happened. His mouth had gone dry and he felt as if he was about to pass out. He needed to get out of there and get some air. He turned away from the casket and that was when Freddy's hand grabbed the sleeve of Bobby's black blazer. Bobby turned and saw Freddy sitting upright again looking at him with eyes that were wide open; eyes that were ghostly gray and still innocent as the day he died on their street. "Cooommmeee wiiittthhh meee, daaadddyyy," Freddy said in that sinister voice that was just above a whisper. "FOREVER!!" Freddy screamed.

2

Hours away from Claxton, Tennessee, in South Carolina to be exact, a sixteen-year-old kid was running for his life in the dead of night. The woods he ran through were dark and foreboding. He had no idea how he had gotten there nor how to get out. When he found himself smack dab in the middle of the woods, something inside of him told him to make a run for it—it did not matter what direction as long as he started running. The entire time he ran, he felt something behind him; something reaching for him. That voice inside his head that told him to start running was also the one that told him not to look back. Ben did as the voice instructed and did not look back.

He stumbled and fell a few times over some deadfall but managed to get back on his feet rather quickly. Ben's legs were getting tired but knowing something was chasing after him kept him going. Inside the pit of his stomach, he knew that his life probably depended on it; depended on evading whatever it was chasing him. He kept running through the trees; dodging low-hanging limbs and jumping over long-ago fallen logs trying desperately to escape whatever it was that was behind him. How did he get himself into the woods? Ben had no idea. He just opened his eyes and there he was. He did not have time to assess the situation or environment he was in. All he knew was that a faint voice had told him to start running.

Through the limbs, Ben could see something ahead of him. It looked like an old house, something that by the looks of it could have been in a horror movie. He was not afraid of it but he felt as though he should be. Seeing the house off in the distance gave the young boy a sense of direction. Scary or not, Ben knew that the house was where he needed to go…somehow. What awaited him inside was no better than what was chasing him in the woods.

The woods gave way to an open field. Across the field was the old creepy three-story house that time had forgotten. It might have been white a long time ago; maybe back when it was newly built and fresh. The moonlight cast an eerie silver glow on the home showing that the white paint had faded and chipped. The front porch looked as if it might just fall apart if anyone with any kind of weight at all would dare step on it. Across the front porch, just up the small string of dilapidated stairs, the front door of the house stood open, inviting the young, frightened traveler inside. Inside that house, there was a white glow making it look as if lights were on and people lived there.

Ben ran up the rickety front porch steps to the creepy house from the field. The steps groaned and creaked but did not fall away like he thought they might. With a hop, skip, and jump across the small front porch, he made it to the open front door. Ben dared to take a glimpse behind him. He wanted to see what was chasing him. Behind him, there was nothing but darkness and woods. No creatures of the night out there. No nothing. Ben turned his eyes towards the inside of the house where the white glow was. Feeling that the inside of the house was the last stop on this strange journey, Ben stepped through the front door cautiously and entered the home. The front door smacked angrily shut behind him. Ben jumped at the sound and screamed out with fright.

Inside the house, Ben found himself outside again in the dark but this time he was standing in a cemetery. There was a cool chill in the air as the wind swirled around him. Ben turned around to see if the front door was still there because he wanted to get out of there. When he turned around there was nothing but the darkness of the countryside. The kid turned back and saw several ghosts walking around the graveyard in ghostly white glows. They walked about the tombstones seemingly to conduct private business amongst themselves until one of them noticed Ben. It was a kid about his age, had to be. The girl walked up to Ben. He wanted to turn and run but could not manage to turn his body around and head for the hills.

"You're here for the new one, right?" she asked.

"I don't understand," Ben replied, frozen in fear by the ghostly girl.

"I think you do. He's waiting on you over there," she told him. She raised her arm slowly and pointed toward the end of the cemetery. Although he could not see that far through the darkness of night, he knew where she had pointed. Suddenly, Ben knew where he was. The tall standing angel statue with its arms wide open, welcoming those that visited, was a landmark that Ben had never forgotten. It was one of the first things that caught his eye on that terrible rainy day. He had been there before, of course he had. It was the Oak Grove Cemetery. It was a bad place not only for him, but for everyone that had to ever come there.

The ghostly girl stood pointing towards his destination. "He's waiting on you," she whispered to him. He could feel the hairs all over his body stand on end. He finally relented and walked in the direction of the end of the cemetery. The ghosts that milled about the place stopped to watch him go by; dead of years gone by keeping an eye on the living person that dared trespass on their sacred ground in the witching hour. Ben kept his eyes averted from them as he passed by. He knew where he was going.

As Ben got closer to the end of the cemetery, closer to that lone tombstone, he could hear something. At first, it was very, very faint but he could make it out nonetheless. It was a low muffled scream accompanied by a dull banging sound. Ben knew who was making that racket, those screams, and banging. He walked slowly toward the end of the cemetery with all the ghosts watching him. Ben could feel their spiritual eyes upon him, judging him. He did not dare to look over his shoulder, much like he did not dare to look over his shoulder when he was running through the woods.

The tall standing angel statue stood to his left with its stone arms open wide, hands splayed. Ben stopped, or maybe it was something that stopped him, and he looked at the angel. The screaming and the low banging sound was still audible. Ben shot a glance at the end of the cemetery where there was only one tombstone standing lonely. He knew who it belonged to. The screams and banging came from that direction. He looked back up at the angel statue and saw to his horror that it was gone off its stone pedestal. With his eyes wide and his heartbeat trip hammering inside his chest, Ben turned to look back across the graveyard. The ghosts were gone; probably back inside their graves. Ben turned his head back around and the angel statue was back on its weatherworn stone pedestal with one notable difference: blood was streaming from its eyes. The screaming and banging from the lone tombstone at the end of the graveyard had stopped.

That voice inside his head that had told him to get going out of the woods blasted loudly in his brain and told him that he needed to get the hell out of there. Ben turned and before he could get his body going, his dead father was standing in front of him, "Where you going, Benny? Want to play catch?"

Bobby Downey woke up screaming in his bed alone at approximately two forty-three a.m. He rose up in the bed, leaned against the headboard, and was breathing so hard that he thought surely he was about to pass out. Sweat dampened his body and he could feel the sheet that he was tangled up within had a thin dampness, too. Bobby closed his eyes and tried to count to ten like his years of therapist training instructed when waking from those types of nightmares. It usually worked, the counting method. By the time Bobby reached eight, his breathing was slowing down, just like he knew it would. At ten, Bobby was breathing slower, not breathing like he had just run a full-on sprint. The pills had kept Bobby awake for much of the day like he wanted; maybe needed was a better word. The pills had kept him up, kept him going for a good twenty-two hours, sometimes twenty-four hours a day. He would eventually crash out from exhaustion.

When he did crash, sometimes he dreamed nightmares so lucid that when he woke he still felt the dream on him as if he never left it. Bobby had been getting worse lately; like not being able to tell the difference between his dreams and being awake. He knew full well that he had some issues going on; mental ones that were made worse by his drinking and prescription pill abuse.

Bobby got out of bed and walked out of his bedroom and down the hall into the bathroom. There at the sink, he turned on the cold water and cupped his hands underneath, splashing it on his face three times. He looked at himself in the mirror, water dripping off. Bobby looked at the man looking back at him and he did not like what he saw. What he saw was a man that did not look like the Bobby Downey of old; not even the Bobby Downey of January of that year. Too much had happened for that… too much stress, too much everything. There were far too many cracks in the glass that was nearly about to break into a million little pieces. He knew his mind was getting worse and waited for the day that it would go full-blown certifiable crazy. "I might be closer than I think," Bobby said to the man in the mirror.

Bobby knew that he had to get a grip on things. He was trying. That was the tagline of his life recently, "he was trying". It was not easy. The easy part of life was long gone when Freddy got killed out playing in the street; the same street that Bobby could see out his bedroom window. Looking out the window at the street where Freddy was killed, he could see his son out there playing catch or basketball on the hoop that was stationed temporarily on the sidewalk of the Phelps' property. He avoided looking out that window as much as possible and had put blackout blinds and thick curtains to keep the image of a window from his eyes. What lay beyond that pane of glass was nothing but misery and pain; ghosts of a time that he wanted to forget.

He might have prevented his eyes from having to see out the bedroom window at the street where Freddy was killed, but he still had to walk out of his house; he still had to drive down that very street. Bobby found it difficult to avert his eyes at the exact place where he held his dead child in his arms that Saturday afternoon in March. No matter what Bobby did, that part of the street was always going to be there; a painful reminder of what happened; a painful reminder of what was, and what will never be.

He was trying to take his son's death day by day: one minute at a time, one day at a time, one week at a time. In the loss of his son, Bobby suffered another profound loss when he and Dana split up. That hurt, too. He dealt with the crumbling marriage which came on the heels of Freddy's death the best he knew how. Many a late night while in deep thought, Bobby wondered if he chased Dana away. It was a question he never really could answer. He knew what it was; had nothing to do with him, but everything to do with what happened to Freddy.

Dana ended up moving away a few months after that terrible day. Not long after the move, she and Bobby divorced. There were no wrong parties, no cheating spouses, none of that usual bullshit other people had. It just simply came down to neither of them could honestly deal with their son's death. They both fell apart but Bobby felt most days that Dana had given up on him. He could forgive a lot of things but giving up on him and their marriage was unforgivable. What he did not know, or chose not to acknowledge, was Dana felt the same way.

Bobby dealt with the loss of his son by staying in the house that had the memories of when Freddy was alive and still growing. He refused to abandon their home. Dana dealt with her son's death by moving far away. At a certain point in time, neither one could forgive the other for abandoning the other. Neither one of them would meet the other in the middle. Dana could not handle Freddy's memory in the house and when Bobby started drinking and abusing Ritalin, the lines were drawn, boundaries were determined, and choices were made.

4

Ben woke up screaming loud enough to wake the dead there in the safe confines of his bedroom. He was wrapped up in his sheets and tried to untangle himself from them still thinking that he was in the dream. He rolled out of bed and landed on the hardwood floor with a crashing thud, face first. With a busted nose and teeth that he just knew for sure were loosened by the fall, Ben opened his eyes and saw familiar things about him: posters on the walls of baseball players, girls half-dressed, posters of his favorite movies, Ghostbusters and The Goonies, a red Corvette on the other side of the wall across his bedroom. In the corner sat his TV and Super Nintendo. Ben got to his feet and pulled his shirt tail up to his nose to help stop the bleeding. It was another nightmare…just a nightmare. Just another nightmare was all, Ben thought to himself.

Benjamin Medlen, Ben to his friends, was at the time of Freddy's death living in Seneca, South Carolina. He, too, was in the category of Bobby Downey of "he was trying" to deal with things much too big for him. Ben's father had passed away at the age of forty-two. The death came out of nowhere and took everyone by surprise—especially Ben. The death of his dad a mere six months prior, a man that he idolized, was difficult enough, but the dreams that he had in the wake were the worst. The dreams were not garden-variety dreams of yesterday and days gone by; they were not of him and his dad playing catch in the front yard where the sun was out and no worries were around. The dreams that Ben started having after his dad passed away were nightmares; ones that caused Ben to spring up from bed in a dead sweat shaking and screaming.

Sometimes his mom would come bursting through the bedroom door to see what was going on when he woke up screaming. Those were the days when his father's death was still fresh. Ben's mom would reach out and grab her screaming son and hold him close trying her best to calm him down. After a while, it worked and the two of them would sit on his bed and talk about what had just happened. Ben would tell his mom about his dreams and try to recount them before they dissolved away like some dreams do. Those dreams that Ben had did not dissolve and fade away like most of his dreams did. The dreams about his dad hung around his neck like a noose for days before they would evaporate.

Chapter 2

1

Ben Medlen sat outside on his back porch doing much of nothing on the already hot afternoon. There had not been much to do lately since he and his mother moved from South Carolina to Claxton, Tennessee. The house that they were now living in was a relic of the past; it was his dad's childhood home that he had grown up in. Talk about ghosts of days gone by. This house had them all, his dad and grandparents. Sometimes Ben felt their presence inside that house, especially when his mom was out running errands or whatever and he was alone. Sometimes he would hear footsteps; sometimes he would hear someone talking in a far-away muffled voice in another room; twice he had heard a door open and then close. There was no doubt to Ben that the house he was now living in was haunted by the Medlens of the past.

The house, a nice two-story with an attic, sat on a corner lot surrounded by a white picket fence that screamed the American Dream was alive and well. The home and the yard were well-maintained and the envy of most in the neighborhood. Ben's father had grown up there, played there, and slept in the same bedroom where Ben now laid his head. Sometimes he could feel his father's presence in that room. Hell, most of his dad's stuff was still hanging on the walls or tucked away neatly in the closet; maybe that was the cause of the presence he felt. Ben could feel something in that house when he first moved in. It felt cold. He had been in that house many times before back when his dad was living and they would come for a visit; living there now was an entirely different feel. Ben did not tell his mom about feeling his dad's presence inside the home as soon as he walked in that first day of their new life away from South Carolina. He figured that would be too much on her at the time.

Ben and his mother, Bailey, had moved from their home in South Carolina shortly after the business was finished after Ben's father had died. With everything signed, papers processed, checks cashed, and the house sold (much to the protest of Ben) the Medlens moved away. Bailey Medlen's intent was not to move into the house where her late husband had grown up as a boy. She wanted to get away from the memory of Steve Medlen. Not because she was a terrible person, but the tangible memories of him lingering, like the house they all lived in, the car they all drove on Sunday afternoons, pierced her heart with so much pain that she could not bear it any longer. That's why she had to get away from their home and go as far away as she could. What Bailey was doing was trying desperately to run away from everything she had lost. Sometimes she wondered if Tennessee was far enough or did she need to go further, maybe out west. Those thoughts of a new life after Ben left for college flooded her mind with fear and anxiety, keeping her up most nights in those early days of the move.

She had put a deposit on an apartment on the other side of Seneca but really did not want to live there. She told Ben that the apartment was a temporary solution. The apartment across town was still too close for her. Steve had driven down those roads countless times and if she stayed in town, her mind's eye would see him; window down on a hot summer day, right hand on the wheel, and his left arm propped up on the door with his elbow pointing out. She knew that those images would be too much to see in her mind, not to mention feeling them in her broken heart.

What she needed was to get out away from their street, away from the neighborhood, away from the town, the county, the state, and even out of the region and drive as far as she could away from the memory of her late husband. Bailey was not too sure where she and her son were going to go, anywhere but there would be nice. She found a nice apartment for rent through a lady she worked with at the pharmacy. Bailey went and looked it over without Ben. Knowing that it was not her ideal place to be, being at home was no longer an option due to the mental strain she was under. She needed out. The apartment fit the bill for a change of scenery. Bailey signed the six-month lease and that was that. "Maybe in six months I can figure everything out," Bailey told herself.

When hearing of their impending move into the apartment, Stacy Topher, Steve's sister, told Bailey that their childhood home was empty and had been since mom died a few months before Steve had. Bailey was trying to get away from Steve's essence and evade all the sights and sounds that came with him because remembering hurt; hurt a lot. Moving into the home where her husband had grown up was not exactly getting a fresh start in her mind. However, it was something far away until she could figure out where to go next and plant the Medlen flag for good.

Besides, it was a free house that was just sitting there collecting dust. Bailey liked the house when she visited it to see Steve's mom and dad and it had such a pleasant feel to it. It felt like home to her. Besides, the house was not where she and Steve lived for two decades. Right then, after talking to Steve's sister, Bailey made another big decision. She called the landlord of the apartment building and asked if she could get out of the lease. She explained the situation to Mr. Cho and he tore up the lease and wished her and her son good luck.

Bailey had spoken to Ben about moving to Tennessee and staying in Grandma Medlen's house until she could figure things out. Ben was not game for it at all because he did not want to leave their home to begin with. Leaving was more for Bailey than it was anything. She could not cope with the loss and being in the same house, a museum of what was when Steve was alive, was too much for her to bear. She had to get away and if Ben did not want to, too damn bad, she concluded. He'll adapt… we'll both adapt.

Bailey had taken Stacy up on her offer last minute sitting behind the moving van and she and Ben headed to Tennessee to try to mend and put things back together as much as they could. In essence, try to put Humpty Dumpty back together again. However, it was going to be a difficult task trying to mentally and emotionally get past Steve's death, especially in the house that he had grown up in. "What's the difference," Ben asked his mom as they drove towards Tennessee. "Dad lived there, too, just like at home."

He was right. He had. There was a difference to Bailey; a huge one. She had not shared the house with him, had sex with him in that house, planted flowers in the yard with him, fought in that house with him, or just lived in that house with him. There were no memories of their marriage in that house. The Medlen home of yesteryear was a piece of Steve's history, but not of Bailey and Steve's history and that was the motivator for her taking Stacy up on her offer. Plus, moving to Tennessee put miles between her and the past.

On the drive to the Medlen home, Bailey knew that Ben was probably right when he told her that Steve had lived there, too. In her mind, she figured that she could deal with that better than dealing with living in the same town. Ben thought it was stupid and that the move would not change anything. But who was he to question? It was not as if she was asking for his input. He was just along for the ride. "You know, staying there is just temporary, right?" Bailey told Ben on their way to Tennessee.

Ben kept looking out the passenger side window sullenly, "It's not temporary."

"It is. I promise. I just need…some time to think clearly is all. You'll see. By the end of the year…you'll see. I'll have everything under control and we'll be gone."

Till the end of the year? Yeah right, Ben thought to himself.

2

Ben sat on the back porch that August afternoon that overlooked the enormous shaded backyard and allowed his mind to drift. He looked around the yard; the lush green grass had just been cut thanks to the landscaper that his Aunt Stacy had hired to take care of the house since his grandmother passed. He was a good man, the caretaker, a little bit too old to be out in the Tennessee heat mowing and trimming, but he seemed to hold up well there in his overalls and skinny frame. He kinda reminded him of Grandpa Jed, Steve's father, what he could recall of him anyways.

Ben was five when he died and did not remember very much. What he did remember were from pictures he had seen thumbing through the family albums. Grandpa Jed looked to be a happy man and in several of those pictures, he was holding Ben as an infant and as a young boy. Of course, Ben had no memory of those pictures the two of them were in. They might as well have been of him and a random stranger.

Ben sat back in his chair and looked around the yard like he had done so many times before. He and his mother had planted their flag at the Medlen home for two and a half months now and that idea that they would pick up and head somewhere else by the end of the year was a distant notion; a broken promise made by a woman who was trying to adapt to a new normal. The longer that they stayed there, the more his mother began to feel at home.

Little by little, they emptied the storage container with all their stuff from South Carolina into the house that summer. With Aunt Stacy's permission, Bailey sold most of the furniture from the previous Medlens during several weekend garage sales making the house with their stuff seem more like home. Pretty soon the old Medlen house began to look like the new Medlen house. All the changes that Bailey was doing to the inside of the house suggested to Ben they were there to stay.

The house for Ben had too many ghosts; too many memories. Sure, there were memories of his father, mementos of his long-gone youth, but there were other memories that hid between the walls; memories of his Grandma Medlen for example. Memories of an old woman that always smiled and hugged Ben when he came to visit three times a year: Christmas, Grandma Medlen's birthday, and a week during July. Each time Ben showed up with his family and along with Aunt Stacy's family, Grandma Medlen seemed so happy, so content, with all her family home with her.

Ben had a lot of adjusting to do in this new house. It was not that the home was a new place or foreign to him, but it was different. Grandma Medlen's home was a place to visit and then leave; not come there and stay forever. The only way Ben was going to leave that home was to leave for college. Then he would have another adjusting period to go through. That had become Ben's life these days, adjusting and adjusting some more.

3

Ben sat on the back porch doing much of nothing. He had a book in his lap that he intended to finish reading that day, but he only held it loosely in his lap as his mind wandered a bit. His thoughts were scattered at best, but one thought clung to his gray matter so tightly that it could not be avoided, school. With it came more adjustments.

He knew that eventually enrolling in a new school was coming. He saw it coming down the road a mile away and knew that there was nothing that he could do about it. That was the frustrating part; not being able to or old enough to stop school from coming or halting the end of the summer. Both, Ben knew, would become an eventuality in his life.

Back in South Carolina, school was not a big deal because he knew how to deal with it. He did not like school all that much because he did not fit in. But that was okay. He knew which kids accepted him and which did not; knew who the kids were that would mess with him and the ones that would leave him be. Back home he was a face in the crowd; a kid that never talked or laughed out loud, one that never drew any attention to himself. Ben liked to consider himself in the details. Most of the kids in his old high school never gave Ben Medlen a second thought. To most of them, he had become just a fixture within the school much like a desk or a locker. That was just fine with him. He liked it and was comfortable with it.

He had friends that he was leaving behind and knew that he would not see them any time soon. There was Jason Clark, his best friend since fourth grade in Mrs. Shatters' homeroom. The two of them had planned out their entire high school class schedule together back in eighth grade when they had to pick classes they wanted. The two of them were inseparable in high school and leaned on each other for emotional support when battling the trials and tribulations of teen life. Jason was a big help when Ben's dad died. He sat and listened to Ben talk about his dad. But Ben never cried on Jason's shoulder. He just talked.

There was another friend that Ben was leaving behind, Danny Howser. Danny was the first friend that he made in high school that freshman year. Ben, Jason, and Danny all become best friends and hung out after school at Ben's house mostly. They would play Nintendo and ride their bikes all over their part of town. It was not uncommon for the three of them to go camping out in either Ben's backyard, Clark's, or Danny's. On the weekends, the three of them would spend Friday nights at the other's house.

Ben hated leaving them but told Jason and Danny that he would stay in touch. "I'll come back eventually," Ben told them in separate discussions before he left. Ben vowed that he would come back in two years to stay after he graduated high school. His friends smiled and said they couldn't wait. On the ride to Tennessee, Ben swore that he was going to make it back home somehow; to get back to things that were familiar, back to his friends. He felt a pang of depression when a thought raced across his mind: what if his friends changed when he came back? What if they moved on without him? What if he truly had nothing to come home to?

In Claxton, however, he was not going to be in the details at his new school. He was going to be the new kid. Although it was high school and the kid pool was larger, people would still see Ben and make snap judgments about him, his clothes, the way he wore his shaggy hair, his face, (which was dotted here and there with acne but not bad at all and no worse than some of the other teens) and the way he spoke when spoken to. All these things were judged by kids and those judgments, warranted or not, decided the school's opinion of him; which was fine to a degree. He had already been tried and convicted at his old school which was why he was just in the details; comfortably in the details.

A new school, a new home, a new town, and a new environment was heavy for Ben. He was not ready for any of it. Hell, he was not ready for his dad to die early either. But here he was trying to do the best he could with what he had. There were times when Ben wanted to break down and cry his eyes out in the aftermath of his father's death. But he could not. He had to be there for his mother at the time. Not that he minded but who was there for him? No one. Ben had to take on the role of man of the house and give his mother someone to put her back up against. That back was a sixteen-year-old kid that was getting a big dose of reality and slowly coming apart at the seams. He wondered when he could finally have his breakdown. Then he wondered who would be there to put him back together.

Ben knew that the world was rough. At least that's what his dad had always told him. "Ben," Steve Medlen said to him one day, while the two were out in the driveway working under the hood of his father's car, "the world is rough, son. Things can change your life in a second and you'll never see it coming." He was right. Ben never saw his father's death coming. No one did. There were no warnings, no alarms, no red flags that said when Steve Medlen was going to die. He was right, Ben thought at his dad's funeral, the world is rough.

4

Ben's mother seemed to be doing better than Ben since the move. On the outside, she seemed fine, slowly adjusting to her new life. On the inside, she was still broken to pieces, unsure of herself and her place in the world. She had figured out some of the scattered puzzle; putting pieces together, she could almost see the entire puzzle take shape. Still, there were countless pieces splayed all over the table but she was taking them piece by piece in her hand and trying to see where they fit into the bigger picture. The bigger picture as it was, was her starting over at forty. Not the best place for anyone to be starting over but there she was. She had no choice. Bailey never thought her husband would die at forty-two, in the prime of his life.

It was not the natural order of things, she thought to herself time and again. She and Steve were meant to grow old together and sit out on their front porch waiting for an older Ben and his wife to bring the grandchildren over for a visit. That's how it was supposed to be, right? When Ben moved out that meant more time for her and Steve to finally be able to dial down and live the life they wanted together. That was the plan. Then Steve up and died and ruined everything. All those plans, all those preconceived notions, were tossed up and thrown into the blowing wind scattering it all. "Planning your life is for suckers," Bailey told Stacy one night when the two of them were talking about life. "You think you have it figured out… then something like this happens and you realize just how dangerous that thinking really is."

Although Steve had been gone for several months, the sting and stark reality of his death still resonated with her profoundly. Everything had happened so fast that she did not have time to just sit and think when the news came. There were funeral arrangements to make, a casket to buy, a cemetery to find, a grave plot to bury him in, insurance papers to fill out and mail off, etc., etc. Everything in her once stable and placid world had turned topsy-turvy. Bailey, for the first time in twenty years of marriage, was alone. She had Ben, sure, but Ben was not her husband. There was a profound connection that she and Steve had that seemed to transcend simply being married; they were soul mates, not bound by mere flesh and bone but rather by time's infinity.

She had met Steve one day in May at Camp Cherokee where they, along with several other eighteen-year-olds, were hired on as camp counselors. Being from different schools on different life paths, Steve and Bailey met that fateful day in May at the archery range where Steve was showing his group of kids how to safely and accurately use a bow and arrow. Bailey stood by and watched Steve, who was good with kids even back then, teach her girls the same techniques that he was showing the boys in his charge. As he stood there helping a girl pull back the cord on her bow, Steve snuck a peek over at Bailey and smiled. Bailey smiled back.

After the archery lesson was over, the kids all ran over to the mess hall for lunch and Bailey hung back as Steve collected his bows and arrows. Eventually, Steve approached her with some stupid bow and arrow joke that went something like, "So did you hear about the blonde that shot an arrow in the air?" Bailey, who was a gorgeous blonde, grinned, thinking that she had heard all the stupid blonde jokes ever told. But she found out Steve had one she had never heard of before.

"No, I haven't," she replied, wanting to laugh right then and there.

"She missed," Steve replied as he laughed. That made Bailey laugh. The one thing about Steve, her future husband, was that he had a wonderful sense of humor. After that, the two of them sparked a deep relationship over the weeks there at camp. The relationship that began with a joke lasted until the day the news came that Steve was dead after twenty years of marriage. When Bailey found herself thinking of Steve, which was more often than not, she would smile with tears in her eyes and laugh thinking about that dumb joke he told her that day. "She missed," Bailey would whisper the punch line.

5

Ben missed everything: his old life, his old bedroom, and the way the carpet felt on his feet when he first got up in the morning. He missed coming downstairs to eat breakfast with his mom and dad before everyone darted off to school or work. He missed walking to school, which was only two blocks away from his house, and he even missed his school which was something that he thought he would never, ever say let alone think about. But he did. The fact was that Ben missed everything. Mostly he missed his father.

Ben sat on the back porch looking across the backyard and listened absently at the birds chirping in the full trees. Things looked different to Ben in Tennessee; maybe it was the way the trees looked, perhaps even how the birds sang. Whatever it was, things were not the same, not like back home. Nothing could ever be the same anymore. The way things used to be were way back in the past and that past was growing further and further back in the rearview mirror with each day that lurched by.

Ben wanted to cry sitting there by himself but he could not just let go. The want was present, but the tears never came. They tried to come pouring out when the news came about his father, but he had to dam them up and turn to stone for his mother because she had nearly fallen apart when the news came about Steve. Ben, at sixteen, had to be the man of the house and he hated that. He just wanted to be a carefree kid, a teenager. Being strong for his mom was not included in the brochure of being a kid.

He hated the fact that he had to be the post for his mother to lean up against. Where did that leave him? Who was he supposed to lean on? In the end, there was no one…just himself. While everyone seemed to seek comfort from someone else, Ben stood alone trying to fight the feelings of emptiness, sorrow, and sadness that were left in Steve's wake. He found no comfort like the comfort he offered his mother. He was a little resentful of that. It should have been the other way around; Bailey picking up Ben. It did not happen that way.

6

At his dad's funeral, he stood there next to the casket with his mother receiving friends and the scant few family members (neither Bailey nor Steve had many left) shaking their hands, hugging them, and engaging with them all the best he could. He had no choice but to be brave because there was no one else to do it. His mother was in too bad of an emotional shape to do it. She stood up there an empty shell of what was. Ben had to smile bravely and be the man of the house. He hated it. He wanted to go away and cry somewhere where it was dark, cold, and lonely. It was all he wanted.

After everything was over, and when Ben was by himself alone in his bedroom back in South Carolina, he wanted to cry and cry hard. But the tears never came. They were behind his eyes ever since the news broke about his father's death, but he had to be brave; be brave and hold his mother up. Looking out his bedroom window that night into the darkness, things looked different even though he could not see. The feeling that things had changed hung in the air as heavy as the house. He wanted to cry…and yet could not.

7

Ben sat on the back porch and was about to start reading again when the back screen door opened up and out stepped his mom. Bailey seemed refreshed these days, Ben noticed with condemnation. Was it fair to walk around there lately like everything in the world was right and that the past was exactly that…the past? Not to Ben. If he should have to suffer emotionally so should his mother. What gave her the right to just up and move on? What right did she have to act as if nothing had ever happened? What right did she have to move them to their dad's old home? I could've grieved better at home than here, he thought a million times.

For so long he kept his mother propped up during those days and weeks after his father's death. Had it not been for him she would have surely collapsed within herself perhaps dragging Ben down with her. The boy had sacrificed himself, and his mental state, to be there for his mother. And now there she was, walking across the huge porch carrying a glass of iced tea in her hand, wearing a baggy shirt, baggy shorts that were a little too short, and flip-flops. "Who was this woman," Ben asked himself as he often did recently. There was a change, a stark one, in Bailey from her attitude down to the way she dressed and talked. Ben realized a couple of weeks ago something that staggered him: he had lost his mom, too, and he was now desperately alone.

"What are you doing out here, kiddo?" she asked, taking the chair next to him and sitting down.

"Just sitting…thinking, I guess. Thinking about reading this book," Ben replied, not really up for conversation.

"A little too hot out here already, isn't it?" That was an absent statement as she sipped on her tall glass of tea.

"A little bit, I guess," Ben said, shifting in his chair. This was the first conversation the two of them had in a few days. Ben tried to avoid her in the big house, and it was easy because of its size.

Bailey realized what Ben was doing and decided to let it go and not say anything. "Just give him his space, Bailey", Stacy told her as the two talked about Ben's avoidance of her as of late. And she had given her son his space, but the space did not seem to fix anything. If anything, it just made things stay the same and that was not what she wanted. Bailey wanted things to progress with her son as they had with her. To be honest, she forced the progression of her life as it did not come organically. Ben recognized that and saw what his mom was becoming even if she did not or chose not.

"Start school next week. I've already got you enrolled, and all the paperwork filled out. All you got to do is show up Monday," Bailey said, looking vacantly out in the same backyard that her son was staring off into.

Ben did not say anything in reply to that. What could he say? That it was not fair that he did not have a vote in staying in South Carolina? That it was not fair that his father died young? That it was not fair that he had no one to talk to about the way he was feeling in the aftermath of his dad's death? That it was not fair for her to be smiling and acting all cavalier about everything. It was like she was desperately trying to reinvent herself into being twenty again by the way she talked on the phone, dressed, and even walked for God's sake. Ben hated all of it. She was not like that when his dad was alive. She was a mom, not a tired forty-year-old assuming that she was in the second act of her life and she was going to get hers. Ben was well aware that his dad's death had repercussions afterward for both of them. His mom had undergone some pretty big changes of late and those changes he did not cotton to one bit.

"Okay," Ben simply said. It was all he could manage to say; was not much more that he could say about the subject. It was not like he had a vote. If he did it would not count anyways.

"I know it's not going to be easy there," Bailey said after a few moments of silence between the two of them, "but you're a junior and it's just two years. Two years is a blink of the eye these days," Bailey said, putting the glass of tea to her ruby-red lips. Ben sat there looking across the backyard and a thought slammed into his brain at what his mother had said: What happened to temporary? What happened to only staying here until the end of the year?

Ben knew that was a lie when she told him in the car ride to Tennessee that this move was just temporary, but hearing it as matter of fact drove Ben deeper down into despair. What he knew was going to happen was now clear: they weren't going anywhere. Ben wanted to laugh out loud but he held back at his mom waxing philosophical in saying "two years is a blink of the eye these days." Two years to an adult and two years to a teen are like apples to oranges. Two years for Ben might as well be a life sentence.

The new school posed a problem for him. The closer the date came for him to go there the more the butterflies fluttered inside his stomach. The high school, which he and his mother had driven by a week or so ago, was not nearly as big on the outside as his old one was back home. It seemed as big as his junior high. Although he had not walked into the building itself to give it a once over, Ben knew that the school was not that large. And it being smaller was going to make it more difficult for him to blend in and be unnoticeable. Ben was ill at ease.

However, unbeknownst to him sitting there on the back porch listening to his mother ramble on and on, he would meet someone that would change his life forever in that school. That person would go on to make such a profound imprint upon Ben's life that he strived for the rest of his life to do it just like Bobby Downey did.

"Just you wait," Bailey told Ben, "Things are going to get a whole lot better for us." That was one of the emptiest promises she had ever made; one that Ben would remember for years to come once he eventually made it back to his hometown.

Chapter 3

1

While Ben Medlen was battling the unwelcomed newness of his life, Bobby Downey was battling the stagnation of his. His life had become a museum of sorts as everything remained the same: the house and the way it was arranged; the same car he drove; same foods; same clothes; same toothpaste; same baseball team he rooted for; same curtains on the windows and what little furniture Dana had left him; the same job as Central High School's guidance counselor. The only thing in his life that was different was that he was no longer married to Dana or a father. Those titles were long gone, turned into dust, and thrown into the wind. The father title he could not help and the other title…well, he might have been able to fix that one...maybe. Fixing things would have required Bobby to get the cobwebs out of his mind and get back to actual life, instead of just existing.

On the day that Dana moved, Bobby stood out there on the front porch watching it all happen. Dana had been moving things out of the house slowly, hoping that it was slow enough for Bobby to stop her. She wanted her husband to stop her and for them to work something out because, in the end, she still loved him. But he let her go. The death of their son, Freddy, had been too much on their marriage. Dana wanted to move away because seeing his room, all the rooms for that matter, taxed her too much. She was too close there in that house and she felt as if she needed to go away. Maple Lane, the street where he was killed, was always going to be there and it was never, ever going anywhere. Seeing that street, that particular spot where her son was run over, was just too much for her to stay. Dana needed to break away and desperately wanted her husband to flee with her. He refused.

"I can't do it anymore," Dana told Bobby one night in the house a couple of weeks before she decided to leave for good.

"So you're just going to pack up and just bolt right on out the door, huh?" Bobby asked with the taste of Wild Turkey still fresh in his mouth.

"You want me to keep losing what little bit of sanity I have left, Bobby?! I can't keep looking at this house and seeing him! And when I go outside…I see the…," Dana stopped and began to breakdown again. Bobby knew what she was going to say. He knew how she felt because he felt the same way ever since that day. It was not easy for him to see everything that Freddy was once a part of. He felt the sting of his son's absence every second of the day and knew that she did too.

"This is our home, Dana! This is where we brought Freddy in from the hospital! And you just want to up and leave like he never existed?!" Bobby yelled. Yelling was how things had gone in the Downey house as of late. When the numbness had abated some after the loss of their son, those feelings, the ever-changing ones that weaved in and out of the five stages of grief, always landed more times than not on the anger part. Anger was the only way they communicated toward the end of the marriage. It was all they had left to give.

"Don't you dare!" Dana raised her head and wiped the tears from her eyes. "Don't you act like I forgot about him! I cannot handle this anymore! You know what your problem is?! You know why our marriage is failing?! You gave up on us! It was supposed to be me and you until the end of the line!"

Bobby and Dana stood some length apart in the living room that night when the line of demarcation was drawn. Bobby knew there was nothing else to do but call the marriage. It had never been the same since Freddy's death. "How did I do that, Dana?! Tell me exactly?! How the hell did I give up on us?! I'm not the one wanting to leave our home!"

"When I said that I think we need to go see a grief counselor or a marriage counselor…"

Bobby turned his head and paced about the room. "For what?! Tell me?! What are they going to tell me that I don't already know?! Huh?!"

"Oh, that's right, since you have a Master's in Psychology you know it all, right?!" Dana replied.

"I know what they'll tell us, so yeah!"

"We lost our son and now our marriage is dying, too! Don't you care?! Or are you so out of it you don't even notice anymore?!"

"Of course, I care! But you're wanting me to just up and leave the house and start something new! Like Freddy was never even here! That's bullshit!" Bobby shouted.

"And you want me to stay and fall apart with you here?! You think that I like having a husband who's living in a bottle all the time now and abusing pills?! You think that I like having a husband who won't talk to me about what happened that day?! You think I like having a husband who won't help me through this?!" Dana yelled at the top of her lungs with so much force her throat hurt.

Bobby stood there knowing that some of what his wife was saying was right. But he would never tell her. In Bobby's mind, drunk or sober, what Dana was doing was treasonous leaving the house where the family was. To him, it was treason upon Freddy's memory. "Then maybe you need to leave," Bobby said plainly without any rise in his voice. Dana was not ready for that he could tell. He could see it in her eyes the hurt of those words. "Maybe you just need to do whatever it is you need to do to help you cope. How about that? You want to abandon the marriage? Fine. You want to leave the house where our family is. It's whatever. But just remember, you chose this path…not me." Bobby then twisted his wedding band off and threw it across the living room and walked to his office slamming the door. Dana should have cried because it was then that everything was over. She knew it was the end of the line…end of the marriage…the end of everything. She took her wedding ring off and dropped it on the floor and she left out the front door.

In the months alone, Bobby did not change anything in the house. He thought it would be a terrible thing to do to the memory of what was. He hated that his wife turned her back on him, on Freddy. Bobby refused to leave the house because "leaving is leaving Freddy behind!" Bobby screamed at Dana one night when she first brought up the subject of moving away. In Bobby's heart of hearts, he knew that he should not have said that to her, but he could not stop his mouth from doing it.

He stood on the front porch and watched the last of what Dana was packing up go into the moving truck there in the driveway. Dana and her best friend, Suzie, got in Dana's car and drove away. She never looked back as far as Bobby could see. Jackson pulled the door closed on the back of the U-Haul truck and walked over to the front porch where Bobby was standing. "I think that's it," Jackson said lowly, hating being a part of the move.

"Yeah, looks about it. Thanks for helping her out."

Jackson lowered his head, eyes fixed on the grass, and nodded, "Yeah, well, maybe it ain't for long. I think you guys will eventually fix things. Suzie does too. With all that's gone on…maybe ya'll need a break for a while."

Bobby looked at Jackson and considered what he had said. "She made her choice and sometimes choices have bad consequences. Drive safe." Bobby walked back into the house closing the front door behind him.

2

Bobby cleaned his office at Central High in a matter of an hour that first week before school began. He had not been inside his office, let alone the school, since Freddy was killed. Going back to work felt odd to him, foreign. The last time he was in his office, he was married and had a son who was alive and well. Now, the office seemed strange, and he felt out of place. Looking at his desk, Bobby noticed that someone else had been fooling around with it while he was away. "Well, let's get this back in order, shall we?" he said to himself.

Most of the cleaning was dusting and rearranging things for no reason at all but for the sake of moving. He moved his stapler from the left side of his desk to the right; went through the papers that were left in small stacks across his desk in no rhyme or reason. His calendar blotter that was lying in the middle of his desk was still stuck on May. Bobby tore the May, June, and July months off and wadded them up, and tossed them into the wastebasket beside his desk. The month of August was clean with no inked words, reminders, or dates circled as of yet. That would come later.

Bobby adjusted the height of his chair behind his desk and sat on it, several times bouncing up and down and sitting up straight on it to see how the new height found him. Several smaller adjustments later, he nailed it. Bobby wondered who had been sitting in his chair. "I wonder if it was Rachael Stevens. She's pretty short. I'll have to ask her later."

School was set to begin shortly, and he still had a lot of stuff that he had to do. Mostly getting the files ready for the new intake of freshmen and doing the class schedules for all the kids in the school. It was a job that he literally hated but over the years he had a computer program that had pretty much done it for him. Sometimes he still had to rework the class schedules for those kids that dropped classes the first week or two, which was fine. It was a pain in the ass, but it was fine.

Bobby opened all his filing cabinets and began to shift all the files into the next set of cabinets. In his office, Bobby had a run of four, five-foot-high, four-drawer filing cabinets. One cabinet was for the freshman, the second was for the sophomores, the third was for the juniors, and the last one was for the seniors. The last cabinet was the one that Bobby needed to open. It was the seniors' files for the 1993-94 school year. He intended on doing it before the school year was over that May, but with what had happened to Freddy in March of that year and then his wife leaving in June, Bobby had just forgotten and didn't care. Work was the absolute last thing on his mind. His job for today was to move the classes down the line and free up the freshman cabinet for the incoming class. His goal was to have everything in order by the end of the day.

As he emptied the seniors' cabinet, he looked through the names on the tabs and did not recall some of them. After you'd been through so many kids they tend to run together, Bobby thought to himself, thumbing through the files and names of the kids that had graduated a few months ago. Some of the names he barely recalled. Some he saw and recalled with sharp and violent imagery; such was the case with William Glass. William was once an at-risk kid who had his own special red folder, as did all the other students that Bobby felt were at-risk. Bobby remembered him very well…

3

William Glass was a messed-up kid. Bobby tried for four years to reach him and maybe repair some of the issues. He spent extra time with him just to get him to address his problems. His job was to guide these kids in the right direction during high school and post-high school, but Bobby had gone above and beyond that. And it was that attention to the kids that made Bobby Downey a popular guy with the students in the hallways. He was good at making the students feel like they counted; even the nerds, geeks, and non-popular, non-sports-playing kids. Most, if not all, the students like Bobby Downey.

William Glass, Willie to those close to him, had come into Central High and began to fight his way through. He was the typical rough end: always wore a black leather jacket, smoked in the boys' bathrooms, cussed like a sailor, was suspended for a variety of things, etc.; you know the type. Most kids tried to stay out of his way and that's how Willie liked it.

Bobby had been seeing Willie just as he had seen all the other kids, especially the freshmen, more than once a month. Bobby took the freshmen under his wing and tried to acclimate them to the bigger school. Some adjusted well because of their parents' contributions to the school's booster clubs or the kids' playing sports. Some just did not fit in. That was where Bobby saw the need to make them feel at home. Not only did he set them up for the future there at the school, but with his "Four Year Plan," Bobby felt that he had set them up for the rest of their lives. That was his hope anyways. All they had to do was follow his advice…sometimes they did and sometimes times they did not. Sometimes you can't get them all, was what Bobby would remind himself at times when he saw kids fail either in school or outside of it.

Each kid, the troubled ones especially, Bobby took their failures personally. He always judged himself harshly thinking that maybe he could have done something differently, maybe said something differently, or maybe a different approach would have fit the bill. Bobby wished that he could have developed a suit of armor to protect him from all the times that his kids failed. Bobby let things hurt. It was his nature to feel. He did not want to end up like some of the other teachers at his school—burned out by years of teaching and just hoping to make it through another year. That was all school was to some of them; just another year. Bobby wondered sometimes lying in bed while Dana slept how some of those teachers could think that way. He hoped to God that he did not end up jaded and cynical like they were.

4

Willie came into Bobby's office for the first time fresh off a suspension for smoking in the boys' bathroom. It was his first offense there at the high school and was not going to be his last. Willie came into Bobby's office and sat on the chair across from his desk all relaxed, legs straight out and crossed at the boots, one arm on the chair arm while the other draped over the back of the chair. Bobby thought that he was way too casual for a freshman.

"Where do you see yourself in four years, William?" Bobby asked after the "hey how are you doing" greeting was completed.

Willie looked up at the ceiling for a minute or two and considered Bobby's question, "I don't know. Don't really think about it."

Bobby leaned back in his chair and looked at Willie. He knew the type and had dealt with the type over and over again. The thing was, there were always Willies and there will always be Willies. It was just a fact of life and once Bobby finally got that nugget of truth understood, he was able to move on. It was hard at first, early in his career, but as time went on, the Willies came and went. It did get easier for him to cope with. Not that he liked it, but he learned to deal with the notion that not every kid could be fixed or for that matter wanted to be fixed. Bobby simply could not fix everyone and put them on the right path. Sometimes they had to cut their own paths.

"Your grades were really good in the fifth, sixth, and middle part of the seventh grade. A-B student. What happened in the eighth and now?"

Willie, still relaxed in his chair, glared at Bobby. He sat there silent for a few minutes in his bad boy pose. "I don't know."

Bobby sat and soaked in Willie's reply. "Listen, I've given a lot of advice to a lot of kids over the years. I've seen your type and I'll bet you a million dollars I'll see it in another freshman next year. You need to listen to me, William…you need a plan for your life because this, whatever this is (hand gesture toward Willie) ain't going to work after high school. So, what are you good at?" And that was how Bobby began to thaw William Glass. It would take Bobby four solid years to chip away at Willie.

As the years rolled on by in freshman, sophomore, and junior years, Willie began to gradually ditch the bad boy image. He stopped cussing the teachers, stopped fighting, and stopped smoking in the boys' room. During his senior year, Bobby and Willie had a good relationship going that was built on trust and honesty. The guidance counselor could see Willie righting the once-troubled ship he was on. He started hitting the books again and then his grades came up. All the teachers that Bobby spoke with about Willie marveled over the fact of how much he had changed. They accredited that change to Bobby's time with him.

As senior year came both for Willie and Bobby Downey, the two of them saw less and less of each other. That was usually how it was when the once wide-eyed freshmen had gotten older. Bobby would meet with them weekly as freshmen, bi-weekly as sophomores, monthly as juniors and every two months as seniors just make sure they were still going straight or needed any help. Bobby would sometimes have some of those seniors who thought they had it figured out pop into his office unannounced. They would come in, shoot the breeze and ask for some advice about something. Bobby would do the best he could in dispensing that needed advice. For the students in that high school, they had no better advocate than Bobby Downey.

During those four years, William Glass had turned the ship around and cut his own path for sure. His grades improved and his future looked bright. What was he good at? Auto mechanics. William excelled and was perhaps the most gifted kid the school had ever seen in the auto mechanics classes. William had plans, with the help of Mr. Maples—the auto mechanics instructor— and Bobby himself, to attend the most prestigious automotive school in the country. Things for Willie were heading in the right direction. Bobby was very proud. Then, two weeks right before graduation, dark news came. William Glass was killed in an auto accident on his way back home from a friend's house where they were working on a car. The future that was once wide open for Willie was to never be.

Bobby put Willie's file in the shred pile along with some other faceless names of kids that he had guided for four years. Sometimes he knew what became of them and sometimes he didn't. There was a temptation to put the word out and find them just to see for himself what kind of adults they had become. But Bobby never did want to look behind the curtain, because sometimes when you look behind the curtain there was nothing at all or nothing at all that you expected. Sometimes behind the curtain were things you were not ready to see. Bobby Downey had a habit of keeping the curtain closed.

5

It was mid-afternoon on a Friday as Bobby sat in the auditorium listening to the new principal, Mr. Glick, talk about the upcoming school year. Bobby did not really like Glick from the moment he saw him. There are just some people you don't like on sight, just human nature, Bobby surmised. Glick was one of those people that rubbed Bobby the wrong way almost

immediately. Maybe it was his tone when the man talked; perhaps it was
the way he looked at people trying to size them up; could have been the
way he walked like he was better than you. Whichever it was, probably all
three attributes, Bobby did not cotton to Glick.

Bobby had met Mr. Glick on Monday earlier that week. Glick was older
than Bobby and wore spectacles that seemed to hang on the end of his
nose. He looked more like an old Southern judge from the 1950s; sitting
up on the bench and looking down at people with his eyes floating above
the top rim of those glasses. His voice commanded respect and attention.
Maybe that was why Bobby had a problem with him.

Peter Brooks, the former Central High principal, was a man of the people.
Teachers, janitors, hell, even most of the students, liked and revered the
man. He was an institution at the school. He was a student there on the very
first year the school was built and came back fifteen years later to serve
as principal. He retired last year, after fifty years of being associated with
the building. No one man had done more for the teachers and students at
that school than Brooks. He and Bobby had gotten along very well and at
least once a week, he and the principal would walk around the track at the
school's football field just shooting the breeze. Never anything important,
just catching up on current events, mainly sports. The two men shared an
affinity for the Atlanta Braves and during the long baseball season, the
two would converse about the ups and downs of the team and their place
in the standings.

When Freddy was killed back in March, Peter Brooks reached out to
Bobby. He did not do it with an impersonal phone call but rather a visit to
the house a day later. Brooks was like a father figure to Bobby, as he was
to most of his younger faculty, and he and Bobby spoke at length there
at his house and cried a lot out in the backyard. Peter was there for the
funeral, the burial, and after everything was said and done. Brooks told
Bobby to "take the rest of the school year off" and if he "needed until the
end of the year then he would work it out with the new principal and the
district office". Bobby thanked him and the two hugged one final time.

6

Mr. Glick stood at the school's entrance meeting with all the faculty,
janitors, cooks, etc. that were coming into the school, his fiefdom. When
Bobby opened the school's heavy front entrance door, he was met with

Mr. Glick, the new man in charge and assistant principal Rover. Terrance Rover and Bobby had always gotten along and never had any cross words; they were friends. Terrance was up for the job after Brooks had left but something had happened, and Bud Glick got picked. Terrance was still burning from being overlooked for the position but did not allow it to show. Bobby and Terrance had many conversations about how Glick probably had gotten the job. The consensus between the two men was that he was a friend of a friend of the superintendent, and it was the Good Ol' Boy Club at work.

As Bobby stepped into the school's cool air-conditioned building, Mr. Glick extended his hand while Terrance stood off to the side. "I'm Mr. Glick, the new principal." It was the first time that Bobby had a face to put with the name. Glick had been at the school during the summer getting a lay of the land and had met several of the staff here and there but not all at once. Bobby took the hand and was surprised that the new man in charge was standing there to meet and greet. He'd never seen anything like this before. Neither had Terrance for that matter by the look on his face.

"Bobby Downey. Your guidance counselor." Mr. Glick shook his hand and broke the handshake and looked insulted by Bobby. Terrance noticed it, too. So did Bobby, felt it in the handshake as he introduced himself.

"Guidance? So, you're not a teacher?"

Bobby stood there and looked at Terrance and then back over to Glick not knowing really what to say. "I can teach history if need be. But um…I just prepare the kids for the next four years and help them get their post-high school life going. You know, helping them with colleges or trade schools. Help them with any problems personal or social or whatever. High school can be hell and mental health is just as important as physical health."

Mr. Glick smiled and turned to look at Terrance and then back to Bobby, "I know what guidance is, Son. You ain't got to explain it to me like I'm stupid. I always thought all that psychology crap was a waste of time if you ask me."

"Well, I help the kids get adjusted around here and stay adjusted; make sure that their high school career is trending in a positive way both academically as well as emotionally. And if it's not, I have to find out a way to fix it because it's all of our jobs to make sure that these kids hit the real world with everything, they need to be successful, right?" Bobby told his boss.

"A lot of new age mumbo-jumbo sounds to me," Mr. Glick said, already not cottoning to Bobby. "Anyways, welcome back." Mr. Glick turned away from Bobby and started to talk to Terrance. Prick, Bobby thought as he walked away down the hall to his office.

7

Bobby sat amongst all the other teachers in the auditorium later that morning listening to Mr. Glick stand up at the podium talking—rambling actually—about who he was, how educated he was, about his plans for the school year, and what his expectations were as well as the state's expectations. Most of them knew nothing about the principal that was hired over the summer. All they knew was that he was from the state's Department of Education office in Nashville. The rumor was that his best friend was Dr. Haden Franklin, the superintendent of the school district and that was used to gain him the job of principal of Central High when Brooks retired.

None of the teachers had much to go on about him other than what he was telling them at the podium that morning. He was the replacement chief and came in during the summer when all the staff was away. Glick came in, set his office up, which was nearly voided of the old regime's knickknacks and mementos, and began his reign in July. He acclimated himself to the classrooms, the hallways, and the lay of the land as it was. He studied each and every teacher in his school on how efficient they were as well as effective through test grades and evaluations.

"One thing I do want to touch on," Glick began in his state of the school speech, "is that we need to be better in the state in terms of test scores for reading, math, and English. I will be meeting with the department heads of those subjects next month to come up with a plan of action to raise our test scores for the end-of-the-year exams. In the next five years, I'd like for us to be in the top ten percent of the state. It's a goal that we can reach if we try. We cannot afford any teachers going forward to be satisfied with just coming in. Those days are over. Your job is to educate and if that doesn't sound like something you want to do, then maybe you need to find another career," Glick expressed in his most authoritarian voice that demanded compliance from his staff. The teachers sat there in repose and listened while Bobby watched their body language. From his training on the subject of body language a few years ago at Amherst College by a former FBI agent, Bobby knew that the teachers in attendance were not engaged with the new man in charge. He doubts they ever would be and his veiled threats on their jobs did not worry them one bit.

Glick, Bobby presumed, was one of those guys that liked to wash over you like a tidal wave, throw his weight around and let you know your place. Hearing him stand there and talk about his credentials, Bobby wondered to himself who he was trying to impress or convince; them or Glick himself.

Most of what Glick spoke about was of no concern to Bobby. He sat there like most meetings and pretended to listen. He was good at that. He was the school's guidance counselor and an all-around good guy. He was not a teacher, nor did he care to be grouped with some of those teachers in that school. Bobby hated meetings with a passion. He always viewed them as a complete waste of time. Glick, however, loved them because he loved to hear himself talk, and more importantly, he loved to make people listen to him; nothing better for a narcissistic person in charge to have a captive audience.

8

Listening to Glick drone on and on, Bobby kept his eyes up at the podium where Glick was speaking. His mind began to wonder. He looked like he was listening carefully, but Bobby's mind began to think about the teachers there in his school. In every school, you had teachers who were battled tested and should have retired a long time ago like Janice Green. She was once an engaged teacher in the years of long ago, Bobby was told. Somewhere she lost that fire that she had when she was new and young. Then it happened: she refused to change with the times, and she was left in a time where the refusal to change began to affect her profession.

Eventually, she got bitter, and eventually the most beloved teacher in the entire school morphed into the monster at the end of the story. Bobby looked at her with contempt because she did not even attempt or care to help with the students' education one bit. Green just came in, sat down, did the very minimum teaching, the least that she could get by with, and did whatever it was that Janice Greens did all day. Bobby had an inclination in thought that if Glick was who he thought he was, Green would not survive his reign. Especially if he demanded that the teachers in his school bring the test scores up and stop phoning their job in, so to speak. Central High may be looking for a new Algebra 1 teacher soon, Bobby concluded.

Then Bobby saw the newbies; the teachers that came there right out of college after their student teaching was completed and had this starry-eyed notion that they could change the world one kid at a time. This, of course, lasted for a few years until they figured out that they are just some kids you cannot save no matter how good your intentions are. It was a hard lesson that Bobby Downey himself had to learn. Those types of teachers eventually let themselves get defeated and just mailed it in until they retired. Sometimes they would recapture that fire of teaching like they had when they first began their careers only to have it stamped out by the end of the day. Slowly, most of the teachers that Bobby knew had turned into the very teachers they hated when they, themselves, were young. Eventually most of them, a high percentage at least at his school, became a Janice Green.

Bobby sat and listened to Mr. Glick talk about the state's expectancy for this year in academics more in-depth and thought about how effective the teachers in his school were. About three of them were high-level teachers. Those were the teachers that Bobby held in high regard. The other teachers hated them but deep-down Bobby thought that it was not hatred they possessed, but jealousy. These three educators were what the others used to be and somehow they fought back the temptation to relent and fade to black and mail it in. Whatever it was that Mr. Jamerson, Mrs. Doolittle, and Mrs. Lowery had, it never went away, never dulled. Years and students did not burn them out. Those were the teachers that Bobby loved; the ones that called their career a calling instead of a job, a steady paycheck.

Bobby sat there being lulled nearly to sleep by Glick's monotone voice that never rose or fell. His mind began to open locked doors inside his mind. It happened sometimes with locked things. One of those forbidden and locked doors concerned his family and about the tragedy that had befallen them several months ago on a sunny Saturday afternoon in March. Even monsters can come into the daytime.

Once the thought of his son's face appeared in his mind's eye, Bobby began to shift in his chair in the auditorium. Seeing Freddy smiling and laughing through different flashes of different events in Bobby's mind caused his breath to accelerate and his palms to get sweaty; his heartbeat got faster and faster. Freddy was something that he wanted to never think about again not because he hated his young son, but because it hurt too much to remember him. Remembering him hurt to no end and the booze and pills he had abused in spades over the months after his son's death helped to ease the pain but it never erased it.

It was always there, that pain, locked up behind a door. It was the only place to tuck Freddy away in. Bobby had done well at suppressing the memories of his son. They would come to him on nights when Bobby's inhibitions were at their lowest, like around bedtime, or when he would walk by his son's bedroom which was still the same as it was when he walked out of it for the last time that March afternoon. The holidays to come were going to be a bitch to manage and that thought alone, the empty Halloweens, Thanksgivings, and Christmases, were enough to make Bobby want to strongly consider ending his life. He had not gotten there to those holidays just yet, but they were coming. Bobby was scared to death about how he was going to manage it. He had no one to put his back up against. He was all alone.

9

The horrible events of that day began to once again replay in Bobby's mind. That day in March was a memory that he knew he would never erase but Bobby had no choice but to get up and hurry out of the auditorium while everyone watched. Glick never stopped talking and watched with harsh eyes as the guidance counselor fled the scene. Bobby needed to get out of there while he could still hold it together somewhat. His breathing began to get crazy, and he started feeling like he was going to throw up. He did not care one bit what the staff or the new principal would say about him getting up and running out of the meeting.

Outside in the hall, Bobby leaned over the water fountain and splashed cold water onto his face. He felt as if his face was burning hot. With cool water bringing the temp down on his face, Bobby straightened up and dried himself with his hands. Just as soon as the flash of his son's final minutes out there lying on the street came to him in his mind's eye, it was gone. Thank God, Bobby thought as he stood there alone in the hallway.

That's usually how it went with that day in question: Bobby would just be sitting in a chair reading or driving home, and that day would sneak up on him and replay. Sometimes that day came while eating dinner. Freddy's death would come to him in the bathroom and even taking a shower. The recording in his mind would somehow press PLAY and the events of that day would begin. It would take everything that Bobby had within himself to shut it off and hit the STOP button before he got too far. Too far was him running from his house, across the front lawn, and down the street where the commotion was. That was where Bobby had managed to press the STOP button every time. He would manage to take that memory and wrestle it back into a room and close the door and lock it. The problem for Bobby was that the locked door would always somehow open, and that terrible day in March would come rolling out.

Bobby stood outside in the hallway from the auditorium and could still hear Glick from his microphone drone on. He noticed that his breathing was still going hard and looked down at his hands. They were still shaking. He made fists with them to try to get them to stop. Bobby walked down the hall and out the double doors that led him outside. It was hot that August morning but there was a breeze blowing some rain in from the west side of the county. The wind felt good against his face as he closed his eyes and tried to not breakdown into an emotional heap.

Chapter 4

1

It was Sunday night and the first day of school jitters were beginning to get to Bobby. He had popped several Ritalin pills throughout the day to keep him going. He popped several more when it got dark outside washing it all down with some Wild Turkey. He did not want to sleep because of what dreams would come. Those dreams were the reason that Bobby started abusing Ritalin to begin with shortly after the death of his son. When he slept, he had the scariest dreams he had ever had, and they always involved Freddy in some fashion. When he figured out that all he had to do was sleep maybe two to three hours a day and be doped up on Ritalin the rest, he would be fine.

The scant few hours he did sleep was not ever deep enough for him to dream or if he did, he never remembered them. Bobby's destructive method to cope was in the fifth month with no signs of slowing. His body was beginning to show wear and tear along with his mind. Hallucinations were becoming somewhat of a normal thing where Bobby had to question if what he was seeing was real or just a trick of a tired, sleep-deprived mind.

It was not like he would have been able to sleep anyways; tomorrow kids would be filling the halls with all their sounds of youth. Being nervous was not a new thing for Bobby but an understood thing. He once told one of the older teachers, Mr. Darting, "You know how I think you know when you're burned out?"

"How," Mr. Darting asked, sitting in Bobby's office shooting the breeze that day long ago.

"If you don't get nervous on the first day of school. That's when I think you know you're done." Bobby still got the nerves…thankfully.

Mr. Darting laughed, "Then I must've been done a long time ago."

2

Ben Medlen found himself standing in his "new" bedroom looking in the full-length mirror. At that precise time, Bobby back home had decided to put on Prince's, Purple Rain, vinyl record on his player and turn the stereo up to ten. Sleep was not coming anytime soon for him. Ben stood there and looked at himself and hated what was looking back at him. He wanted to cry and felt the tears coming but for whatever reason, he held them at bay. He wanted to sneak out of the house and hitchhike all the way back to South Carolina.

Jason told him the other night on the phone, "Dude, I'm sure that if you wanted to come back here and live my folks would put you up. No problem there I don't think."

"Mom would never go for it," Ben told him. "I'll just have to deal with being here for two years. After that, I'm moving back. I don't know how yet but I am."

It was not Ben's bedroom he was standing in and sleeping in. His bedroom was in South Carolina in a house that was up for sale. Soon, he thought, new people would be living there and changing everything. He imagined kids playing games in his old bedroom. He thought about all the TV watching in the living room. He just knew that a family would be gathered around the dining room table for dinner like his family had not too long ago. Ben also wondered if the new kids would have a dad that would go out in the huge backyard and throw some baseball like he and his did often.

It wasn't fair, Ben often thought. As the late night grew later in the bedroom that was not his, Ben thought of it again: It wasn't fair. Up in his room at the Medlen home, Ben stood there looking in the full-length mirror that was hanging on the closed bedroom door. He looked like his dad when his dad was Ben's age. The similarities were striking. The pictures that were still in his grandma's picture albums showed Steve Medlen as a young man through the years. In another picture album, Ben thumbed through and fetched photos of himself and took those out along with his dad's and held them side by side. They could pass for twins. Looking in the mirror, it was like Steve was back in that bedroom somehow not dead but back in time. The thought of that with his reflection looking back at him gave him chills.

Ben stood there in front of the mirror lost in his head, gazing at himself. The longer that he looked at the depressed kid that looked back at him, the more that he did not recognize him. His hair was a mess, his acne was a little more blotchier than normal, and he was looking thinner than when he lived in South Carolina. Not only was Ben's mind under heavy duress, but his body was buckling, too. Ben knew that he needed help but where was he going to get it? His mother? Yeah right.

Ben stood there wearing a plain white tee and a pair of cargo shorts and looked at the boy that was looking back at him. He used to smile some; used to laugh some; used to feel happy and cling to the ideology that the future was going to be okay, that adolescence was just a stop in the road that would lead him to something bigger and better. He held that idea close to his heart. His ideology was blown apart, and the stop on the road seemed to be a final destination. God, how he wished his dad was still alive. Things would be different. Yes indeed.

Had Steve Medlen been alive, Ben would not be standing there in the bedroom looking at himself in the mirror wondering where the kid that was looking back at him was headed. Had Steve Medlen been alive, Ben would be up playing video games late into the night while munching on Doritos and dreaming of the blonde girl that sat beside him in history class. Ben and Ashley had talked from time to time at school, mostly in the hallways and sometimes at high school football games but never anything major. It was always just normal teenage stuff. They never could get into anything major because either Ben was with his friends or Ashley was with hers. The timing was never right for the two of them to be alone. When Ben was forced to leave, there went any kind of chance he might have had with her.

She was not his girlfriend by no stretch of the imagination but could have been if Ben had gotten the nerve to ask her. Ashley had waited for him to ask her for her phone number, but Ben was too shy. At some point, he was going to ask his dad how to approach a girl like that, but Steve was not around to ask; he had died before he could do it and took his secrets to the grave with him. Before he moved away to Tennessee, Ben thought about going to her house and confessing his feelings for her. She lived pretty close to him, maybe a five-minute bicycle ride, but Ben could not muster the nerve. He had seen stuff like that done in movies, but Ben was not a movie star talking lines that were written for him and being directed on what to do. He moved during the summer without a goodbye to her. Ben wondered what she was doing now while he stood in the mirror looking at the reflection that looked a lot like his dad back in his teen years.

Ben at sixteen had perhaps the biggest tragedy to befall him: the death of a parent. He was close to his dad and the hole that Steve's passing created was huge to the Medlen family. Ben thought about that hole inside him and wondered how in the hell he was ever going to fill it in. Did he even want to? Most importantly, how could he fill it? With what? A new dad? Nope. Ben was wounded, his soul had been cut to the quick and he was still bleeding for his lost dad. It had been five months since the news came about Steve; five months since Ben's world changed; five months since his mother became something else altogether; a woman he did not recognize any longer. He had lost his mom and that was another scary part of all of this. Ben felt it deep inside his soul that his dad's death had altered everything in his once safe and secure family. Matter of fact, he knew it did.

Had Steve been there he would have told Ben to "stop moping around and pick himself up and get moving on." Steve would have wanted it that way. Ben knew his dad would have said that and God did he try to do what his dad would have wanted. He tried so hard until he was exhausted from trying. He could only block out the hurt for so long before he gave out again. Each time he gave out, Ben wanted to die. The hurt came from the memory of the day of his dad's death and the memories that followed. That was when suicide first came into Ben's mind. When that dark seed of suicide grew inside Ben's mind, it grew tall and blossomed in there. There was a lot of fertile ground for it to grow.

Ben was going through a lot: his father's death, moving to a new town, a new place to live, a new school, new everything. Ben was not wired to deal with all of what was happening to him. The kid was hurting and dying at the same time. No one was around him to help. Even if there was, could anyone really help Ben Medlen? Probably not. He knew one thing for sure: he was on his own. This was shaping up to be the biggest test of his young life. Ben did not think that he was up for the challenge. The issues that he had going on seemed too big for him to shoulder. Problem was, Ben was getting weaker and was falling down more. Getting up off the floor was getting much harder to do as the days rolled by.

Ben wanted to kill himself. It was not some teenage, "nobody understands me" bullshit where all he did was play the Cure's music in his bedroom and wear black. What Ben was going through was real. The problem was real, so the solution had to be real. Where was the solution? Ben figured it had to be suicide. It was the only way that the pain was going to stop from his head and his heart. He had brought up the carving knife from the kitchen drawer and laid it on top of his dresser. It had been lying there in the open for days. He knew that his mom was not going to come into his bedroom and nose around, so it was safe to sit there and look at. She had her own life to look after nowadays, and that new life was getting away from the ghost of her husband and her son that looked like him.

The silver and shiny knife sat there waiting for the time when Ben would grip it and start slashing his wrists. Ben had thought a lot about suicide and numerous ways to commit it. There were all kinds of ways to die, and all Ben had to do was pick one and just do it. He had to get the nerve up first. That was something that he did not know if he could do. Getting the nerve up to kill yourself was not easy. He guessed if you wanted out of life badly enough you would just do it, not giving it a moment's notice.

Ben took the knife from the dresser and looked at himself in the full-length mirror again. Ben stood there, his heart beating, thumping against his chest so hard he could hear it in his ears. He was shaking a little as his grip on the knife handle tightened a bit. He did not turn his gaze away from himself as the mirror reflected the broken kid in the mirror. He was convinced at that moment in time that this was it; he was checking out.

Sweat began to crop up on his forehead as he raised the knife a little bit upward. He held out his left arm and turned it over to where the thin skin of the wrist and underneath the forearm showed. In all the suicide research he had done, he knew that if he wanted to slash his wrists, he had to do it vertically. Horizontal was only a cry for help, for those that wanted attention. Ben did not want attention. He wanted to ease his pain, to bleed out and die. He wanted the pain to go away. He wanted to get away from the life that had somehow fucked him over in a matter of seconds when his father died. Most of all, Ben just wanted to stop feeling the way he was feeling. He was sick and tired of being sick and tired.

4

He stood there, a kid of sixteen, holding the knife with his right hand and ready to slash his left wrist. As he stood there eyeing himself in the mirror, he recalled something that he had read in a book: if you wanted to let the blood flow, you needed to be in a hot bath or shower so the blood got circulating so the slashes would just open up the red flood gates so to speak. Ben thought about going into the bathroom and getting into the tub but decided that killing himself in the bedroom where his dad had grew-up was symbolic.

Ben slowly moved the knife over to his left wrist all the while he kept his eyes on the kid in the mirror. He was doing it slowly because if he wanted to back out he could before he felt the sharp steel on his skin. Going too fast would stamp out any notions of objections and it would be too late. He wanted to make sure…it was do or die.

5

Across town at that very moment that Ben was trying to convince himself to slash his wrists and leave the cruel world, Bobby Downey was sitting alone in the dining room at the table with papers scattered across his desk. Prince was playing loudly in the background. His table looked like a mess, but it was an organized one. The day before school was always a little messy for Bobby. He was not tired, far from it thanks to the Ritalin. Now, he was up and going and ready for anything.

In all the mess that was on the big oak table, a chicken parm sandwich, half-eaten, with a glass of sweet tea nearly gone sat to his right. He had picked up the chicken sandwich on his way from nowhere in particular earlier that night. The truth was that Bobby was not eating much at all. When Freddy got killed out there in the street, Bobby did not eat for a few days; just was not on his mind. In the weeks after his son's death, Bobby had lost thirteen pounds and was looking bad, an unhealthy thin. He had to force himself to eat something just to keep going.

When he started popping Ritalin, his appetite became less as the calories burned away. By the time Dana packed up and left, Bobby's weight had gone from two-twenty down to one-seventy-two. He caught a glimpse of himself in the mirror sometimes during that summer before school and after Dana left the house and did not recognize the man looking back at him. He had bluish-black bags under his tired eyes, his face looked thin, and when he stepped back from the mirror, he could see the rest of his body; thin and looking like it was in a state of starvation. Bobby cried looking at what life had done to him.

Bobby needed some fresh night air to clear his mind some. It worked most times and was a good distraction when he felt the walls were closing in on him. He had thought about cooking something at home but decided against it last minute. He had it in his mind briefly to make cheesy chicken breast wrapped with strips of sugar maple bacon; God how Freddy loved that dish, Bobby remembered. He had not made that meal since a few days before Freddy was killed back in March. Before he opened the fridge door all the way to get the bacon and cheese out of the crisper, Bobby closed the door and decided he did not want to go through all the trouble of making it. It was not that though; what it was, was that he could not eat something that his son loved. That was what it boiled down to…Freddy; always Freddy.

Bobby decided to get into his car and take a drive that August evening to maybe find something to eat. Driving around town and then out into the county where the roads all led somewhere, night had taken over for the daylight and Bobby found himself driving aimlessly down back roads. Maybe he knew where he was going. He had forgotten all about getting something to eat at the moment. Eventually, he would pick up a chicken parm sandwich combo #2 from Clucky's. Stuff was on his mind that night other than food. It was not his son, but his best friend, Sam Wells.

6

Bobby and Sam were the best of friends. Sam was a little older and had been at Central High School for five years before Bobby showed up. Sam was the U.S. History teacher and the History Department head. He was the one that took Bobby under his wing and showed him the ropes of Central High. Sam gave him a rundown of the good teachers, who he could talk to, and the ones to steer clear of. The stuff Sam taught him he still used today. He was the one that came up with Bobby's filing system in his office. "That's pretty smart," Bobby said after Sam showed him how he would do it.

"I know. That's why they keep me around."

Through all the good times and bad, Sam and Bobby's friendship stood upright. When Freddy was killed, Sam and his wife Clarissa, were there night and day for the Downeys. Those were the darkest days their friendship had ever seen. Bobby had never forgotten the tears Sam let him cry on his shoulder or the endless talks they had on the back porch about why God was so cruel. Sam never interrupted his friend, he let him talk, let him cycle through it. He was there, always there, for Bobby…until he was not.

Sam left a few months after Freddy's death. It was right before Dana and Bobby split apart from the damage of that day out on Maple Lane. Sam had called Bobby and asked if he could come over. Bobby said that he would be expecting him shortly. Sam showed up and could tell that when he entered the Downey's home that the tension was so thick that he nearly choked on it. Bobby and Dana had been fighting again although Sam did not hear the argument, he knew what had been going on from Clarissa because she and Dana talked a lot. It was how Sam knew that the marriage probably was not long for the world.

Of course, he never said anything to Bobby. He tried to help him talk things out, but Bobby had started drinking and it scared Sam because he was changing right before his very eyes. He had told Bobby that maybe he needed to slow down a few weeks before this visit, and Bobby said, "I don't drink that much. Just a little bit when I need to forget."

"You need to forget a lot lately, huh?" Sam replied out on the back porch. Bobby did not turn to look at Sam. He knew that he was right. Why argue with the truth?

It was a Saturday during the summer when Sam Wells came to Bobby and Dana's house to break the bad news. He did not want to do it over the phone. He respected his best friend too much to do it coldly like that. He wanted to see Bobby in person, not his voice over the telephone.

On the back porch, where most of their profound conversations seemed to take place, a sober Bobby Downey, sober at least until Sam left that was, sat there looking off across his privacy fenced-in backyard. "Man," Bobby began letting the news sink in for a bit, "I can't believe it."

Sam nodded his head. He could not really believe it himself. "I know. I never thought that I'd get it, but here we are."

Bobby sat there and wondered what he was going to do next. It was selfish thinking on Bobby's part. He knew that. But where else could his mind have gone? Maybe congratulations? "You sure this is what you want to do? I mean, that's pretty far away, right?"

"Other side of the country. Nearly three thousand miles give or take some," Sam replied rocking back slowly in his chair.

Bobby licked his lips and sat in silence. He was thinking of everything but nothing at the same time. He was losing his best friend, the only friend he had since he was an adult. The friends that he had made when he was a kid did not last. Do they ever? Maybe a precious few, but not his old crew from back in the day. Sam was like a brother to him and when he said that he was taking a principal's position in the state of Washington of all places, he was stunned. He knew that Sam had talked about doing something like before, but Bobby always guessed it would be somewhere close; not on the other side of the fucking country.

"Joey had this position come up and thought of me and I interviewed with their super and Joey pushed. I honestly didn't think that I'd get it."

"Clarissa onboard? Because she's never been out of the state." Bobby was secretly hoping that she was not. Maybe that would cause enough tension for him to give it up and not force a move.

"Yeah, ever since her mom died there's nothing tying her here. She's kind of looking forward to it, I guess. Money that I'll be pulling down she can quit her job and have more time with Brit."

Well, there that goes, Bobby thought.

Bobby chewed on his bottom lip. He was getting anxious and sad at the same time. He hated seeing Sam go. He was the one Bobby could go to when things felt tight inside his head and boy did they ever feel tight those days. He did not know exactly where he would have been, probably not sitting there talking on the back porch with him, had Sam not been there through all of Bobby's tears and bouts of depression.
"By mid-August, huh?" Bobby managed to ask.

Sam nodded, "Yup. Joey has me and the family a place to stay until we find a house out there. He's been great. I owe him a lot. I wouldn't have even gotten into teaching had it not been for him."

Bobby knew that his brother Joey was a good man and that once he moved out into the Northwest, he would eventually get his little brother out there, too. Bobby sat there and was heartbroken by his best friend's news. He knew this was the end of the Sam and Bobby show. The series was canceled, and the characters would be in their separate spin-offs after the move.

7

Bobby and Dana did not talk very much in the aftermath of their son's death. When they did talk Dana called it empty talk. Bobby knew all about empty talk—empty talk that never went anywhere. That was exactly where it was going when Sam moved away. Bobby knew deep down that the two of them were probably finished. At least they had finished on good terms, right? Yeah, they did.

Over the months that ensued, Bobby and Sam tried to make a long-distance friendship work. It did somewhat. Bobby would call and just miss him, and Sam would do the same. Even Dana, when she still lived at home with Bobby, would miss Clarissa when she would call, and the same with Clarissa when she called the Downey home. The four always just missed the other in that grand old game of phone tag.

After several frustrating games of phone tag, Bobby was getting the big picture: Sam was slowly sinking into the sea of his life out there in Washington and was too busy for him. Sam was a friend, a good one, honestly his best, but Bobby was not out there, was he? So, Sam had to make new friends to replace Bobby. Bobby knew this and was not happy about it, but he accepted it. He knew that his last best friend was gone, only a ghost rattling around inside his head with others he had lost along the way. That was life; sometimes hard and sometimes good, always fluid and forever changing.

It would have been nice to have Sam around, especially after the day he had at school replaying the day his son was killed. It was too much. There was no one to tell this time around when it happened. Bobby would always talk to Sam about his dreams of Freddy and how they affected him. Sam would listen. Just sit there and listen. That act of kindness was invaluable to Bobby. He was able to vent and say whatever and there was no judgment whatsoever from Sam. He just listened. One thing he never told Sam was about his Ritalin abuse. Sam had known about the alcohol but the Ritalin? No chance. Maybe he did and he didn't say anything.

I'm sure Dana said something about it to Clarissa. Maybe Sam figured it wouldn't matter what he said to me and that I was going to do whatever I wanted.

8

In the months after Freddy's death, Bobby would dream about his son. He would swear on a stack of bibles ten high that he could hear him in the house laughing or just simply calling out "Dad?!" There was no one at home but Bobby and Dana. On those tough days and nights, he would call and talk to Sam and cry it out or talk it out; whatever was needed at the time. Sam would always be there and when Bobby and Dana finally called their marriage, it was Sam that was at his house to help him through it right before he left for the Northwest forever.

Bobby had no better friend than Sam Wells. Now, Sam was gone and the feelings, the bad ones, were coming back; his dead son, Glick, and Dana being gone were all things that were wearing his mind out. Of course, Sam was just a phone call away if he was even home which was a big IF these days. Bobby had left messages on the family's answering machine sometimes. His messages were always returned when Bobby was gone with Sam leaving one on Bobby's machine. It was phone tag in its basic form.

Bobby sat at the dining room table head propped up on his hands listening to Sam Cooke's, "Bring It On Home To Me" on his old record player off in the distance. Prince had ended and Bobby was feeling mellow. With elbows on the table, Bobby looked at the stack of papers, most of them not important, but still needed to be signed and organized, and filed away in his office tomorrow. He glanced at the telephone that sat next to the plate of cold chicken parm and fought back the desire to call up Sam and tell him what a dick the new principal Glick seemed to be. But he didn't. Bobby knew that his calls would probably hit the machine and by the time Sam called back, probably later on because of the time difference from there to Washington, the moment would have passed.

Bobby was all alone. Being alone was a frightening proposition for him. When he was alone, he got to thinking and thinking led him to dark places that he did not want to go. One of Sam's major friend functions as a best friend was to keep Bobby on the main highway and not let him take a left or a right down some country back road that only would lead to sorrow and dead ends. Sam was not there anymore to keep him on the road, and it was up to Bobby to keep going down the safe and familiar stretch of life's highway. It was something that he was going to have to get used to because there was no one else to do it.

He had made it to bed around eleven-thirty. He lay there on his king-size bed right smack in the middle of it staring up at the ceiling. After getting tired of staring at the ceiling he turned to stare at the walls. This was his new normal: a man without anyone to prop up against; a man that might as well be washed up on a deserted island. Dana had been gone for a little bit now and her emptiness in the bed was felt keenly. Sometimes he would wad up the covers and hug them pretending that they were her and cry. He missed her so much. He missed Freddy. He missed his old life and hated the new normal. He was alone and had been for what seemed to be forever. Honestly, ever since his son died and his wife left it was Bobby and the house. It was only a house now. Home was what it was when the family was there.

He often thought about just selling the house and leaving all the memories behind and starting over and rebuild his life. That was what Dana had tried to get him to understand. Bobby now realized what she was trying to tell him. She could not do it anymore there. Bobby? Well, he was beginning to finally get it; finally getting what she was trying to tell him. God, why did he not listen to her? Leaving back then seemed treasonous to Freddy's memory is why.

Rebuilding would be hard, starting over from scratch was not in the cards. But essentially, that was what Bobby Downey was doing but just in the same house. He would never admit it to anyone, but he considered Dana brave for leaving. That took some guts, he thought to himself. Bobby just did what anyone in his position would do—he just kept on keeping on…by himself. Lying there in bed he wondered if there was more to life than just living and dying. Could there be a point to it all? And if so, what was it? Was life just a thing we did before we died? Bobby wondered. His thoughts wandered all over the subject. Eventually, sleep did finally capture him as the effects of the Ritalin wore off. It was four forty-five a.m., an hour before his alarm would go off for the first day of school.

Chapter 5

1

Ben had dropped the knife to the floor. His emotions had finally caught him by his throat and forced the issue. Tears poured out his eyes and he fell backward, hitting the floor hard, almost knocking the breath out of his body. He cried so hard that his stomach stayed in a constant state of tension as he looked up at the ceiling through lenses of water. Looking through his eyes was like looking through a dirty plastic bag filled with water; nothing came into focus, and everything was blurry.

Ben lay there on his back and cried heavily for the first time in a very long time. He wanted the pain to go away; the pain that started when his dad died. All he wanted to do with that knife was to take the pain away and feel something other than depression and guilt. "Why did he have to die?" Ben blubbered over and over on his bedroom floor. Ben wanted his dad back—his life to be normal again where his family was whole as it had been. But he knew that it would never be like that again…ever again. A change had come into the Medlen household and things were different. So much so that Ben did not want to live anymore.

People had told him that it would take time to move on and that eventually, he would. The secret that those people did not know was that Ben could not move on. He did not have the strength to do it. He was knocked out coldly in the boxing ring, lying on the canvas as the ref counted slowly to ten. Ben was not getting up to fight anymore. There was no more fight left in him, no more punches to throw. In the spring of his youth, the springtime of his existence where things were planted and tended to, where experiences would be made both good and bad, Ben was ready to give up and die away like the fading embers of a dying fire.

He was alone and could feel it all around him. It was the most alone he had ever been, lying on his back looking up at the ceiling and crying. No one could pick him up, dust him off, and set him anew. He was alone on that cold iceberg drifting on the water in the dark towards nothing; emptiness. If he ever needed someone it was at the very moment when the thought of suicide was fresh and inviting. He was desperate and nobody knew how desperate Ben had become.

It was that desperation that had led him to the mirror holding the knife. It was that desperation that had convinced him that life was not worth living. It was that desperation that was the sum of the problem. When his dad passed away, he and his mother moved into the home where dear old dad spent his youth; things had only gotten much worse from there. His mother had no clue how desperate her son had become, and she would never because she was fighting, too, in the wake of her husband's death early on. It was a different kind of battle that had fundamentally changed who Bailey was. Bailey Medlen, as she and her son knew it, was never more. A newer Bailey Medlen emerged from the wreckage. Maybe Ben was different, too. He felt different inside; broken down mentally with no fight left in his spirit.

2

Ben was not obtuse about how the death had affected his mother. He could see it in her eyes; see it in her movements and speech. They had both lost something special but on different, varying degrees. Ben lost a parent, a mentor, a person that he could go to for advice any day, any time of night, three hundred and sixty-five days a year. His mother had lost the love of her life as far back as when they were young at the summer camp. Bailey had lost someone that she had a child with and someone that she was supposed to grow old with on the front porch.

That was the plan: to grow old together and watch as Ben and his wife brought their kids, their grandchildren, over for a visit. When he died, plans had changed and left her and Ben holding the bag of what was supposed to be and forced to deal with a new bag: what will never be.

Ben lay there on the floor of his dad's old bedroom, the hardwood cool against his back through his shirt, and eventually cried himself to sleep. His last conscious thoughts were of how empty he had felt, how insignificant he was in the grand scheme of things. He wanted to die.

The pain was intense deep down in his heart and it grabbed a hold of his soul and gripped it so tightly that sometimes Ben could not breathe. That feeling, he had come to know, was a panic attack. Those had become more often in the days after his father's death. He had heard about them in his health class in school back home, back when everything was great and sunny, but had never experienced one. Nowadays, he was having them often, but he avoided telling his mother. Besides, Ben had resigned, would she even care?

Killing himself would end all the pain, and maybe a trip to see his dad, but when he fell onto his back and cried on the floor looking up at the ceiling, he knew that he never could because of his mom. It was his mother somewhere in the house that had prevented him from taking that knife and slashing his wrists open to collapse on the floor to bleed out. Had it not been for her he would have done it.

That was the bitch of the bunch. He was ready to die and needed to leave his life of pain and sorrow, but his mother, unbeknownst to her, was the stopper. Even though she was undergoing some strong changes within herself inside and out, Ben held back from slicing into himself because of her. He did not want her to have to lose another. Had he known what was coming in the future in terms of his mother, Ben would have gone ahead and opened himself up.

With nothing else to do to alleviate the pain, Ben lies there on his back and cried, not latching onto any of the fast-flashing images going through his head at the time. Eventually, sleep found him. He had cried himself to sleep and that was good. He needed a release, temporary as it was, from the exhaustion. He was going to need some rest because tomorrow was the first day of school.

3

Sleep was thin all night. That was exactly how Bobby wanted it because that meant the Ritalin had not let him down. Bobby tossed and turned throughout as he thought he would. It came as no surprise that when his alarm went off that he felt tired and ran down. He knew once he got out of bed, got dressed, and got some caffeine and Ritalin into his system that he would be good to go. Five forty-five had come early on that first official day of school where the kids flooded the hallways and went about their business. He was ready to face the day as it was. It was his first real day of school without his family and that was a weird sensation as he began to get out of bed. It was the first day without Sam, too. Today was about adjustments; the new normal.

Bobby put on a blue button-down shirt, black striped tie and slipped on his black slacks tucking his shirt. He snaked the belt through the loops of his pants, and then buckled it and reached for his glasses and put them on. He combed his hair; swaths of gray were beginning to shimmer this season of school. That's new, Bobby thought to himself as he leaned over the sink to inspect his hair more curiosity; gray around the sides. Nothing major. But certainly not there a couple of months ago. Or was it? Bobby did not think so but could not be entirely sure either. Did it really matter?

Bobby was not vain and thankfully that was a character defect that he was glad he never acquired. Gray gave those that bore it a look of distinction. He was okay with it because good Christ he was not twenty anymore. Not even in his thirties. The forties had come and so had the touches of gray. Standing there looking at himself, a different version of months ago, Bobby nearly didn't recognize the man in the mirror. Time and change could be seen on Bobby Downey.

4

When his mom came knocking on his bedroom door, Ben found himself lying on the bed, his dad's bed, under the covers. He stirred about raising up on his right arm, eyes half open, still hurting from crying the hours before, and looked around the bedroom. How did I end up here, he wondered as his mother knocked on the door, "Ben, you need to get up. You've got about thirty minutes before we've got to leave if you're going to make it to school on time." School had finally come and that was something that caused Ben a great amount of fear. Being new was something that Ben had not been in a long time, not since he was a freshman at his old high school. But even then, he was not what you would call the new kid. He was there with his friends from junior high who he had gone to school with for years and played little league sports with. But here in a new town, his dad's town, he was going to be the new kid on the block. That filled him with immense anxiety.

Ben was not good at being new and honestly did not know how to be or how to act. Ever since they moved into his dad's old home, he dreaded the day that he was going to have to go to a new school. His mother had lied to him and vaguely promised him that staying at his dad's house where he grew up was only temporary, at least enough time to figure out what their next play was. But he knew what the next play was: it was staying at the Medlen home, the original Medlen home because his mother had gotten complacent.

Stirring about in his bedroom, Ben opened his closet and reached in, grabbing a South Carolina Gamecocks tee shirt and a pair of jeans. Over at the chest of drawers that used to be his dad's, Ben opened the drawer and retrieved a pair of balled-up socks. With clothes in hand, he walked over to the window and looked out into his neighborhood. It was quiet and peaceful, and the sun was already in full view spilling light into the room. He looked over at the clock on his nightstand and saw that in under an hour he would be in a new school. That thought made him shudder and caused butterflies to swarm inside his stomach. He fought the urge to vomit there in his bedroom. Then his eyes fell onto the knife lying on the floor. Ben looked at it for a moment before being snapped back into reality by his mother's voice from downstairs yelling for him to "get going!"

5

It was eight-thirty in his office as Bobby sat at his desk going over a list of freshman names that were new to the high school. In one pile were those new names and in another pile were the sophomores, a third and fourth stack were juniors and seniors. Perhaps it would have been much easier to enter all of this into a computer program and keep up with it that way, but Bobby put it off. Even Sam had gotten on his ass about stepping into the land of organization and computer technology. Bobby was organized, just not electronically. He was still tethered to the old ways, the good ways.

"You know," Sam began one day while sitting in his friend's office looking at the filing cabinets and stacks of papers on Bobby's desk, "they'll come a time, and it's here now, that you won't need all these papers and filing cabinets. It'll all be on a computer. All's you'll have to do is punch in a name and that person's file will just come up. You actually can do it now. I can show you. Let me lead the way," he said with a laugh.

Bobby sat behind his desk smiling, "Nah, you know me, Sammy. I'll do it the old way until I can't do it anymore. Besides, I think I remember these kids better this way. Writing stuff down sort of brands it into my mind. But I do use it for making class schedules. That's at least a step in the right direction."

"You know, technology ain't a bad thing," Sam reminded.

"Until it all goes down and then where are you?" Both men laughed. "Seriously though, I use my computer quite a bit contrary to popular belief. I do plan on putting all these files into the computer next year. I plan on coming in during the summer and doing it." That summer Bobby never made it to school to do anything. Freddy was dead and his marriage was not long afterward.

Bobby saw that there were approximately two-hundred and fifty-two freshmen this year, up by forty from last year. It was the biggest incoming freshman class since he had been there and pushing the school's total enrollment right at a thousand. Bobby leaned back and looked at the four stacks of papers on his desk with the names of every student, their class schedules, what sports they played, and medical docs. Within those stacks, highlighted names in red meant there were at-risk students. Those names and files were given to him from the schools before them coming to Central High. Bobby was a stern believer in trying to have everything about the new kids coming in that he possibly could from the eighth-grade teachers. He felt that if he knew who was who he could help them all better, especially the at-risk kids, the ones that liked to fight and could not care less about their academic careers.

An at-risk student highlighted in red was a signal that Bobby needed to keep close tabs on them. He and the teachers, the ones that still cared some, would communicate throughout the school year on grades and behaviors for the at-risk students. Of course, some teachers were so burned out they never communicated back to Bobby how they were doing until he came calling to see how things were. Bobby would even go as far as contacting the parents or whoever it was that was in charge of these kids if something was going on at school. A lot of the parents or those in charge, sometimes aunts and uncles or most of the times grandparents, did not know anything about the kid and in some sad instances did not seem to care. That made Bobby's job that much more difficult. He cared about the kids in his school, especially the wayward ones that were headed down dead ends.

Some of the at-risk students had personal issues at home or were on the verge of criminal activity. Several had a looming drug problem. Some were at risk of not graduating. At any rate, whatever the case may be, Bobby had to save as many as he could. What he called his save record was standing at twenty percent; two out of every ten names written in red he helped get through the trials and tribulations of high school and teenage life. He wished it was more, but he knew that there were just some kids, some situations, that not even he could fix.

"A lot of kids," he told Sam in his office one day, "don't want to be fixed."

Leaning back in his desk chair, he was contemplating on starting his interviews with the freshman today, starting in alphabetical order when Rich came knocking on his half-open door. Bobby leaned over and saw Rich and motioned for him to come in.

"Have you seen Laurie today?" Rich said, sitting down in a chair in front of Bobby's desk. "Fuck me. She's wearing this skirt that is probably illegal in some states. I'd love to be in her class sitting in the front. On the first day of school and she does this. Killing me, man!"

"Shouldn't you be in class?" Bobby asked incredulously at his work buddy. Bobby never called Rich Wilkerson a friend. That word was reserved for Sam who was three thousand miles away. Rich was young, mid-twenties, and had been teaching for only three years at the school. He was an assistant football coach and already going bald. Probably in the genes, Bobby guessed. At any rate, Rich was your typical already past-his-prime ex-jock. When he saw Rich around the school, he was always laughing it up with the male student-athletes and flirting with the young girls.

"Eventually," Bobby had told Sam one day last year, "him flirting with the girls is going to catch up with him." Sam agreed.

"Yeah, probably, but it's Driver's Ed. I just handed out some papers they need their parents to sign and told them to keep their voices down to a dull roar," Rich said. "But you need to see her, dude. Make an excuse to go into her class sometime today and you'll see what I mean."

"I'll take your word for it," Bobby said, hoping that was enough to get Rich out of his office.

Rich drummed his fingers on his knees and looked around Bobby's office. "So, what's with the papers there?"

"Just files of all the kids and such. Kids I've got to keep up with. Mostly at-risk kids."

"You like being in guidance?"

Bobby sat there and wondered if this was the real Rich Wilkerson speaking or if he was leading up to another riff on Laurie Duckworth. "Yeah, most of the time I do."

"I only got into teaching so I can coach football. The rest of it I don't really care about. I'm just hanging out here until Coach Reedy retires so I can be the HC one day." Bobby had figured that was the play long ago when Rich first started. Actually, it was Sam who called it. It was a well-known secret that Rich Wilkerson was not really committed to the profession of teaching. But then again how many educators there at the school were? Bobby could count them all on his right hand which were legit teachers that taught and cared.

"Everybody's got to have a goal," Bobby replied emptily. Before Rich could reply, Bobby's phone on his desk rang and he picked it up. It was old Mrs. Nixon at the front desk. She wanted to know if Bobby had time to speak to a student. "Of course, send them in. Richard, I've got a kid coming in here. Do you mind?"

"Not at all, duder," Rich got up but before he walked out of the door, he turned and looked back at Bobby, "I'm serious about Laurie. Tell me what you think later." Bobby did not think of himself as an irresponsible person by no means, and true he had his share of mistakes and missteps throughout his life, but one of the dumbest things that he ever did was give Rich his phone number and the illusion that they were good friends. It's not that he disliked Rich, but he did not like the persona of the man. He did not think Rich was fake by no means. What you saw was what you got. In all honesty, Rich was probably the most honest person aside from Sam he had ever met. He was who he was, warts and all. You either liked him a lot or you didn't. There was no in-between when it came to Rich Wilkerson.

6

Ben had gotten out of the car on that first day of school and his mom put her hand to her mouth, kissed it, and flung it to her son who was standing there wanting ever so badly to get back into that car and drive all the way back to South Carolina; back to his home, back to his friends, back to his life. But that notion was knocked out of his mind when a fat kid bumped into him causing Ben to stagger back a few steps. "Watch it, bitch," the fat boy said, lumbering to the steel gray double doors to the school. The first interaction he had was terrible at his new school.

Watching his mother's car drive away through the exit gates where other cars and yellow buses had gone through, Ben tried to get a handle on his nerves and turned around and walked to the double doors where all the other kids, walking in tandems and triples with their cliques, were going. He was soon enveloped in the sea of teenage population and was just a face in the crowd.

When he got into the school, the smell of clean was the first thing that he noticed. The next thing was that the front of the building had opened up into the humongous cafeteria. It was circular with classrooms outlining the oval-shaped eatery. All the classroom doors were open and some of the well-dressed teachers were standing at them to greet their students when they approached or to guide them to where they needed to be.

Ben reached into his jeans pocket to fish out his class schedule and to his utter surprise he came up empty. He tried his other pocket and the only thing there was an ink pen. He frantically checked his back pockets. Empty. He took off his backpack at the double doors. He quickly found out how much of a bad idea that was as he knelt on his left knee and unzipped his backpack. He plunged his hands in and took out notebooks of paper. It was at that moment when a herd of kids came through the doors, laughing, cursing, talking, and yelling the way teenagers often do. None of them paid any attention to the kid on his bended knee searching for, in vain, a piece of paper that his mother had given him on Friday when she enrolled him.

Where was that daily schedule? Who knew? Probably on his dresser. Ben was knocked around by those traveling kids and eventually his notebooks were knocked out of his hands and then kicked by the shoes of those teens across the floor. His entire backpack was quickly scattered across the cafeteria floor, under chairs and tables by the time the last few kids came in through the double doors. This day keeps getting worse, he thought to himself, scrambling to recover the contents of his backpack.

By the time the late bell rang out that morning, Ben had retrieved all his notebooks of paper and pencils and other such school stuff. He was late according to the bell but late for where? He had not a clue. Ben stood in the silent cafeteria and looked at all the classroom doors that were now closed. His only refuge was the school front office which was easily identifiable by its see-through glass walls. Besides, the header in blue above the office archway read OFFICE. It looked eerily similar to the one back home in South Carolina. Zipping up his backpack, and shouldering it once again, Ben went for help.

7

A knock on his open door by Mrs. Nixon's frail hand brought Bobby out of his train of thought about Rich, "Mr. Downey, I've got Ben Medlen here. He's a junior. It's his first day and he doesn't know where to go… to what class, rather." Mrs. Nixon slowly moved to the right and Ben appeared, meekly, head lowered with his backpack strapped to his back.

Bobby spoke friendly, "Well come on in, my man!" Bobby got up from his chair and walked around to meet Ben with his hand extended. Ben walked into the office and shook Bobby's hand limply with eyes not looking at him directly. "Please, have a seat. The chair is pretty comfortable, made it myself back in my days when I was a small Panamanian child laborer." Ben did not laugh or even smile but that was part of Bobby's routine. He tried to make a joke to loosen up the tension most kids had when they came into his office.

Ben sat down on the chair Rich had just moments ago gotten up from. "Thank you, Mrs. Nixon. Tell Dick I think he got a raw deal."

"Who's Dick?" the old secretary asked, confused. The "Tell Dick I think he got a raw deal" joke started when Bobby began his career at the school. When a younger and more alert Mrs. Nixon used to run the office, it was a President Richard Nixon joke between them, an inside joke, that they both laughed at. Over the years the old woman began to forget things and with age, the inside joke between them had been lost to time. "Never mind, Mrs. Nixon. Thank you."

Bobby closed the door and went back to his desk and sat down. "Well, Mr. Medlen. What brings you by this time of the morning?"

"I don't have my class schedule. I think I forgot it at home," Ben managed to say through chewing his nails, looking down at the floor of Bobby's office.

Bobby nodded his head, "Okay, not a big problem. You said your name was Bill Clinton?" Another intentionally failed joke. He looked at the kid sitting in front of him biting away on his nails not getting the reference.

"About a nine on the tension scale there, Ben. You understand comedy, right?"

Bobby turned to the right of his desk in his chair and started to thumb through the stack of junior class files. A few moments later he pulled out Ben Medlen's bio folder. He opened the manila file folder and thumbed through the papers that his mother had signed last week when she enrolled him. "South Carolina, huh? Played golf in that state once. Wasn't the PGA tour or anything like that. Don't get the wrong idea here. I ain't that good."

Ben's class schedule was placed in the very back of all the important papers. He took the schedule, got up and went to his copier and made a copy of it, and handed it to Ben while putting the original back into the folder. "Here you go, Mr. Medlen. Use it in good health." Ben avoided eye contact and rose to take the paper from Bobby and shouldered his backpack on again.

"Thanks," he sheepishly replied.

"You're welcome," Bobby replied. Before Ben could walk out, Bobby said, "You lose that one it will cost you a finger. That's how I run things around here. Tell your friends. Now get out of here, you talk too much," Bobby said, turning back around to his desk to look at his computer.

Although Bobby did not see it, Ben smiled for the first time since being in Tennessee at the guidance counselor's snarky, playful demeanor. It would be the highlight of the day for Ben, meeting Bobby Downey, as his first day of school went exactly as he thought it would go. Even with the class schedule, he was still confused about exactly where to go, and where the classes actually were located within the school. To Ben, the school was laid out way differently than his back home. This one seemed to him like a maze.

8

The school was sectioned off into the science pod, which was circular with a science office in the hub of the circle. Classrooms, five of them, surrounded the science office hub like the classrooms that surrounded the cafeteria; then came the math pod, the English pod, the business pod, and the history pod on the far left of the school. The classrooms that were on the rim of the cafeteria were elective classrooms like art, shop, music, auto mechanics, and drafting. All of it was confusing for Ben who tried to navigate the best he could. He dared not ask anyone for help. Nobody helps the new kid, he thought. He was a stranger in a strange land. Eventually, Ben would figure it all out. He was late for most classes that first day, but he used his wits and figured out where to go.

As he roamed the halls of teenage life in between fifth and sixth-period class change, he spied Bobby Downey, the man that had helped him earlier that morning, posted up by the main office wall drinking out of a Braves coffee cup alone. There was something about Bobby that Ben liked. He could tell that he was a warm soul, the type of person who you could just sit around and talk with. Personable would-be what Steve Medlen would have called him.

Bobby looked around and saw Ben standing there trying to figure out where what direction to go. He and Ben locked eyes and Bobby held up his left hand and wiggled his fingers "Don't lose that schedule. Fingers, remember? I cut them off." Ben smiled for the second time that day. Bobby half grinned and before Ben could walk over and ask Bobby for directions, a female teacher came over to Bobby whisking him away by his arm, the both of them laughing at whatever it was she was saying to him as they walked down the hall. "Let's just try to find these next two classes," Ben told himself.

Chapter 6

1

Ben's first day at his new school was in the books and it was not a rousing success. He did not think it would be. The teachers were different than back home: they talked a little differently, acted a little differently, and taught school a little differently. It was all different for the transplant. Ben went the whole day avoiding eye contact with everyone and tried to keep his head down. It was not ideal but it was all he could manage to do. He was not confident to look anyone in the eye, at least not yet, not like back home.

In class, Ben only looked up when the teacher was speaking. Not once did he look around and scan the room for a friendly face. He did not think he would find any if he had. In a room full of people, Ben never felt so lonely, so betrayed by his mother as he did at school that morning. Everything, his dad's death, moving and now a new school was bending his mental state. He could hear the floorboards cracking in his mind every once in a while, and worried when the floor would give way underneath his feet. He had nearly ended it all the night before and wondered how much more he could take.

School, the first day of a two-year odyssey, was in the books. The bus ride home had pretty much gone like the day at school had. He had gotten on the wrong bus to home to start with and although he was not familiar with the streets and neighborhoods, he knew enough that he was on the wrong bus. When the bus driver stopped to let some kids out, Ben slowly walked up the bus aisle to the overweight alcohol-smelling driver and told him that he thought he was on the wrong bus. The driver told Ben pretty much that was his problem. Ben stood there as kids were getting off at this stop bumping into him and his bulging backpack causing him to sway around as the driver thought of how to get Ben home. "Where you live, kid?"

Ben stood there and thought for a few seconds, "1456 Morgan Street."

"Morgan Street?" the large driver replied. "That's all the way across town." Ben and the driver stood there looking at each other like they were in some sort of Old West showdown out in the street. "I can't take you that far," the driver said. Truth was, he could have if he wanted to and if Ben or his mother had raised the issue to the school about it, Ernie, the bus driver for bus sixty-seven, would have more than likely been suspended for not looking after the welfare of a student. But as it was, Ben nor his mother reported the incident.

With the driver not offering to help the kid out, Ben decided for him. He got off at the stop, in a strange but well-maintained-looking neighborhood, and said that he would call his mother for a ride. The driver said not to worry that this was a safe place and closed the door and relaxed the air brakes and drove away leaving Ben watching the kids look at him through the windows of the bus. He looked around and had some relief thanking God that this was not the bad part of town. At least he did not think that it was.

"Okay," Ben said out loud to no one but himself, "you're stranded in a new town, and you have no idea where home is or what direction even. What to do?" Ben stood there, backpack hanging off his shoulders, thinking…

2

Bobby was finishing up some after-school stuff in his office when a knock came lightly at his half-open door. He looked up and his heart dropped thirty thousand feet. It was April Murray. She had been there as a teacher, of American History, for around eleven years if Bobby was remembering that correctly. A year before he had started Central High.

Bobby flashed a friendly smile and waved her in, "Shouldn't you be gone by now?"

"I could say the same thing about you, Bobby Downey," April said, leaning her shoulder against the metal door frame, arms crossed in front of her chest, smiling back.

"I'm just trying to get some things ready for tomorrow. I'd write it down on a Post-It and do it in the morning but then I'd forget where I put the damn Post-It." They both laughed, it wasn't funny but that's how people laughed when they totally liked each other.

"You're such a dork, you know that?" April said playfully, just more small talk in the dance.

"Yeah, well. What are you going to do, Ms. Murray?" he returned from his desk.

The two of them locked eyes for what seemed hours. April finally broke the enchantment and looked down at the floor and then back at Bobby, "So, the reason that I came to see you was to ask if you'd be interested in walking the track at the football game with me Friday night. Jackson ain't going now and I was like, 'I might know someone who maybe was a little willing,'" Walking the track at the game was exactly what it sounded like. The football field where the Yellow Jackets played was surrounded by this long oval running track that was used for the high school track team.

During home games, two teachers were to walk around the track and keep an eye on the kids that were walking around it instead of watching the football game. They were to make sure that nothing got out of hand, no fights, no drug use, things like that. Most teachers did not like doing it and it before the year got underway in terms of sporting events, Terrance would assign random teachers to walk the track or be at the ticket window or concession stands at the events.

Those teachers could get out of it only if they had another teacher stand in for them but that usually came at a fifty-dollar fee. Some teachers did all the sporting events, racking up fifty bucks an event. Mr. Evans, the shop teacher, one year made nearly fifteen hundred dollars selling his time to those teachers that had asked him to take their place for whatever reason. Bobby and Sam had walked the track a few times back in the old days. They would walk around, watching teenagers making sure there was not anything crazy going on.

There was this one time when Bobby and Sam had to intervene in a fight there on the track one home game. Two greasers, a term that rough-end guys at their school were called, had gotten into a fight around the end of the third quarter. Over what, no one afterward was really sure. It happened on the visiting side of the track and when the crowd swooped over to where the two dudes were throwing down, much like teenagers do when a fight breaks out, Bobby and Sam ran quickly over to the brawl and weaved and pushed their way through the crowd. Bobby grabbed one and Sam the other. They pulled them apart despite them swinging and cussing the other. That was the last time Bobby had walked the track, November of 1993, the last home football game he did. That was back when Freddy was alive, and Dana was still his wife. Those were the good ol' days.

"Wow," Bobby replied. "First home game. Going to be a lot of people. What are you going to be packing?"

"I thought a Smith 360 Taser. You know, release the lightning if I have to." Bobby smiled and raised his eyebrows at her witty retort as they were now just being funny with each other. "Lot of lightning there for a history teacher. Sure you know how to handle that?"

"No, but I'll have fun trying if anybody gets out of line. I may just have to practice a time or two on you. You know, to get the feel of it," April returned Bobby's verbal lob over the net.

Bobby leaned back in his chair and thought about April's proposal. "That sounds like a regular Saturday night at the Downey house," Bobby smiled. He could not help but to smile around April. "Yeah, I'll go with you. You make a compelling argument."

"Good. Glad I could talk you into it," April said, smiling.

"I'm going to let you know up front, that I'm not a cheap date."

"Really?"

"Really," Bobby replied deadpan. It was his signature humor at the school. Bobby Downey was regarded as one of the most sarcastic, snarkiest, and funniest guys in the school, probably in the entire county school system and that was partly why people liked him; partly why April liked him and was drawn to him. "I'm going to need at least a hot dog, with the works and a bottle of water. Room temperature at the very least. If it's not room temperature, then I send it back."

"That's fair," April said, playing Bobby's game.

"I'm not finished. You don't get off that easy, Ms. Murray…"

April interrupted quickly, "I've never met the right man."
Bobby closed his mouth and smiled and was stunned by her comeback and threw his hands up in the air in a give-up gesture, "I've got nothing. Can't follow that."

"Okay then, Mr. Downey. I'll be seeing you around." April her pulled her shoulder off the metal door frame and turned to leave his doorway.

"You may indeed, Ms. Murray! We do work at the same place, you know!"
Bobby yelled out to her as she disappeared somewhere behind the walls of
the hallway. He could hear her distant laughing all the way to his office.
Bobby sat and thought to himself, what a girl.

3

Ben had finally gotten home after he called his mother from a house that
had a beautiful white picket fence and well-maintained lawn. Ben had
wandered around the neighborhood for about thirty long minutes in the
hot August sun trying to figure out what to do when he finally just gave up
and approached a woman who was tending to flowers at the edge of her
front porch. Ben walked up the walkway from the street and cleared his
throat as he stood before the woman. She looked up, frightened some, and
asked what the kid needed.

"I'm new to this town and I got on the wrong school bus and the bus driver
wouldn't take me home. Is there any way I can call my mother to come
to get me or maybe you could call her?" The lady smiled and invited Ben
into her house to make the call.

It actually was not that bad standing there waiting on the sidewalk in front
of Mrs. Jefferies' house. She had given Ben some cookies and a Coke and
told him that he could stay inside until his mom arrived. Ben appreciated
the hospitality and told her that he ought to wait outside so his mom could
see him. He thanked her for the phone call, the cookies, and the Coke
which helped quell his thirst on that hot day. Ben stood on the sidewalk
in front of Mrs. Jefferies' house looking around at the nice homes and oak
trees that were standing sentry on both sides of the street. The limbs of
those trees had given the neighborhood street a shady and cool canopy all
the way down as far as the eye could see. It seemed to be a nice place to
live. Where he now lived was nice, too, but it was just as foreign to him as
the neighborhood he was stranded in.

Ben walked up and down the sidewalk a bit, taking sips from a nearly
empty Coke can, looking around trying to make the time go faster. Was
it getting hotter as the day progressed? Ben could feel his hair get sweaty
and felt the beads of sweat roll from his hair down his back. Ben could
have easily stayed in the nice climate-controlled home of Mrs. Jefferies,

but she talked way too much and had way too many cats. Ben was allergic to cats that triggered itchy and watery eyes with a sneezing fit. Although not ideal, Ben opted to hang outside and wait for his mother to arrive, not telling the nice old lady that he was allergic to her cats as to why he could not stay inside. He thought that would be rude somehow.

About fifteen minutes later, Ben saw his mom's car turning onto the street. Ben was walking down the sidewalk when he spotted his mom's car. He was excited and relieved to see her. Ben opened the passenger side door and got in as she stopped the car in the street. "Are you okay?!" she asked. Ben could sense the panic in her voice.

"Yeah, I'm good."

Bailey wanted to know how in the world he got on the wrong bus. "Why couldn't that bus driver not bring you home?! You just wait, I'm going to contact the school board over this! Dropping a student off in a strange neighborhood! Doesn't he know that you're literally brand new to the area?! What if a pedophile kidnapped you?!" On and on she went until they reached home. Ben just sat, looking out the passenger side window listening to her.

Later that night in the Medlen home, Bailey was at the dining room table working on a crossword book, chewing on her pencil trying to figure out the clue: Rush Drummer Neil five letters across. She should know this because she was a music buff and had totally forgotten who the drummer was for Rush. How did that happen? She had listened to all of their records at various points in her life and knew all of the band members by name. She could rattle off stuff like that about music like nobody's business. That was one thing among many that she and Steve had in common: a love of music. Steve was gone and she was stuck there at the table trying to figure out who banged the drums for Rush. It was on the tip of her tongue, right there on the edge of her memory.

Ben was up in his bedroom, more particularly, at his small desk, which you guessed it, used to belong to his dear old dad. He had a small radio playing lowly on the window seal of his bedroom. The only station that he could get in clear was WIMZ out of Knoxville. It was a classic rock station and it sounded like the one back home in South Carolina, WZRM.

Sitting at his desk leaning back in his chair, Bob Seger's, "Night Moves", came on. That song took Ben back to South Carolina, back home, where that song was playing one night out in his dad's garage.

Inside that garage, Steve was working on his 1981 Chevy Malibu Classic. God how he loved that car, Ben remembered. Steve was under the hood ratcheting something or another when Ben came in, maybe twelve at the time, and that song, "Night Moves", was playing from the radio of that Malibu. As the song played in his bedroom, Ben teared up and nearly cried at the recollection of the memory. He could see his dad in his mind's eye, leaning over nearly all the way into the engine. He could hear the sound of the ratchet in his dad's hand turning, making that clicking sound as he was tightening or loosening something. Even though he wanted to cry at the hurt of mentally seeing his dad brought on by the song, Ben smiled.

4

As Ben was listening to Bob Seger and remembering a special point in time, and with Bailey finally recalling the name of the drummer for Rush, Neil Peart, Bobby was sitting in his recliner in his living room watching the Braves/Phillies game. He hated the Phillies. Always did. The house was quiet, like it was always those days, especially at night. The walls sometimes seemed to close in on him, making him feel claustrophobic. That used to never happen. That was because the house was a home with a family, a fully functional family at one point.
Eventually, the plan was to add another kid or two but that never came to pass. Instead, Bobby lost a kid one terrible day and a wife that walked out the door in the wake of it all.

His first day at school went okay. Having the students there had taken some of the edge off. He had a lot of work to do with the kids and being back in the saddle again so to speak, Bobby was good mentally. He had something at school that he did not have at home: distractions. The school offered many distractions throughout the day to keep his mind off of Freddy and his washed-up and dead marriage. Not to say that the thoughts did not slip through the filter and cause him to think back on the past, but for the most part, his first day was okay. Better than he thought it would be. However, being at home, there was not much in the way of distraction because the entire home smacked of his life past and present. Everywhere he looked he saw the ghosts of what was. For better or worse his house had become a museum of the Downey family.

He would not consider leaving the house for another. He was the stalwart. He felt it was his duty to keep what was going even though there was nothing left but charred remains, ruin, of what was and what will never be again. Bobby felt he had to keep the light on at the house. He had to. What choice did he really have? Leave like Dana did? Out of the question. Leaving meant closing the book on their family and Bobby was not ready to do that. He did not know if he ever could just pack up and leave the house. Sometimes, when deep in thought, he wondered if he would feel better if he did move from the house, away from Maple Lane where Freddy was killed. Sometimes, deep down, he wondered if staying was killing him.

Dana had been gone for a bit now, but it felt like yesterday when she shut the door on him, leaving him behind to deal with Freddy all by himself. He was a counselor and should know how to deal. But it was different when it was you having to deal with the fundamental destruction of the family. Dana could not or would not accept Freddy's death, Bobby could never tell which because she switched perspectives every thirty minutes it appeared. And she had the right to do so. It did not matter how many times she switched, Freddy was still dead.

Thoughts of the day that Dana finally left the house for good, leaving him to fend off the coming monsters inside his mind and the ones that lurked in the shadows of the house in the dark of night, always caught up with him when he was home trying to wind down. The house had very few distractions and keeping his mind off of things was a challenge, to say the least. No matter how engrossed he got in a book or a movie or a ball game, his mind eventually wandered over to the destruction of his life. In all of that destruction and ruin came the monsters.

When they came, those horrible monsters, they hunted him, growling and snarling in horrific audible sounds that echoed throughout his mind, bouncing around up there like a silver pinball in a pinball machine. Bobby would be thinking about something totally different and then a random memory of his dead son, his wife leaving, or the day that Freddy died, came from the locked room inside his mind. When the memories came out, touching his mind, those monsters would love nothing more than to pull Bobby down and eat him alive. He would run all night and day to evade them: the memories, the hurt, and the rawness of everything that happened to Freddy and everything afterward with Dana.

Feeling that the door was about to unlock itself, Bobby quickly got up from his comfy recliner and walked over to the end table on the other side of the room and picked up the phone. He was going to call Sam to see how his old friend was doing. It would do him good to hear a familiar voice, a voice of the past as it was now. He took his bottle of Ritalin and shook out several pills from the pill bottle. He tossed them into his mouth and swallowed them dry.

When Sam picked up on the third ring, Bobby started talking, and just as quickly as the locked door started to open, it closed. The monsters that were ready to stalk and prowl his mind stood down. There was no worry for those monsters. There would always be another time; another time when Bobby was relaxed and his guard down. That was all it would take.

5

After "Night Moves" went off and the DJ played some more oldies from the classic rock era, hours went by up there in his bedroom. Ben was feeling tired. His first day at school had taxed him so. He had planned to go through his backpack and review all of the papers that had been handed out throughout all of his classes. He even had homework on that first day in Mr. Richards' Physical Science class. That was a dick move for a teacher handing out homework on the first day, but it didn't matter. It was homework that was due by Friday.

Sitting on his bed, music playing lowly from his small radio with a bad antenna over on the window seal, Ben was organizing all his papers into folders. He considered himself pretty organized. Back home, his real home in South Carolina, he was an A student, 3.7 GPA. Smarts just came naturally to him. His father had been at the top of his class in college, and his mother was as well. Ben came from good genes.

The thing with Ben Medlen was that he did not have to think too much about schoolwork. You know the type because you probably sat beside them in school. All they had to do was review the material for a few minutes and then ace the exam. And pop quizzes? Forget get about it, get out of town. Ben was never taken off guard by those. He seemed to be always prepared but never studied for anything. That was his gift he reckoned. But what good was it now?

His dad was dead, he was in a foreign land in Claxton, Tennessee, and was barely holding things together. Holding things together mentally was something that he did not know if he was smart enough to do. Even intelligent people killed themselves. Sometimes intelligent people just broke. Miles apart across town, two people, Bobby Downey and Ben Medlen were fighting internal battles which were wearing them down by the hour. Days and nights were mere battles but the war, ah the war, trudged on. Bobby had been battling for what seemed forever and Ben was fighting the same war, just over in another theater. The mental strain on the two of them had weakened them both immensely to the point of mental exhaustion. Both of them wondered when the dam would finally break and if the end was near.

Chapter 7

1

The rest of the week for Ben Medlen did not get much worse. Of course, it did not get much better either. He had memorized his class schedule by Wednesday and did not need his paper schedule, but he kept it in his back pocket just in case he had a memory lapse. On Thursday, he had gotten a better handle on how to quickly navigate the halls; swimming through the schools of people like they were fish going from here to there.

Ben made sure to get on the right bus that was to take him to his house. Monday and Tuesday he somehow managed to get on the wrong home buses again but by Wednesday he was finally on the right one. No more getting off in a strange neighborhood. This time around he knew exactly what bus to get on…seventy-eight, thanks to asking the front office for help the next morning after his last mix-up. He first checked to see if Bobby was in his office. Ben felt as if he was a point of reference, a guidepost of sorts, and although they had only met for just a few moments, Ben felt comfortable with him.

Bobby was always there for any of the students in the school and they all knew that. That was what made Bobby Downey one of the more popular people in the place. When Ben walked to Bobby's office door it was wide open, but he was not at his desk. So, Ben walked back up the hallway and talked to Mrs. Nixon, asking her about what bus he should get on. When she didn't know the answer she called another secretary, a younger one by at least forty years and she made the appropriate calls and figured it out for him with a smile.

By the end of the week, Ben was a master of the school and had even begun to file away teachers' names on the various classroom doors in the other areas of the school. Since it appeared that he and his mother were going to be in Claxton for some time it seemed, he might as well begin to get a lay of the land. It did not mean that he accepted the new school or his new position in life, but he knew that he had to, at the very least, figure out how to traverse the school. He had a handle on things now.

Friday came and went and so did the first week of his new school. He still hardly ever looked up, keeping his eyes glued to the floor even when he was walking through the halls as people bumped into him, jarring him from left to right. Even at the cafeteria, Ben sat nearly alone at the end of a table, the one he sat at on Monday, and ate his food. There were people close to him and perhaps would have talked to him if he had looked up from his food and paperback. He tried to blend in as much as he could, but he also was well aware that he was sticking out sitting there alone. It was a double-edged sword if there ever was one.

Ben had gotten a handle on his teachers as well. As the first week went by, he understood their styles and their personalities. Mr. Hodges was the Algebra II teacher and was a hard ass from the jump. His expectations were huge of his students, and he did not take anything off of anyone. Especially disruptions as he was at the dry-erase board writing formulas and talking about the various ways to arrive at the correct answer. One kid in that class had been laughing at something someone beside him had done and that was it all had taken for Mr. Hodges' fuse to be lit, which was a very short fuse to begin with. He told Mike Acres, a jock from the football team to gather his things and leave his room. "Off to study hall with you!" Ben had had a teacher similar to Hodges back home and knew how his temperament was. Ben would have no problem in this class because he was not a kid that partook in disruptive behavior. It's not that he did not find stuff funny, but he was a new fish in the pond and did not want to make waves.

His Physical Science teacher, Mr. Richards, was another high-strung educator. He was tall, monotone in speech, and talked so low that you had to practically lean toward him at your desk to hear him. That was if you did not fall asleep first, which a lot of kids did in that class. At one point, Mr. Richards was looking right at Ben like he was the only kid in the room. Uneasy about this, being singled out, Ben Medlen looked around the room, a cursory scan, and saw that nearly everyone, save about two more students, had fallen asleep at their desks. Some were even snoring and most had their heads down on their desks with drool ponding. It did not seem to bother Mr. Richards in the least bit. He must have been used to it by now with that low monotone, boring voice of his.

Shop class was something of a joke. In normal shop classes, you learn how to build things like birdhouses, lamps, and things like that. It wasn't that he thought he was too smart to be in there and thought it was a gimme grade. He did it because he liked building things with his hands. He guessed it started when he and his dad had built him a tree house out in his backyard up in a huge maple tree one summer when he was ten. He was fascinated by how much his dad knew about building and the skill that it had taken to make something out of nothing. Mr. Hammonds' shop class was a joke on every level. The teacher, an old man of seventy and way past retirement age, always sat in his office and read a newspaper and practically allowed the students, usually no more than eight to ten a period, to do whatever they wanted. They could build stuff if they liked, they could stand around and talk, they could use those forty minutes as a study hall, or just whatever they wished to do. Ben knew that the class was going to be an automatic A. Mr. Hammonds addressed the class on the first day and told them that they had to make something so he could pass them on; just one solo project. That was it. That would be easy enough. Five months to build something, whatever they wanted. It didn't matter. Ben was going to build a nice triple-decker birdhouse with attached bird feeders. Bailey loved birds, or at least she had back home in South Carolina.

His junior English class was taught by Mrs. Doolittle. She was a twenty-something teacher whose passion for literature practically vibrated off of her. She would get into these discussions with the students in the class over the book they were reading, and it felt that it was not a classroom at all; more like a book club discussion. It was one of the more intriguing classes that he had ever been a part of. If he would have had something like this back home, he would have liked it. He wanted to come out of his protective shell in that room and engage in the discussions. Mrs. Doolittle could see it in his eyes and tried to fish him out several times, but Ben was not ready for that just yet. He was still too timid to do so. He loved the way she taught. Ben found that most teachers he had encountered throughout his school career that were younger had more of a spark in their eyes, a sincereness in their voice and movements. It was the older ones that Ben had seen that had been beaten down by years of kids and monotonous workloads that never changed much from year to year. He was not even sure if some of those teachers were that smart to begin with. Ben concluded that even he could be a brilliant teacher if he taught the same thing over and over for thirty years. Intelligence was nothing more than repetition, Ben often thought to himself.

Mrs. Lowery's World Geography class was decent, too. She was a middle-aged teacher who still had her looks going for her and she appeared to know her stuff. You could tell in her voice, much like Mrs. Doolittle's, that she was passionate about geography. When she introduced herself on the first day to the class, for those that didn't know her already from being at the school freshman and sophomore years, she did not neglect to inform them all that she had been in Egypt on many archaeological dig sites and had traveled the world over and that in a few years she would have her Doctorate in Archeology. That was amazing to Ben because he had never known anyone that had done the stuff like she had. When she began her chapters of teaching that first week about ancient Egypt, it was as if she was giving a firsthand account of it. That made everyone in the class that much more involved. Ben loved it.

For his final class of the day, Ben had Art History with Ms. Simpson. She was an ex-army vet and knew her stuff when it came to art and the history of all the artists the world over. She was also a master in discipline. She could handle her classroom like nobody's business and that was made apparent to Ben when another kid, Mike Morgan, who had long flowing hair and wore a black Danzig tee shirt, had disrupted her while talking. Instead of doing what Mr. Hodges had done and telling the football player to gather his things and go to study hall, Ms. Simpson made Mike do twenty push-ups, military style. Ben found that punishment was nothing sort of intriguing.

2

Bobby's first official week went about as they all had for the last decade. He got the piles of papers that were on his desk sorted into his huge black filing cabinets, alphabetized them, and sorted them by grade. He even began using his computer more and keying in the files. On Tuesday, he took out all of the past seniors who had graduated in May and put them into the shred pile, which he shredded at the end of the week on Friday. His desk looked like a desk and not the catch-all it had been earlier.

On Wednesday, he finished moving all the files down the line in his row of filing cabinets. The freshmen from last year had gone into the number two cabinet marked SOPHOMORES; the sophomores went to the third cabinet marked JUNIORS; the juniors from last year went into the last cabinet marked SENIORS. In each of those filing cabinets, there was a red folder amongst all the manila ones: At-Risk Students, Bobby called it. They were students that needed help in the worst kind of way. Those at-risk students were either kids with bad records, bad grades, bad overall attitudes, or ones that were in danger of not graduating. Most of the time they were all four rolled into one. Bobby's job was to try to reach them and get them back on the main road. It didn't work all the time.

That red folder had been created since the at-risk student's freshman year and followed the line of cabinets until those students either graduated or dropped out of school entirely. Every freshman class had at-risk students. Bobby's goal was to reach the senior year with none in the red folder. It never happened.

In the senior filing cabinet this year, Bobby had gone from fifteen names that freshman year down to four. That was progress for him. It was a win. It seemed like he was doing good around there and to the best of his knowledge this was the thinnest the red folder for seniors had been since he'd been at the school. There were four names that he probably would not be able to get set right no matter what and he knew that; accepted it. He still had the rest of the school year to give it one last push; one last miracle mile to get them turned around before they graduated and were released into the wilds of society and adulthood. In his line of work, there were just some truths you had to understand: you just can't save them all. Bobby was down to four names. He thought that maybe, just maybe, this school year he could reach them.

3

Melaine Stubbs was one of the at-risk kids in that new senior cabinet. Bobby encountered her after her epic brawl in the school's cafeteria back in October of her freshman year. She had come back from her week of out-of-school suspension and was sent to Bobby's office for counseling. She was a hard case, a tough nut to crack, but not the hardest in Bobby's career. That distinction belonged to David Roth, a kid that was so full of rage and hate that he eventually dropped out of school and wound up in federal prison. Bobby knew that would probably be the fate of David. Sometimes sitting at his desk, leaning back, he looked at those at-risk kids and could tell what would eventually befall them.

Melaine Stubbs was a pretty girl but had pretty big problems at home she was dealing with. One of the problems for Melaine was that she had a robust sexual reputation. That branded her as a slut to most of the girls and she took exception to that. That's essentially what started the first brawl; someone called her a slut and she went bananas on them. By the time she was finished, well, pulled off by Mr. Hixson and Mr. Culberson, she had bloodied the girl's nose and pulled a chunk of her hair out. To boot,

Melaine had blackened both of the girl's eyes. That fight was a showcase that Melaine was not going to put up with things. Those that tested her resolve had better beware because Melaine Stubbs was a fighter.

Through the years, Bobby and Melaine notched a twice-a-week, counseling session in his office. She was guarded, defensive. She was vulnerable at times and showed that she did have some issues at home with her parents that had divorced the summer before she entered high school. Her father was abusive both mentally and sexually, which Bobby was going to turn over to the authorities, but it was a matter that had already been addressed sometime before Melanie came to school. Her mother was an alcoholic. "A high functioning one," Melaine told Bobby as if she was defending her mother's name for whatever reason. Perhaps it was out of some misguided loyalty, Bobby figured.

Bobby and Melanie had a good working relationship as counselor and patient/student there in his office. Melaine, as the meetings and years rolled by, had gotten more comfortable with Bobby. Eventually, she told him things about how her home really was (a house of horrors that gave Bobby nightmares) and her relationships with boys at the school. She talked about drinking and smoking pot. She talked about her sexual relationships there at school. And through it all, she talked about her dreams (wanting to be a lawyer) and where'd she like to live (Boston), what kind of house she saw herself in (a nice two-story Cape Cod), what kind of husband she wanted (one that worked, who was loyal, and was nice) and how many kids (just two).

She wanted a better life than the one she had. As time rolled on, that girl that had those dreams could not get out of the cycle of violence and self-deprecating tendencies she was chained to. Melaine Stubbs was like a record with a nick, and it skipped every time, never going anywhere but the same place. Bobby felt bad for her and cried a few times on his way home from school after the meetings between them. This girl never had a chance with her monster father and her alcoholic mother. Melaine had nobody to pick her up and dust her off and tell her it was going to be okay. Bobby tried, but he was too late. If only someone had come to her rescue earlier maybe things would have been different early on in high school. Melaine Stubbs was in that red folder and Bobby hoped and prayed that maybe one day she would not continue to be in that red folder of life; that maybe she would get better, do better, and become something better than what she had been exposed to over the years. Bobby held out hope for her…

4

Another student that lived in the red folder from sophomore year was Alexander, Alex to his friends, Reed. He was not violent, nor did he come from a bad and broken home. He was the opposite of Melaine Stubbs. Alexander's parents were prominent citizens of the town. His dad was a deputy mayor of Claxton while his mom was an accountant for a major law firm in Knoxville. A kid could not have come from a better, more helpful environment than Alexander had. In all that he had at home; it was not enough for Alex.

He was a kid that liked to just float around the school, not do the work that he was assigned. By the time he was a junior, he was already identified as one of the few that were in jeopardy of not graduating. He was far behind in credits. Bobby tallied it up in his office during his weekly meeting with Alexander that he would have to pass everything his current year, which was impossible now because of his lackadaisical view on academics and was certainly heading for summer school…again. If he passed everything in summer school, he would have to pass everything in his senior year and still would have to have a class or two in summer school to barely graduate. Alexander sat on the chair across from Bobby's desk, slumped down in it so much that it looked like he was laying straight, legs stretched out. Alex did not and would not take his schoolwork seriously. That did not stop Bobby from trying to get through to him.

Bobby had spoken to Alexander's parents, and they were immensely concerned about their son. Alexander's sister, Julie, was a freshman at the school and she was the exact opposite of her brother. She loved academics, was in the district's math bowl, was a cheerleader, was in several school clubs, had a GPA of 3.5, and was one of the more popular kids at her age. Bobby often wondered if Alexander acted out because of his sister. He tried to fish that out of him in secretive ways hoping that it would give him some insight on how to better steer him the rest of his high school career, but he would never give it up. Bobby began to think his theory of sibling rivalry was unfounded and that Alexander just liked being difficult. Not unheard of for kids his age.

Bobby and Alex met each Monday for thirty-minute sessions from his freshman year until his junior year when it was clear to Bobby that

Alexander was not going to change. Over the years, the meetings had been pared down to ten-minute bi-weekly sessions based on Bobby's notion that this kid wasn't going to care no matter what happened or how much he talked to him. They talked about different issues and such. Alexander had no issues at home. He was pretty popular with the kids around the school. He caused no trouble at school aside from the few pranks that he pulled on various teachers that Bobby thought were genius. Alexander was not a troubled kid nor was he a troublemaker. He was at his core a lazy kid who would turn out to be a lazy adult. "Brilliant but lazy," Bobby said, looking at his junior high and freshman year grades. Somewhere inside that kid was an intelligent mind, but he had grown lazy somewhere in his freshman year and it spread to the rest of his high school career.

5

Another red file name was Georgia Wannamaker, another senior, who transferred in from Blount County after her first baby was born. She first came to Bobby's office via April Murray in February of her junior year, several weeks before Bobby was MIA after Freddy's death. April had been concerned that her student, a pregnant girl with her second baby on the way, was heading down some blind alleys if someone did not help her. Bobby was willing to talk to Georgia. They met every Wednesday once a week. Georgia, just like Melaine and Alexander, was unique. She was a smart and funny girl, but her fatal flaw was that she could not stop having kids. Bobby had even asked her if her parents had discussed birth control for her and she had responded to him that they had. Even the school health class had an entire seminar about it. Not that it was an epidemic there at the high school, but it was a national concern and one that the school and the district felt it needed to address.

Georgia had the tools to be a successful individual and was when she was not pregnant or tending to her children. Her grades were steady, C student at best but Bobby felt that she could have done much better if not knocked up all the time. When Bobby asked her what her long-term plans were, she responded by saying, "Taking care of the kids, I guess." Bobby asked her about college, and she laughed, "When I get time. I'm just trying to make it through high school." Bobby had worried, along with April Murray, that Georgia would eventually get overwhelmed and then quit school altogether. Bobby saw potential in her; that she could do it all, even with two kids, but she remained in that red folder because she warranted observation.

When Bobby had gotten back to school that August, he was surprised to see that Georgia was still enrolled. He figured that she had already had the baby and wondered if she was coming back to finish out her senior year. Eventually, Georgia would withdraw from high school that December.

6

Last, but not least, was Stu Grissom. He was already by Bobby's standards on the cusp of being lost forever. He came to Bobby in his junior year, a transfer from another school. He was damaged goods from the get-go: a foster kid in and out of homes, fights, suspensions, run-ins with the police, you name it. This was the type of kid that Bobby wanted to see win. He was the underdog, never given a chance to realize his potential. At least that's how Bobby saw him as he met with Stu on Monday mornings for forty-five minutes weekly. Honestly, Stu needed more time, but Bobby was already stretched thin as it was. He had thought about recommending Stu to a therapist pal up in Knoxville. She was good. However, he knew that Stu would not take the offer. It would be a waste of a recommendation.

Stu was all bad boy but deep down he was a shattered kid that was trying his very best not to be dragged down by his past. His damaged past was his parents who gave up their kid to the foster care system when he was five. He told Bobby that he did not remember much of his parents. The only thing he did recall was that they didn't want him. That abandonment had stung Stu greatly and shaped his life up to that point. He wanted to be better and had even conveyed that to Bobby, but he did not have the tools. Bobby supposed that even if Stu had the tools early on, he would have never been taught how to use them properly.

During those meetings in his office, Bobby tried to keep things light and positive. They would discuss things like sports (Stu was a big baseball fan but was never able to watch any because his foster dad was a prick) and philosophies on life in general. Stu was a well-read kid, a romantic at heart, but his persona in school and out and about was that of a hardcore dominating rough end. In Bobby's office, Stu could be himself. The more they talked, the more comfortable he became...the more relaxed.

"One day, I'd like to work at the FBI," he told Bobby. At the rate he was going in school it did not bode well for him to make it there. Bobby told him that he needed to bear down and get with the program in academics.

He even set up some practice exams for the SAT for Stu to take. Bobby would go on to tutor him after school for a bit.

Bobby knew that Stu wanted to chart his future in a newer direction, and although the teachers in that school had given up on him a long time ago, Bobby was not about to. He wanted all the kids to win in life, especially the ones in his red file. Stu was a reclamation project and one that Bobby wanted to win. Stu was the underdog, the guy that shouldn't be successful. There was something, maybe in his eyes, Bobby thought, which made Stu Grissom someone not to give up on. When Bobby thought of Stu he smiled. He smiled because he could see Stu being one of those success stories. At least he hoped so…

7

On Thursday of that first official school week, Bobby had sent out a memo to all the freshman teachers in the school and asked them if they had any of what they would consider "at-risk kids" to please get with him so he could arrange a meeting with them. Some teachers thought it was a great thing that Bobby was doing for these kids. Others didn't care. They were the burnouts, beaten down by a system they once loved; beaten down by the ever-changing youth from year to year. To hear some of the teachers in that school, the old ones that had been in the game for three decades or more, kids were worse. Worse than what, Bobby often wondered. The year before? Maybe that was true. Worse than when they were kids? Sure, that could be, but times were different back then, much like they are different now. Maybe society gets worse every generation.

In twenty years, kids would be perhaps worse than the current year. Bobby chalked it up to attrition; it was just the natural way. He guessed there was an outside chance that sometime in the future he would say what the old timers were now saying. That thought scared Bobby because he never wanted to be an old man that hated everything and everybody like Mr. Seitzer that taught Economics. "I get like that, fucking shoot me dead," he once told Sam.

"Shotgun to the dick," Sam said as he laughed.

On Friday, Bobby finalized his meetings on his computer (it was becoming of good use for him it appeared the more he used it) for the rest of the school year for his small red file folder group. He gathered his paperwork and placed it in his backpack as the dismissal bell rang. He walked out of his office, closing the door behind him for the weekend. He was walking down the hallway in the office area when Mr. Glick, the arch-villain in Bobby's world already, approached him. "Mr. Downey…a minute?"

Bobby stopped, "Of course."

"I was at the district budgetary meeting earlier this week and it looks like some cuts are coming…some that will take hold after this school year," Glick said in his old Southern drawl.

"And I'm guessing that since you stopped to tell me, those cuts will be affecting me somehow."

Mr. Glick smiled a little, but not too much. He did not want Bobby to see how much he relished the looming cuts. "As you may or may not know, I sit on the school district's budget committee, and I offered some ideas where the school district could save some much-needed money. I won't bore you with the particulars of it all, but there are several positions, for lack of a better word, in schools that are not necessary. They'll be a vote close to the end of the year to make the final decision on what those proposed cuts will be."

Bobby stood there for a moment and thought of what to say next. "You're going to try to cut the guidance counselors out, I'm guessing. Which is why you decided to stop and talk to me. And I'm going to also assume that you're going to push some of the borderline ready-to-retire teachers out and consolidate the rest of the teachers to make the student/teacher ratio per class, bigger. Which would keep you from having to hire any new teachers. How close am I to being on target?"

Bobby was on point because he and Sam had that same speculative conversation years prior that something like that would happen eventually. When it came to the school's inner workings, everything was and is eventual, especially when it concerned money.

Bobby wanted to punch Glick's lights out there in the hallway. He was not a violent man in no way, shape, or form, but he could make an exception this time he thought. Mr. Glick stood, arms crossed, daring Bobby with his eyes to say something else. What was there to say? Glick had made it clear that he did not see the need for a guidance counselor in schools and saw it as new-age mumbo-jumbo. Of course, when it came time to drop the axe to cut some stuff away from the schools, Mr. Glick could not have been more helpful in finding ways to shave some fat off the budget.

"Listen, Bobby, it's nothing personal. It saves the twenty schools overall in the district an annual savings of a million dollars. When I served at the state in the Department of Education…"

"I see a big fat raise coming your way eventually. Maybe even some sort of promotion," Bobby interrupted Glick, turning to walk down the hallway. "Let me know how that vote goes at the end of the year. I can't wait to see how it turns out. I'm on pins and needles." There was that vintage Bobby Downey: snarky, sarcastic, thumbing his nose up to authority.

8

That afternoon Ben came home through the front door while his mother was on the phone talking to someone. It seemed business-like but he could not tell any particulars because as soon as he entered and closed the door quietly, Bailey had ended the call with a "thank you". She walked across the living room and over to her son, "I've got some good news."

"We're going back home? Dad's haunting our house and the new people are giving it back to us?" Ben said sarcastically.

"No," Bailey said, pushing her lower lip out to blow her hair out of her eyes. "I got a job offer."

"Where?" Ben asked, walking past his mother and into the kitchen. He took off his backpack and slung it down onto the kitchen island listening to his mother as she talked.

"Huffaker Pharmacy. Their pharmacist just retired, and they saw my resume that I sent them and called and asked if I was available for an interview. Which I was, of course. And I totally nailed it! We should celebrate! Tonight! Dinner!" Bailey said excitedly. Ben wanted to be excited for his mother but found it difficult to do so. Her getting a job here, a job like she had back home, meant that they were never leaving, that roots were beginning to take hold. It was more evidence they were not going to leave that house or that town anytime soon.

When Ben did not share in her joy, Bailey asked what was wrong. "I thought you'd be happy for me?"

"I am happy. It's just that…I don't know."

"I couldn't stay out of work forever, kiddo. All day I just sit here and think about your dad and stuff. I've got things around here to do, but it's not enough to keep me occupied and my mind off your dad. I need to get back out in the workforce. The insurance money ain't going to last forever. I just need…something else right now. I don't expect you to understand what I'm going through."

Ben got it. He had thought about his dad day and night. He always crossed his mind and was sure that he did in his mom's as well. Ben had noticed that his mom had started changing a lot, the way she was acting, the way she was dressing, everything about her old life was slowly disappearing as if she was becoming someone else. Her old life was gone, and so was his, but he did not see the need to change everything that was connected to the past. He knew that she hurt and hurt badly since his dad was gone, but that did not give her the right to act as if she was this brand-new person who was never married. Also, Ben had noticed for a while now that Bailey never brought up his dad in conversation.

It was as if to Ben that she was trying desperately to put distance between Steve's death and her new life. That angered her son that much more, but he never said anything about it; the things he noticed her doing and not doing for that matter. She wanted far away from dad's memory, but we ended up in the house he grew up in. What was the difference between being here and staying home? Ben often wondered.

"I understand, totally," Ben said, after looking at his mother from the other side of the island in the kitchen. He wanted to hate her for it, hate her for selling the house and hate her for moving them into where dad grew up and lived and breathed. He wanted to hate her for forcing him into this new high school; hate her for ripping him out of his comfort zone and putting him into a foreign land known as Tennessee. But through all that hate, Ben could not hate his mother. Not yet.

"I hope so. Because I don't want you to think that I've moved on. I'm still…you know." Ben wanted to say that she had moved on since she sold the house they shared, gave away practically all of his dad's stuff, and moved away. Eventually, Ben saw them leaving this house one day because the memory of his dad was here, but not like it was back in South Carolina. His biggest fears were not on the horizon just yet, but he knew that they were coming; forming someplace where no one could see.

"I'm happy for you, really. When do you start?" Ben asked, moving the conversation down the road. He hated talking in circles.

"The lady wants to meet me on Monday morning. And from there I think it's all good. Just a formality."

Ben nodded and smiled. What else could he do? "Cool," he replied.

9

When Bobby got home, he was so upset that he called Sam at his new school. When Bobby called him, he was on lunch from the time difference where they lived. Bobby told his friend about his run-in with Mr. Glick.

"I'm not surprised at all. Remember, we talked about this a while back?" Sam replied. "If a school district can save a mill a year, then they'll do it. Hell, here, they've cut out music, drama, and soccer, and they've threatened to cut after-school programs. It's savage around these parts. Since when did education become an option to fund in this country?"

"Yeah well, Glick didn't like me from day one. I could tell. He sees what I do as nothing important at all."

"People like him usually don't," Sam replied.

"I guess I'll be looking for another job someplace else by the end of the school year."

"Maybe not. It might not even pass. Just because he suggested it doesn't mean anything. You could be offered a job as a teacher someplace else, too," Sam said.

"If he intends to collapse and consolidate teachers and up the class size, the district ain't going to be looking at hiring any new teachers. They'll make do with what they have until they can't."

"I wouldn't worry about it. Not yet anyway. Call Pete Samples. His dad is on the school board. He'll be able to tell you something. That guy can't keep his mouth shut about anything."

"That's a good idea, man. I didn't even think about him."

"I know. It's a shame I've got to keep an eye on you way out here. And here I thought you were ready to spend the night home alone."

"Yeah, thanks, Dad," Bobby said, laughing on the other end.

"So, what's going on with you this Friday afternoon, Mr. Downey?"

"Going to walk the track tonight." Bobby half-heartedly replied.

"What?!" Sam said, nearly choking on his fish sandwich. "Who roped you into that?"
"April Murray," Bobby replied, pacing around his living room.

"Ahhhhhh. Good choice. Good choice. You ask her?"

"No. She asked me, Saddie Hawkins style. Apparently, she recognizes the talent," Bobby
smiled as he said that.

"Whatever. She's just hard up for companionship. It's good though, man. She's a good one, you know," Sam told.

"Yeah, I know. It's just walking around on the track. Not like it's a date."

"Okay… glad to see you're changing things up a bit. You deserve a win."

It was still a touchy subject although its sensitivity was waning some. Bobby and Sam had discussed Dana many, many times in the past, in person, with Sam going over to Bobby's house to be with him for support. But now he was thousands of miles away and the best they could do was a phone call. Talking about Dana was hard for Bobby at first. Freddy was even harder. Sam never brought Freddy up in conversation unless Bobby did. Then they would talk about it. Otherwise, Sam kept his mouth shut on the subject and stuck to the trail that Bobby was leading him on.

"I know. I'm just not ready. Dana just...," Bobby struggled for words much as his students did in his office during their meetings. "She just burned me down, man. I don't even know if I can rebuild after everything that has happened," he said, walking out onto his back porch.

"Hey, listen," Sam said, putting his fish sandwich down on his desk and swallowing the last big piece in his mouth, "April is a good woman. About the best I've seen. Certainly, the best there. She may be exactly what you need. At least give her a chance to help."

Bobby and Sam sat there silent on the phone. Nothing was said. Thoughts ran through Bobby's mind, and he knew that maybe his friend was right. "Maybe you're right... right about everything."

"What?! Hang on a sec...I am writing down that you said that on my calendar as we speak."

"I would because it will never happen again, you know."
"That's why I'm writing it down. And hey, Bobby?"

"What?"

"There are these things called condoms. What you do is when the moment is right with April and you two are alone, you might get these feelings... it's okay, it natural..."

Bobby laughed, "Get the hell outta here!" he said with a fake Brooklyn accent and ended the call on his cordless phone. He stood there looking around his backyard and missed his friend already.

10

Ben was up in his bedroom and had hooked up his dad's old Atari game system to the TV. He had discovered the game system a couple of weeks ago before school started up in the attic. He had never gone into the attic before and knew very little about what was up there. What was up there, most of it was of no interest to Ben; old paintings, tables that had been bought at some point in time only to be banished to the attic and forgotten. Most of what was up there were boxes stacked on top of boxes. The boxes ranged in sizes from small, big, to very big. Some of the boxes had words written on the sides letting the explorers of the attic know what the contents were. Over in a far corner was a medium-sized box that simply said STEVE. Ben walked over and took off the three other boxes that were stacked on top of his dad's box and pulled the container to the middle of the attic.

There was an old beat to hell dark brown Rawlings baseball glove. There were a few trophies from his baseball days; a blue Atlanta Braves hat where the cursive A on the front had been dusted to something darker than white; there were cassette tapes, most of them dating back to the 1970s and early 1980s; a few car magazines; pictures of Steve and his friends when they used to be in a band. Ben remembered his dad telling this story of the time he and his friends formed a band. "We couldn't play worth a damn," Steve told his son one night out in the garage working on his car. Looking at the picture of Steve and his three best friends young and dumb, Ben smiled a little. It was as if the picture confirmed his dad's story.

Ben had brought down the Atari, along with a few game cartridges, cassette tapes, and a bigger stereo that used to be Steve's from a long time ago to his bedroom. He blew the inches of thick dust off of everything and coughed when the dust hung in the air like thick smoke around his face. He honestly didn't know if any of the equipment he had brought down from the attic would work. It had been decades since they were last in operating condition. He was not hopeful.

Ben had finally hooked up the Atari and turned his TV on. The Atari screen came on. He put the Pitfall! game cartridge in the game console and it worked, too. Success! Ben walked over to the window seal where his small radio was and replaced it with Steve's old stereo. He plugged it in and hit the power ON button. It worked, too! Ben opened the cassette tape deck and thumbed through the tapes of music to find which one he wanted to listen to first. He settled on the Cars' first album. He popped it in, turned the volume up, and the first song, "Good Times Roll", came on filling the bedroom much like it did back when Steve was a teenager. He went downstairs to gather some food and drinks for his night.

Bailey was sitting on the couch reading a paperback while the TV was on showing a rerun of last week's episode of Law and Order lowly in the background. "What are you up to tonight?" Bailey looked up momentarily from her book.

Ben, stopping with a bag of Doritos and a half-full two-liter bottle of

Mountain Dew in his arms, said that he had found his dad's old Atari game system and his stereo with some tapes. "They still work?" she asked.

"Yup. So far so good," Ben replied, heading up the stairs.

"Have fun, kiddo."

Ben smiled and walked back up the stairs and into his bedroom. Retro Friday Night was underway.

Chapter 8

1

That Friday night was the first football game of the season for Central High. It just happened that it was their first home game. It was packed full of fans, students, teachers, and past players of the days of old and not-so-old. It was sold out and standing room only as there was not a seat to be had in the stands. The first game of the year was with their arch-rivals, Park City High, who had beaten Central ten games in a row, a losing record against them that stretched back an entire decade.

The adults in the stadium seats came to watch the game while the students, for the most part, came to walk around the track, eat, and socialize. Bobby and April had met at the football field ticket booth earlier before the place started to fill. They made some small talk and April said that they ought to start walking around seeing that kids were already gathering in various parts of the track and off in the shadowy grassy places near the home and visitor bleachers. Before Bobby and April knew it, the game had gotten underway, two minutes in and the track was so full of kids that it was hard to walk with all the people walking aimlessly. It was so loud there that you could not even hear yourself think. It would eventually get quieter as the night wore on, especially if their school was losing, which they normally did. Usually, around the third quarter of each home game, the game itself was already decided by the visiting team. For whatever reason, Central High's football team fell apart after halftime. It never failed.

2

Bobby and April walked closely, side by side, strolling and looking all around making sure nothing out of the way was going on. Bobby was nervous walking by April. She was a stunning woman and was one that most of the men and even boys of the school had talked about in some sexual way or another. She was conservative in dress and in tone and mannerisms. She only loosened up around those she really liked. Bobby had never really seen April out of the element of the school. This was a first for him. He liked it.

"How was your first week?" Bobby asked.

"Oh, you know. Same old, same old. It never gets any different. The names change but it all stays the same. You?" April asked while they made the first turn on the track.

"Same. Got everything lined up for the rest of the year. Checking on my at-risk kids, but otherwise, a normal year coming, or I guess I should say what passes as normal around here anyways." Bobby did not tell her about his run-in with Glick earlier that day when school had dismissed. They were not there in their new friendship for Bobby to tell her small secrets... not yet.

"How's Sammy doing?" she asked.

"He's good...doing good over there. He seems to be adjusting to everything. You know, it's a time difference, different climate, different everything for them. Good move for him and his family though. Good for his career."

"That was a bold move to just up and move your family across the country. I don't know if I could've done that," April said, putting her hands in her shorts' front pockets.

"Me either. But Sam is a bold man. I want to be him when grow up." April chuckled at his remark.

"Would you ever leave this school and go someplace far away like he did?" April asked.

I may not have much of a choice soon, Bobby thought. But he answered honestly, pretending that Glick had never mentioned anything about cuts', I love it here; been here for a long time now. I want to be here so long that they name something after me. What about you?"

April walked with her head down and considered Bobby's question, "I don't know. Depends on if I had anything here worth staying for, I guess."

"Fair enough," Bobby said, sort of picking up on what April was really saying in between the lines. "So you think you'll be at this school forever? Like retire from here?"

April shook the hair out of her eyes and looked around, "Probably. I guess.

I don't intend on going anywhere anytime soon. Like you, I've been here for a long stretch. I don't want to start over at another school. It just seems exhausting to start over at our ages, you know?" They both laughed at that and agreed.

"Any family? We've worked together for so long I don't really know you is why I'm asking." Bobby asked, knowing that that question wouldn't be volleyed back to him because April knew what the entire faculty knew: that his son had died in an accident and that his wife moved away afterward leaving him behind to deal.

April shook her head, "No. Mom and dad are both dead. Car accident. They were coming to see me graduate that day they were killed. My older brother, Ray, lives in England. I don't see him much at all…hear from him just as much."

"Sorry about your parents. I didn't know… England? Wow. When's the last time you guys saw each other?"

"Mom and dad's funeral. After that, it was, have a nice life, call if you need me. That was it."

"You guys not get along?" Bobby hated asking questions about family because he hated fielding questions about his, especially from those that did not know the history.

"We used to, but after he moved away when he turned eighteen to join the military, we became strangers. The only reason we ever did see each other was because of mom and dad. Since they've been gone…we just don't," April told as they walked the straightway of the track in front of the visiting set of bleachers.

"I'm sorry. I didn't know. If I upset you…"

"No, you didn't. It's not something that I advertise. You didn't know."

3

Bobby and April lapped the track ten times at a slow crawl as the game reached the third quarter. They had not paid any attention to the score because they were so wrapped up in their conversations with each other.

The large crowd that had filed in there earlier had thinned out considerably. When they rounded the track's upper curve, the one next to the admission gate, Bobby said, "Didn't we speak about me getting a hotdog and bottled water at some point?"

April laughed, "We did, sir. We did. I totally forgot…. hotdog with the works, right?"
"Yeah. But I was just messing around." The both of them stopped there on the track and stood facing each other with big goofy smiles on their faces. They really liked each other, but who was going to come out and say it? It was felt between them. For April, was like being hit with a jolt of electricity. For Bobby, it was butterflies flying around in his stomach.

"No, Mr. Downey. I'm a woman of my word. I'll be right back. Don't go anywhere," she said to him as she walked backward toward the concession stand. She kept her eyes on Bobby as he smiled wide and chuckled.

"I can't really go anywhere because I don't have the food that I was promised," he said with a big smile. They were both hooked on each other. It did not take long.

4

As the game drew to a close, a blowout where their school was beaten down 49-10, Bobby and April walked out through the entrance gate side by side slowly, much slower than they did while walking the track. Most of the cars that had been packed into the small spaces had all but gone leaving about twenty scattered cars that probably belonged to students.

 "Where's your car?" she asked.

Bobby looked around and saw it way off in the darkness, under a street light. "All the wayyyyyyy over there…right next to the gate there. At least I think that's mine."

"Do you want a ride?" April asked, as the two stopped at her car.
Bobby lowered his head and laughed a bit, "Ah, you and those loaded questions."

"Hey, I can't help that your mind is in the gutter."

"Oh, my mind is never in the gutter, Ms. Murray. Matter of fact, as a somewhat trained psychologist, I think I might need to see you. You know, treat you. Because you have some self-destructive tendencies that I'm picking up on."

"Is there a treatment that works for nymphomania?" April asked, wanting to laugh but kept it together somehow.

Bobby laughed out loud and started walking backward, hands in his front pockets, into the dark empty parking lot towards the far end, "I think a walk will do me good, Ms. Murray; gives me time to figure out a course of treatment for you. I'll have to read some psychology books; got a long night ahead of me; probably the whole weekend if I'm being honest. Your condition is going to take me some time to figure out."

April laughed at his playful comeback. God, she loved him right there. "See you Monday?"

"Unless I win the lotto. Have a good weekend," Bobby said, still walking backward looking at April who stood there in the glow of the artificial light, arms crossed smiling by her car.

Bobby faded into the darkness of the night and walked to his car. April eventually got into hers and drove past him beeping her horn at him. He waved as she was nothing but red taillights blurring past him in the darkness. Bobby stopped and watched April drive through the open gate and down the road; nothing but taillights. For the first time in a long time, Bobby felt good. Not just good, but good on the inside. Good in places he hadn't felt in a long, long time.

He got into his car and sat there for a few moments thinking about the night that was. It was a good night and one of the first where he did not think about Freddy or Dana. It was a nice reprieve for a few hours. He reached over to his center console and opened it up pulling out his Ritalin bottle and a half-full bottle of Wild Turkey. Popping the white cap off the pill bottle, he shook three pills out into his hand and tossed them into his mouth washing them down with the liquor. Bobby Downey sat there in the darkness letting the pills do their thing.

Chapter 9

1

August had turned into September pretty quickly it seemed. Both Bobby and Ben were utterly blown away by how fast the first few weeks of school had zoomed by. Ben loved it because it meant that he was that much closer to the school year being over in May. It was a long way off, but it didn't matter to him. He was counting down.

Bobby had nothing to count down towards. He was here to stay, well, maybe not to stay if Mr. Glick had his way in the looming school board budget vote. Bobby, during the month in between that run-in with Glick, had been sitting on the info that he was given and had only told Sam and that was it. He had come close to spilling it to April one day while the two of them walked the track again during another football home game. News flash: they lost. Bobby decided against it and thought it would be better if he waited and talked to Pete Samples, the guy that was notorious for not keeping anything a secret. He was a phone call away, but Bobby had not had time to call him. Maybe it was because he did not want it to be true.

2

Both Bobby and Ben went through the motions of school. Ben was still keeping a low profile in his classes, still sitting by his lonesome at the lunch table during lunch. He kept his eyes glued to the floor when he walked through the halls. It's not that he did not want friends, it was because as smart as he was, he just did not know how to make friends. His interests were not the interests of this generation. Ben was a retro kid and did not quite fit into the mid-nineties' social norms. As kids around him were changing with the times, Ben stayed safely in the 1980s when he was a kid. That was his comfort zone. While everyone was abandoning that decade and running into the unknown, Ben was staying put, watching kids his age move on to new things and talk a new language and act a different way. It seemed there in 1994, his junior year of high school, Ben was witnessing the total change of the world as he knew it.

Ben, in his first month of school, did eventually begin to settle in somewhat. Although settling was nowhere near like what it was at his old school. "Work with what you've got," Ben's dad always said. Ben did manage some gains in his classes over the last month. In English class during a class discussion over that month's book, Moby Dick, Ben listened intensively and actually made eye contact with some of the kids in his class as he turned to watch them talk about the book. He interacted a bit with the discussion, too. Even Mrs. Doolittle was impressed by Ben Medlen coming out of his shell, albeit slowly, but it was a gain.

Other classes had about the same benchmark as his English class. He was looking up a little more, not yet acclimated to his new environment but he was getting warmer. His confidence that he had left back in South Carolina had not traveled with him to Tennessee but that was okay, Ben thought to himself, he would have to summon up some confidence here, but had no idea how in the hell he would do that. Small gains were okay. Eventually, small gains would turn into big leaps.

3

Bailey Medlen had gotten that pharmacist job a few weeks ago and was picking up right where she had left off in that profession before her husband died. It was a totally different pharmacy, but it was "pretty much all the same thing," she had told her son when Ben asked if she thought she could do the job or not. She could and was. Like a duck to water. Life was going on without the patriarch, without the man that taught Ben the game of baseball, how to adjust a carburetor on a car, how to ride a bike, and girls. Life was moving on without Steve Medlen and it did not matter if Bailey or Ben liked it or not. That's how life is; it never stops just because you had a setback or a death. Life marches onward, never stopping because you cannot seem to go on. Life, Ben was learning at a young age, does not care about your pain.

One of Ben's problems that he had, there were so many, was that he watched his mom move on without Steve. He got that to a degree, he did because life had to keep going and could not stop just because someone you loved died, went away, or whatever. On one hand, Ben understood his mother. She was still beautiful, still young, and if she made it to her life expectancy, she still had thirty-plus years ahead of her God willing that those years would be spent in good health.

On the other hand, Ben hated that his mom was moving on. He hated seeing her dress the way she was dressing; she was trying too hard at looking like she was twenty-something again. Makeup was always on full display; her clothes were different; her hair was different than what it was years prior; her mannerisms seemed to be different as well. Most of the time Ben felt as if his mother was a stranger to him. She had changed since her husband's death, and those changes Ben did not like. He wondered sometimes up in his bedroom when his mom would try to replace his dad. He knew that it was coming; could feel it deep in his bones. How was he going to deal with that? Ben was not sure.

They had never, not once, discussed that possibility, but it was a possibility, right? Did Ben think that she would go the rest of her life and not have a date with another man or a romantic notion about another man? What about sex with another man? That made Ben shiver in more ways than one. He ran over in his head the impact of seeing his mother with another man that wasn't his dad. Would he be ready for that?

The big worry was what if Bailey had met someone, fallen head over heels in love with them and they got married. How would Ben deal with that? How would Ben deal with seeing another man touching his mother that wasn't his dad? Living under the same roof? Kissing his mother like his dad used to? How would all that go for Ben Medlen? He knew how it would go: he would reject it and maybe bolt for South Carolina earlier than he had planned before his senior year was over. To Ben, that would be a betrayal of his dad's memory, treasonous.

Ben knew that he was getting ahead of himself with all of those thoughts of what his mom may or may not do. But if she did what he thought about to the point that it made him hurt and angry, then he was finished there. She would have made her choice and he would have to make his eventually. His dad's memory was up for grabs and Ben was going to honor his dad's memory and not bend if Bailey had found someone else and remarried. No way. Ben did not want a stepdad and was never going to accept such an abomination to his father's memory. Ben was okay with his mother moving on in some aspects. Fine. But when it came to finding another man and replacing his dead father, that's where Ben drew the line in the sand. She does that, Ben thought to himself, that's just nothing more than being a traitor to his dad's memory.

Ben had kinda broached the subject of them moving on since his dad died. They had talked about it but not to his satisfaction. Could he ever be fully satisfied by anything that she said? Perhaps not, not anytime soon. Steve's death was still raw in Ben's mind and he still caught himself looking around his bedroom at what used to be his dad's from time to time. Sometimes he could swear that he could feel his dad in there. Maybe he was. He felt the cold drafts swirl around in his bedroom on those hot September nights and could feel his dad's presence. Was it in his head? Ben didn't know. He liked to think that his dad was with him in some form. It was a comforting feeling and one that he liked, no matter how much it freaked him out sometimes.

4

Just as Ben was wrestling with his demons, so was Bobby. When the nights were lonely, and there were many of those, Bobby would run out of things to do, things to keep his mind out of forbidden and locked rooms up in his mind. In that one locked and forbidden room was where his dead son lived. There was a lot of hurt behind that door that somehow unlocked itself and opened to invite Bobby in for a look. Bobby hated going into that room. He knew what was awaiting him in there but sometimes it felt good to hurt so bad.

It had been six long months since Freddy was run over and killed out in the street in front of their house on Maple Lane. Freddy and his friends from the neighborhood had been playing in the street that day. It was not unusual for the five of them; Freddy, Cameron, Timmy, Warren, and Jack to go out into their street and play street hockey or pass baseball. Sometimes Timmy and the rest of the gang would roll his portable basketball goal to the side of the road from his house and they shoot hoops. With the street having tall standing trees on either side of the road that grew into each other up high, intermingling their branches and leaves during the spring and summer creating a canopy, it provided ample shade all the way down Maple Lane. Sometimes when the winter was gone and the leaves were coming in on those trees, Bobby would sit out on the front porch and remark to no one but himself that Maple Lane looked like something out of a Norman Rockwell painting. It was beautiful.

None of the parents that lived on Maple Lane ever really worried about their kids being out in the street. It was not busy and most of the cars that did come down the road were neighbors and they always watched out for the kids. It was perhaps the safest street in America. No one would have imagined what would happen on an unassuming March afternoon that would change all of that. After the incident, kids stopped coming into the street. They stayed in their yards or on the sidewalks. Parents, who were normally going about their business in their homes, now watched their kids when they were outside, the ones that did let them out that was. Freddy Downey had become the cautionary tale about parents watching their children because you just never knew. If it could happen to Freddy, it could happen to anyone.

It was just a normal Saturday, nothing unusual about it at all. Run of the mill. Same old, same old. There was nothing, no harbinger of what was to come. No strange dreams. No strange feelings. Nothing. The Downey family woke up and got ready for their Saturday like normal. Freddy woke up early as usual to watch cartoons. Bobby and Dana tried to sleep in, but it was never really any use. They were creatures of habit getting up around five in the morning to get ready for their workdays. Sleeping until seven or seven-thirty was like sleeping all day long to the two of them.

Bobby had planned on mowing the grass, the front and back at some point. The only point of decision was when did he want to tackle it? Before or after noon? That was indeed the question. Dana had planned on going into town and picking up a few things for supper that night. Pot roast was what she and Bobby had planned on. They had not had it in a few months and when Dana mentioned it to Bobby, he gave the thumbs up. Freddy, after he watched his cartoons, got out of his PJs and put on his shorts and Braves tee shirt, Braves hat, and bolted outside to play with his friends. It was an everyday thing, especially on Saturdays when all the neighborhood kids had the entire day to do whatever they all wanted.

5

Bobby, Dana, and Freddy went about their day like always. Nothing out of the ordinary. Dana had gone to the grocery store and did some shopping and decided to go get her nails done. No big deal, nothing unusual. Bobby was outside in the backyard, deciding, after all, to cut the lawn around noon after Dana left for town. Freddy had already been out of the house to visit his neighborhood pals and sometimes Bobby could hear the kids playing down the street. He was outside going around and picking up sticks and medium-sized limbs that had fallen from the trees around his house from the spring storm a few days prior. Mowing over the limbs would do nothing but dull the blade of the push mower and Bobby had just replaced it two weeks ago.

The Saturday afternoon there on Maple Lane was just like every other

Saturday: nothing unusual, nothing out of the ordinary…just a regular day with people doing regular things.

Bobby was nearly finished with the backyard when Dana pulled into the driveway and parked beside Bobby's car in front of the garage door. She got out and was gathering the several plastic bags of groceries in her hands when her husband appeared from the side of the house.

"You're back?"
 "Yeah, I am."

"Let me help. It's what I get paid around here for," Bobby said, rushing over to his wife. He took most of the bags in his hands while Dana only had two in each of hers. "Like the nails," Bobby remarked as the two of them walked up the walkway to the front door.

"Thanks. I wanted pink this time."

"Was it busy at the store?" Bobby asked, making the usual husband/wife conversation as they walked.

"Yeah, it was," Dana said. The two of them made it up the front porch and through the front door. "I went in there for just a few things but came out with all of this." She and Bobby walked through the living room, through the dining room, and into the kitchen where the bags were placed on the island in the middle of the room. "How's the yard?"

Bobby walked over and took a glass from the dish strainer and poured himself a glass of cold chlorine-laced tap water and downed the entire thing in no time flat. "Good. Still wet from the storm a couple of days ago though. Five full bags of grass clippings already."

"Good thing you changed the blade, huh?" Dana asked, absently putting the food away into the fridge and cabinets while Bobby leaned against the kitchen counter cooling off, watching her.

"Yeah, I know," Bobby watched as his wife bent over here and there and the thought hit him like it did every once in a while at how pretty Dana was. Sometimes he wondered how in the hell he got so lucky at having her and with that thought, wondered what he would ever do without her.

Dana raised up from her squatting position in front of the opened fridge and saw that Bobby was looking at her. "What'cha looking at, mister?"

"Just you, missus."

Dana felt what Bobby was feeling: that Saturday afternoon lust that seems to only happen between a happily married couple whose kid is out of the house for a bit. The two walked towards each other and met at the kitchen island and kissed, holding onto each other. These were happier times and times like those happened more often than not. Before Freddy was killed out in the street, they were a near-perfect family. They were not a fairy tale sitcom family whose troubles and disagreements would be over in twenty minutes. Life was never that simple or easy. Real life never worked that way. They were a real deal American family with just as many issues as the neighbors had in their neighborhood, in their own homes. Some of those problems their neighbors had, and even the Downey's themselves, were worse by comparison, but everyone had something no matter how things appeared on the outside. Nothing was perfect. But the Downeys were close.

"Freddy at friends?" Dana asked in Bobby's arms.

"Yeah."

"Well, I've been thinking about you all day and it has been driving me crazy," Dana said, kissing her husband.

"Well, you must be a hell of a guy then to get you all hot and bothered. Is you the Asian guy at Yomoto's behind the grill? Because I can't compete with that, so as you know."

"You're funny. Let's go before Freddy decides to come back inside." Dana took him by the hand and led him upstairs for one of those spontaneous afternoon special meetings. It would turn out to be the last time they had sex together. It turned out it was the last time for a lot of things. The Downey family would never be the same shortly after the event out on Maple Lane.

6

Ten minutes later, the two of them lie on their backs looking up at the ceiling from the floor. It felt good, both of them touching each other, kissing each other, being consumed with each other. Everything on the outside of their closed bedroom door had ceased to exist for that moment in time. Both lay there on their backs staring up at the ceiling, naked, talking about how long it had been since they did it on the floor. "Probably before Freddy came along," Dana replied.

Dana got up to go to the bathroom and Bobby got up from the floor which was hard because now all he wanted to do was take a nap. Not a long nap but just a short one but he decided against it. He reached over and gathered his clothes, stood up, and put them back on: boxers, shorts, socks, and a plain white tee.

Bobby walked down the stairs as the AC kicked on in the house. He was cooled off and relaxed after his sexual encounter. He went through the kitchen and out the back door. He had to start Round Two with the yard. But it was okay. He felt good, felt relaxed. As he pushed the mower around to the front lawn to put the final twenty-plus minutes on his chore, he saw Freddy and his son's friends playing out in the quiet street. Then, out of nowhere, Bobby heard something loud and menacing before he ever laid eyes on it. As he bent over to pull the cord to start the mower, Bobby Downey saw it.

7

A red Pontiac Firebird that Bobby had seen on the street go by from time to time was flying at what Bobby had told police officers later was "at least sixty". Bobby felt as if something was not right for whatever reason, perhaps nothing other than parental instincts, he turned his head towards his son and his friends down the street. It all happened so fast that at first, he didn't know what had happened until he heard the screaming and the unmistakable sound of tires screeching on the pavement. Then he knew…

Bobby stood there to the side of his mower with the cord in hand. He could hear the roar of the engine. He let go of the mower's starter cord and walked quickly over to the edge of his front lawn where his grass stopped and where the sidewalk that spiraled throughout the neighborhood began. Bobby watched as the kids turned and saw what was bearing down behind them. They all, the five of them, Freddy included, tried to scramble out of the way. Most of them had gotten out of the way except for Freddy. Freddy must have been frozen, that's all Bobby could come to think of.

He did not move. His friends screamed for Freddy to move but in that split second there on Maple Lane the Downey family was over thanks to a red Pontiac Firebird.

8

Bobby screamed and ran toward where the kids were, where his son was. He was too late, and he knew that he was too late. He jumped over the Wilson's knee-high white picket fence that lie as a property border between their yards. Bobby wasn't even aware that he had jumped over it. His eyes were focused on what was happening in front of him. He ran as fast as he could on legs that were feeling like jelly. He nearly fell but caught his balance and corrected mid-stride. His eyes never left the horrible scene in front of him down the street.

Bobby was running as fast as his feet would go, screaming Freddy's name at the top of his lungs. The car that had come screaming down the street had landed into a huge maple tree on the sidewalk in front of Gary Glazier's house. Had the tree not been there the Firebird perhaps would have gone through the house there was no doubt. The kids, Freddy's friends, were standing on the side of the road with stunned faces, trying desperately to process what had just happened in a matter of seconds. They were silently looking at the mangled car as a cloud of smoke poured from the hood that had been smashed in when it hit the tree.

The boys had been playing a game of Wiffle Ball out in the street, something that they all had done for years without incident when the red Firebird came screaming down the street. Freddy was playing behind a washcloth that was used as second base. When Timmy was up at bat, he swung the plastic bat and crushed the plastic ball high in the air; a routine pop up. Freddy camped under it, barehanded, and was about to catch it when he heard all of his friends screaming at him. At first, he had no idea what they were yelling about until it was too late. He caught the ball and he no sooner turned around behind him and saw the car's grill bearing down on him. That would be the last thing Freddy Downey would ever see.

Bobby was running down the street yelling, hoping that his eyes were wrong; hoping that this was some strange nightmare and that maybe he had fallen asleep after he and Dana had sex on the bedroom floor. Lying on the pavement, his right leg bent behind him, blood coming from his mouth and nose about fifteen feet from where he caught the pop-up, lay Freddy. His head lie still on the pavement, busted, in a pool of dark blood that was slowly filling around his head like a macabre halo of sorts. His right eye was still wide open the other had already been knocked out from the violent hit. His left arm was bent and broken in what looked to be in three places. His small collarbone had managed to rip through the skin exposing it. It was the most gruesome scene anyone, especially Bobby, had ever seen in real life.

9

Bobby finally reached his son and fell to his knees. He didn't have time for his mind to register that his son was already dead and that his last breaths were just before his dad could get to him. Bobby knew by the sight of him that it was bad; way too bad to walk away from this, way too bad to just walk it off like he had told him when he would get hit by a pitch up in the batter's box. Freddy couldn't walk this one off. Freddy was dead and all Bobby could do was gather his limp son in his arms one final time as he screamed.

Bobby sat in the street holding his bloodied and dead son in his arms. The Firebird was smoking from the smashed car hood. The car itself was wrapped around the maple tree. Freddy's friends stood silent on the sidewalk still trying to process in their little minds what had just happened. Neighbors began to emerge from their homes slowly at first to see what had happened on their quiet little street. Soon, nearly all the neighbors were out of their homes and gathered at the scene. The parents of the kids that were still alive gathered them in their arms crying, hugging them tightly because they knew that it could have been their child lying dead in the street. Timmy's mom tried to move him away from the scene, but he was not having any of it. He pushed his mother away and watched Bobby hold his best friend ever since first grade.

10

A couple of months later, after it was all over, Dana wanted to move away from where their son was killed by the driver that was on meth in the fast Firebird. Bobby couldn't do it. He was well aware that his wife could not bear to be there since her son was no longer there in the house. Bobby couldn't either but there in that house were the memories of the good times, the times when Freddy was alive: the birthday parties, the cookouts, the family get-togethers. This was the place where they first brought Freddy when he was born. This house was where Freddy lived and breathed and was a kid. This was where Freddy was then…and now. One night Bobby would swear on a stack of Bibles that he saw the ghost of his dead son in Freddy's bedroom. It was just a glimpse, but Bobby knew what he saw; he saw Freddy standing there in the middle of his bedroom just staring as Bobby passed by. Bobby stopped and backtracked and looked into the bedroom and did not see anything.

Bobby could not entertain the idea of moving away. He was a hostage to the home; a hostage to Freddy's memory that lingered there in the Downey home. He couldn't imagine tearing himself away from the place and if Dana could not understand that then he didn't know what to tell her. She was free to go but Bobby would never and told her that out loud. Maybe he didn't have to. It was a situation of Bobby being the unmovable object and Dana being the unstoppable force. Something had to give… eventually it did.

Bobby and Dana had been shattered beyond belief. Instead of relying on each other for support, both of them sought refuge by diving deep within themselves and cutting the other out. Both were battling with Freddy's death and how it was unfair for him to be cut down in the spring of his youth; how unfair it was that they would never see such benchmarks in the kid's life like his first serious girlfriend, graduating high school, or maybe even college. They would always wonder what kind of man he would have eventually grown to be. In the long future, they were going to miss when he got married, bringing the grandkids over. All of that, all of that future, was now gone forever thanks to a red Firebird.

Chapter 10

1

Months rolled by since Freddy had been run over and killed by Jim Thompson, who survived the accident. He was arrested and later convicted and jailed for the vehicular homicide of Fredrick Downey and was serving his twenty-five-year prison sentence in Pinewood State Prison. It wasn't enough, nowhere near for what he had done to Freddy and the Downey family. Nothing ever would be enough as far as Bobby and Dana were concerned.

The trial was quick and there was not much of a fight from Thompson's court-appointed attorney. It was cut and dry, the incident. The only thing that was in question was how long Jim Thompson, who had a rap sheet a mile long, would be penalized for what he had done, and what he had taken away. At Jim's sentencing, it was the first time that Bobby had laid eyes on his wife since she left.

They say that time heals all wounds. But those they say that probably never held their dead child in their arms, Bobby thought. Time had indeed gone by and put some distance between that day and Bobby, but every time that Bobby pulled onto their street, he saw the ghosts of that day before him through his windshield. He could see all of them playing Wiffle ball. He could hear Jim Thompson's Firebird screaming demonically down the road fishtailing from side to side uncontrollably toward the kids. Sometimes Bobby would close his eyes and just hope that he pulled into his driveway without hitting the mailbox. Most times he did manage to get into the driveway, eyes closed.

Under normal circumstances he would have told Dana "Hey look at what I can do now!" but doing that was under duress. Sometimes he understood what Dana was talking about. He did even back then when she could not handle living there anymore. Bobby got it. He just could not move away. Staying did hurt Bobby's mental state as months went by. There was no doubt about it and he knew it; could feel it.

When Dana left for good, she and Bobby did keep communication somewhat. As time rolled on, each of them charted their separate ways. Both of them hurt but neither knew exactly how to comfort the other.

Dana had suggested a therapist at one point again and Bobby said that he was one and there wasn't anything that anyone could do; at least not for him. Dana eventually went and found someone to talk to. It helped some, but Bobby was right, it did not fix her. The tools she was given by her therapist could not repair how she felt after what happened. But she moved on, somewhat, and if that meant being away from Bobby and away from their home then that's how it had to be.

Bobby harbored some ill feelings towards his estranged wife. How could she up and leave their home, especially where their son had lived, played, and slept? How could she? Bobby knew the mechanism and the inner workings of why, but he refused to acknowledge them. He was a smart man, an educated man in psychology, but all that went out the window when Freddy died. No amount of psychology training in the world could fix Bobby. His only fix was to stay in the house and think of how Dana betrayed Freddy's memory, betrayed the marriage.

Dana and Bobby eventually stopped talking altogether over time, and before either of them knew it, they were strangers to each other. Dana had contacted Bobby a while back and said that she thought it was best if they officially divorced. Bobby agreed.

After everything was signed at the bottom of the decree, the two of them stood outside the courthouse and talked a bit; caught up some, but nothing major. "You look like you've lost a lot of weight," Dana remarked, looking at her now ex-husband.

"Happens when the people you love the most go away from you."

"I'm not getting into this with you again," Dana said, ready to walk to her car. "You made a choice to stay where I couldn't be."

"And you made a choice to leave me there alone to deal with everything!"

"You could've come with me and we could've…"

"Could've what, Dana?! Move on past Freddy?! Forget all about him?! That doesn't work for me!"

Dana stood there emotionally rocked back on her heels by her ex-husband's accusation of her wanting to forget all about her son. "I didn't leave because I was trying to forget about him. I left because I couldn't see his bedroom anymore or the backyard or…" Dana started to cry there on the sidewalk as cars passed by.

Bobby's initial instinct was to go over there and comfort her as he had in years past, but he elected not to. He stood there and watched the tears fall. In some parts, he was happy that they did. God knew he cried a lot from the pain.

After a few moments, Dana wiped her tears, sniffled big, and moved her hair from her eyes, looking at Bobby, "I couldn't stand to see down the street where he was run over, Bobby. I can't be like you and see that part of the road every day."

Bobby stood there knowing that his ex-wife was partly right. However, it always came around to the same place. It always did in Bobby's mind. "You left me behind. You walked out. You betrayed our son's memory because you "can't be like me" and stay there in our house. You walked out when I needed you the most. Do you think it's been easy being there at home where Freddy is just a memory and my wife just up and moved away? I lost two of the most important people in my life, Dana."

The two of them stood and looked at each other. The end had already come and gone between them and anything that was spoken afterward was going to be nothing more than hurt. Nothing was ever going to repair the relationship. Dana felt as if Bobby gave up on her by not coming with her to try to pick up the pieces, while Bobby felt Dana gave up on him by leaving him and forfeiting Freddy's memory.

"I'm sorry that I wasn't what you needed," Dana finally spoke, breaking that cold silence.

"You made a choice not to be. This is on you. You're the one that voted NO on us," Bobby said, as he turned to walk to his car. He did not turn to look back at his ex-wife but he knew that she was standing there, head down looking at the sidewalk as if she was searching for a response. There was no response.

2

Steve Medlen died when he was forty-two years old. A massive heart attack or stroke was what was assumed but it was never officially confirmed. "Ninety-nine percent it was a heart attack though," Bailey would say. She batted around the notion with Steve's sister about whether or not to have an autopsy performed to find out what had killed him so young. After some discussion, the decision was ultimately hers and she decided not to go on with it. It would remain a mystery, but the usual suspects were always in play.

Steve was a relatively healthy man. He was not overweight by much. Of course, he did have a dad body, he was forty-two for God's sake. Who was he out there trying to impress? Bailey was the only one for him. He kept himself in shape good enough to keep the blood pressure down to respectable numbers and avoided going to doctors at all costs. Even at the behest of his wife, Steve refused to go citing that "they just make you sick when you start going".

Steve would have normal aches and pains from time to time in his chest, sometimes waking him up in the middle of the night because they were so bad. Bailey worried even when he asked her not to. Sometimes Steve would worry if he was having something in the way of a heart attack, like the one that had killed his dad at the age of sixty-six. His dad had been "healthy" too. The pains would pass and Steve would feel invincible again until the next pain came. And they always did come. Bailey worried much as wives often do about their husbands and their health.

In the days leading up to Steve's death, Ben didn't notice anything odd about his dad. Steve talked the same, acted the same, and did the same day in and day out. He was a creature of stern habit. Knock him out of his routine and you'd see a man on fire. It's not that Steve Medlen could not adapt to change; he could, once he discovered a new routine within the change, then he was good to go until another change occurred. "Life is mostly about how you can adapt to stuff," Steve once said to Bailey.

Ben looked back, and how could you blame him, on the weeks and days before Steve died. He tried to search his brain to see if he had missed something that his dad had done or said; a clue as to why he had just up and died. Did he ever clutch his chest? Did he sweat for no reason? Did he ever show any pain whatsoever? No to all of it. Ben never saw anything out of the way from his dad. Steve was just Steve: joking around, coming home from work talking about his day with Bailey. And if Ben was in the room he'd listen and laugh at some of the stories his dad shared from his day at work. His dad was a great storyteller. Ben's friends, when they would come over, would talk to Steve.

Ben would lure his dad to tell them all the stories about when he was growing up. The guys all laughed and loved the stories Ben's dad told. What made the stories so great was Steve's gestures and delivery of the funny parts of the stories. That always made Ben and his friends howl with laughter. The stories were great, but Steve's delivery and comedic timing were what made them better.

Steve was normal: just Dad being Dad. The Sunday before he died, he was in his garage tooling around with his 1981 Chevy Malibu Classic. It was a project car that Steve and his dad had started ten years ago in his dad's garage. Now that car was in his garage and he and Ben tinkered with it here and there when Steve had the time and was not worn out from work. He noticed that since he had hit forty, he was getting tired more. He wondered if that came with the job of being middle-aged. Probably so.

On that Sunday, with a Braves spring training game on the radio, Ben walked into his dad's garage that was attached to the house and saw the hood of the baby blue car up. His dad was standing at the front of it, tee shirt and jeans with a dirty white rag hanging loosely from his back pocket. He was studying the motor. Ben walked up next to his dad and looked in. "What's wrong?"

Steve rubbed his jaw, which always meant he was in deep thought, and answered his son absently, "She's running rough. Might be the carburetor."

"Didn't you adjust that already?" Ben asked, becoming mechanically savvy since his dad had shown him a few things about this car.

The car was going to eventually be his one day, Steve told him, and it was best that he knows about it, and how to fix any problems that may come about. And so far, he was holding his own. His dad was a great teacher; not just about cars, but about life in general in those times when Ben and his dad talked as father and son. Ben appreciated the way that his dad talked to him like he was an equal. That made Ben love the man even more.

"I'm going to adjust this thing again…better yet, you do it this time. Show me what you know," Steve said to his son. Ben was up to the challenge. That day in the garage, Ben showed exactly how much he had been paying attention to his dad as he adjusted the carburetor. When he turned it on, Steve stood back and saw his son in the driver's seat revving the engine up and letting it idle. "She's running good now, ain't she?" Steve said as the two of them smiled.

In the garage later on, as the Braves game was still going, now in the eighth inning with the Braves out in front, 8-5, Steve and Ben leaned up against the back of the car after their tinkering was complete for the afternoon and looked out into the neighborhood. The two of them were holding their glass Coca-Cola bottles and stood silently letting the peacefulness of the neighborhood wash over them. It was the last Sunday Ben would ever have with his dad.

3

That day Steve Medlen had been found, everything changed in Ben and Bailey's world. The world as they had known it, was turned upside down and nothing would ever be the same going forward. The patriarch was dead, the leader of the band had died. That morning, everything started out perfectly in South Carolina for the Medlen family. There was not even the slightest notion that anything horrible was going to come for the family.

Ben got up from bed, got ready for school, and got on the bus like he had every year since second grade. Bailey went to work and so did his dad that morning. In the kitchen, Ben grabbed a pop tart and dashed out the door telling his mom and dad he loved them and to "have a good day, see ya'll later!" He would only see his mom later at school. When he saw her, he knew something was wrong because his mom showing up at the school to pick him up never happened.

Seeing her standing there through the glass wall of the office as he came walking up from the hallway with her head in her hands, Ben knew something terrible had happened. All warning bells inside his head went off putting him on high alert. He braced himself for whatever news she had.

Ben walked into the office and Bailey raised her head away from her hands and looked at her son with big red eyes. She had been crying and by the looks of it for a long time. She opened her mouth and tried to talk, tried to utter the words that would alter his world forever, but she only looked like a trout trying to breathe out of water. That's when Ben got scared.

"Mom? What is it?" Ben asked, standing there feeling as if he was going to throw up from nerves.

"We need to go." He went numb and the best he could later describe it was like his ears had a loud ring in them. Ben already knew without his mom saying another word; something had happened to his dad, something terrible. In the back of his mind, he knew that his dad was dead.

4

The sheriff's department was called out on Highway 39 around eight-thirty that morning to investigate a car that had been spotted off in a field a few yards from the highway up against an embankment. A passerby had called it in. A deputy sheriff responded, Deputy Reagan, and he approached the car finding a man inside of it slumped over, lying to the right of the driver's seat, airbag deployed. Deputy Reagan tried to open the door, but it was locked and after several attempts to get the man to respond, the officer took his six-cell Mag-Lite flashlight out of his belt and busted the window. He reached in and opened the door. He grabbed the man and pulled him up and check for a pulse. Nothing. He was dead.

Bailey was at work at the pharmacy talking to an elderly patient about her medicine side effects when Deputy Reagan and another deputy by the name of Scudder waited on her to finish up with the old woman. When the old woman turned to leave, Deputy Reagan stood there at the drop-off desk and asked if she was Bailey Medlen. "Yes? How I can help you, officers?" Both officers lowered their eyes and steeled their nerves for the bad news they had to break.

They asked her if Steve Medlen was her husband. "Yes," Bailey responded.

They began to tell her about the accident as delicately as they possibly could; told her that she needed to come down to the hospital to identify the body. Bailey did not hear anything after that. She went numb, the voices of the deputy growing more distant with each passing second. Her mind was blank, and her reality forever changed.

Chapter 11

1

October

Bobby milled about the crowded hallways of his school in between the class change of third and fourth period; always a busy time as the guidance counselor emerged from his office with a meeting with Alice Masterson, a freshman that had been deemed trouble from her junior high. Bobby didn't think she was trouble at all, maybe a little misunderstood is all. All Alice really wanted was for someone to listen to her, and from Bobby's experience, that's what the underlying issue usually was: just for them to have someone to hear them vent. Bobby was always there with a good ear, but he put Alice in a red file in his freshman drawer because he wanted to make sure that he kept an eye on her throughout the rest of her career. If she even made it all the way that was.

Walking slowly down the hallway, patrolling as he called it, he smiled here and there to kids that would speak to him, tipping a wave to others that made eye contact. On some days a few kids would approach him and make conversation. That was the comfort level Bobby had cultivated over the years. It pained him to think that all of this, the career that he had built over the years, would likely be gone by the end of the school year. He had yet to call Pete Samples to see if Glick had just been running his mouth or if what he said was the truth. People like Glick never just ran off with their mouths, did they? Nope, not in Bobby's experience. People like Glick liked to talk about the stuff they were going to do and did it. Those types were talk and action.

Walking aimlessly around the halls, doing nothing more than stretching his legs really until his next meeting with Ben Medlen, a transfer from South Carolina, Bobby looked over from across the way and spied April Murray. The two of them had locked eyes. There was something about her that drew Bobby in. It was a magnetic pull of sorts. It was early, but Bobby was feeling things for April. He liked her: she was easy to talk to, seemed to smile all the time, was beautiful inside and out, and most of all appeared to like him.

The two of them had talked a bit here and there since they walked the track at the first football game on Friday night but nothing serious at all afterward. Matter of fact, they had walked the track at two more football games since the first home opener. Kids and other school faculty had been noticing that the two had been together at football games and had even watched them stand and talk to each other in-between classes. People were beginning to make assumptions and neither did Bobby nor April take umbrage to that. They didn't care. They were smitten with each other but nothing from either the Bobby or April camp had confirmed it. The mystery of it all was fun and exciting. Most of all for Bobby, it was a nice change of pace to have something else to think about while at home. April was one of the best distractions he could have asked for.

Last week, Bobby and April were standing by the vending machines during a class change from fourth and fifth period watching all the kids come and go; some of the kids that walked by looked at the two, giggled, or smiled. Bobby had even gotten a high five from Markus Stratlen, the wide receiver from the football team as he walked by in his group of friends.

"What was that about?" Bobby asked April.

"Oh, you haven't heard? We're an item now," she said matter-of-factly with a smile across her face.

"Really? Well, how are we doing?"

"I think good. People think we're a good couple," April replied.

"Like maybe a shot at Homecoming King and Queen this year?"

April laughed, "Maybe. I'd say fifty-fifty odds."

"Oh, I'd go better than that. I'd go sixty-forty." Bobby and April looked at each for what seemed an eternity until Bobby broke the enchantment. He always did it seemed. He did not want to but something made him do it each time. It was like an involuntary reaction.

The two of them had not gotten to the point where they exchanged numbers. All the playful flirtations and looks across crowded rooms and meetings were nothing more than a subtle form of foreplay. It made Bobby feel something that he had not felt in a long time, not since Dana walked out on him. He felt as if someone was interested in him, him, for some reason and that made him glad all over. It had been a very long time since someone had wanted him.

Out there in the hallway, Bobby smiled and waved, and April smiled bigger and waved her hand back. He could tell that she was really into him. She did not hide it very well. Why would she? She knew that she liked Bobby for a long time but he was married. She stayed a respectful distance because the one thing that April Murray was NOT was a home wrecker. In Bobby, the adage applied that all the good guys were taken and Bobby was. That was until the news had hit the school that Bobby had lost his son in a terrible accident and later…his marriage. April was in total shock as well as the rest of the staff when the news of Dana Downey had moved out not long after their son was killed. No one knew the particulars, but how could she do that to him, they all asked in different ways.

It was heart-wrenching to watch as Bobby bravely came to work and try to deal with the aftermath of his son's death and the death of his marriage after the summer break. April wanted to go to him a million times that new school year, but decided it was for the best to just stay where she was. She didn't want people talking. Even though Freddy was killed back in March, and his wife left him a bit later on, Bobby was still fresh from it all, still raw. You could see it on his face there in the school. Bobby did the best that he could while at work, but sometimes the pain flashed in his mind so brilliantly that he had to take walks outside to grab some fresh air. Sometimes for Bobby, the walls closed in on him a little too fast in some of the worst times.

2

Even though Bobby had felt good about himself again somewhat; felt good about this budding relationship with April, he also felt guilty about smiling and feeling happy. That was because Freddy was dead, in the ground and he could not smile or be happy ever again. That thought caused Bobby to reassess what it was he was doing with April and his intentions. Thoughts like that came when he was alone at night, struggling. Sleep never came easy for Bobby; he kept himself hopped up on Ritalin to keep sleep to just a few hours. He knew a few hours was nowhere near enough. Two to three hours a day was not feasible in the long run. His body and mental condition were already feeling exhausted.

He took Ritalin to stay awake as long as he could on the daily to keep from sleep, to keep from the nightmares of that day, but in staying awake, his thoughts were too much for the man to bear at times. It had gotten to the point where he would get up in the middle of the night and run on the treadmill in the next bedroom. Bobby would run on that treadmill full bore with tears in his eyes thinking about the past, just months ago, when Freddy was alive and his marriage to Dana was still strong.

Bobby thought that he could outrun his thoughts, that maybe he could run so fast that the thoughts of Freddy and that terrible day would go by the wayside. He tried to outrun the thoughts of the day when Dana walked out of the house for good. He ran as fast as he could at one in the morning on that treadmill crying from the pain that stabbed his heart with every beat. Sleep would eventually come when Bobby got off the treadmill and lay on the floor whimpering for the days of past; sobbing and crying for the son he lost and the wife that left. Those were the bad times for Bobby; the weeks and months after Freddy and then the Whammy! from Dana's exit. Those were indeed the darkest days. But there was a light in all that darkness. Faint as it was, there was a light; that light was April Murray.

3

Ben sat in Bobby's office. It was his introductory meeting with the school's guidance counselor whom he had only met once and that was on the very first day at school. Ben had seen him in the hallways here and there and the both of them had exchanged waves. Ben had come a long way from that day when he was lost when Bobby had given him a copy of his class schedule. Now, he was able to navigate the school like a seasoned pro. Even the buses were no problem after a few days.

Ben looked around the office waiting for Bobby to come in. On the wall in black picture frames behind Bobby's desk were a bachelor's and master's degree from the University of Tennessee given to Robert Jackson Downey. On his desk were stacks of papers, a blotter calendar, a Ghostbusters cup that had pencils in it, and a printer and computer on a smaller side desk next to his big one. In the corner of the office was a bookcase with books that Ben didn't think he would be very interested in reading.

Ben saw two pictures turned away from him, facing Bobby when he sat down. Looking around at the half-opened door of the office, Ben reached over and took one of the pictures. He turned it around to see who was in the frame. It was Bobby and a kid, probably his kid, at what looked to be a Braves baseball game. At least the guy has taste, he thought to himself. His dad liked the Braves. He picked up the other picture and it was Bobby and a woman. Ben figured that it was his wife. He put the picture back in its place on the desk when he heard whistling coming from down the hallway. In came Bobby Downey.

4

Bobby came in and flashed a smile to the kid that he had met on the first day of school, for sure had seen him about the hallways of the school during class changes. By this time, Ben had fixed his eyes on his shoes only looking up when Bobby came in. The guidance counselor sat down behind his desk and leaned back. Bobby pulled out a file on Ben from his drawer at his desk and opened it. Bobby had already gotten the cliff notes from Ben's old school and was impressed with the kid that sat quietly across his desk.

Bobby had gone around and asked the teachers what Ben was like in their classrooms: shy, great grades, polite. They all told him that he seemed like a good kid, a good student, no problems with his conduct at all. Bobby noticed that Ben did not have any friends he walked around with or that he belonged to any clubs, nor did he play any sports. Not that he had to, but Bobby wondered if young Mr. Medlen was adjusting well in a new state and new school. He had been meaning to meet with Ben several weeks ago, but other students, some recently new red-filed ones from the new freshman class, had garnered his attention in the few weeks of the new school year. Since Ben was not deemed a risk by his grades or teachers, he put off meeting with him, to check in on the kid.

"From South Carolina?" Bobby opened up.

Ben nodded his head, looking down at his shoes. He was nervous talking to Bobby for some reason.

"I used to visit family in Columbia. Had an aunt and uncle that lived there…many moons ago."

Nothing from Ben.

"I was looking over your transcripts from Culver High School. Impressive, man. Grades here are really good, too. What's in the secret sauce?"

Ben shook his head, "Nothing really?"

"Whatever it is keep doing it…smarter than I was at your age. Ever given any thought to what you want to do after all this is over? I mean, you're a junior and I'm going to tell you, time will fly by so fast that you'll be out of here in no time."

"Not really. I haven't thought about it much."

Bobby sat in his chair and rocked back a little looking at the kid that refused to look up. He had kids in his office before like Ben and sometimes they warmed up and sometimes they did not. Ben, it appeared, was going to be one of those kids that were going to take some time perhaps.

"I wouldn't recommend a guidance counselor at a high school. No money in it. Dog fighting, that's where the money is. Gambling. Being a pimp…"

Ben smiled a little bit and wanted to laugh at the obvious joke. He could tell that Bobby was a joker guy. He had heard people in his school talk about him from time to time and all of it was good and positive. He liked Bobby and didn't get a bad vibe off of him whatsoever.

"So, all jokes aside, McFly, how are you adjusting to life here? In this school?"

"Okay, I guess," Ben said after a moment of consideration.

"I like you. Man of few words. Most thinkers are. What's been the biggest difference from here to Culver High School back home?"

Ben considered this question for a few moments; moments that Bobby thought were going to extend well into the end of the meeting. To his surprise, it did not. "Just some of the teaching styles here are different."

"Better or worse?"

Ben considered again, still looking down at his shoes. "Better in some places."

"It's funny because no matter what school you go to you find practically the same type of teachers: the hard cases and burnouts, the way too lax ones, the 'I'm more intelligent than you'll ever be', or the ones that make you want to get up in the mornings and come to school because they really care."

To this Ben raised his head and looked at Bobby for the first time, "Yeah. A lot of people don't see that."

Bobby knew that he had Ben hooked now. All he had to do was reel him into the boat. "Yeah, right? I've been here for a while," Bobby said in a very brief moment of reflecting, "and all those types are right here in this school. In others as well across the world I guess. If I'm being honest, they were the same types when I was in school."

"Kids are the same. Same types, I meant," Ben was trying his best to keep his eyes on Bobby and not stare down at his shoes all meeting long.

"See the same types here and back home?" Bobby asked.

"Oh yeah: same jock types…same bullies…same preps…same nobodies… same nerds."

"High school has been around forever but the students never change, just the faces, you know. Teachers, too," Bobby articulated.

"You asked what I wanted to do after high school. I have no idea," Ben said after a minute or two of silence.

"Well, that's why you've got me here: to guide. You're a smart kid. Can do anything from what I've seen in your grades."

Ben shifted on his chair to get more comfortable. There was something about Bobby that just made him feel at home. It was the first time that he could feel his guard, his knight shield, being lowered since he started this new school as it came to talking to people. "I've had so much happen over the last little bit that thinking about the future…I just…I don't want to think about anything for a while," Ben said, struggling to put into words his thoughts on the subject of life after high school.

Bobby, still leaning back in his chair, nodded slowly, "I got it, man. I do.

Most people at forty don't know what they want to be when they grow up. I don't think anyone really is doing what they want to do. I think they're doing what they have to do and hope they figure it out along the way."

"I've never heard it put like that before," Ben said, liking that statement from his high school guidance counselor.

"Stick around me and you'll get all kinds of bumper sticker-worthy tidbits."

"You like it here? I mean being a guidance counselor?" Now it was Ben asking a question. Bobby loved it when kids in his meetings engaged. He liked a good back-and-forth. He did not get much of that in there and always welcomed it when it did sparsely occur.

Bobby considered Ben's question before answering, "Yeah, it's rewarding at times. Other times, you feel that you're not making a difference, not like I thought I would be making when I first got out of college and into this job…but like anything you have to take the good with the bad."
Ben sat, hands now in his lap thinking about what Bobby had said. He supposed he was right. "What would you be doing if not this?"

Bobby smiled, "You should be a reporter, Medlen. Let's see," Bobby looked up at the ceiling from his leaned-back position in his chair and thought for a second or two. "Professional bull rider. You know, a big belt buckle that looks like a boxing championship belt? Or a Ghostbuster."

Ben chuckled, "Ghostbusters is one of my favorite movies."

"Mine, too! The greatest film of all time!" Bobby exclaimed with excitement.

"I watched it with my dad for the first time when I was six."

"Man has good taste. Seriously though, I don't know what else I'd be doing or want to do. The guy that might've known is twenty-plus years gone down the road. A lot of miles have been put on since then. I'll keep doing this until I can't," Bobby said, thinking about Glick and how he was going to cut him out of the picture and others like him around the district.

"It seems like you do a good job here. I hear kids and teachers talk about you sometimes."

"Well, I try. So, I got to ask, why here? How did you end up at this school all the way from South Carolina? Did you pull out a map, close your eyes, and point to a place?"

This was a tough question but one that he would eventually have to answer. He was surprised that he had not already fielded the question before and would have if he had any friends in this school. Ben steadied himself to tell Bobby why he came, and what had driven him and his mom out of there. Was it the both of them being driven out? No. Ben did not want to leave his safe confines. His mother did. She was the one that had the problem with being there. She had a problem with being in the same house they all lived in. Ben was just fine staying.

In the end, he did not have a say in the matter. He spoke up about it, what his mom was planning but she did not listen and didn't seem to care because at the time it was all about her feelings and how she was dealing with the death of her husband. Before Ben could open his mouth, the bell rang out loudly causing the both of them to jump in fright.

"Well, until next time, I guess."

Ben smiled at the invite and got up from his chair, "Is it cool that we can talk anytime, Mr. Downey? It's just… I've got some issues…and no one really to talk to." It was the first time that Ben had ever reached out to someone. He felt that Bobby was the guy to talk to. There was a certain relaxation between him and the guidance counselor.

"Of course. Of course, it is. Anytime. I'm here for you. Whatever you need."

Ben nodded his head, "Cool."

Ben was about to leave the office through the half-open door when Bobby said something that caused him to pause and turn around. "What?"

"There is no Dana…only Zuul," Bobby repeated, quoting that famous scene in Ghostbusters.

Ben smiled back and threw him the next line, "What a lovely singing voice you must have."

He walked out and Bobby clapped and shouted, "There you go! Knew I liked you! Now get out of here you're bothering me."

5

Ben walked from Bobby's office with his head up and he was doing so really and truly for the first time since he had been at the school. He did not catch himself doing so until he was actually meeting people's eyes as they hurried past. It was as if Ben was seeing the school for the first time. It was much different than watching the green and white tile floor flow by. Keeping his head up he saw lockers, other classrooms, and the large concrete pillars dotted throughout the first floor of the school that extended up to the ceiling that held the floor of the second floor. It was strange how much different the school looked from this point of view.

Ben was not sure why he had confidence coming out of Bobby's office. It was like a newfound sense of self. It was the first time since he had been there in the school, and in town, that he felt somewhat normal. It would never feel like it felt back home, never. However, right now, the here and now, Ben felt good. It was best to hold onto that feeling for as long as he could.

In his next few classes, Ben kept his head and eyes up. Now, he was one of them, one of the kids in the classroom. He was like a kid with a new bike on Christmas. He was seeing things from a whole new perspective now. Sure, he had been engaging a little bit more in class discussions before Bobby's meeting with him, and sure he was not looking down at the floor as much, but after talking with Bobby, an adult that appeared to be interested in him and his life, Ben felt a rush of confidence. It was not the comfortable confidence that he had back in South Carolina, but at least it was a start.

6

Bobby walked the hallway that ran between the school's main office and the English department. Kids were thinning out trying to hurry into class before the tardy bell caught them. With his hands in his pockets, he walked up to Millie Strafford and Danny Okaford, both seniors of the school. They were posting bright orange cardboard signs on both sides of the school's walls down that particular hallway.

"Costume party? This is a first," Bobby read, standing there looking at the poster that was made by Millie in art class or probably, most likely, in her spare time at home. She was that kid.

"That's right, Mr. Downey. Isn't it awesome?!" Millie said excitedly, walking over to Bobby as she carried more orange poster board signs.

"How did you get Glick to OK this?" Bobby asked, in awe that the stuffy old man would even go for something like a costume party.

"I don't know. Mary talked to Mrs. Hooks and Mrs. Hooks talked to Mr. Dean and Mr. Dean talked to Mary and the both of them went to Mr. Glick and laid it all out there. And so here we are!" Millie said at machine gun speed.

"October 30," Bobby read the poster that was written in the girl's handwriting. "The First Annual Halloween Costume Party. Free Drinks. Music from DJ Ferris. 6:30-10:00."

"It's kind of nice to be a part of something people around here will be doing for years to come," Danny said, walking over to Bobby and Millie.

"Yeah. This is awesome you guys. Great job."

"You should totally be our chaperone, Mr. Downey," Danny said.

"And Ms. Murray. I think you guys make a cute couple. I mean, if you two are," Millie broke in with that machine gun quick statement.

"Can you do it, Mr. Downey?" Danny asked a little bit too enthusiastically.

Bobby considered for a moment and looked at the two doe-eyed kids, "Why not. I'll round up Ms. Murray and see what she's doing on the thirtieth." Both kids' eyes grew wide, and they smiled with excitement. Millie and Danny walked away from Bobby and down the hall plastering more of those bright orange signs on the walls. Those were the nicest kids at the school. So nice and sweet that he was just sure that he got Type 2 diabetes from them.

As Ben was answering a question in class out loud for everyone to hear, Bobby walked down to April's classroom. He was going to ask her if she was interested in coming to the costume party with him. He knew that she probably would. At any rate, he was still nervous. She made him nervous. Not that she was difficult to talk to, quite the opposite. She was great to talk to. He was nervous because he was falling in love with her more and more as the days went on and a part of him hated that because he had not totally stopped loving Dana.

Bobby wanted to call her a million times and tell Dana that he still loved her, but he could not do it. He knew that even though she may love him, she'd never be back, and he could not leave the house. They were never to be a married couple anymore. It was over. So why could not Bobby move on from it? How come he could not move on from Freddy? How had Dana moved on so fluidly like nothing had ever happened, like the entire marriage was just a mirage and Freddy meant nothing? Truth was, Dana was spiraling herself. She just never let Bobby know how much after she moved away.

Bobby caught himself before his thoughts went further down the train tracks. It was not fair to say that Dana had moved on from Freddy. Bobby knew that Dana would be forever locked in that room inside her head and the day of Freddy's death would replay for the rest of her life. He felt bad for her because the death of a child hit the mother harder. Bobby theorized it was because they carried the child inside of them for nine months and there is a bond there that a father could never fully understand. Just as much as Bobby could not leave the house where they all lived once upon a time, Dana could not bear to stay with the memories. Bobby and Dana's resolve was too strong for the other to give in.

Bobby walked up to April's door and through the long rectangle of glass in the door, he pressed his face to it and breathed heavily, fogging up the glass. Her students were looking at this from their seats and some giggled. April, confused at what they were lowly giggling at turned to look at the door and saw through the fogged-up glass it was Bobby Downey. She smiled and told the class she would be right back. They all giggled and made catcalls when she opened the door and saw that it was their guidance counselor and the man that people had been saying was Ms. Murray's boyfriend. She stepped into the hallway closing the door behind her.

"Fogging up my glass now?"

"Better than knocking I thought."

"What brings you by? Would you like to sit in my class so I can teach you a few things?"

"Oh, I think you could probably teach me a whole lot, Ms. Murray."

April laughed, "You never darken my door, Mr. Downey. This must be serious," she said, crossing her arms in that sexy way that drove Bobby wild.

"It is, kind of," Bobby nervously scratched the back of his head and cleared his throat. April thought he was cute being nervous in front of her. This seemingly confident man with a profound wit and deadpan sarcasm was jelly when he was around her. "Have you seen the posters up for the costume party the kids are putting on?"

"Yeah, those bright orange posters? No, I must have missed those all over the walls. Tell me where they're at so I can understand what you're saying," April wanted to laugh at her sarcasm. Bobby did the laughing for her. He loved her sharp wit and great comebacks.

"Oh, that's why I like you. Millie and Danny wanted to know if I would chaperone the party. But it'd be a lot cooler if I had someone to do it with." Bobby and April locked eyes and neither one broke away.

April stood there and considered for a bit, "I don't know. We'll see. See if I can find you someone," April said deadpan. Bobby caught onto what she was doing.

"Well, when you find someone, you let me know. I'm so hoping that you can talk old Mrs. Corbett into going with me. I've got some moves I want to try out on her. Saw them in a book once," Bobby said, as he slowly backed away. April had put her hand on the silver metal door knob and turned it as she watched Bobby backing away.

"I'll do my best, Mr. Downey. She's pretty committed to her relationship though. I hear she's been married fifty years now."

"Great," Bobby said loudly across the hallway, still walking backward not taking his eyes off April, "she must be tired of him by now. What's his name, Gilbert? Yeah, tell her it's time to trade up!"

"Go to your office," April said, laughing and smiling as she disappeared back into her classroom.

8

As Ben was walking out of the school at the end of the day amongst the sea of kids fleeing the prison, Abby, a blonde girl that Ben had noticed a few times in his English class, ran right into him from the left causing him to stagger to the right a bit. She was looking at some papers and was not paying any attention to her surroundings and Ben was walking with his head up looking around, seeing the sights; not that he didn't know what they were, but it was the first time since he had been at Central High that he actually took in the environment.

Abby fell down, her papers scattering across the sidewalk. Some kids saw her and the papers and just kept walking, a few of them walking right over the sheets. Initially, Ben thought that Kevin Banks, one of the high school's more notorious bullies, had run into him on purpose. Butterflies instantly filled Ben's stomach as he just knew that he was in for a fight. It would not have mattered if he ran into Kevin by accident or not. There would be a fight because that's just the way Kevin was.

When Ben looked down thanking God that it was not Kevin, he saw Abby. It was love at first sight. There she was, glasses askew sitting down on her but looking around at her papers and then up at Ben, "I'm so sorry. I didn't mean to run into you. I wasn't watching where I was going." Ben kneeled down without even really knowing that he was doing it. He gathered her papers and took her hand and helped her up. The two stood face to face and she adjusted her glasses and blew the hair out of her eyes. She had the biggest hazel eyes he had ever seen. She was beautiful in a dorky sort of way.

"It's totally okay. Here are your papers," Ben handed her.

Abby took them. "Thank you," she said nearly in a whisper.

Abby was not good with talking to guys, especially ones that she nearly knocked over. As one of the school's nerds, she usually kept her head down like Ben had and just tried to make it through the day without incident. The two of them looked at each other for a few seconds more and Abby pushed her glasses up tighter to her face with her index finger on the bridge. They were not down on her nose, nowhere close, it was just a nervous habit she had. She was nervous standing there in front of Ben, "I'd better get going." She walked by Ben.

Ben knew that he had to say something because things like this only happens in the movies he thought, "Hey you!" Ben yelled.

Abby turned back as kids were walking all around obstructing her view at times, "Me?"

"Yeah, let me know the next time you're coming that way so I can leave the building a little later." It was a joke and he hoped it landed.

Abby stood there holding her papers and at first, she did not know if Ben was being a prick or not, and then she saw him smile. That's when she knew this cute guy was making a joke. "I will."

She turned and walked away wondering to herself where that sudden burst of confidence had come from. It certainly had come from Abby Maddux. She smiled and bit her lower lip as she walked to her mom's SUV. Ben watched her get in and was thunderstruck by what had just happened. In one day, he gained some confidence which surely had something to do with Bobby's meeting in his office and now a girl, a knockout, ran into him causing butterflies to swarm down in his stomach. What a day at school. Things appeared that they were getting better…or were they?

Chapter 12

1

October 30th

The night of the school's Halloween costume party finally came. The turnout was much bigger than expected. The thirtieth fell on a Friday and Halloween was on Saturday; a lot of party stuff to do for the teens of Central High that weekend. A couple of weeks previous, Bobby and April had been talking to each other when they could around the school. They were not trying to be obvious about their mutual affection for each other, but both had a difficult time keeping their eyes off the other when they passed in the hallways. Their smiles could not be contained either. Neither Bobby nor April had the courage to exchange phone numbers at that point in time just yet. Bobby wanted to but was still dealing with the mental baggage that weighed him down. April wanted to but did not know when the right time was to bring up the subject. She figured it would happen when it was supposed to happen.

They volunteered to walk the track at the last two home games of the football season that October. The other teachers were happy about that. Big shocker, they lost…again. Not that Bobby and April noticed. They were too busy with each other, talking about things: their likes and dislikes; favorite music and movies; typical dating questions people asked. The football games were their date nights without them having the pressures of actually going out in town doing the whole dating thing.

The school was where they felt the most comfortable. On those football games during the fall, Bobby was falling harder for April. April could say that she loved Bobby Downey, but she dared not utter those words to him. She knew that he was as broken as anybody she had ever known. She could see it on him, in his eyes, and the way he carried himself like his thoughts were much too big for him. April knew the pain he was trying to work through and kept her feelings to herself. She was sure though that Bobby knew how she felt about him, but what did Bobby think about her? Well, April was about ninety-nine percent sure he felt the same way.

On the last home game of October, there was a fight on the far end of the track. Kevin Banks, a kid that Bobby and April knew all too well, was involved in a brawl with Preston Malone, another punk kid that was nearly out of school; not because of him being a senior, but because he was loading up to drop out and chase that GED dream. Bobby and April saw from a distance a crowd had swooped over to the far end of the track, which from where Bobby and April were located was the entire length of the football field. Bobby took off running, hoping that he could get there before too much blood had been spilled. April was left behind on her walkie-talkie calling for someone to get one of the deputies that were standing at the entrance gate to respond to the fight across the way.

Bobby had gotten there and broke through the circle of onlookers and found Kevin getting the daylights punched out of him. Preston was on top of him, left hand wadded up in the collar of Kevin's shirt and pounding him with his right. Bobby reached over and grabbed Preston by his raised fist and dragged him off. He pulled him away and through the already thinning circle. The deputy had finally gotten there and taken Preston. Bobby went back over to Kevin who was lying on his back breathing hard and muttering something Bobby could not understand. His face had been busted up pretty good. To be honest, Bobby didn't care. Serves you right, he thought to himself.

He had seen too much over the years that Kevin had done to kids, usually smaller and weaker than him. He had inflicted pain everywhere he went. Bobby used to, a long time ago, had Kevin in the at-risk folder. Eventually, he shredded it because Kevin was too far gone for his kind of help. Kevin needed anger management. Bobby had recommended that very thing after talking to him when he came to Central High as a freshman from Claxton Elementary. No one cared to listen. When Bobby was able to get a therapist friend of his in the next town to take Kevin on as a patient, Kevin refused to go. It's not like his parents tried to convince him to go and get help; they were just as bad as he was… probably where he learned it. "Some kids", Bobby said to Dana one night in bed, "are just rotten to the core…can't save'em." Kevin was one of those kids.

The Friday before the Halloween costume party, Bobby was in his office eating his lunch; a small bowl of Trix in a small plastic bowl. Bobby called himself a cereal slut. He loved nearly all fun cereals and had eaten them all over the period of his life. When it came to lunchtime, Bobby preferred to stay in his office alone with his cereal of the day. He would take that time to catch up on some news reading or something other than schoolwork. He used that time to decompress from the day if only for an hour. When he came back to work in August, he had heard the whispers of how much weight he had lost and how tired he looked. He thought it would be best to start the school year off right and at least eat lunch. Cereal was his preferred choice.

A knock came on his office door, which was always customarily halfway open. It was April with an apple and bottled water. Bobby always got nervous when he saw her. Always. That's how he felt with Dana, especially early on when they dated and at times while they were married. "Want some company?"

"Come in," he said with a mouth full of Trix. April came inside and sat down on the chair across from his desk.

"Trix today?"

Bobby nodded, "Yup. Love'em. But they're not my favorite though."

"What's your favorite?" April asked, rubbing her apple on the right sleeve of her pink blouse.

Bobby considered. "I'd have to say Honeycombs. Frosted Flakes is a very close second. I like Apple Jacks, too. Sometimes I have a hard decision to make in the mornings."

"I bet you do," she said, biting into her red apple.

"How's school today?" Bobby asked, leaning back in his chair holding his small bowl of cereal.

"I teach history…how good do you think it is?" she quipped, smiling behind the apple.

"Never get tired of those smart-ass comebacks," Bobby grinned, putting the spoonful of Trix in his mouth.

"So…did you find a date for the costume party?"

"Struck out every at-bat, you believe that? Just could never get the one that I really wanted," Bobby said, putting another spoonful of Trix into his mouth.

"That's a shame," April said, taking another bite of her apple. "What did Mrs. Corbett say to you when you asked?"

Bobby returned April's serve, "The usual excuses. I go to bed by seven-thirty…my hip ain't what it used to be. But there's someone I want to ask, but I just don't know about it."

"Why not?"

Bobby shrugged his shoulders, "I don't know. Don't want to ruin a friendship, I guess. Especially if she doesn't feel the way I do. I have no idea how she really feels. I think I might, but sometimes signals get crossed…assumptions get made. Understanding signs was never my strong suit."

April chewed on her apple, "Well, maybe the two of you need to get together and hash it out… like adults. She might surprise you, but I think you got a good hold on things. I think you guys both know what you might want in the latter stages of your lives."

Bobby considered and smiled as he finished his cereal and put the bowl down with the spoon inside, "You're probably right." Bobby leaned on his desk, elbows on the wood, right hand propping up his head looking at April. "Listen, if you're not doing anything next Friday night, how's about doing a guy a solid and help me keep an eye on these crazy kids, huh?"

April took another bite from her apple and playfully considered Bobby's request. She kept him hanging for a little bit while she chewed her fruit. "Okay. I think I can help you out there. It just so happens that I have nothing at all to do next Friday night. Lucky you."

Bobby smiled, "Lucky me."

2

Ben sat in Bobby's office talking on that same day after lunch just as he did during their first official meeting. Bobby had not scheduled a meeting with Ben, but Ben had dropped by earlier that morning in between the

second and third period and asked if Bobby would be busy sixth period. "Nope, not at all; clear dance card. You need to see me?"
"Yeah," Ben had said, "if that's okay?"

Bobby nodded, "Who's room are you going to be in sixth period?" he asked, already scribbling an excuse for the teacher to allow Ben to see him. Most of the teachers were cool with Bobby's request.
 "Ms. Simpson. Art."

"Yeah, I know Simpson. She owes me ten dollars," Bobby said in his funny, dry way, "Here you go, captain." Bobby handed Ben the note on a school letterhead. "If Joyce has any issue with it just tell her to talk to me and we'll work something out, okay? Might play Battleship…Vegas rules."

Ben took the paper and nodded and walked out of the office not understanding Bobby's sense of humor at all.

3

Bobby sat behind his desk looking across at Ben leaning back in his chair. "What did you need to see me about today? Everything okay?"

"Getting better, I guess. Getting more acclimated around here."

"Must be, you're using bigger words. Grades okay?"

Ben nodded, "Yeah, picking up where I left off at Culver."

Bobby and Ben sat in silence for a few minutes. Bobby was waiting on Ben, who had requested the meeting in the first place, to state why he had done so. Bobby was not pushy, but he knew that there was something on the kid's mind. So, after waiting some, Bobby finally started fishing.

"Something is clearly on your mind. Anything that I can help with because I quit mind-riding after I left the carnival in the eighties."

Ben shifted in his chair a bit and caught himself from looking down at his shoes, a nervous habit that he had been doing much better at getting rid of. For whatever reason, he was trying to revert back to bad habits all of the sudden. Maybe it was because he was about to start peeling back some layers of what was really going on with him on the inside. "I feel like you're a good guy. And I need a good guy to talk to. I don't have anybody. There's my mom…but I don't think she'd understand, and since my dad is gone, I don't have anyone to get advice from."

"Where's your old man? He up and leave?"

Ben looked around a bit before he answered. It was the first time that he was going to tell someone around there that his dad was dead and gone. People in South Carolina knew, his friends and family knew, but not in his new environment.

"He died back in March…forty-two… heart attack on his way to work. At least that's what everyone thinks anyways." Just saying out loud that his dad was dead, not something he had actually done since it happened, stunned Ben a bit and his insides began to feel like jelly for some reason.

Bobby didn't know how to exactly to respond to this. Ben had totally taken him off guard because usually, in his experience in talking to kids, they either had one parent because the other one left or no parents and a family member was looking after them. Turns out that Ben's father had died. Ben was the first person that he could relate to. Bobby could see the haunted look on Ben's young face and Bobby knew that haunted look all too well because he, too, had the same look when he saw his reflection in the mirror. He probably should have seen it earlier on Ben and would have if he had been fully paying attention like he used to at his job. But things had changed. Everything had changed.

"I'm sorry for your loss," Bobby said lowly. "You guys close?"

Ben thought about all the stuff he and his dad had done together over the years before he answered. The answer came easily, "Yeah. We were."

There was silence between them in that office for a few minutes. Then Bobby said, "Coming to Tennessee wasn't your idea was it?" Bobby figured not.

Ben shook his head no, keeping his head up and eyes focusing on a bookshelf in the office, "My mother's. I didn't want to leave our home but she decided that she couldn't live there anymore since dad was gone. Too many memories, I guess. But that's where the memories were, you know?" Bobby did know. Dana left because of the memories and Bobby stayed because of the memories. Ben would have stayed because of the memories just like Bobby had. The parallels in their lives were frightening, to say the least.

"I do. You feel betrayed by your mother because she moved away from home, don't you?"

Ben did not have to take any time to reply, "Yup. Every day. I mean, that was our house, and now we live in my dad's house that he grew up in and man…sometimes I think I can feel him in there. I know that sounds crazy. Mom just walked out of there, sold the place, and didn't even look back… didn't even consider my feelings at all. I didn't want to leave. I mean, every square inch of that place had a memory of my dad, but why would I ever want to leave it? And then I get this crazy notion, and I know it's crazy and irrational, but what if he was a ghost back in our old home and was watching us there in the house and when we moved out, he got lonely not being able to see his family? That thought creeps in sometimes." Ben seemed to be on the verge of tears. This kid should have been talking to a grief counselor a long time ago, Bobby thought to himself, but he knew precisely how he felt.

Bobby felt the same way when Dana left. Freddy was why Bobby could never leave. What if he was still there? Sounded crazy, just like Ben had said. Ben had just said what Bobby felt some nights. Some nights, Bobby would sit in his dead son's bedroom and just lie there on his bed and think about life before the incident in the street, right outside his windows. Sometimes he sat in Freddy's bedroom at night to see if he could feel his presence. He thought that he did on a few occasions. It could have been the immense grief that he had mixed with sleep deprivation and alcohol. Sometimes Bobby did not feel alone in that house and saw things…saw Freddy, heard him.

The mind could play funny tricks on you sometimes. It was cruel. Like the time when Bobby was reading a book, probably a few weeks after Freddy had been run over and killed, he could have sworn he heard his son laughing in the kitchen. It was so rattling that Bobby put his book down and eased up from his chair and walked slowly into the kitchen. Of course, there was nothing there, but he knew that he had heard Freddy laugh. Bobby thought himself crazy, but he heard what he heard. There was no explaining it away.

Bobby snapped out of his thoughts as Ben was talking. He did not mean to ignore him, but he had because he was swallowed up by Freddy's memory again. It happened often and when it did, it enveloped his mind, body, and soul. His mind had gone on a field trip while his body stayed.

"That's a tough break, kid. You ever speak to your mother about how you feel?"

"She doesn't understand. I mean, I know that she's going through stuff too, you know. Because we've both lost the man we love, but that loss has hit us on different levels. She lost a husband, and I lost a dad. I'm at a disadvantage because I'm sixteen and can't really do anything about it. If I'd had my druthers, I wouldn't have moved here, especially in my dad's old home where he grew up."

"That's got to be hard living in the house your dad grew up in. How did that come about?"

Ben shifted on his chair again and got more comfortable. "My Aunt Stacy. She told Mom that the house she and Dad had grown up in was empty and just sitting there. Since my grandmother died nobody had lived in it. Aunt Stacy said that if we wanted to get away from our home we could live in grandma's old one until we got things put back together. It made no sense to me. Mom was just looking for a way out I think not having to deal with Dad in our house."

Bobby nodded slowly. He knew what this young man was saying. "Most people don't know what to do when death comes knocking. People scramble… they panic." Bobby said in a moment of reflection and profound thought, "Does anybody really know what to do?" It was a rhetorical question as Bobby thought about Dana walking out of his life for good. God, it seemed like a lifetime ago. The funny thing was sometimes it felt like it just happened yesterday. Time was tricky that way.

Ben thought about what Bobby stated. "No. I doubt any of us do. I still don't know."

"Me either. It's been seven months since Freddy was killed and…I still can't get a grip. That's like what, two hundred plus days and nights?"

Ben sat and for a very brief moment, he wondered who Freddy was. Then it clicked into place: that was the kid in the picture on Bobby's desk. Freddy must have passed on. Bobby had forgotten at that moment that Ben was new to the school and Freddy's death was old news to everyone that had known about it. Bobby thought Ben had known about it, just assumed.

"Freddy was your son?" Ben asked, opening the door slowly to that locked room in Bobby's mind to take a peek at what was behind it…lurking.

"Yeah. He was killed out in our street playing Wiffle ball. A meth head ran him over. He was just outside on a regular Saturday afternoon. No different than any other day." Bobby reached over and took the picture off his desk and handed it to Ben for him to look at. Ben had already seen it but had taken the gesture anyhow and looked again. What he saw was two happy people, a father and a son, no different than him and his dad. "That was at Fulton County Stadium back last year…Braves game."

Ben smiled at the memento and handed it back to Bobby. "Yeah, me and Dad went there. Saw the Pirates come in April."

Bobby grinned, "No way. We did, too. It was on a Tuesday when we went… night game."

"Yup. We did, too. Where'd you guys sit?" Ben asked.

"Right behind the Braves dugout in the first row. You?"

Ben laughed a bit, "We sat in the second row up from you guys in the same place, the first and second seats from the aisle. That's crazy." The two guys laughed about how small the world was. For the rest of the meeting, the two talked about the Major League Baseball strike and how they thought it was total bullshit to the fans. "A lost season," Bobby called it. Ben agreed.

4

In the subsequent days, after their conversation in Bobby's office, which Ben really liked, it felt good talking with someone that got what he was saying, especially an adult. Bobby not only could relate with Ben, but he had some experience in the world of death because his son had been killed on just an ordinary day much like his dad. The two were connected and Ben began to feel a certain kinship to his guidance counselor because Bobby had a lot of the same characteristics as Steve Medlen. Bobby felt like an old comfortable shoe to Ben almost as if he had known him his entire young life.

As the next week rolled on, the school chatter was focused on the upcoming costume party, the first annual one at that. Ben would hear kids talk about what they were coming dressed as and whatnot. Some of the girls had been discussing some provocative dress. A few of the teachers had gotten wind of the plans and reported this to Mr. Glick, the ruler of Central High. He had gotten on the school-wide intercom and addressed this potential with a stern warning "that if anyone tried to enter the costume party with anything scandalous, they would be turned away and suspended."

Most kids did not think he had that kind of power but who was stupid enough to challenge Glick? Glick also announced that Mrs. Booker was going to be working the front table at the entrance doors to make sure anything provocative was not permitted inside. Mrs. Booker was a stuffy old woman and looked to be a hundred. She taught Biology I at such a snail's pace that students had not finished anywhere close to halfway through the book in five years.

Ben had been keeping tabs on Abby Maddux ever since she had run into him outside the school on his way to the bus. She was in his World Geography class in fifth period and sat two rows of desks over in the third seat, a perfect place where he could see her. He had seen her before in those quick glances around the classroom when he thought no one was watching. He had seen Abby before, but she did not stand out to him. Maybe it was because he was just scanning the room so fast his mind did not have time to register her. After their meeting outside the school building, Ben made it his job to see her.

On Wednesday of that week, Ben was walking through the crowded hallway to the cafeteria for lunch. He was walking in the direction of the school's main office to see if Bobby was standing outside of it or walking slowly up and down the corridor as he was prone to do during class change. He did not see him at first but saw him eventually as some of the crowd thinned down. Bobby was standing there talking to the head baseball coach, Coach Ritter, about the still lingering Major League Baseball strike that claimed the World Series. Ben stopped a few yards away and waved at his guidance counselor. Bobby saw him and patted Coach Ritter on the shoulder and said he'd see him later, "What's up?"

"Need some advice," Ben said.
"Okay?"

"I'm thinking of going to the costume party."

"Hey, awesome! Glad to see that you're getting social," Bobby said.

"But there's a girl I wanted to ask, and I don't…" Ben was cut off abruptly by Bobby.

"Just do it. Don't think about it, spaz. Do you know this girl?"

"Kinda."

"What do you mean, kinda? You know her or not?"

"Well, she ran into me by accident a while back and nearly knocked me down not looking where she was going. We share a class in World Geography. She always catches me looking at her, but I'm not doing it in a weird way."

"Yeah, because watching people is never weird," Bobby said in that patented sarcastic way that only Bobby could do.

"You know what I mean."

"Do I? I don't watch people. I may observe, but never "watch" people, as you put it." Bobby used his fingers to do air quotations on the word watch.

Ben just stood there looking at Bobby waiting for him to stop playing around, "For real? What do I do?"

"I told you already. You just do it. Ask her out to the costume party. Or ball, I think that's what the more elite in the school are calling it."

"So just go right up and ask her out, bare bones and all?"

"Have you never watched TV in your life? A John Hughes movie or anything? You just pick a time and ask her. Probably do it after your World Geography class is over."

Ben drew in a deep breath and exhaled. He was not good with girls not even back home in South Carolina. He was not what you would call a ladies' man by no means. "All right, I think I can do that. Maybe. I don't know."

"Good. Now go get something to eat. Matter of fact, bring me back a chocolate pudding cup…in my hand in five minutes," Bobby said, holding out his right hand. Ben shook his head and grinned and walked to the cafeteria. "I'm not kidding, you know?"

5

Ben waited until Mrs. Lowery's class was over to make his move. The bell dismissed her class and all the students scrambled up from their desks and made a beeline for the last class of the day. Abby had taken a little extra time to get up as she gathered her books and papers and put them in her backpack. Ben was already ready, hanging back on purpose waiting on Abby. The classroom was nearly empty except for Mrs. Lowery at her desk looking through a book. There was a line of kids at the door slowly pouring out into the hallway. Abby and Ben were the last two in line. Ben stood there behind her, nervous as he knew he would be. "So, Abby…long class today."

"Yeah, it seemed that way," she replied, looking back at Ben as the line was nearly gone into the hallway.

"I'm just glad we've got one more class left. I'm ready to get home." More small talk leading up to the main event. The two of them spilled out into the hallway where they were engulfed by all the other students talking and clamoring going to and fro. Abby and Ben walked side by side, dodging kids here and there. "So…what do you think about this costume party thing?" Ben asked.

"Sounds neat, I guess. I bet people are going to have fun dressing up."

"Yeah, I think so, too. I thought about going."

"Yeah? What are you going as?" Abby asked, pushing her glasses back up on her nose with her index finger, a nervous habit.

"I don't know yet. Got a few ideas maybe. Are you planning on going?"

The two of them walked in silence for several slow paces before she answered, "I doubt it," she replied.

"Oh. Okay." Ben felt rejected and took her "I doubt it" as a brush-off. "Well, I gotta go down this hallway to art. I'll see you tomorrow." Ben broke away from Abby and was slowly walking down the hallway to the right, another crowded one when he heard Abby's voice tower above all the confusion.

"Come here for a minute!"

Ben turned and battled his way back to where he left her, "What is it?"

"I only said 'I doubt it' because no one ever asks me to stuff like that. If that was what you were doing? If not then I totally feel like an idiot."

Ben was stunned by this admission because Abby Maddux was a knockout. At least he thought she was. "That's totally unbelievable. Are you serious?"

Abby nodded and looked around and pushed her glasses up that didn't need it. They never needed it.

"I was trying to ask you out to the party, but I didn't think you'd want to go with me."

"Of course I do. I think it would awesome. I'm just used to people never asking me," Abby said, biting her lower lip. She was clearly happy but at the same time, nervous.

"Okay. Can I have your number maybe? So we can talk more…sometime? Maybe…maybe later tonight," Ben fumbled nervously. Abby smiled and gave him her number. She was nervous, too.

6

On the night of the costume party, or ball, depending on whom you asked, the gym was packed. The get-together on the day before Halloween was a rousing success. Things were loud thanks to DJ Ferris at the music controls and the gym floor was packed with boys and girls dancing to the new music that was foreign to forty-year-old plus teachers, Bobby and April. The gym was dimly lit and jack-o'-lanterns with candles inside of them glowed ghoulishly about the place. Streamers, orange, black, and green hung everywhere. Life-sized paper skeletons hung on walls as well as witches on brooms and black cats and full moons.

"The kids did a really good job in here didn't they?" Bobby remarked when he and April first walked into the gym long before the costume party started.

"Yeah, they sure did. I'm excited for them. Hopefully, this goes off without a hitch and we can do this for years to come."

Bobby, who had shown up dressed as a Ghostbuster, in full uniform and detail rendering proton pack strapped to his back with all the lights and sounds, was standing alongside April, who showed up as the bride of Frankenstein. She was stunning. The two of them were told how awesome they had looked all night by the kids that walked by. Millie, the girl that had coordinated the event, who was dressed as an eighteenth-century Victorian queen, had snapped a picture of her and Bobby for the yearbook.

Things in the gym were flowing well that night. It was not like when he and April walked the track at the football games. No fights would break out because even though this was not an exclusive party, the troublemakers of the school did not come to things like this. Parties like this were usually reserved for the better-behaved kids, much like the prom and other school dances.

7

Ben came to the party dressed as Special Agent Fox Mulder from The X-Files. He was dressed in a suit and tie and on his front suit jacket pocket was an FBI photo ID with David Duchovny's face on it. Ben had convinced his mother to drive him to the costume store in Knoxville a day before to see if he could find the X-Files FBI badges for their costumes. He was successful.

When the two of them, Ben and Abby, talked about what they were going as to the costume party, Ben asked her if she had ever heard of The X-Files. As fate had it, she had and was a fan of the 1990s sci-fi show.

She came to the party as planned dressed as Special Agent Dana Scully. Ben had found and bought FBI photo IDs of both Mulder and Scully and affixed Scully's FBI badge to Abby's front suit jacket pocket before they walked into the gym. None of the kids there at the dance knew who they were supposed to be. It was okay, they didn't care. "I think we look great," Abby said, as the two of them opened the doors to the gym and entered.

The two of them had danced some, and when they were songs on that they did not want to juke and jive to, they went over to where the tables and chairs were at the designated areas and sat down. The two of them had a lot in common with each other. Ben was glad that he had spoken to Bobby about how to approach Abby about if she wanted to come to this party.

"There's a lot of people here tonight," Ben remarked, as he and Abby sat by themselves.

"Yeah," Abby replied. "Believe it or not but this is my first party."

"Mine, too. I didn't go to these things back home."

"Why not?"

Ben shrugged his shoulders, "I don't know really. Never seemed interesting, I guess."
"Did you have a girlfriend back home?" Abby asked.

"Nah, not really. There was a girl that I hung out with that worked at the arcade sometimes, but she really wasn't that into me. Sometimes you can tell, you know?"

"I would say yes, but I never had any boyfriends."

"Why?" Ben was shocked. Abby could hear the shock in his voice and that made her feel wonderful inside. She could tell that Ben saw something about her that she always hoped someone else would see one day.

"I don't know. Nobody ever really saw me much, I guess. I'm just this nerdy girl who reads all the time and doesn't talk much."

"I think you're pretty great, and I'm glad that nobody got you." For the first time, Ben felt as if he knew what love was at the age of sixteen. Abby, sitting beside him, felt it, too.

8

Bobby and April were talking when a song, a slow one from DJ Ferris, came from his musical pulpit up on the stage there in the gym. April looked at Bobby. The two of them locked eyes and April reached out for Bobby's hand as couples that wanted to slow dance with each other hit the floor while others went to sit down in the low-lit gym. Ben and Abby went dancing.

Bobby allowed her to take him to the gym floor, gently pulling him, and leading him to the floor. The song that came on was "Never Tear Us Apart" from INXS. "This is for all you ghouls and ghosts that are in love," DJ Ferris said deep and seductively over his microphone. April and Bobby pressed their bodies close to each other. Bobby felt a body against his that was not Dana and it felt good, natural…like it belongs there.

"I'd put my arms around you, but I can't get it around your proton pack," April said.

"It's okay. This is fine." April's hands were on his shoulders as the two of them swayed slowly to the song.

"Can I tell you something?"

"Yeah, fire away," Bobby said, nervously awaiting what she was going to say. He had an idea about what it was. Bobby was not stupid.

"I like you a lot. I'm kinda crazy about you. I think you feel the same way about me, too. Am I right about that or is my mind playing tricks on me here?"

Bobby held her and swayed back and forth with her and thought for a few quick moment."You're right," Bobby admitted. This was what he knew was coming. "I really like you, too. I think you're a knockout: great person, beautiful soul, the whole nine." Bobby paused speaking as he looked into her eyes. "This is all new to me, you know? I'm trying to figure out… how to do things again. Still trying to figure out how to get going after everything that's happened. Sometimes…well, most times, I'm a mess."

"I know," April said, looking into his eyes.

"I wasn't…I'm not in the best of places these days. I haven't been in a long time. Not since Freddy…not really. Dana was just the cherry on top…still drowning most days, I guess."

April nodded sympathetically and put her head on his shoulder. The two of them swayed slowly to the music, holding each other close. Somewhere through the crowd of kids dancing and in love, someone whistled and shouted, "You go, Mr. Downey!"

Bobby smiled and closed his eyes, "Kids."

The two of them laughed. For a moment everything was better. For a moment he was a million miles away from Maple Lane and that day Freddy was killed; a million miles away from all the pain and loss that had defined his life up to that point. He could have stayed on that gym floor with April for the rest of his life and that would have been just fine.

9

As the costume party began to wind down, Bobby stood over next to the entrance leaning up against the wall watching April talk with some of the female students and laughing. She was having a good time. Watching her, Bobby felt that connection with her. It was not the same connection that he had with Dana, but what was ever going to be? What me and Dana had was special…or at least was, he thought leaning up on the wall and watching April. But not special enough to survive Freddy's death.

He knew that he was falling for April, but should he? He was not in the best mental frame of mind and although he had told her that, she didn't seem to mind at all, but he did; he minded a lot. She had no idea how bad the nights were at home alone or the dreams he had where he woke up screaming…when dreams did come on those couple of hours of sleep. April had no idea of the alcohol and Ritalin abuse. There were a lot of things that April didn't know.

Before he could go down the rabbit hole inside his mind any further, he saw Ben coming over to him. He had seen Ben earlier with Abby Maddux and thought she was a great choice. She was a well-rounded student, not very vocal at all, and quiet. She was actually one of the biggest nerds in the school. Bobby felt that the two of them would somehow bring out the good in each other; that somehow they would counterbalance the other and amplify their best qualities. "And you came as…I got nothing. What are you supposed to be? A mortician?" Bobby teased.

"I'm Special Agent Fox Mulder of the FBI. The X-Files TV show?" Ben replied, taking a place along the wall beside his guidance counselor.

"Right. Glad that you didn't go overboard with the costume. So, Abby Maddux, huh?"

"Good choice?" Ben asked.

Bobby kind of shrugged his shoulders a bit, "Eh, I mean obviously you've gotten past the glass eye."

"She doesn't have a glass eye," Ben said, knowing that Bobby was messing with him.

"That's what I heard. You hear so much stuff in bathroom stalls these days. They are the school's biggest rumor mill."

After a few seconds of silence between them, Ben tried his hand at being funny. "So, Ms. Murray, huh?" Ben froze and forgot what he was going to say to Bobby. After trying to recover the fumble, Ben just said the first thing that came to his mind. "Glad you could get past her… glass eye."

Bobby smiled and turned his head to look at Ben who was embarrassed, "You can see that? She has one, like, for real, dude. I didn't notice it until we were dancing and the damn thing never moved."

"Are you serious?" Ben asked with concern.

Bobby threw his head back and chuckled at Ben's question. "Do you get comedy, Ben?"

"Yes," he replied sheepishly.

"Sometimes I wonder. But all jokes aside, because you clearly can't get them or give them, Abby is a nice fit for you. Good girl, good family."

"Yeah, I like her a lot. She's pretty cool. So how long with you and Ms. Murray?"

"Not long. Honestly, I don't know if I can let my guard down long enough to let anyone in. I mean, I feel something, but should I? Got a bag of emotions going on at the moment. I mean, I like her…but what do I do with that, you know?" Bobby said, watching April stand and talk to a group of senior girls.

"What's keeping you from letting your guard down? Maybe we need to explore that some."

Before Bobby could think of a reply, April saved the day by walking their way taking Bobby out of the conversation. "Have Abby home at a respectable time, Mr. Medlen," Bobby pushed off the wall and walked to meet April midway on the gym floor.

Chapter 13

1

It was night. The moon was full, drenching the landscape in a ghostly silver that is seen only in horror movies. Ben was not scared. He should have been. At night, the place was different, felt different. Stories were told about this place and places like it ever since stories had been told. Ben was sure of it. It was not the place that frightened him so much, but the eerie silence that covered it all. That was the scariest thing to Ben.

The Oak Grove Cemetery where Steve Medlen's body was buried was a sprawling sixty-acre plus bone yard that a person could get lost in. If you made a wrong turn here and a mistake there, you'd be lost for a bit even in the daylight. There were landmarks throughout the cemetery to keep you on your course. Landmarks such as a tall standing statue of a bronze man in a three-piece suit from decades gone by; a set of five American flags to mark the veteran's area; an above-ground mausoleum for the BOOKER family; and a landmark that gave Ben the willies. It was a tall stone angel. Its stone wings were open behind it, arms open and inviting as if it was taking in the visitors. Ben walked around the cemetery, lost in the eerie silver moonglow amongst the tombstones.

Ben knew that his father was buried in proximity to the tall statue of the angel at the far end of the cemetery. He dreaded seeing that statue because there was something about it that made Ben want to close his eyes and walk by it. Ben walked past it and did not dare once shoot the statue a gaze as the moonlight bathed the stone in a silver haunting aura. He could feel it looking at him as he walked by, could feel its stone eyes upon him. Ben wasn't wrong. The angel was watching him, turning its head as the boy went on by.

Ben walked due west from the angel and was looking for a grave that should look newer there if there was such a thing. Off to his left was a grave that had a mound of dirt. It was a clear signal that a recent burial had taken place right there. Has to be him. Ben rushed over to the grave. The marker read Harold Dempsey Killenbrew: 1942-1994. Nope, not Dad. Ben stood there and scoped around the cemetery.

The rows of monuments, some tall like the stone angel, others medium-sized and mostly small, stood sentry-like about the cemetery watching over the dead. The tombstones themselves seemed to reflect that ghostly moonglow and made the entire place seem to just light up. Ben could see ghostly silver radiating off of every marker in that necropolis. Ben did not know how he had even gotten there; no memory of coming to the place. It wasn't important. What was important was that he located his father's grave; that was why he was there.

Ben walked around the graveyard, stopping to look every once in a while at the tombstones hoping one of them read STEVEN MARKUS MEDLEN. He saw a lot of Andersons, Smiths, Waters, Culbersons, Brentwoods, Applegates, Woodards, Duckworths, Von Hopes, Logans, Seagles, and Ryders. Looking out across acres upon acres, Ben could see what looked like to be thousands of glowing tombstones. Just what was the approximate number of dead in this place? Ben wondered what that number would actually be if someone had taken a count.

He walked around in the graveyard of mystic and wonder for what seemed hours until he finally happened upon his dad's grave. It was located on the far reaches of the cemetery's border where a chain-linked fence drew the line between Oak Grove Cemetery and whoever owned the land on the other side. It was his dad's grave all right. It was the only tombstone out that way. Something was not right. He knew where his father's grave was located, so why did it take so long to find it?

When he and his mother had visited the guy that owned the graveyard, he told them that they were "plum full except over on the far end but you might not want to bury him that far. Be a helluva walk to visit him," the old man in overalls said to them.

"It doesn't matter," Bailey Medlen told him. "He wanted to be buried here. I think he'd be fine with it."

"Well, okay then. I hadn't planned on putting any out that way but I reckon I'll reconsider it now since there seems to be a market for it."

Ben stood before his father's grave and a chill came through the air that caused chicken skin to flash on his arms and neck. Ben had found what he came there to find. Now what? Why was he looking at his father's grave? Ben could not remember. He stood at his father's grave, which looked like it had been covered up for decades instead of several months, searching his mind on why he had come to the Oak Grove Cemetery.

3

Ben knelt on one knee and placed his hand on top of the soil of Steve Medlen's home. He felt something pushing, faintly from underneath the dirt. How was that possible? Ben retracted his hand and looked down at the dirt. Was it moving? Ben put his hand back on top of the dirt again and yes, yes, it was moving, like something underneath it was trying to… come up.

Ben rose to his feet and began to backpedal some and watched in horror as a hand came from the grave. Then another. Both hands, from the wrist up, could be seen wriggling around, grasping at whatever they could find to grip. Then they placed themselves flat on the dirt, much like Ben had just a few seconds ago. In the middle of where the hands were, something else, something bigger was coming to the top. It was a head, then shoulders, and an upper torso. Soon it was a man that had dug himself through the dirt and into the moonglow. It was Steve Medlen rising from the dead, rising from his entombment.

Ben turned to run away. He did not get very far because he ran into a rather large tombstone that had not been there before; knocking him down, knocking the wind out of him. Ben scrambled to his feet. He did not dare look back at his dead father who was stiffly walking behind him not with a shuffle like in those zombie movies, but with a brisk stride. Had the kid been brave enough to sneak a peek back behind him at his dad, he would have seen that Steve Medlen was nothing but a near fully decomposed animated corpse coming for him. Ben made a break for it through the rows and rows of glowing tombstones knowing that he had to make it to the gates of the graveyard's entrance. It was his only chance. As Ben ran past the tall angel statue, it turned its head to watch him run by.

4

As the kid ran for his life, other dearly departed loved ones came out of their graves to give chase to the visitor of their necropolis. Not the ghosts he had seen before in dreams when visiting the cemetery, but full-on decomposing corpses like his dad. Ben saw this and did not have time to gasp from terror. He kept running through the boneyard dodging the undead and those eerily glowing tombstones.

Ben ran up to the entrance gate and it was locked with an old rusty log chain and a padlock in the middle connecting the two ends. How in the world did I get in here, he thought frantically. As he turned around, toward the cemetery, everything was as it should be. The tombstones were no longer putting off that silver ghostly glow. The dead that had come from their graves, all gross and rotting, had gone back to their long slumber underground. It was just a cemetery and nothing more. Ben, with his back to the black iron gates, drew a sigh of relief and just as he did, hands grabbed him from his right side. Those skeletal hands were Steve Medlen's.

5

Ben tried to scream but nothing came out. He was shaking and felt himself pissing his pants as warm fluid poured down his right leg. Steve was not looking so good; being buried will do that to you. He was badly decomposed, had long hair and nails, and was bloated. The smell of his dad made Ben want to throw up had the fear not overridden his state of mind. Through wide eyes, Ben could see that his dad was missing an eye and the clothes he was laid to rest in had been eaten away to nothing more than strips of fabric hanging off him.

Ben tried to squirm away from his dad's grip, but it was no use. Steve's undead hands appeared to have some strength behind them. Steve got in front of his son and leaned down to Ben's face and looked him in the eye. The singular eye was deadly gray and where the other eye should have been a green puss-like liquid streamed down on the rotting meat that was his face. Ben wanted to scream but nothing came. His throat closed. He just shuddered and pissed there at the iron gates of the cemetery. Ben could smell his dad's breath and it smelled like death itself. Steve looked his son in the eyes and opened his mouth to speak. But words did not come out of the zombie that was once Steve Medlen. They were just mouthed words. From what Ben could tell they were the same words, the same sentence, over and over and over. Why did you leave our home…why did you leave our home…why did you leave our home.

6

Ben woke up in his bed drenched in sweat. He sprang up and jumped out of the bed looking around his bedroom, and panting heavily. He could feel that the crotch of his boxers was soaking wet from pee. It was a nightmare and nothing more. He looked around his bedroom, his dad's old bedroom, and everything was where it should be; nothing out of place. Ben ran his fingers through his hair like a mad scientist and felt of himself, making sure that he was not still at the Oak Grove Cemetery and that his dead father was not face to face with him.

Ben had dreams about his dad since he passed away, but nothing as vivid as this in a while. The last one he had about the cemetery was one for the books, but this one was a howler. This one left the poor kid shaking and covered in sweat. He looked at the alarm clock on his nightstand and it read 4:32 am. Ben decided that he would just stay up the rest of the morning because sleep would not come; not now. As far as he was concerned, he did not want to close his eyes, at least not until the nightmare had a chance to burn away. Happy Halloween, Ben Medlen.

7

Bobby was up to his bad habits on that Halloween night. The habits never really stopped. He slowed down some but some nights, especially a night like this, Bobby needed something to take the edge off. It was Freddy's birthday that Halloween night. April had asked Bobby after they stayed at the gym and cleaned up from the costume party the night before if he was free for the weekend. "No, I've got some things I got to take care of for a bit." Those things that he had to take care of were sitting alone at home and disconnecting himself from the rest of the world. The next day was Halloween, Freddy's birthday. He would have been eleven. He would have been trick or treating had it not been for Jim Thompson.

That Halloween night, Bobby had shut the lights off in his house. He wanted nothing to do with the trick-or-treaters from the neighborhood. Back in the good old days, every kid in the neighborhood knew that the Downey house was the place to go for all kinds of candy. Their house was the only one on the block that was decorated for the ghostly holiday. This time around the Downey house was just plain Jane, like all the others on Maple Lane.

Inside the house, Bobby had been drinking for most of the day. He was feeling it, too. It had been seven months since his son was killed out in the street and the day still hurt. The whiskey had taken some of the edge off and made the memory of Freddy more manageable, while at the same time inside his mind making his son's memory more hurtful. Just as the large consumption of alcohol made Freddy go away sometimes, the same alcohol caused Freddy to come back with a vengeance, especially as his defenses were down.

Feeling himself start to doze, Bobby got up from his recliner and staggered into the kitchen where his bottle of Ritalin sat on the kitchen counter. He fumbled with the bottle, dropping it several times, and wrestled with the cap for a bit. Finally, he was able to get the white cap off and turned the bottle upside down. He only had a few left, enough to get him through the weekend; enough to keep him from getting sleepy. Bobby took three pills and swallowed them dry. He stood in the kitchen, hands upon the counter keeping him steady as his head and body swam. Eventually, his knees buckled and he crashed to the floor where he lay there on his back laughing. Laughing turned to heavy sobs.

Bobby, in a matter of a few weeks after Freddy's death, became a high-functioning alcoholic. As the drinking helped, Bobby knew that eventually, he would need something else to get him away from Freddy even if it was temporary. Temporary was better than being besieged all the time with his son's memory. After Freddy, Bobby could not sleep and eating was just a formality, sometimes not even doing that for a couple of days at a time. Then came the pills to help him along. Ritalin and Wild Turkey was a combo that seemed to help.

Bobby's prescription drug problem was created by his son's death. He knew that for sure. At first, he just needed something that would keep him awake because of the nightmares, the same ones that came to him over and over. He could not escape them. He was afraid to sleep and had even told Dana. He started simply enough in those weeks and months after Freddy's death. He started on gallons of strong coffee. That kept him up, kept any potential nightmares from coming. Over time his tolerance level had grown and the coffee, even different kinds, and potencies seemed to not have lasting effects on him. So he went to the next level.

That next level was over-the-counter stuff like No Doz and Jet Alert. Those worked great for a while, too, until he was taking way more than recommended. At one point for a couple of months, Bobby was taking five times the recommended dose. Then, just like the caffeine in his coffee, his body had built immunity to it. When he would fall asleep, the nightmares would come to him: the same slow-motion underwater dream; the same scene; the same dead kid in his arms out on Maple Lane.

Bobby had kept his problem secret as best he could, but Dana was dealing with the aftermath of her son's death differently. She had stayed with her mother for a few weeks off and on just to get away from Freddy's memory inside the house. When she did return full time trying to make a go of still living there, she found that her husband was worse off than she had known before. Dana knew that Bobby was falling into that abyss and was afraid that he would never come back fully after the death of their son. Would I ever come fully back? Dana already knew the answer to that. It hurt her staying in the house where Freddy had lived and it hurt watching her husband fall off the cliff of despair. The two of them were hurting and dying on the inside, but neither one reached out to the other for support. Dana turned inward and Bobby turned to drink and pills.

8

She eventually confronted him about his abuse of Ritalin when she found a half-empty bottle in his nightstand drawer. It was an honest mistake really; Dana had been looking for some tax papers and had gone through all the usual drawers in the house, especially the desk drawers in the office. She went into their bedroom and searched the one place she had not looked. Pulling out the drawer, Dana discovered the bottle. She took it out and read the sticker. At first, she was mad that Bobby had not told her about going to the doctor. Then she was upset because the thirty-day supply, which was prescribed to him a few days ago, was nearly gone. That meant only one thing. Standing there in their bedroom, Dana began to put the clues together and arrived at a frightening conclusion: the reason Bobby was losing weight, looking like a shell of a man and not sleeping, becoming more manic by the day was that he was abusing pills along with the drinking. She was going to confront Bobby about this. She dealt with the drinking but the pill abuse was something entirely new. To her, it was major.

9

"What are you doing with this?" Dana asked one day when Bobby came back inside from sitting out on the back porch. She was sitting in his recliner in the living room waiting on him holding the prescription bottle.

Bobby just looked at her, hyper-aware, "Four a day keeps the dreams away. Just something to keep me going is all; nothing to get up in a twist about, hon. Besides, you know I have ADHD."

"This ain't good. This is supposed to last all month its reads and it's nearly empty. How long has this been going on, Robert?" When she said Robert he knew she meant business. It was what his mother had called him when he was in deep trouble.

Standing there with his hands on his hips, Bobby considered her question for a few moments. "A little bit. Don't worry. I just need a little help. That's all. It's totally under control. Good Christ, you act like you're my mom all of a sudden."

"So this is why you aren't sleeping at night? Why you don't come to bed?"

"I sleep at night!" Bobby sharply replied.

"Yeah, a couple of hours in the recliner. That's not sleep," Dana spoke with concern in her voice. Bobby knew that voice well. Dana was worried about him and Bobby felt terrible that she had to feel that way, especially with her having to deal with Freddy. It was not fair and he knew that. What was really fair those days?

He felt that he had a handle on things, but did he really? He went down roads, blind alleys, that he tried to direct those at-risk kids in his red folders from going down. The irony was that Bobby should have his own red folder in his filing cabinet for being at risk.

"I can't sleep because I'm afraid of that nightmare that happens from time to time," Bobby finally admitted after trying to catch some of those random thoughts that were flying through his mind.

"And you guess that if you can stay awake all day and night that you can somehow, what? Escape it?" Dana's voice of reason sounded solid, smacked right. Bobby knew that what he was doing was not the right way to go, but all the psychological training that he had over the years was out the window when it came to his demons.

"No, but if I can limit how long I sleep then maybe I can close the window on whether or not the nightmare comes."

"And the drinking? You know that's a deadly combo, right? I mean, I shouldn't even have to tell a grown-ass man that…, especially you," Dana said sharply.

Bobby stood there as if he was on trial. He did not even try to defend himself, not much really. "The drinking," he replied, "is to get some peace of mind sometimes…because he's in here…so much, Dana," Bobby pointed to his temple and looked to his wife as if he was going to break down and cry. The matter of fact was that Bobby was nearly there, tears collected in his eyes making them look glassy to Dana.

"Yeah, I know," Dana replied. "He's in my head, too. Or have you forgotten that I lost him?"

Truth was Dana was having a hard time as well. She just was not abusing things like her husband was to temporality escape. She had nightmares, intense ones, where she would wake up in a state of panic after seeing her dead son in her dreams. Dana would be okay one minute and then the next a total wreck during her days and nights. She would sob into her hands at home and at work and even at the grocery store. She had nowhere to go, no refuge from the events that happened outside her house on that fine Saturday afternoon.

Dana sat back and looked at her husband. She knew that he was still in pain and was not dealing with it properly if there was such a thing. She wasn't anywhere near putting any distance between her and her son, and she never would, but at least she was trying to by dealing with it every day. Bobby was not coping, at least not the right way in Dana's eyes. Bobby was abusing prescription drugs and whiskey at the same time hiding behind that snarky sarcastic demeanor that his colleagues found witty and charming. Not Dana. She knew what lay beneath that smile and charisma; a broken man that refused to get help and get fixed; if being fixed was possible after all that had happened.

"You need help."

Bobby stood in the living room and looked at his wife, "I think maybe eventually the nightmares will go away. I've got to get some distance between me and Freddy somehow…that's all I'm trying to do here. I swear," he spoke somberly.

Dana doubted it. She had been there in the bed with him in the early days; fresh after their son was killed. Numerous times when those nightmares came they caused Bobby to spring up from the bed screaming, shaking, and crying. He had PTSD, she had no doubt. She had even talked to her therapist and he wanted to see Bobby, but he, being a big strong man who had a master's in psychology, refused to go.

"And Dr. Katz?" Dana shook the bottle rattling the few remaining pills inside against the thin walls. "He's a pill mill." Dana knew about the doctor who they in the Blue Cross office called, Dr. Feelgood because he was notorious around for writing his patients whatever it was that they wanted. "He gives his patients whatever they want and you want to be associated with this? This won't stop because eventually this won't work and then you'll have to move on to something else stronger. It's the evolution of things."

Bobby stood there and considered her argument. She was right, he knew that, but it didn't matter. He knew what he was doing. "This ain't going last forever; just a temporary thing."

"Yeah, because at the rate you're going, you'll end up killing yourself with these and the alcohol. I don't want to see that happen." Dana said almost in tears.

No amount of tears could change his mind. The pills were working, they were keeping him up twenty-one, twenty-two hours a day, sometimes twenty-three and even all day. That's not to say he was functionally coherent. There were times when he saw things, hallucinations he knew for sure, but they seemed so real. Seeing Freddy mill about the house was a usual occurrence those days. Most times Bobby could close his eyes and count to ten and when he opened them Freddy would be gone. Seeing Freddy was much better than dreaming of Freddy. In those dreams, he could not simply close his eyes and make his dead son go away. Seeing him about the house or outside was better than dreaming of him.

The one that was the most vivid hallucination, or maybe it was not a hallucination, lines were blurred even back then, happened one Monday morning a month after Freddy was killed. Bobby had walked outside to get his Sunday newspaper that had sat on their sidewalk since Sunday. He tried to never look down Maple Lane where the incident happened. On that particular morning, Bobby saw Freddy riding his bike like he did all the time up the sidewalk. Bobby stood there in his robe holding the damp newspaper and watched as Freddy rode his bike by his dad, "What's up, Dad?" Freddy asked, passing him by and down the sidewalk without looking back. Bobby closed his eyes, counted to ten, and shook his head, hoping to shake the image out. When he opened his eyes, Freddy was not there on his bike. Bobby eventually determined that he was dreaming awake. He preferred it much more to dreaming asleep.

"I'll be fine. This is just…to get me through, okay? Relax about it, would you?" Dana severely doubted it as Bobby walked out of the living room having enough of the conversation, the road to nowhere, shaking a little. Dana threw the bottle against the far wall and sat there and cried. She had lost her son and felt as if she was watching her husband systematically kill himself in the process. Being in the same house where Freddy was alive was getting to be too much for her to handle. Watching Bobby was the breaker for her. She made her mind up that she needed to leave Bobby and the house for good. She had asked him to leave with her awhile back, but he refused and it turned into a fight; a bad one. Dana, on the verge of falling off the mental cliff herself, decided that she had to focus on saving herself. She knew it was probably selfish not to drag Bobby from staring out at the abyss, but things were different…everything was different after Freddy's death.

His shaking was another side effect of taking the pills as often as he did. He was supposed to only take two a day for his "ADHD", but he was taking four and then eventually five. Bobby ran out of his prescription usually in a week. So he did what every addict did: he went to another doctor and asked for them. He had four doctors in total that he could see once a week, each month a different doctor and pharmacy, and no one was the wiser. It was 1994 and the term "doctor shopping" was not exactly defined and the computer software the pharmacies used had not caught up to people like Bobby yet. Eventually, technology would evolve and catch people like Bobby Downey.

10

On Halloween night, Freddy's birthday, Bobby Downey was sitting in his living room in the dark. What light did come through the blinds and curtains was from the street lights. He was sitting in his recliner, a bottle of nearly gone whiskey stuffed beside his leg and the side of the recliner. He had already taken five Ritalin pills an hour before he started drinking and was feeling fake, felt like he was in a dream state. He was not tired, should be, but was not thanks to the pills. Bobby laughed out loud as the thought crossed his mind that maybe he was in a dream.

Then as quickly as that thought came, another took its place. Maybe I'm dead, Bobby wondered. Bobby's heartbeat increased as he sat there thinking that maybe that was why he felt so loose. Maybe I am dead, he thought in a panic. This is exactly what Dana was afraid of.

"You're not dead, Dad," Freddy's voice came from down the hall. Bobby's thoughts ceased at once when his dead son's voice cut through the darkness.

Bobby rose slowly up from his recliner. The bottle of whiskey fell into the seat spilling what was left. He stood there and looked around the house. It was still, dark, and quiet. He could hear his heartbeat through his ears and feel his heart smacking against his chest.

"Freddy?!" Bobby screamed. Nothing came in reply.

Bobby stood for a few more minutes and awaited his son's voice. Nothing. Just as Bobby had given up and decided that maybe he needed to get some fresh air, Freddy's voice came again.

"Yeah, come outside, Dad. I'll be at the swing set." A distinct shudder chilled Bobby to the bone. That was Freddy, Bobby panicked.

He thought he was now dreaming and had passed out while drinking, but didn't the Ritalin keep him going? It was supposed to. Bobby grabbed his hair and pulled it harshly. He winced some from the pain. I can still feel… so maybe this ain't a dream, he concluded. Bobby closed his eyes tightly and counted to ten silently. When he opened them there was nothing; the house looked the same in the darkness. Bobby began to relax some and then Freddy called out, "Are you coming?"

11

Bobby reluctantly walked outside from the backdoor on that Halloween night and saw across the yard a shadowy figure sitting on a swing. It looked like Freddy but who could really tell? Bobby stood there watching the small dark figure and then his son's voice spoke, "Over here." Bobby's heartbeat was loud in his ears again. His chest was hurting and for a brief minute, he thought that maybe he was having a heart attack. His eyes were locked on the figure over at the swing set and again he wondered if he was dreaming all of this.

"This ain't a dream, Dad," Freddy told him as if he was inside his head somehow.

Bobby walked across the yard in bare feet. The backyard was already cold and dewy on his skin. He could see his breath hang in the air in puffs of smoke from the cold. This ain't a dream, Bobby again concluded. It feels too real. As he walked closer to the swing set, the shadowy figure came more into focus: it was indeed, Freddy. That revelation gave Bobby pause.

"Freddy?" Bobby spoke weakly while the spit inside his mouth dried out. Freddy turned his head to look at his dad, "Come over here and sit in the swing beside me."

Bobby stopped for a few minutes trying to figure out in his scattered mind whether to obey Freddy's request or just turn tail and run into the house, bolt the door, and hide under his bed. Bobby found himself sitting in the swing beside his son. Bobby could not take his eyes off him. He just stared. Freddy, who was now eleven, well, would have been had it not been for Jim Thompson, looked the same as he saw him before he went outside that Saturday afternoon to play. In fact, he was in the same clothes. How could this be, Bobby wondered, still gazing at his son in disbelief.

"Where's Momma?" Freddy asked, looking at Bobby.

"She moved away," he replied in a state of utter wonderment and confusion.

"Why?" Freddy asked, looking out across the backyard.

Bobby sat there looking at Freddy and was enchanted by his son's return. He heard Freddy's question and knew that he should answer him, but looking at Freddy had caused Bobby's mind to go blank, numb…void of thought. "Why, Dad?"

Bobby snapped out of his trance when Freddy spoke, "What?"

"Where's Mom and why did she move?"

Bobby tried to wet his lips but the saliva had not returned as of yet. " I don't know where she went, Son. She um…couldn't stay here anymore after…what happened to you… what was happening to me. I think it was too much for her."

Freddy sat there for a few moments and looked as if he was thinking about what his dad said. "But you'll never leave, right?"

Bobby smiled and shook his head, "No, Son. I won't leave you."

"Good." Just like that, Freddy vanished into thin air. Bobby sat there and could see his breath in the dark backyard. He rose from the swing and called for Freddy to come back. After minutes of calling for Freddy, Bobby felt an overpowering emotion of sadness and he broke down and started crying loudly sitting himself back on the swing. He sat crying the rest of the night at everything. He was crying over Freddy; crying over Dana; crying over the mess his life had become. He cried because he wanted everything back to the way it was before that day in March when Jim Thompson changed his family forever. Bobby wanted his old life back.

Chapter 14

1

November

It was the Tuesday before school broke away for Thanksgiving. Some positives were finally happening in the lives of Bobby Downey and Ben Medlen in the weeks after the costume party at school. They still had their demons; Ben with his dreams and the growing distance his mother seemed to have put between them and Bobby's drinking and prescription medication abuse that kept right on trucking. They were doing better, it seemed in other regards, and the weekly meetings they held in Bobby's office benefitted them both.

It started out with Bobby being a friendly, non-judgmental ear for Ben, but in an unlikely turn, something he had not had since Sam had bolted to Washington, Bobby had someone that he could talk to. Even though Ben was a lot younger, he seemed to be wise beyond his years. They both had lost so much and were both on the brink at times with themselves. Those meetings, the mental health check-ins, helped.

Bobby asked how things were going with Ben, who seemed a little bit more cheery than he did when he first came into his office a while back. He was more open and smiled a bit more. Even in the hallways of the school, without Bobby being noticed by Ben, he watched as the kid held his head up in the air, eyes ahead, and actually talked to other students. Even at lunchtime, he was sitting with his new girlfriend, Abby Maddux. He's getting there, Bobby thought to himself observing this. Even Ben's teachers told Bobby that Ben Medlen was doing so much better than when he started back in August. That was great to hear for the guidance counselor. It put a smile on his face.

Bobby on the other hand was back and forth. After the event on Halloween night when he talked to Freddy out at the swing set in the backyard, he still had trouble figuring out what that scene actually was. Was it a hallucination brought on by his pills and alcohol mixed with zero sleep? Or was it the ghost of his dead son? "Does it even matter at this point?" Bobby asked himself.

Bobby had to start making some personal changes or he was indeed going to do what Dana had told him earlier: he was going to end up killing himself. He knew that he should cut back on the drinking. A half bottle of whiskey during the weekdays mixed with pills and a full bottle on the weekends mixed with those same pills had to have an eventual ending. He knew the ending when mixing stuff like that was never good.

Bobby knew that he might be in trouble and also knew an addiction when he saw one. He was a counselor for Christ's sake, how did this even happen? He should have known better, hell, he had read case studies and written papers while in his psychology classes about addictions. He knew that he should have gone to see a fellow therapist and get a handle on his issues but he had too much pride. Bobby was convinced that he could overcome his addictions and he knew what to do. He just had to finally decide to stop. He had it in him to quit it all…he just had to be committed to doing so.

November first came, that morning after Freddy came either as a ghost or a hallucination, Bobby did not drink a full bottle of whiskey. He only drank about half, the set usual that he did during the weekdays after school. The pills, instead of five, he only took four. They were small steps, but steps nevertheless. Through the next few weeks, Bobby made some progress. He made a vow that he was going to get clean.

2

Bobby and April were still dancing around each other into the new month; still interested in each other. They had finally exchanged phone numbers. They had finally gone out on a date that was not on school grounds. That first official date went really well. The two of them went to dinner at Bert's, an Italian pasta place there in Claxton, and afterward, in the cold November night, they took a walk along the bridge that stretched across the Big Bend River.

The date ended at April's front door around midnight. They kissed for the first time. April's heart was all a flutter while Bobby's stomach had butterflies swarming inside. She noticed that Bobby was a little shaky and thought that was from the nerves. It was not. Bobby was shaking because his body needed alcohol. It was going through withdraws. It was a matter of fact that Bobby had known nearly all date long. He knew that he had to do something later to get himself under control.

The kiss they shared was so electric that when they pulled their lips apart, the two of them looked at each other and grinned really big. It was the best kiss that either of them had ever had. They stood there in silence and if April would have invited Bobby inside he knew what would happen next. He did not want to go that far…not yet. Besides, April never invited him in even though she wanted to; he could see it in her eyes through her glasses.

"I'd better get going," Bobby said, trying to mentally override his body withdrawal.

"Yeah, I guess so," April replied.

Bobby walked off the front porch step and turned to her as she watched him go, "That was good right?"

She nodded, "Amazing."

Bobby looked around the dark street-lit neighborhood, "Yeah, I thought so, too. Goodnight, Ms. Murray."

Bobby walked down the sidewalk backward watching as April stood there watching him leave. She watched him disappear into his car and drive away until he was nothing but faded red taillights.

3

"So…things are good with Abby?" Bobby asked, sitting in his chair, arms on his desk looking at Ben.

Ben smiled and nodded, "Yeah. Really good. She's so nice. Sweet. Mom likes her, too."

"Oh, wow, you already took her to see mom? Must be love," Bobby quipped.

"Yeah, she's a keeper. I think dad would've liked her, too. So what about you?"

"What about me?" Bobby asked.

"You and Ms. Murray?"

Bobby considered this for a moment. He had been honest with Ben and Ben had been honest with him. The two of them were friends, he felt. Were they supposed to be? Student and counselor? "I don't know. She's pretty awesome, I guess."

"You seem to spend a lot of time around each other here at school."

"Yeah, I guess we do."

"You guys went out on a date yet?" Ben asked.

"Yeah. It was really nice."

"People around here think by next school year she'll be, Mrs. Downey," Ben said with a smile.

"I wouldn't go that far. Been married once."

"Really? I thought you were married. What happened?"

Bobby sat there and thought about revealing some aspects of his personal life with Ben. He was young, and might not get it as Sam would, but hey, Sam was not around anymore and barely got a hold of him on the phone these days. He could not talk to April and dump all his baggage on her; that would end up drowning the poor woman.

"She left after Freddy was killed…I'm beginning to think she might have been right."

Ben sat there and his face had gotten red with embarrassment, "I'm sorry. I didn't know about any of that."

"It's okay. It's common knowledge around here. I guess I assumed you'd known."

"Oh, man. Dude…I'm sorry. Let's talk about something else."

"It's okay," Bobby waved him off. "I'm dealing with it, I guess. Some days are better than others. Dana, my ex-wife, wanted to move out of the house and I wanted to stay. Freddy's death killed our marriage. We weren't strong enough to sustain that kind of blow. Hell, maybe I wasn't strong enough for her. I don't know…I don't know much about anything these days. I just couldn't leave the house."

"Because that's where your family was: the memories, good times, and bad," Ben broke in, knowing how it felt to leave his home back in South Carolina.

"Exactly. I mean, how could she want to move away from all that? I mean, I get it, I do, but she and I never could agree on what to do. She couldn't stand to see the house without Freddy and I couldn't stand the thought of moving away from his memory. Plus, she wasn't too happy with me on some other things I was doing. We just…" Bobby stopped as he noticed his hand trembling a bit. He took it off his desk and made a fist, something he had been doing a lot lately. "We just couldn't make it. Wasn't anybody's fault," he said with some regret in his voice that Ben picked up on.

Ben asked, "What else were you doing that she wasn't happy about?"

Bobby sat there and considered whether or not to tell him about his Ritalin addiction to keep him awake or his excessive drinking. Confiding in the wrong person could be disastrous; could end his career potentially if word ever got out. Wasn't his career at Central High ending anyways? Wasn't this his last run, his last mile, at the school? It was if Mr. Glick had anything to say about it. He still had not called Pete Samples to get the scoop.

"I've got a pill problem and a drinking problem…it's been running pretty bad lately. Actually, if I'm being honest, since Freddy was killed," he revealed, not looking at Ben but rather up at the ceiling.

"What kind of pills?" Ben asked, after a few moments of reflecting.

"I've been," Bobby chuckled a bit at the impending admission of his problem, "abusing Ritalin pretty heavily."

Ben nodded his head, "I know what that stuff is. I had a friend back home that had to be on it for ADHD. You got that?"

"A very mild case. Then I discovered that I could use it for other things.

I started seeing multiple doctors to get them, and different pharmacies filling my scripts. I run through a lot. Basically, I use it to keep me awake… keeps my mind from wandering around which always leads back to Freddy. I take too much…more than I should, but I take it to keep me going because I'm afraid to sleep. I have dreams about that day my son was killed…about him being in the house…out in the yard…doing random Freddy things.

"So, I take the pills to keep me awake. I sleep, but it's like a couple of hours a night when my body finally just collapses. But these dreams… when they come, they're never good. You know, they always feel so damn real, like I'm there all over again that day he was run over. Or he's just randomly in the house in these dreams. I don't know…just a weird situation."

More silence between the two in the office. It seemed to stretch out for five minutes, maybe longer until Ben asked, "Have the pills worked?"

"For the most part, I guess." Bobby left out the part about the hallucinations of Freddy, or if they really were hallucinations at all.

"It doesn't seem that all healthy for you."

Bobby chuckled a bit, "It's probably not. I'm trying to dial it back some."

"How's that working?"

Bobby thought about Ben's question and felt the trembling hand that he still held into a fist. "It's still early; my body doesn't seem to want to cooperate much, probably because I got it used to the liquor and pills for so long. But hey, I've been able to cut down from taking pills here at school."

"Sounds like you have an addiction."

Bobby nodded, "Yeah, I think so, too."

"So what's your end game here? I mean you surely can't do this for the rest of your life?"

Bobby never thought about his end game. He didn't know if he even had one. "I don't know. I never thought of the end, I guess. I just try to deal day by day; have since Freddy and Dana."

"Do you think you need to see a therapist?"

"I know what's wrong with me," Bobby defended his role. "I just got to figure out how to better deal with it." The dismissal bell rang loudly causing both Bobby and Ben to jump a bit. They did not realize that school was over and the Thanksgiving break was now. "Have a good turkey day, Mr. Medlen."

"You do the same. Listen," Ben said, shouldering his backpack, "you need to take care of yourself, okay? I've been down some bad roads, too. Something that you don't know about me is that uh…I'm suicidal. Or was. Maybe still am, I don't know. But I totally understand about how bad things can get."

It was the first time that Ben had ever said that to anyone. Why Bobby? Maybe it was because he trusted him. He reminded him of his dad in a way. There was an authentic vibe that Ben had gotten from his guidance counselor and he felt comfortable talking to him.

Bobby sat there stunned about Ben's admission. "We for real need to talk about this," he said with concern. Ben could see it on his face. He was covered with it.

"Next time. Promise," Ben said and walked out of his office for Thanksgiving break.

4

Thanksgiving at the Medlen home was different than in years past: this was the first without the patriarch, the first in another state, and in another home. Steve Medlen was gone, dead roughly eight months now. For eight long months, Ben's father had been in the dirt at Oak Grove Cemetery and Ben had only visited his gravesite a couple of times. Once before he and his mother left for Tennessee and the other the day school broke for the summer. Of course, he had been there in his nightmares.

Ben hated going to the cemetery to see where his dad was resting. And why did they call it resting? He wasn't asleep down there. He was dead, not breathing, with nothing going on at all. So why do they say final resting place? Ben thought to himself time and again over the subject. Nevertheless, Ben had gone to the cemetery on his bike both times to pay his respects to the man that had shown him basically everything in his life.

Ben did not like the graveyard; not one bit. It was lonely both times he came to visit. Even on the day that Steve was buried, Ben did not recall seeing anyone else around milling about the cemetery or paying their respects to a loved one. But were graveyards supposed to be teeming with people? No. They were cold places, places of sorrow, and pain. That's how Ben saw the place he came to: full of pain and sorrow.

Sometimes when he was alone, Ben debated in his mind if he should have visited his dad's gravesite more. He did not see the point because his dad was not really there. But still, he felt bad that he did not go more than he did. But should he have felt guilty? Some days he did and some days he didn't. It depended on how he felt that day as he went back and forth on the subject. But what did it matter now? He was in Tennessee, miles away from South Carolina, miles away from everything that he ever knew.

5

Bailey Medlen had seemed, at least to Ben, to be in good spirits those days in November. She had not moved on fully, but it sure did look like it to him. She liked her job a lot and appeared to be acclimated to it quicker than Ben had to his new school. Plus, Bailey had a purpose again. It was true and Ben did have to remind himself of it from time to time, that Bailey did not do so well there at the beginning. She was a mess. Her whole world had come crashing down in flames when the officers arrived at her pharmacy back home to tell her the horrible news. From then on, the funeral arrangements, the visitation, the burial, and the wake at their home, Bailey Medlen was not good; not good at all.

Ben had helped her along the way the best any kid his age really could. So did Stacy, Steve's sister. Ben was concerned about his mom: the way she looked afterward, the shocking weight loss, the depression, the uncontrollable crying events. Bailey nearly fell into the abyss. It was by the sheer grace of God that she did not. Ben was so worried about his mom in the months after his dad's death that he tabled his issues until later. When she got somewhat better, that was when Ben started to slip. The bad part was that there was no one to pull him from the edge of the abyss. His mom was going through a transformation while Ben was falling apart at the seams. There was no one to pull him out of the despair.

6

It was not until after a few weeks of Bailey getting back to work that she began to look at herself again. The weight that had been lost was slowly coming back. Her eyes had some life in them again. Her voice was returning to that cheerful place that it seemed to always stay, at least that's how Ben had always seen it. Bailey was coming back, but would never be fully all the way back. The Bailey Medlen that Ben had known since forever would never be fully whole again. He had to settle for the 2.0 version of his mother. 2.0 Bailey Medlen was not an upgrade that Ben really liked if he was being honest with himself. Even though there was some of his mother still in the new upgrade, there were some new upgrades he could have done without.

On that Wednesday, after Ben had come home from school for his Thanksgiving break, he noticed that his mother was already home from work. It was odd because she never got home until five or seven depending on how busy the pharmacy was. Ben walked through the front door, just as always and his mother was in the kitchen cooking. He could smell the food immediately and it instantly made him hungry.

"Mom?" Ben called as he walked into the house and through the living room.

From the kitchen, Bailey called out, "In here!"

Ben went into the kitchen and saw his mother taking a pie out of the oven and placing it on the counter. "What's all this? And what are you doing home so early?"

"They shut the pharmacy down early today. And I thought that I'd get a jump on cooking for tomorrow," Bailey explained.

"Okay," Ben said, looking at all the stuff that she had on the counters. Pies, empty pie shells, mixing bowls, a bag of flour, and a bag of sugar and the list went on. "There's just two of us you know? Aunt Stacy and Uncle Tommy coming down to eat with us?"

Bailey stood there, looking at the food. She seemed to be considering something. Ben knew by her slow response something awful was probably coming. He was bracing himself. "No, not them. We're going over there on Friday night I think. We've got a guest coming to eat with us."

Ben's heart dropped into his stomach. He knew what guest meant: a guy. He knew it. He just fucking knew it. This was what he was afraid of.

7

Over the last several weeks, nearly a month and a half or so, Ben would come into the living room and could his mom laughing and talking to someone on the cordless telephone; sometimes at all hours of the night. There were times that he did not see his mother unless the phone was affixed to the side of her head. Ben knew that it was probably a man that she was talking to. You could always tell because she had this way she talked to Aunt Stacy and her friends from South Carolina, but when it came to this guy she was always on the phone with, she talked differently, even spoke differently. Nothing like it was with Steve. That was just one of the many changes that Ben did not like in Bailey 2.0.

"A guy?" Ben already knew the answer to that question but wanted verbal confirmation.

Bailey nodded and then turned her back to the counter and started absently mixing flour like she was busy. Ben knew that she did not want to face him and his wrath. He stood there looking at the back of his mother. He was growing madder by the second. How dare she?

"Dad's been dead eight months and you're already moving on to the next guy?" Ben was trying to keep a lid on his bubbling rage. But it wasn't working…not at all.

"Chris is just a friend, that's it. His wife died around the same time as your dad…"

"He has a name. Steve. Or did you already forget?" Ben zinged her good with that one.

Bailey did not say anything back, no reply was needed. She knew how this was going to go but she had to come clean because she had invited

Chris, which he accepted, and eventually he would darken their front door with his presence; an unwanted presence in Ben Medlen's eyes.

"I don't expect you to understand but…"

Ben lashed out and walked out of the kitchen, "Yeah I'm too young to get it, I guess! I knew this was coming! I fucking knew it! I won't be here when your boyfriend comes!"

Bailey turned and began to follow after Ben, "We need to talk about this! And don't raise your voice to me!"

Ben kept walking and then went up the stairs and into his bedroom. Bailey stood down at the landing, her hand on the railing and tears forming behind her eyes. She knew this was how it would play out. She ran this scenario around and around in her mind a million times and it always came to this, or something close. This was nearly dead on, on how she thought he would react. She understood. She did, but where was the median here? Bailey was not going to compromise with him because the way she saw it Ben was the child and who was he to dictate who she was with or not? Lines were being drawn whether the two of them knew it or not.

8

Up in his bedroom, Ben fell onto his bed face first and buried his face into his pillow. He wanted to cry, he was there right on the verge of tears, but he forced them back. Instead, he screamed as loudly as he possibly could into his pillow so loudly that it hurt. He ran the gamut of emotions lying there: rage, sadness, grief, and hatred. He wanted to punch something, beat the hell out of whatever it was he could get his hands on, something to blow off the steam that had built from the kitchen to his bedroom. He was fuming.

Ben rolled over on his back and stared up at the ceiling. The tears were in a holding pattern, they were ready to flow when the word came. Ben refused. He jumped up from the bed, walked over to his dresser, and pulled out a knife, the same one from a while back, from the top drawer. He gripped it tightly and put it to his wrist. He was done. He pressed the blade to his skin. He felt the coldness of it, the non-discrimination of the instrument. The tears were in his eyes, pooling, ready to stream at any minute and Ben hated that feeling. He hated that he was on the brink of tears because that meant once again he was standing on the edge of the abyss.

Ben hated crying because that was a sign of weakness and he had been tired of being weak. His dad was not weak. Steve Medlen was the strongest man Ben ever knew. Standing there, steady and ready to slash and bleed out, Ben closed his eyes and tears trickled out. Suddenly, his mother yelled for him from downstairs. "Ben! Abby is here!" Abby would have no idea, but she was just in time to save his life. Had she been a second or two later, Ben would have been lying on the floor leaking out; just a second or two later.

9

It was freeing telling someone about his Ritalin habit. Only Dana had known about it and that was only by sheer chance. Otherwise, Bobby would have not said anything about it to her. It was not something that he could have kept a secret for very much longer. He was wearing out mentally and was posting physical signs such as shaking and weight loss. There were dark circles under his eyes that told the story for anyone that looked; that story was that Bobby had not slept a good night in a very long time.

No one else knew what went inside the Downey home, not even Sam, not all of it. Now, for whatever reason, Ben knew his secret. Why did he tell a kid something heavy like that? Maybe it was because Bobby saw something in Ben Medlen; something that he could trust, an understanding in his eyes. Ben had the look of a man that had been thousands of miles in his body and was only sixteen. In a way, Ben reminded Bobby of Freddy. Maybe that was the connector.

10

Bobby started seeing Freddy more and more after hitting the Ritalin harder and staying awake for stretches of twenty hours or better. Three pills a day at first, one hundred and eighty milligrams combined; eighty more than he should have taken daily. When the three weren't hitting all the right buttons, Bobby started taking five to six pills a day to get by. It was at that point that Bobby began doctor shopping, getting his prescriptions, and taking them to different pharmacies to have them filled. As long as he could stay awake and keep his mind focused, away from thinking about

Freddy, he was okay. At least that's the lie he told himself. The Ritalin wasn't by no means the end all to thoughts of Freddy.

On one of the first times that Bobby had seen Freddy, a Saturday that was, Dana had gone to see her mother for the day leaving Bobby to his own devices. It was about a month after Freddy's death. Bobby sat in the recliner drinking aimlessly, already tuned up on Ritalin watching an afternoon Braves baseball game. Up to that point, Bobby had not moved on really from that day their son was killed in the street. He was still stuck in a maddening loop. Bobby was drowning in his sea of despair while Dana was desperately trying to keep her head from going under in hers.

Sitting in his recliner on that innocuous Saturday afternoon in his living room, something happened to cause panic in his heart. He heard Freddy's voice coming from his bedroom. Bobby took the remote and muted the TV and sat there listening. It was muffled, but it was Freddy all right, that he knew. Was it a ghost? Had Freddy come back from the dead somehow?

Bobby slowly rose from his chair and crept across the living room's hardwood floor. There it was again, Freddy's voice, muffled. Bobby went to the landing of the stairs and looked up. He could hear his son talking. But how was this even remotely possible? His son had been run down like a dog not too long ago. Bobby stood there lost in the entanglement of his racing thoughts when he heard Freddy's muffled voice again. With nerves jittered so much that his hands were shaking, Bobby put his loose grip on the staircase railing and began to ease up the stairs, trying to keep quiet, listening for his son's voice as he went.

Halfway up, Freddy's bedroom door opened, and out stepped Freddy, looking the same as he did right before he was run over by that red Firebird. He looked happy, as much as a kid his age could. Freddy walked down the stairs, "Hey, Dad," and walked past Bobby. Bobby stood there terrified feeling as if he was going to pass out. Freddy disappeared into thin air at the bottom of the stairs. Bobby looked back up at Freddy's bedroom door. It was closed now and had been since that day out in the street. Bobby slid down against the wall and sat on a rung of the stairs and cried. He had seen his son and his son had spoken to him. But was Freddy a ghost or was he a hallucination of his mind brought on by his immense abuse of Ritalin, alcohol, and grief? Bobby sat and cried; shaking, feeling as if he was losing his mind, what mind of his was left to lose.

Bobby had continued to see Freddy here and there over time before Dana had finally walked out of the door forever. Bobby recalled there was one time when he saw Freddy in an odd place. His dead son was not restrained just to the house. One morning going to school, the first unofficial week where teachers had to report, Bobby was driving to music from The Cars, blaring them through the speakers when something out of the corner of his eye caused him to turn to look. Sitting beside him in the passenger seat was Freddy, sitting like nothing was going on at all, looking out the window. Bobby was electrified with profound fright, jerked the steering wheel, and over-corrected it there on the empty highway. If there would have been any oncoming traffic close by he would have crashed into them head-on. There was absolutely no doubt about that.

Another time, this was when he and Dana were still married, still grieving each in their own ways, he and his wife sat in the living room on the couch. Even though they sat on opposite ends of the couch, they might as well have been on the East and West Coasts of the country. Both were thinking about things, going over things, tilling the garden of their minds so much that the dirt was as thin as baby powder. Dana was reading a paperback love story and Bobby was sitting there watching the evening news when out of the blue he heard footfalls coming down the stairs.

It was Freddy. He came off the last rung and onto the landing and walked casually to the recliner and plopped down to watch TV with his family. Bobby looked at his wife. She did not see her son nor did she hear him. He wanted to get her attention but it would be no use. Only he could see their dead child, and there was the question: was Freddy haunting Bobby or was Freddy a hallucination brought on by his overconsumption of Ritalin and alcohol abuse mixed with sleep deprivation and grief?

Bobby could easily answer the question by gradually taking himself off the medicine, and easing back the drinking as coping mechanisms, but the nightmare of that day would flood back to him when the night came. That was what Bobby was afraid of; having to relive that day. Once was more than enough. It was better to let sleeping dogs lie, he decided. So, he continued to abuse the pills, doctor shop, drink heavily, and not get any sleep as a way to deal.

11

Bobby sat at his desk in his office on that day of the Thanksgiving holiday dismissal thinking about Freddy, his drug problem, and his failed marriage. He was lost in a trance when April came knocking on his half-open door, cutting him loose from the tie that bound him. "Leaving or staying here through Thanksgiving?" she asked, flashing that beautiful, playful smile.

She looked so wonderful in her purple top and black knee-length skirt. How a woman like that wanted him he would never know, not in a million years. How did Dana for that matter?

"What? Oh, yeah? I lost track of time, I guess," Bobby said, snapping back to the land of harsh reality and looking at his watch.

"Are you still coming over tonight?"

"Of course. You want me to bring anything?"

"Just yourself. I'll see you later." She walked out and Bobby could hear her high heels spiking the floor as she left his office.

"Yes, you will," Bobby whispered as he sat there and looked at Freddy who was standing at his bookshelf looking over his collection. He dug into his pocket and pulled out his meds. He took another pill and swallowed it dry. It hung in his throat, he could feel it. But it was okay, it would dissolve eventually…everything dissolved in time.

Chapter 15

1

Ben had collected himself and walked out of his house with Abby. Bailey, still in the kitchen preparing food for Thanksgiving, jumped a little bit at the sound of the slamming door. Ben wanted her to hear his emotion as he pulled the front door shut. He shut it so hard that he thought for s second that he cracked the frame on the outside. Bailey knew that her son was upset, and he had every right to be. Ben did not like the notion of her talking to another man, a possible replacement for his dad. He saw it as another betrayal of his memory. How did Bailey Medlen see things? It was not so cut and dry for her. Nothing was cut and dry since Steve died.

Bailey knew that eventually she would find another man. She was still young, still had her looks, and was in a career where she could support herself. She certainly did not need a man to financially prop her up. Bailey and Steve, throughout their good marriage, never once broached the subject of what the other should do if the other died relatively young. It just never came up between them. Steve was not the type that sat around and talked about his feelings and neither was Bailey. They had no deal in place, no will to be read by an attorney on what to do if the other died. What did she think her late husband would have said to her if he knew about what Bailey and this guy Chris were doing?

Bailey had no way of answering that question. She tried to put Steve out of her mind most times. It was the only way she could cope with the staggering loss she had taken. Bailey, for the most part, had reinvented herself. She looked as if she had to because her old life, the one she had with Steve, was gone; a new one came about and Bailey at times was not too sure about how this new skin of hers felt. Sometimes, looking in the mirror, she looked at the woman that was looking back at her and she wanted to cry. Bailey Medlen was gone…

Steve was dead and gone. In their wedding vows they made a long time ago they told each other til death do we part. Steve parted that morning on his way to work. He was the one that left her to figure out how to go forward in life. Feeling overwhelmed there in the kitchen with emotions nearly choking her, she picked up the glass mixing bowl and smashed it down onto the floor in the kitchen, and started to cry. It wasn't fair. Life wasn't fair. Nothing about any of this was fair. Bailey stood amongst the food, the bowls, and the broken glass and cried.

2

Ben and Abby sat side by side in swings out in her backyard that waning afternoon. The swing set, which had been a staple in her backyard since Abby was six, had seen its better days. The evening air was not cold, but it was rapidly cooling as the sun began to dip down behind the pine trees. Rays of red-orange sunlight in straight wide paths shone through the skeletal limbs of the trees. The evening was approaching, ready to steal the light from the day and cool the temps down.

Ben had told his girlfriend about what had happened at home; about how his mom had another man coming that she met from wherever it was and that he was coming over to eat Thanksgiving dinner. Abby sat there in her swing and listened as Ben rattled on about how things had turned sour earlier at home. Ben had opened up to Abby through their blooming relationship about his dad and his home back in South Carolina, and how he was adapting to life in Tennessee. She was interested in her boyfriend, her first, and wanted to be there for him during his crisis.

After Ben finished his venting, he sat there, hands holding onto the rusty chains of his swing, feet touching the ground looking around the backyard of the Maddux home. The sun had lowered further down behind the pines and the light of the day was giving way to twilight. "So what are you going to do?" Abby asked, with her hands in her lap.

Ben shook his head, "I really don't know. I mean, I don't want to be in that house. I don't want to be there when this Chris guy comes over."

"It's a tough spot," Abby remarked.

Ben nodded his head. It was a tough spot. It seemed like his life here lately had been nothing but tough spots. "I guess I'll just stay up in my bedroom the entire time."

"Well you're more than welcome to come here for Thanksgiving, you know? My parents asked me earlier today if you would be interested in coming over, if you didn't have plans; which, by the sound of it, you don't."

Ben laughed, "Yeah, not now anyways. You sure they wouldn't mind?"

Abby smiled, "Of course not. You coming over was their idea. They like you a lot."

Ben, sitting there and considering her invitation, reached for her hand and held it on the swings, "Yeah, I'll be here. Thanks."

3

On the other side of town, Bobby and April sat outside in her backyard in chairs warming their bones by the fire that night before Thanksgiving. The night air had gotten colder but it was not as cold as it should be for that late in November. Bobby was sitting there looking into the fire, legs crossed holding a tall glass of sweet tea. April, who was sitting close beside him, was covered up in a red and black checkered flannel throw. Even though the fire was warm, she was not. She was always cold, and chilly even the temps outside were in the low eighties. She blamed the genes that her mom had given her. She, too, was always cold. "Must be where I got it," she told Bobby one night at the football game while they walked the track.

The two of them had gotten close since the costume party at school. Bobby knew that he liked her that first night at the football game where they walked the track. She was easy to talk to, easy on the eyes, and most of all uncomplicated. Being uncomplicated was a welcomed attribute that Bobby desperately wished he had. April could match wits with Bobby, often going back and forth with him in his smart-ass, sarcastic ways. Bobby liked that a lot.

Bobby and April had talked about a lot as their relationship had grown like flowers in the spring. However, Bobby was withholding on some things. He did not want to be. He wanted to be open and honest with her, and for the most part, he was. With April, he saw a chance to be happy, much like he was with Dana years back. That was back before Jim Thompson and his red Firebird killed their son. He still loved his wife, but Dana had chosen to leave and walk away forever. Sure, he could have gone with her and salvaged some sort of life, but what about Freddy? In the end, it all came down to Freddy.

He and April had gotten into some deep conversations over the weeks they talked. Bobby avoided talking about certain things: things like that day

Freddy was killed, Dana leaving, and the eventual divorce. April did not press; she respected his privacy. Bobby wanted to start pouring himself out to her, but he always slammed on the breaks when he felt as if he was oversharing in some aspects. Bobby tried his best to keep things in his life put into their own compartments: the Ritalin, the booze, Freddy, and Dana were all in rooms up in his mind behind locked doors.

April, herself, had a string of disappointments when it came to relationships over the years. She told Bobby several of her low points with those guys. A couple of them were from school, that had moved on. Bobby knew Bill Miller and Nathan Bradley. They were nice guys and had from time to time sat with Bobby at school meetings and the such. Bobby never saw himself as the type April would go for, but hey, what did he know?

Bill Miller was a U.S. History teacher there at the school for five years. He moved on when he met his future wife at a car wash of all places. He and April had dated off and on for a year and a half until she called it quits. When Bobby asked why, April just said, "That it wasn't working anymore." When Nathan Bradley came up, April said practically the same thing; "Wasn't working anymore." That got Bobby thinking: what if this doesn't work anymore?

Bobby was worried about that notion, worried that if he lowered his guard down and bared his soul to her that she would eventually knock him out. How devastating would that be to him? He was already broken mentally. After all, he had a drug problem, his son was long gone dead and his ex-wife was gone and perhaps with another man. Bobby could feel deep in his bones that he and April were good for each other. It felt right, but what if that was another one of those illusions of the mind that Bobby had?

He wanted to open up to April but found himself reserved. She knew that. She did not pry and that was good. She thought that Bobby would eventually come around; if he didn't, so what? She enjoyed his company. He was the best guy that she had ever been around. She had always noticed Bobby in school and knew that he was off-limits because he was married. But that did not stop her from looking. Even when she was with Nathan and Bill, April had this unspoken thing, an attraction, to Bobby. She did not know precisely what it was, but it was something cosmic for sure. She just knew that she wanted to be around him. Bobby had that way about him; people just wanted to be around him for whatever reason.

When news came about his son, she was devastated for Bobby. She knew that this would be something that he could never fully rebound from. Who could? The death of a child was a backbreaker, a life-altering experience. She attended the funeral and hurt for Bobby. When the news came that Bobby's wife had left him, she wanted to reach out to him and take the broken man in her arms and tell him that things were going to be okay; that she was there to help. She stayed away because she did not want the perception that something was going on between the two and that was why Dana had left the marriage. Small towns tend to gossip no matter what was going on.

So, April stayed back and waited until the end of the summer when he reported back to school that unofficial week in August before the students filed in. She, along with others, watched while the days and weeks rolled by as Bobby tried to keep it together. She saw his fake smile and heard his fake laugh at the school. She saw the weight loss; how his clothes didn't fit him anymore. She saw the haunted look in his eyes, the graying on the sides of his hair. She, as well as everyone else, noticed that Bobby looked as if he had not slept a good night's sleep in years. April even noticed the trembling hands but never said anything. She heard other teachers, mostly female ones, talk about how everything had worn down Bobby Downey, a handsome man in his own right who was looking haggard in recent times. They all were right, though: Bobby was weak and broken down and had the look of a man that had walked a million miles without a rest.

April knew that he needed help and she decided that she was going to be the one that tried. She felt that if she did not do something quickly, Bobby might not last much longer. Funny thing was, Bobby thought the same thing. He felt that his mind and body were wearing out and with his sleep deprivation, his Ritalin abuse, and drinking, it was a matter of time before his heart just gave up. Sometimes, while in his office, Bobby could feel his heart pounding, chest constricting, and shortness of breath. Several times he thought he was having a heart attack and probably was. Truth be known, he perhaps had several attacks on his heart since that day back in March out on Maple Lane.

He battled through all those heart palpitations and self-diagnosed minor heart attacks and managed to make it to another day. Bobby knew that eventually, a big one was lurking; a potentially fatal one hanging out somewhere in his arteries. Eventually, Bobby knew, a day would come when something would grab his heart and stop it from pumping. Then there would be no more anything for Bobby Downey: no more thinking about his son, seeing him in ghost form or hallucination, or thinking about Dana and how good they had it over the years until that bad day out in the street.

April loved Bobby, and after that night on the gym floor where they danced, she knew that she loved this severely complicated man. She knew that she wanted to be with him no matter what, through thick and thin, bad times and good. She just felt right when she was with him, complete. April was not brave enough to tell Bobby how she felt. She contemplated on when to tell him, but felt anytime soon was too soon. She did not want to add any more to his load. She could see in his eyes that the load was getting harder and harder to shoulder on his back every day. She wondered if the day was coming when she would wake up and find out that Bobby was dead, maybe died in what little sleep he had stolen.

"So, have you thought about my question?" April asked, pulling the flannel throw to her chin, and watching the orange dancing fire.

"About staying the night?" Bobby asked, knowing what she was talking about. "I don't know. I'd have to ask my mom. She usually doesn't like me staying with friends through the week."

April nodded and played back, "Okay. Well, maybe she'll let you if I ask."

Bobby laughed a bit, "Maybe."

April laid her head over on Bobby's shoulder and the two of them watched the fire flicker and dance in the night. At that exact moment in time, everything was right and balanced in the universe for the two of them. For the first time in a very long time, Bobby thought of nothing in particular.

4

Thanksgiving morning, Ben came downstairs as usual when he was out of school and went into the kitchen. He was hungry and wanted some pancakes. He opened the freezer and found some of his favorite microwavable pancakes sitting in there. Taking six small discs out of the package, he put them on a plate and popped them into the microwave. Bailey came into the kitchen and said, "good morning." Ben replied politely as he usually did. He was still bothered by their conversation from earlier but tried to keep it out of his mind. It was too early for fighting. "I got dinner made for later," Bailey told him.

"That's good," he said.

"All your favorites…all the hits. We're eating at about four. Chris has to be back at work at eight tonight," Bailey said, pouring herself a cup of coffee.

"Oh, okay then. I won't be here," Ben replied, wanting to crush the plastic syrup bottle in his hand. That name, Chris, already made his blood boil and he had never even met the guy.

"Where are you going to be?" Bailey's voice had some rise to it.

"Abby's parents invited me over to eat with them and I accepted before I knew what time you were planning dinner around that guy." The microwave beeped and Ben opened the door and took his hot plate of pancakes, taking them to the kitchen table. He started pouring syrup on them as his mom started talking.

"And you didn't think to ask me if you could go?" Bailey asked, sipping her coffee and leaning up against the sink.

"Not really. Besides, you got that guy to keep you company. You'll be fine," Ben said without looking at his mother who was staring darts at him.

"He has a name, you know?"

"Yeah, I don't care. You have fun with him. I've got plans." There was silence between the two there in the kitchen. Ben kept his eyes ahead, looking at a picture of a wheat field hanging on the wall while his mother sipped her coffee. He could still feel her looking at the back of his head. It felt hot. Was that even possible, he wondered.

"You're not even going to give him a chance, are you?"

Ben chewed on his pancake and then swallowed before he answered, "I doubt it."

"I guess I don't understand your problem here."

That was the opening that Ben was waiting for. He was going to unload. He had a lot of baggage to unpack on his mom ever since she forced him to move to Tennessee.

"My problem?" Ben turned to look at his mother who was still in her pink robe. "My problem is that my dad died and you act like he's replaceable like a cup or something. And then you uproot me from my home and make me move to another state and live in the same house dad grew up in.

"And then I had to start a new school in my junior year of high school. And to top it off, you are dating some guy and I'm supposed to be all good with that? Fuck that!"

Ben got up from the table and left his pancakes sitting. He had lost his appetite. He stormed from the kitchen and ran up the stairs. Down below, Bailey could hear the door slam shut. She jumped a little from the sound.

5

Thanksgiving Day came and went for both Ben and Bobby. Ben went home after staying with Abby and her family as long as he could. He needed some distance between himself and his mother. So, Ben hung out with Abby in her house and talked to her parents at length there in the living room after having one of the biggest meals ever. Things were really good between them all. They liked Ben and he liked them. Her parents kind of reminded him of the way his mom and dad were back home, back in the days when things were normal, when things were good; when death was nothing but a word and meant for those that were old as the hills, not in their forties driving to work.

Harry Maddux was a big burly man in his mid forty's who had a biker's beard and the matching gravely biker voice to go along with that hair. On the outside, he was a formidable man standing six-four, two-eighty. The first time that Ben met him, he was intimidated by the man who shook hands with Ben. Harry's slab of meat for a hand swallowed his. The grip, to his surprise, was not tight. It was loose and pleasant. He was a train engineer and talked about his career there in the living room as Ben sat beside Abby on the couch. It was Jessica Maddux that had told Harry to change the subject because nobody cared about what he did for a living.

Abby's mother, Jessica, was an older replicate of Abby. She was blonde and wore glasses and had that soft-spoken gentleness that Abby had. Standing next to Harry, Jessica looked like a kid. But who wouldn't, Ben thought to himself. Ben could see how much Abby and her mother looked alike in the family pictures that he was privy to viewing. Books and books of pictures of the Maddux family narrated by Jessica who told Ben who everyone was, what they did, and how they died in those photos. By the end of the night, Ben was exhausted.

Ben spent Thanksgiving with the Maddux family while Bailey and that guy Chris stayed together at Ben's house. He wondered how much longer he would be staying at home now since Chris was in the picture. As if things were not bad enough for Ben, here steps in a man that replaces his dad with his mother. He could almost taste the bile in his mouth when he could hear in his head his mother telling him, "He's not here to be your dad because no one can replace him." He knew those words would eventually come. That caused some rage to build up inside his teenage mind.

The dinner was fantastic that Jessica and her mother had cooked. Unbeknownst to Ben, Abby's entire family had come to eat dinner: uncles, aunts, grandparents, cousins, and a few family friends. Ben was introduced to them all. By the time it was all over, he had forgotten all their names, but the faces he probably could remember, if he ever needed to.

Ben did not come from a big family like Abby did. His family, even when Steve was alive, consisted of his aunt and uncle and their two daughters on his dad's side. On his mother's side, both parents were dead and she was the only child, much like Ben was. Ben sat there with wonderment as the house was alive with people laughing and sharing stories of yesteryear. The older people in the group talked about how things in this generation were completely messed up and that back in their day gas prices were cheap, politicians were honest, and music was better. That last part may very well be true.

Ben was asked to join in at the huge dining room table with several others to play Rook. He had never played the card game before and was taught by Abby's dad. It seemed easy enough. After a few rounds, he got the hang of it and played holding his own with the elders at the table. That was really fun for Ben.

Off in the kitchen, Jessica and her mother talked about how nice and good-looking Ben was and wondered if he was a keeper. Abby, standing in the kitchen with her mother and grandmother, of course, blushed red. They could tell that Ben and Abby were more than what she was telling them. More than a good friend? Moms somehow knew everything. Even the stuff that you thought you hid out of sight and out of mind. At any rate, Jessica was happy for her daughter because this was the first time that she had a boyfriend. Abby was, too, and wrote in her journal exactly how much so.

Abby Maddux was not the most popular girl in school. She was never a cheerleader. She was never any boy's fantasy girl nor the Homecoming Queen. Abby was never asked out on a date to the movies or a school ballgame. What Abby Maddux was, was a straight-A student, a member of the chess team, and a retro girl who loved the 1980s. Abby was quiet, unassuming, and never had what you would call real friends. Her friends consisted of some from the chess team that ate lunch with her at the school's cafeteria. She had one true friend, Leigh, but she moved away when she was ten. They still talked on the phone and during summers went to each other's houses to hang out. After Leigh moved away, Abby found it difficult to make friends. She wanted friends, and wanted to be liked, but found it too exhausting/frustrating to try. Besides, she always thought and wrote in her journal, nobody would like me anyway if I actually did try. What's the point?

All that changed when she met Ben. Her weekends were filled with hanging out with him. She went on her first date ever with him. Their relationship began to take root after the costume party in the gym that Friday night. From there, things had just gotten better. The two of them were the same in nearly every aspect. They just fit like a hand in a glove. Their teenage love was sweet. It was honest. It was real. For Ben, Abby running into him was the best thing that had ever happened to him. Good things were few and far between in those days for Ben Medlen. For Abby, Ben was everything. Nothing was brighter and hotter than true love, not even the sun in the afternoon sky. Ben felt the same thing. Abby was the best thing going for him.

When Ben left the Maddux home, full to the gills with food and fun, he came back home later that night through the front door. Bailey was in the living room on the phone, talking to Chris he presumed, and just walked on by her without acknowledging her existence. He could feel her eyes upon him as he walked through the living room and up the staircase. He did not give a damn though. He was still mad at his mother. Maybe not mad, that was inaccurate. Hurt, there it was. He was hurt that his mom had pretty much desecrated his father's good memory like she had. She had crossed a line on that holiday by having another man over…in his dad's old home to boot.

6

Long before Ben had woken up and gone downstairs for his pancakes to get his holiday underway, Bobby was up early that morning, six-thirty or there about, sitting on his front porch bundled up in the cool morning watching the neighborhood slumber. The sun would not be up for nearly another hour. The weather forecast called for a rainy Thanksgiving Day and by the looks of the early morning, Bobby could feel the rain in the air, could smell it. The temps were around fifty-five, mild for that time of morning on Thanksgiving, but East Tennessee weather was known to change on a dime. And it often did.

Bobby did not spend the night at April's house. He was not ready for that leap just yet. The two of them stood in her living room and discussed it when they came inside after the fire went out for the evening.

"I totally understand," April said, standing there facing Bobby.

"I hope you do," he said. "I don't want you to take this as me not liking you or not wanting to spend time with you. Because I'm crazy about you, you know? It's just that I…I um…"

April stopped him from struggling for words of explanation, "You don't have to explain yourself to me. I thought I'd ask knowing probably what you would say anyways. It's cool."

Bobby looked down at his shoes and then back up to April. He wanted to tell her that he was nervous about where they were headed because he felt that they both knew where they were headed. They loved each other, he could feel that. It was that feeling that he had with Dana. And guiltily, he still loved Dana to varying degrees. He guessed part of him always would. Was that fair to April? Should he even tell her? Why even bring it up, he thought to himself standing there looking into her eyes.

If he was going to be honest, then he should tell her how messed up he really is: tell her about seeing Freddy; about his prescription drug abuse; about how he drinks way too much; about how his life was ripped apart the day his son was killed out there in the street playing Wiffle ball; about how Dana just left him and their marriage behind all because she could not deal with things. Was he ready to throw all of that on her? The answer was no. It was too much to unpack and go through. Maybe in increments eventually, he thought to himself. Yes, he had some demons for sure perched upon his shoulder whispering in his ear to do more pills and drink more. He had cut back some; cut back to the point where his body was going through withdrawals. It was okay, or at least, was going to be okay…eventually. Bobby wanted to get better and felt that April was the way back.

If he had spent the night, he would not sleep, and then she would ask questions. He was shaky from not drinking and was wired from the pills that night already. Sure, he would catch an hour or two like he always did of sleep. If he stayed, he and April would probably end up having sex and although that would have been great, Bobby was not ready for that kind of emotional plunge either. He loved April, he did, but he wanted to tread lightly in this new relationship. It would perhaps be the last one that he would ever have. He thought Dana was the last, but fate had something else in store for Mr. Downey.

"I just want to take things a little slow, you know?" Bobby spilled. "I'm still dealing the best I can with things. Sometimes I'm good at it and other times…not so much. I guess I don't want to ruin what this is or is going to be. I'm a handful. I'm a mess. Most of the time, I'm coming apart at the seams. And…I don't want you to have to deal with all of that." It was honest what Bobby said. He loved her enough not to bring her down in his bouts of self-destructive behavior to which he was prone.

April looked at Bobby and wanted to cry for him. She could see that he was broken, and honestly, she did not know if he could be mended, but she wanted to try; wanted to be there. She did not look at him as a reclamation project, but as a beautiful soul that needed someone to pick him up and tell him everything was going to be okay. April wanted to do that. She wanted to be that person Bobby desperately needed. She never loved anyone as much as she loved Bobby Downey right then and there standing in her living room.

"I know you don't. And we'll take things slow. Don't worry about dragging me down. I want to help pull you back up." April was on the verge of tears and Bobby felt as if he could let the waterworks go, too. If only Dana would have been that supportive, he thought standing there. Maybe she was, he debated in his mind. She put up with a lot, you know? She lost her son and husband in this, too. Don't think that it was just you, okay, Bubba? You both lost big in the game of life.

Sometimes Bobby's mind was right, the part that was not in critical condition or foggy from the pills and liquor. Had Bobby taken better care of himself he could think about things logically, but the severe sleep deprivation mixed with everything else had been a taxing toll on the high school guidance counselor.

7

Bobby had slept only an hour and a half that night. No dreams came for a visit. They rarely did in those small sleep sessions and if dreams did come he did not recall them with any accuracy. Maybe it was because he slept so little; not enough REM sleep to even warrant a dream. When he woke up by his alarm, he slowly rolled out of bed and touched the floor with his bare feet, walking across the bedroom and into the bathroom. He took the bottle of Ritalin and took one with a paper cup of water, "Time to get the day going." God how much he wanted to just sleep and get his mind, body, and soul right. All he wanted was a full night's rest. At the rate he was going, he would have to have a year's worth, a Rip Van Winkle situation. Sleeping a full night meant risking having that nightmare and Bobby was not about to throw caution into the wind. It was a fifty-fifty chance of dreaming of Freddy, but Bobby did not like those odds. He needed something more in his favor.

Sitting on his front porch did take some steel will. After all, just down the road a piece was where Freddy was killed. He could still see in his mind's eyes, night or day, that red Firebird screaming down the road towards the kids. There was a macabre peace in sitting there on the front porch, especially right before dawn or at sunset. Dana could never sit out there. She could barely even come into the house through the front door, pull into the driveway, or having to look out a window into their neighborhood. Their home had turned into a true house of horrors for Dana; for Bobby, too.

Bobby surmised often that had he left with Dana they would still be married. His messed up mind often wondered about that possibility. Any regrets? Some. He did not want to leave because of Freddy, but Dana had left because of Freddy. Freddy was the glue that held Bobby and Dana together, and he had been ever since the news came from Dana that she was pregnant with their son.

Ultimately, Freddy pulled them apart. Bobby thought back to when he was talking to Ben Medlen in his office. He was dealing with the same situation in a roundabout way as well. His mother had left the home after his dad's death because she could not handle being there in the memory of it all. Ben was just pulled along with her. It was not fair to the kid. Life ain't fair, kiddo.

8

Bobby showed up at April's house around twelve-thirty that Thanksgiving afternoon. Before he came, he drank a quarter-half a bottle of whiskey and took two more Ritalin pills. The Wild Turkey was to take the edge off and get his tremors under control. He was getting better somewhat at getting off the pills and booze, but still, he had some issues: his issues being that his body had gotten used to how Bobby was treating it. He was feeling okay for the most part.

Bobby was feeling okay, alert, and focused from the Ritalin, ready to go, and knocked on her front door. When April opened it, there stood Bobby with a bouquet of flowers in his hand.

"Flowers?" April asked. She took them out of his hands when he offered and noticed something odd about them. "Plastic flowers?" she remarked with a smile.

"Yeah," Bobby said, walking inside and closing the door behind him, "old lady Wilson next door to my house always has plastic flowers around her house. She went to visit family in Knoxville and I thought I'd get you something nice."

"Wow! Thank you! I'll go get some water to put these in," she laughed and the two of them hugged and kissed there in the living room.

Bobby was feeling good at that moment. He was flying pretty high off the Ritalin he had taken. At that point, he had the energy of someone that had been sleeping for ages. It was what kept him going at school. He would most certainly begin to wind down around eight tonight, but that was okay because he had his bottle of uppers with him. He was prepared.

April and Bobby's, Totally Rad 80's Movie Marathon, was something of legend. Of course, the legend of this marathon did not escape the confines of April's Cape Cod-style house on Barker Lane. First in the lineup, leading off in the VCR was Sixteen Candles. A total classic any way you sliced it. Batting second was The Goonies. Hitting third was Bobby's all-time favorite film, Ghostbusters. In the cleanup spot was The Breakfast Club. Fifth was Ferris Bueller's Day Off, a personal favorite of April's. The two of them sat on the couch and ate snacks and talked, watching flicks well up into nearly midnight, taking pauses in between all the movies. Those pauses gave Bobby time to go to the bathroom and take some pills to pep him up. Starting The Breakfast Club, Bobby was good to go again for as long as he needed to.

With neither of them being tired at all and after the Totally Rad 80's Movie Marathon was completed, April went into a bedroom that served as a junk room in that big three-bedroom home, and brought out a radio with a cassette player.

"I've got some mix tapes if you're interested," April said, bringing back a shoebox under her arm full of old cassettes from that bedroom.

Bobby and April sat at the dining room table and shifted through all the tapes. "Thank Christ you labeled these mixed tapes," Bobby pointed out. "Ballads?" he asked, holding a tape up.

"I think that one has some really cool songs on it. Let's see." April took the tape from him and put it in her radio's tape deck. She pressed PLAY and the first song was "With or Without You" from U2.

It was April's favorite song. Both of them sat there and listened to Bono's voice come through the speakers like soft velvet. They were instantly taken back to March of 1987, just seven years ago; back when things were better, back when Freddy was three, back when he and Dana were together; back when things were…good.

Bobby got up from the table and held out his hand. April smiled and took it and he gently pulled her up from the chair and he leads her to the middle of the dining room floor. They both slow danced to the song. Bobby lowered his head and put his chin on her shoulder and took a deep breath smelling the honeysuckle of her hair. It was intoxicating. This dance was something more than the dance at the school's costume party. This was more intimate. This was deeper.

As the song closed, Bobby pulled April apart from him and looked into her eyes. "I need to tell you something…I love you."

April smiled and mouthed, "I love you, too" but no words came out. Tears of joy welled up in her eyes as she put her face into Bobby's chest. They slowly swayed to the next song, "Pale Blue Eyes" from R.E.M.

Chapter 16

1

December

It was two-thirty, school was almost over for the day while Bobby and Ben sat in his office. It had been two weeks since they last had a meeting. December was in its first full two weeks and the Christmas break was looming on the horizon. Bobby and Ben's last meeting was a good one. That was the meeting before Thanksgiving when Ben mentioned that he was suicidal. Bobby wanted to talk about it more and Ben was hesitant and told him next time. Well, the next time finally came…

Sitting in Bobby's office, Ben appeared off-kilter to Bobby. Maybe it was being out of touch for two weeks. He had only seen Ben walking the halls of the school on occasion after the Thanksgiving break, usually with Abby by his side. Bobby would tip a wave and Ben would do the same. Bobby was eagerly waiting on his meeting with Ben that was scheduled to come up. He was not one of those at-risk kids that he checked in on. Ben was one of those kids that Bobby knew needed an ear, a place to vent given his circumstances. Besides, Bobby could use a little therapy himself. "Talking is good for the soul," Bobby often said.

Ben sat in Bobby's office and talked about Thanksgiving and how he spent it with Abby's family. When Bobby asked about his mother, that's when Ben told him everything about what she was doing and how she was replacing his dad with this Chris guy. He told Bobby how much differently his mother was acting; like her personality was changing so much that he could tell that she was conforming to the way the new man in her life behaved. He called this newer version of Bailey Medlen, Bailey 3.0, a fast upgrade from the 2.0 from earlier when she had appeared to start moving forward from his dad.

"So I'm taking it that you aren't very happy with your mom right now?" Bobby asked, leaning back in his chair.

"Not really. I wasn't all in on the whole dating thing with mom to begin with. But I knew that it was going to eventually happen."

"He not a good guy?"

Ben shrugged, "No idea. I honestly don't care. He's starting to pop in various times now. He's spent the night a few times. I mean, she barely knows him and he's staying over? What's that about? It's just very uncomfortable for me… the whole situation is if I'm being honest."

"So you stay up in your bedroom when he's there or how does that work?"

Ben looked around the room before he answered. He had to think about it for a bit before he told Bobby what he was doing, "I leave and stay at the park."

There was silence between the two in the office for a few moments. "Like sleeping? Like a hobo?" Bobby asked.

Ben nodded. "Yeah. I've done it a few times. I can hear them laughing and talking in that house and it seems so wrong. One night, I went downstairs to get some pizza rolls and heard them having sex. That was it for me. I got my stuff together and left for the night. The only place that I could go was the park. So…I spent the night there. Thankfully, it's not far to walk in case I needed to get back home in a hurry…sleeping bag is pretty warm."

Bobby was stunned. He wanted to scold Ben but how could he? Ben's reaction to the abnormality of what was going on in his house was normal. His mother had turned a bad situation for Ben into a serious one by bringing another man into the home and did not consider, at least it appeared to Bobby, Ben's feelings on the subject. It seemed that Bailey just dumped it on him.

"Have you spoken to your mother about this? Like how you feel with him being there?"

Ben shook his head, "About what, exactly? She ain't going to change her operation. She's moved on from dad and now she's with this guy. I met him once in passing leaving the house for the day and he tried to talk to me. His voice just makes me want to punch him in the throat. When he's there he makes himself at home like it's his or something."

Bobby sat there and felt for the kid. He was in an impossible situation.

He was a kid of sixteen who was so uncomfortable at home that he had to sleep at the park. "You think that this guy is someone that your mom is going to be with for a long time?"

Ben considered this for a minute. "I don't know. Maybe. First guy outside of my dad she's been with as far as I know. It's all new to her. I'm really hoping that she cycles herself out and gets bored and realizes what she has done."

"And if she doesn't?"

Ben considered Bobby's question for a few moments in reflective thought. "Then I don't know. Have to deal with it until I graduate school and move back to South Carolina."

"What about Abby?"

Ben ran his fingers through his hair in uncertainty, "I'm still figuring that part out. I haven't told her my plan."

"I think you should. You guys talk much about your home life?"

"Some. She knows the things you know. Except for the suicidal thoughts that I have."

There was the opening that Bobby had been looking for. He ran for it quickly before Ben could close it or before the school bell could dismiss them. "When was the last time that you thought about killing yourself?"

Ben did not even have to think about it, "The day before Thanksgiving. I was ready, man. I was about to do it. And then Abby just happened to come by. Had she not, then I may not be here." Bobby could have sworn that he saw tears forming in Ben's eyes, but he was not entirely sure.

"Anything since?"

Ben thought about it, "Yeah. A few times. Especially when I look back at everything that has happened to me lately." Ben let out a kind of chuckle not out of amusement but out of disbelief at how bad things were. "I don't know how I've kept it together for so long. It's like…it's like things were beginning to be tolerable, you know. I met Abby. She and I work really good together. And then all this mom and Chris stuff…”

The two of them sat in silence soaking in what Ben had just said. “Sometimes I just want to stop feeling and just go away…like die. I get tired of hurting, you know. It’s like I can’t find a way out sometimes and these thoughts get into my head…and they stick.”

“What kind of thoughts,” Bobby asked.

Ben was lost in thought, deep in the twisting and turning roads that led usually to nowhere before he answered, “Like I’d be better off dead; that all I would need to do is just slash my wrists and be finished with everything. What scares me the most, Mr. Downey, what really scares me sometimes, is that maybe…maybe one of these days I might do it, that I might finally get to that point of no return and just stop being a pussy and just do it.” Ben reached up with his hand and wiped away some tears that had finally broken through.

Bobby looked at Ben and thought about how sorry he felt for the kid; just sixteen having to deal with issues that adults could barely get a grip on; that Bobby himself could barely get a grip on.

“How’re things with you?” Ben asked, turning the tables and getting the spotlight off him for a bit.

Bobby looked at Ben and casually shrugged his shoulder much like Ben had earlier. “On the outside of it…holding up pretty good…inside? I’m a mess.”

“Still taking the pills and drinking?”

Bobby nodded, “Yeah. Cutting back though… body is still pushing back. I’m not drinking as much these days. I’ve managed to drop my pill habit some. Some days are a little worse than others.”

“Ms. Murray know?”

“No. Not been easy hiding that from her, now that I stay with her some nights through the week. It’s helped my drinking a lot. I mean, I can’t just walk up in there with a bottle of Wild Turkey and drink half of it in front of her. So, those nights I stay I don’t drink. I still pop pills because I can hide those. Still ain't sleeping though when I do stay over there. I usually stay up reading or whatever because I've got so much energy from the pills. Sometimes, I grade her papers just to work off the energy."

"You planning on telling her about all this?"

"Eventually…maybe…hell, I don't know. I'm still trying to figure out how much longer I can go doing this." Bobby sat there considering if he should let Ben on another secret, one that he had not told anyone. After a few moments of debate inside his mind, he let it out. " Did I tell you that I see my son sometimes?"

"No," Ben replied, sitting there thinking about what Bobby could mean. "Like he's a ghost or something?"

Bobby looked at his young friend and considered the question for a few seconds. "I'm not sure what he is. Maybe it's a mixture of a psychologically induced hallucination brought on by my pill consumption, guilt, and alcohol."

Ben smiled a bit, "Man, you totally just sounded like a trained professional right there."

"I've been known to sound educated from time to time," Bobby smiled back.

"So what do you mean you see your son? What do you think it is?"

Bobby exhaled deeply as if in frustration, "I don't know. We interact with each other, like it's real…like he's really there but not at the same time. It used to freak me out, but now…nowadays it's commonplace. I just…I don't know…maybe he's haunting me, haunting the house. Maybe he's all in my mind. Alls I know is that I see him sometimes." Bobby had some sadness in his voice that Ben picked up on. Ben could relate to the sadness. There was a silence between the two as Bobby sat there lost in thought. It was easy those days.

"How're things with Ms. Murray?" Ben asked, breaking the silence and trying to get Bobby back on the road of coherent thought.

"Great," Bobby replied, snapping out of his trance with a smile. "She's been really good for me. You know, since Dana left. She doesn't pry into my personal life. We just have a good time. We talk a lot…about life and such. But she steers clear of the subject of my son and my marriage. I mean, we've spoken about Dana here and there. Freddy? No."

"Do you want to talk about him with her?"

Bobby sat and considered before he answered. "I do, but then again I don't. It's a weird paradox, I know. Every time that I go out on the front porch..in the front yard… look out a window, I still see him out in the street playing Wiffle ball that day. And I see that car coming down the road. It's like some sort of memory echo that I see. I should move away like Dana did. But I can't…I just can't do it. I don't talk about my son to April because I don't want to infect her with my problems. There's like a darkness inside me…hard to explain, I guess. It's like nothing is there sometimes. Sometimes I don't care if April is there or not and I think that I'd be fine if she left and didn't fool with me anymore. Other times…I need her…just to have someone pick me up and tell me that it's going to be okay."

The two sat there in silence once again. It seemed that was always the case when one or the other made a poignant case that caused them to ponder. "You should take a chance on telling her. Maybe venting it out. You love her?"

Bobby smiled, "I do, yeah. She's awesome…really awesome. I guess I'm afraid that if I tell her about my drug problem and start in on Freddy that she might leave. Because who wants a basket case, right? I'll be honest here; I don't even know if I'm fixable at this point. I wonder how much damage I've done to my body, and then I wonder how much my mind is damaged."

"I don't think you're a basket case, Mr. Downey. I think me and you are victims of the times. We've both lost a lot. Our worlds have changed and we're trying to figure things out, where we belong in it and stuff as we go."

"Listen…" Bobby said, leaning up from his desk and looking over at Ben. "I know this ain't a normal guidance counselor/student relationship in terms of how things are supposed to be done. But I want you to know that I appreciate you listening. I've got no one else that understands some of the stuff I'm going through and it helps talking with someone that has had some recent losses, too."

Ben grinned a little sheepishly, "Me, too. You're the only adult that I can talk to that understands and won't judge. I've got Abby, but I don't want to hit her with everything that I got going on inside my head. She ain't lost things like I have. She doesn't know about me sleeping at the park sometimes or my suicide stuff. The only one that knows is you."

"Wise beyond your years, Mr. Medlen," Bobby said, as the school bell rang signaling the end of the day.

Chapter 17

1

January

The Christmas holiday break came and for two weeks the students of Central High School were gone to do whatever it was they did during that layoff from education. December had turned into a brand new month and even crazier, a brand new year. It was officially 1995. Bobby had profound trepidation about the new year because in three short months it would be the anniversary of Freddy's death. "God, how fast a year goes," Bobby remarked to himself, turning the calendar in his office over. Just the mere thought of that day getting closer caused him to want to throw up. He was always nervous about it.

During his Christmas break, Bobby and April hung out more and more, but only at her house. She did not ask any questions and figured that if Bobby wanted her at his place he would ask her to come. Being at her house, April thought, was probably for the best after everything that had happened at Bobby's. She was more than happy to always be the host. Besides, she had spent most of her time there in that house alone and it was nice to hear someone other than herself talking.

What was twice as nice was having someone there even if she and Bobby on those rare nights, didn't have anything to say to each other; even if they were just sitting there grading papers it was okay because he was there. April was madly in love with him and she could feel that he was with her. She also knew that Bobby still had a lot of scar tissue that may never heal. He had not gotten into a lot of his demons, but she figured that would eventually happen. He would have to be the one to bring up the subject of Freddy. That was not her place, not her job to peel back the bandage that covered the wound. He had spoken about Dana some, but not a lot. April never prodded, just left things alone. She let Bobby hit on the subject on his own time.

On December first, Bobby and April decorated the inside of her house in festive holiday cheer as well as the outside. It felt good for Bobby to do something that resembled normal festive holiday cheer. He did not decorate his house for Halloween like in previous years, so doing this with

April brought the guidance counselor back to somewhat better times in that regard. By the time he and April hung up the stockings with care, put up her Christmas tree, and hung Christmas cards of holidays past around the walls of the home, the inside of her home looked like a cozy Christmas card itself.

During the two-week break, Bobby had dropped his whiskey consumption down. He was only drinking every other day and only two shots from the bottle of Wild Turkey. His body was getting used to the drawdown and at first, Bobby was having terrible headaches so much to the point he was chewing on ibuprofen by the tens. The shaking in his hands came and went and when they came he clenched his hands into fists to make them stop when he was around April. She saw this several times when Bobby thought he was being sly. She knew that he had a problem. She saw the physical signs on him. She never brought it up. Bobby's complexion was also getting paler and he was sweating a lot more from doing nothing but sitting there in his office or at home. His body was fighting itself.

Despite getting his alcohol drinking under control somewhat, Bobby still had a problem with his pills. He had scaled those back, too. Instead of the five or six that he was hitting a day, he was taking three to four. As a bonus, he had stopped going to one of his four doctors for the meds, Dr. Dean. He still had three that he saw in different parts of the county unbeknownst to anyone at the time. His goal was to clear another doctor by the end of January. Bobby knew how to deal with addiction and felt this was the best method for doing so. Was he a doctor? No, but he knew all about addiction and how to treat it all the same and its operational procedures to break the bewitching spell it had over him.

Christmas came and Bobby and April spent it together at her house. They exchanged gifts; Bobby gave April a red cardigan that she loved and April gave Bobby a book on Native American legends and myths. Both gifts were a hit as they played Christmas music and drank hot apple cider watching A Christmas Story on TV that Christmas Eve night. On the couch, the two of them sat, feet propped up on the oversized ottoman in front of the couch, April snuggled onto Bobby with his arm around her. It was the best Bobby had felt in a long while.

Bobby still had some hard times at home when he left April's house. Bobby came home from his Christmas day with April, closed the front door to his dark home, and stood there staring into the living room. This time of year used to be bright, colorful, warm, and inviting when Dana was there and Freddy was alive. The Christmas tree would be put up with care, ornaments from years past, some store-bought and some Freddy made when he was younger, hung on the tree for all to see. The tree itself was always a source of conflict between Dana and Bobby.

The tree had been in Dana's family for God knows how long and Bobby complained about how mangled it was each year and how hard it was to assemble and take down. He implored her each year they brought it down from the attic to finally give in and for them to buy a new one; one that wouldn't be so damn difficult to put together. Dana refused, citing that the memories that are wrapped up in the tree meant too much for her to just cast aside. Now, Bobby missed that tree that was still boxed up in the attic. He had a notion earlier that month to lug it down and assemble it, just to feel her presence. But he decided against it; wasn't worth the trouble. Besides, seeing those Christmas ornaments that Freddy had made with his small hands would surely set off the waterworks.

Christmas morning was another hard time for Bobby. That was Freddy's favorite day of the entire year. And why wouldn't it be? Freddy had all kinds of gifts to open from underneath that damn tree that Bobby hated so much. Their son would always wake up before they did and come rushing into their room at the first sign of daybreak. He would bounce on their bed waking them both up, screaming, begging for them to get up and come see what Santa had left under the tree.

Blurry-eyed and tired, the parents of Freddy would slowly get out of bed and follow their son into the living room where he slid on his knees in his PJs to the tree. By the time he had gone through each and every gift, pictures being taken by him and Dana, all the gifts were opened in a matter of ten minutes. "It takes us an hour to wrap all of this and he undoes it in like ten minutes," Bobby remarked to his wife one Christmas. Bobby thought he said that last Christmas, but he was not sure. Sometimes the memories of those past Christmas mornings all blended together.

Bobby went inside his home that Christmas night after leaving April's and made his way to his recliner and sat down. His mind was blank. He did not want to think about anything anymore. He wanted to escape. Bobby considered reaching for his bottle of whiskey but fought back the urge mightily. He eventually won out because he had already had his allotted two shots that day. Man, he could use a drink though. Sitting there trying to fight back the memories of his family, one gone and the other dead, Bobby started to cry. He tried so hard to keep from doing that but the memories, the hurt, and the longing for Dana and Freddy finally broke through the walls and flooded him.

By the time he had finished his emotional release, a dim daylight was creeping in from the curtains. Hours had ticked off the clock. Feeling tired, Bobby knew that it was time not to sleep but to take some of his pills and stay awake. Sleep was too scary to try because there was a possibility he might dream, and those dreams that would surely come would only hurt Bobby more. As he got up from the recliner to go into the kitchen, he stopped and listened carefully. He could have sworn that he had heard Freddy talking in his bedroom.

2

The Christmas break for Ben was not as good as Bobby's. Ben stayed away from home as much as he could. He was there mostly by his lonesome until his mother came home from work. When she came home, Chris was usually with her. That was when Ben either stayed up in his bedroom or left the house to roam the town of Claxton and see the sights of his new town. He had gotten an old bicycle out of the garage that must have been his dad's from long ago when he was a teen. Ben had found it a few days before Christmas prowling around the packed garage. It was on the far back wall buried underneath boxes from years past and empty paint cans and other various junk that had not made it to the landfill.

Looking around the garage, for nothing in particular at all, he spied what he thought were handlebars poking out from under some old towels. He walked over there and removed the towels and sure enough, there were the handlebars of a bike. He reached down and pulled the left handlebar through the junk and to his surprise he unearthed an honest-to-God bike. The bike was old and had some treads left on the tires. The seat was a little worn, but the hand grips still looked to be mostly okay. Pulling the bike the rest of the way out of the junk and into the clearing of the middle of the garage, Ben saw that the hand brakes still worked and the chain appeared to be in perfect operational order however it could use some oil.

Ben sat on the bike and it felt good. He bounced up and down on it and noticed that the tires could use a shot of air. If there's a bike here then there may be a tire pump, too, Ben thought. He got off the bike and kicked the kickstand, which still worked, and propped the bicycle up. He looked around the garage, all the walls, moving junk around here and there, searching for a tire pump that may or may not be in there. After a long ten minutes of looking and jostling items of refuse from long ago, Ben was about to give up when over in the corner he saw several pieces of cut two-by-fours leaning against the wall. He walked over there and removed the wood, which he had not done before, and saw nothing underneath. Exhaling in frustration in the cold garage on the twenty-second day of December, Ben turned to go to the bike when up on a shelf above where the old two-by-fours had stood leaning, something that caught his eyes.

Ben reached up to the shelf and felt around with his hand. His fingers found purchase on something cold. It was metal and he felt a rubber hose that was wrapped around it. Excitedly, he pulled it down and it was indeed a dark gray bicycle tire pump. Dust was two inches thick on it by the looks and Ben walked it over to the bike in triumph. He unwound the rubber hose, which looked to still be intact, and found the nozzle part of the hose. He placed it on the front tire valve and locked the nozzle part of the hose in place. Ben stood over the floor pump, shoes standing on the sides of the pump cylinder, pulled the handlebar of the pump up, and then pushed it down, sending air into the tire. It was working. Ben repeated this several times, checking each time how much air was in the tire. After several hearty pumps of air, the tire was ready to go. He did the same with the back tire.

3

For the first time since he had lived there in Claxton, Tennessee, Ben rode around the town looking around. It was not a large town by no means at all. Most of it was rural with spiraling county roads that went to God knows where. There were many neighborhoods, and many streets, to travel down. There was a downtown part of the town. It was nowhere as big as the town he had come from, not by any stretch, but there was something neat all the same about this new town of his, the town where his dad grew up. It was small, readily accessible and he could see his dad being a kid there. I wonder if dad rode down these same streets on this bike, Ben thought as the cold wind whipped him good, driving down past the park.

Ben rode everywhere that afternoon on his newfound bike. He decided that he would do into Wilson's Drugstore for a Coca-Cola. He had always passed by the place and seen people coming in and going out and had never been inside. From the outside, it looked like one of those old-time drugstores that probably still sold milkshakes in the summer that was run by a guy in a 1950's style setting. Ben rolled into the parking lot on that overcast day and propped his bike up against the outer brick wall of the drugstore. He was pretty sure that no one would swipe it. If they did, oh well.

Ben walked inside and saw the layout of the drugstore. It was not what he was expecting. It was small and had aisles of shelves that had various products sitting on them. It looked pretty modern to him. The store was decorated with Christmas holiday cheer and the smell of apple cinnamon was strong. Over to the left of him were a book and magazine area with two arcade video games, Street Fighter II and Excite Bike. On the right of him was the cash register and counter where customers paid for things. In the middle of all that was a spinner rack of comic books. It had all the titles and iconic superheroes that Ben had grown up with over the years.

Over next to the book area and arcade games was a free-standing Coca-Cola fridge with a see-through glass door. Ben walked over there while a kid, who looked to be around his age wearing an Atlanta Braves baseball hat, was standing playing Street Fighter II. By the way he was moving, fingers vigorously tapping the buttons, it appeared to Ben that he was really into it.

Ben walked over and opened the beverage door and got out a plastic bottle of soda. He watched this kid play the game until he finally got his lights punched out and the message flashed on the screen, RYU WINS. "Damn it!" the kid grunted in frustration. He dug into his jeans' front pockets in search of quarters and came up empty. He turned and saw Ben standing there watching him. "You got a quarter I can bum?"

"I just got enough for this," Ben replied, holding up his bottle.

The kid looked back at the machine and let the clock count down to zero before he would have to start all over unless he slid another quarter into the slot to continue. "Looks like I'll have to come back, Ryu. Don't think you've won this," he told the video game character. "I've seen you around school, I think, right?"

"Central High?" Ben replied.

"Yeah. You a…"

"Junior," Ben replied before the kid could get it out.

"Cool. Me, too. I think we got Mr. Hodges together, first period."

Ben stood there trying to place his face in the class. "Oh, yeah, you sit over on the first row, I think, right?"

"Yup that's me. I'm Matthew Morgan."

"Ben Medlen."

"Where did you go to school before Central High?" Matthew asked.

"I came here from South Carolina in August."

Matthew stood there in awe because he had never known anyone from there, "Wow, that's awesome, man. What brought you to this town? It's not exactly a traveler's paradise."

Ben looked out the large glass store window that was behind the two arcade machines and bookshelves and thought about just lying and making something up that sounded badass. He quickly reconsidered. "My dad died earlier this year and me and my mom moved into my grandmother's house."

"Man, that sucks. Who's your grandmother? Chances are I might know her."

"Well, she's dead now. Gracie Medlen."

Matthew held his mouth open in shock and surprise, "Oh wow, I knew her back when I was little. She used to pay me and my friend Curt to rake her leaves in the fall. Man she ruled!"

"That's awesome!" Ben remarked about the connection that was made between this kid in his high school to his grandmother. "Yeah, she was great," Ben said.

"She used to make these homemade apple pies for the Fourth of July

Festival we have here in town. God, they were so good. She was one of the nicest people I ever met."

"She used to make me one of those pies every time that I would come visit."

Matthew looked at his watch, "Well I hate to cut it short, but I've got to go pick Mandy up," Matthew said, walking away from the arcade machines and Ben. "But I'll see you around school after break, Ben! Have a good one!" Matthew said as he hurriedly walked out of the drugstore.

4

Christmas in the Medlen home was forced. Instead of it being just Bailey and Ben, she invited Chris and his folks over. Ben only stayed downstairs for a few minutes, faked smiled at them all as they drank beer and laughed and told crude jokes. To his surprise, his mother was joining in on all of that. She had never done any of that before; at least not in front of Ben. Bailey never cussed as far as Ben knew; never drank as far as Ben knew; never smoked cigarettes as far as he knew, and never seemed to be so desperate as far as Ben knew. His mother was transforming right before his very eyes and had been for some time.

Bailey had been changing since they moved into the house. She had started doing things differently, talking differently, and even dressing differently. Ben did not like that early on but after thinking about it over the weeks with Abby's help, he looked past it some. However, his mother was slowly becoming someone else other than the Bailey 3.0 and the root cause of that was the man sitting to her right with his hand on her knee. Ben hated him and he suspected that Chris hated him. It was okay, it was mutual. There was a vibe that he had gotten off of Chris and he did not like it, not a nary bit. He knew and had even told Abby that this guy was going to be the end of a lot of things.

"Maybe not," Abby told Ben one night when he brought up Chris and how he thought he would ruin his mom, turning her into something worse.

"You don't see what I see," Ben simply replied.

After his forced thirty-minute stay with all of them downstairs, which Ben kind of snuck out without anyone noticing him, he went to his room and closed the door. God how he missed his dad during times like these. It was his first Thanksgiving and Christmas without his dad and he was mentally falling apart. But his mother? Nah, she was fine drinking and laughing with the white trash that was downstairs telling nasty jokes and treating the Medlen home like a honky-tonk bar.

Ben was sitting in his bedroom, the muffled sounds coming from downstairs could be heard even with his door closed. Ben was scared. He was only sixteen, had at least two more years left there at Central High, and had a mother who was turning into someone he didn't even know anymore. And the reason for this newer, more profound change was that son of a bitch downstairs. Ben went over a million possibilities in his head over how things were going to probably go. He saw Chris eventually moving into the house and taking over. That seemed to be his nature, an Alpha male who liked things his way, and Ben suspected that when Chris was challenged in not getting his way he would use violence to get it. He seemed that kind of guy to Ben. He had that vibe off him.

Ben wanted to sit there and cry out his pain, but he held back. He was getting stronger by the day. It was not like he had vanquished his depression. It crept on him most times, but Ben was getting better at managing his mental spirals into darkness. A lot of that was thanks to Bobby. Bobby was a godsend to him and was a man that Ben knew he could count on. Most of all, Bobby listened and never judged. He knew that if he ever needed Bobby that Bobby would be there. Deep down in his gut, Ben knew that times were fixing to change. He could feel it coming from downstairs, could taste it in the air. He was scared. Knowing that he had finally lost his mother caused Ben even more fright. Darker days were coming…

Chapter 18

1

Mid-January.

On an idle Thursday evening after school, Bobby found himself at Food Town. He was in there picking up a few things to take over to April's for supper. It was his turn to do the cooking. He didn't mind. Back in the land of long ago, Bobby and Dana used to split the duties. He was actually a pretty good cook.

Bobby had been spending time at April's house more and more. April had noticed Bobby's ability to only catch a few winks, mostly two hours, sometimes far less, and was in awe at his stamina to be up all day. She had no idea that he was not doing it on his own. A normal person could not keep the pace that Bobby was keeping without a little help from the doctor and the local pharmacies. But he was drawing himself down from the pills. His alcohol consumption had gone from two shots of liquor every other day to one shot every other day. Progress. He had even taken another pill out of his daily needs. Bobby had managed to go to two a day. More progress.

As Bobby turned down aisle four to find the taco shells, he and Pete Samples nearly ran smack into each other face first. The two of them did not recognize each other at first from the embarrassment, and then their eyes focused. They swapped "how you doing" and made small talk. Then Bobby popped the question that he had been putting off for some time.

"So, I hear a rumor about, Mr. Glick."

Pete rolled his eyes and chuckled. He and Bobby moved to the left to let an old lady push a shopping cart by them. "I hate that guy. He comes in from Nashville and wants to move up the educational ladder. He ain't satisfied with just being a principal, you know? He wants to be like a damn state director of education or something. But what's this rumor you've heard because there's so many out there on him?"

"That he had put in place a measure to be voted on about removing all the school counselors in the school district and forcing teachers that are close to retirement out so he can consolidate classes.”

Pete was not grinning anymore because he knew that Bobby was a well-respected counselor, very much liked around the district. Anyone would be hard-pressed to find anyone that did not like Bobby Downey. Even though he and Bobby were not great friends, but mere acquaintances, Pete still respected him and his reputation enough to shoot him straight.

“Well, yeah, that one is probably true. He’s got the superintendent’s ear for sure. I was in the meeting awhile back when Glick made mention of that and he outlined the blueprint of his plan, and when he showed on a graph how much money would be saved cutting people like you out, then that gave Franklin a hard-on for sure. I think Glick even took it up the ladder to the state where he has some friends. I think he can pull something like that off.”

Bobby knew that Pete was shooting him straight. The guy was notorious for never keeping things quiet that were supposed to be left in house. The bitch of the bunch was that Bobby could see in his mind’s eye this very thing happening. “You think they’ll do it?”

“They’ll for sure try. In the end, I’d say it’s very possible. But who knows, right?” Pete nodded somberly, knowing that the news had to be hitting Bobby in the gut. He could see it on his face.

“Look, all this shit has to be voted on and things signed and all that, but in the end, it’s money that he’s found a way to save. If he’s got the ears of the right people and convinces them to consolidate classes and have teachers taking on more kids, and cutting people like you out, then that saves money. And you know money talks. For whatever reason, Franklin loves this fucking guy.

“Bullshit part of it all is that Glick won’t be here for long. I’d give him a year or two more and he’s moved back to Nashville in a better position than he came from. All of this cutting is just for him to put on his resume. That’s it,” Pete said.

“And you think for sure it’ll happen?”

Pete nodded again, “Yeah, I think the possibility is high. At least that’s the feel of it. But don’t tell anyone that I said that, okay?” Bobby agreed. “He figures the cuts will be to the tune of a million bucks, maybe more. And that just lit up Franklin's eyes like a Christmas tree. You should've seen it. But of course, Dr. Franklin is most certainly going to take the credit for this idea. But he'll make sure to take care of Glick, too, on the back end. They're just hitching their wagons to each other is all."

"This really sucks. So, I guess my tenure doesn't mean anything?"

"It may or may not. He's not firing you, because if he was then you could fight it. But these are under budget cuts. He's also, and you didn't hear this from me, he's got another plan for the next school cycle, to hold down raises. And when the cuts to counselors coming…forced retirements…it's just bad times, man. Bad times. They're still getting all the lawyer stuff sorted out, too, to make sure they can't be sued or whatever from those they try to push out. If they can't force out the old, they'll come up with competency issues like low test scores to validate what they're doing. They got all this shit planned out."

"How do you see the vote going on the cuts?" Bobby asked.

Pete looked down at the shiny sales floor that had a newly waxed sheen to it and thought it over for a few seconds. "I'd say five to two. The two will be Wendell Katchem and Grady Keefer. They can't stand Glick or Franklin at all. So they'll vote against the cuts he proposed just because of spite."

Bobby did not know what else to say. It was one thing thinking that you may lose your job, but another thing entirely to hear it from the keeper of secrets. Pete may be a blabbermouth but he was honest. No one could ever accuse him of being a liar. "Well, I better get to finding another place to go then."

"Well like I said, four teachers are retiring legit at the end of the school year. And they might take a look at all the counselors who are cut and see who has been at their job the longest and offer them those positions, I don't know. Nobody knows anything for sure. But if he's wanting to consolidate classes and have teachers taking on more, then I don't know, man. They may just say goodbye. You could probably fight it, but I don't really know how all that would go to be honest."

Pete patted Bobby on the arm that was holding the handbasket in a gesture of goodwill, "I wouldn't worry about it. You're a good guy. And who knows, all this bullshit might not even make it through. I got to get going before Jessica thinks I'm out whoring around. Have a good one, Bobby." Bobby smiled and stood thinking about his future.

2

Just as changes were looming on the horizon for Bobby Downey, some good and some bad, Ben Medlen was facing some changes as well. Abby and Ben were doing very well. Ben had become a fixture at the Maddux home. He was always welcomed and was made an honorary son that they never had by Abby's dad. That made him feel very good inside. That sense of belonging was something that he had not felt, if he was being honest with himself, since the move to Tennessee.

The Maddux home, warm and inviting, seemed to be full of life and pleasantness. Ben's home paled in comparison. Ben had come from one broken home only to land in another, in another state with a woman that he barely recognized. Bailey had changed more so after the Christmas break. She had undergone a surreal amount of change since she had met Chris and those changes were not good ones. Steve's death had changed Bailey to varying degrees, but in meeting up with Chris, Bailey underwent the most change.

Ben and his mother had become strangers in the home where his dad had grown up. They barely talked at all when the day left them together in the house. Ben would make his own supper and eat upstairs in his bedroom while Bailey would nibble on whatever she had brought home from a fast food joint and talk on the phone with her new boyfriend.

The word boyfriend made Ben sick to his stomach. He hated that his dad had been replaced so quickly and felt that it was his duty not to condone what his mother had done to his good name. To Ben, Bailey had crossed a line and was at a point of no turning back. However, Ben had no idea that the line she crossed long ago would be a thousand miles behind her as she and Chris forged ahead together.

Things had been bad lately between Ben and Bailey. So much in fact that the two of them had practically stopped talking; all communication ceased to exist. She did not know what was going on in his life and he did not care to know what was going on in hers. What he did know was that Bailey was loading up to bring her new boyfriend into their home, his dad's old home, and that was not a good thing. Ben was not pleased.

He was not totally sure, but one night towards the tail end of Christmas break, Ben told Abby, "I bet you a million dollars she's loading up to move him in."

"How do you know," Abby asked.

"I heard something the other night when I was walking from the kitchen and up the stairs. Chris said something like 'I'm going to have to find a place to live because I'm so far behind on my rent'."

"You think your mom will actually move him in? She barely knows him."

Ben nodded, "It doesn't matter. He's got my mom right where he wants her."

Ben had already stayed at the park on those random nights where Chris would be staying overnight, and it was just his luck that it was always cold when he did. It was like he was doing it on purpose or something. Those nights in the town's park were not easy for Ben, who had to get himself acquainted with the environment in the darkness. It was not the animals that made sounds around him under the trees in the park that spooked him. It was not the darkness, either. It was the real sense of being alone. It was that lonesomeness that made Ben cry nearly every time he had to stay at the park.

The park itself was only a couple of miles from his home. It was a nice park, full of vibrant trees of different species and various sizes. A smattering of trees populated various isolated parts of the park and made it ideal for someone to unroll a sleeping bag and sleep under the pines. That's where Ben camped when Chris came to his home. Ben would wait until dark and gather his camping stuff, which was his sleeping bag, a bottle of water, and a bag of trail mix. He would sneak out the back door quietly as a mouse. His mother was too immersed with Chris that she never knew he was not upstairs in his bedroom.

He had visited the park during the summer when they first moved to Tennessee. He was taken in by how pretty the landscape was. There was a basketball court that was perhaps the most used landmark in the park.

There was a baseball field complete with two dugouts, one visitor, and one home. There was a huge oval blacktop walking track for exercise enthusiasts that was laid out all around the perimeter of the park. There were numerous park benches dotted here and here. Over on the side of the park, closest to the parking lot and entrance, was a swing set, a jungle gym, a set of seesaws, and of course, the pavilion and swimming pool. Across the baseball field, beyond a tall chain-linked fence was a forest. Ben had thought about exploring it once, but something about it gave him creeps.

3

There was something about Chris that Ben did not like; something that did not sit well with him. Maybe it was the way he talked, walked, looked, or acted. Perhaps it was everything, the whole package. He did not get Chris' last name and did not care to. He did not care what he did for a living. He did not care for him being at his house. He did not care for his mother and Chris laughing and hanging out together. He did not care for the man that was coming in and seemingly taking over what wasn't his. What kind of man did that kind of stuff, Ben wondered. Not a good one.

The nights that Ben had to sleep at the park were near sleepless ones. The first time that he fled his warm and safe home for the dark unknown reaches of the town's park was one of the worst nights of his life. That first night alone in the park, Ben cried big wet tears out in the thin protection of pines. He cried under a canopy of skeletal branches that interlocked above him in the starry night sky. He was cold and lonely, tucked in a sleeping bag that used to belong to his dad. He found it in the attic weeks ago with Steve's name written on the white tag in blue ink. His young mind thought of many things that first scary night alone in the park. One thought was on the forefront: One day I'm going back home, back to South Carolina. I swear to God. Those thoughts of going back home, back to where he belonged, kept his mind occupied that first night. Ben fell asleep to the thought of being back in his old bedroom.

The trips to the park to get away from Chris being in the house were random. But one day things changed. It was Saturday when the change announced itself. One morning, nearly right before the start of the afternoon, Ben woke up and came downstairs for some cereal or whatever breakfast food he could find. When he stepped off that last rung of the staircase, he saw boxes stacked up in the living room. They were moving boxes. He stood there wiping the sleep out of his eyes and went over to inspect what they were. They were taped up. He picked one up and it was heavy.

"You're up late," Bailey said, standing in the archway that was in between the dining room and kitchen. It was the first time that Bailey had spoken to her son in what seemed weeks. That didn't get lost on either of them.

"What's all this?" Ben asked, looking down at the large boxes. He already knew. The weird sensation in his gut sounded the alarm.

"Chris' stuff."

"What's it doing here?" Ben asked, with a big lump in his throat. The thing that he feared was coming true.

"He's um…he's moving in here. Going to help us out for a bit," Bailey said, leaning up against the inside of the archway.

Ben felt his blood pressure rise and it started thumping his head. He could feel his heart pounding against his chest and he was shaking. His body was not handling the news well at all. It was news that he knew eventually would come. Whether it was moving to Chris' house or him to theirs, it didn't matter; neither situation was better than the other in his eyes. It was still treasonous in his view on what his mother was doing and had done long ago by selling the Medlen home back in South Carolina.

"That's great," Ben couldn't have sounded any more sarcastic.

"Like it or not it's happening. It's not your house. You don't get to make the rules," Bailey spoke sharply.

Ben was ready for the rumble. "It's not yours either. It was grandma's house. And dad's house. Or did you forget?!"

"What is your damn problem?! You're acting like a fucking punk!" Bailey snapped. Ben was stunned by her words. He had never heard his mom talk like that before. He had heard Chris talk like that a lot, plenty of times. Maybe she was starting to copy that prick's mannerisms and language; it seemed to fit.

"I don't think he belongs here," Ben said.

"It's not your call now, is it? I decide who stays in this house, not you little boy," Bailey said back.

Ben knew that she had him there. He was only sixteen, about to turn seventeen come March. Nobody listens to a kid even if they are right. Adults always had jurisdiction when it came to kids and they always thought that they knew better. His mother took a cigarette out of her front pants pocket and lit it up with a lighter from the same pocket. She was smoking and had been for a little bit since she and Chris had gotten together.

Had Chris influenced her that much? Apparently so because now she was acting totally unlike the Bailey Medlen he had grown up with. This was the 3.0 version: she was cussing at him, ignoring him, and now smoking.

"Now you listen up, Bennis." He hated when she called him Beniss. She only started it since Chris started doing it because he thought it was funny on one of those nights he was drunk in their living room making fun of Ben's name.

"Don't you try to ruin what me and Chris have got going here. He's the best thing that's happened to me in a long time. And I'm not going to have my son screw this up. You got that?! So, whatever you got to get right in your head, whatever you got to do to get over not liking Chris, you'd best figure it out and quick. Because when he's living here we're going to be a happy family! You understand me?!"

Ben stood there and looked at his mother blowing smoke into the house like a dragon. How he hated that woman standing in the archway. He never in his wildest dreams thought that he could ever really hate the woman. But events over the last several months, after his dad, he did. God help him but he did.

Ben clenched his teeth so tightly that his jaws popped. Never in his life had he wanted to hit someone as he did his mother just then. It was her attitude and her overall change of personality that caused his rage. She had changed from the loving mother that he knew, shared tears and laughs with, successes and failures with, mourned over his dad with to this bitch of a woman that he didn't even know anymore. Ben was afraid now, more than he had ever been.

He had lost his father and now he had lost his mother…for good.

He knew a frightening truth standing right there next to Chris' moving boxes staring at his mother; knowing that truth caused his mind to go into panic mode. When Chris came to live there, things would certainly, most certainly, get much, much worse there at home.

4

"So you get a bad vibe off this Chris guy?" Bobby asked from his usual position behind his desk.

Ben sat there and looked around the office and nodded the truth. "Yeah."

"Why?"

Ben knew a million reasons why but struggled to come up with just one when asked. It was not as if Bobby was just some adult asking questions. Bobby Downey had become a friend of his, a person that he could tell anything to. So why was he drawing a blank on Bobby's question? "I just do."

Bobby nodded his head in acceptance of Ben's reply, "Well, you certainly have a right to feel the way you feel, you know? But usually, there's a beginning point for your emotional response either bad or good. So… where was the beginning of this emotional response you have? Let's trace that back."

Ben sat for a few minutes and ran over why it was that he hated Chris so much. He knew exactly why for weeks now, but sitting across from Bobby's desk all the things that he hated about the man were dancing and darting away from his grasp. Finally, Ben grabbed a hold of one of those reasons. "He's changed my mom to the point where I don't even know her anymore. I mean, she had started changing over the summer when we first got here, you know. But now…" Ben trailed off.

"I'm guessing changed for the worst?"

Ben only nodded and looked about the office. "Yeah, pretty much."

"How so?"

"Like, she cusses all the time now. She never did that before. She's smoking cigarettes. She's drinking. She's just been really gruff with me the last several weeks. And now she's moving this guy into my dad's old house and that sucks. It's like…she's just a totally different person now. I don't even like being around her. I feel like I've lost my mom."

"It's a little fast to be moving in a guy you barely know," Bobby remarked really to himself but it was directed towards Ben.

"Exactly! I said the same thing but mom wouldn't hear of it. What's going to happen is that he's going to come in there and start taking over and then try to control me like he apparently does mom."

"Does he seem like the controlling type to you?"

Without taking the time to consider the question Ben replied, "Yup. He's already got mom whipped and now he'll come after me and try to get me in line. But I'm not going to play that game with him."

"What does your mom see in this guy you think?"

Ben sat there and thought about it. "I don't really know. He's nothing but white trash to me. Barely works; can't manage money. Drinks a lot and cusses like a sailor, smokes like a train. He's everything that my dad wasn't. And it's so weird to see my mom with somebody that's so…just nasty, you know? I mean, if it was with a decent-looking dude and he had a decent job and was not foul-mouthed all the time I might be on board with it somewhat, but not with this guy. It's like she's trying to erase my dad with someone the exact opposite."

"You think Chris is just a stop along the way toward her final destination? Sometimes that happens."

"I don't know. I hope so. But something tells me mom is settling for the first guy to show her attention. That's what I think."

"Sometimes after the death of a spouse, the survivor tends to try to find another partner to fill the void. Sometimes they go out and find someone with the same qualities as their husband or wife."

"And sometimes they go out and get with someone totally different than what they had but in a bad way," Ben remarked.

"You'd be right. But there's not much that you can really do about it though concerning your mom and Chris. You'll just have to try to ride this out as long as you can."

"What if I can't ride this out? I mean, what if it gets like really bad when he moves in?"

"The only thing that I can tell you is that you'll have to figure that out when you get there. Look, we can play hypotheticals all live long day and sing them to the tune of 'Sweet Child O' Mine'. What usually gets us is the stuff you never dream of. Wait and see what happens when he moves in. Maybe you'll be surprised, maybe not. It's a flip of the coin. But you won't know until you get there. And if it does get as bad as you think, then we'll talk about it and figure something out."

"Got to work with what you got," Ben said lowly, defeated, remembering his dad's tried and true saying about life in general.

"Yup…and sometimes it ain't a lot, is it?" Bobby said back.

Chapter 19

February

February came in colder than January and wetter, too. Things mentally with Bobby Downey were running about the same as it ever was. His drinking, however, was down again to twice a week with no set days: just shots now and not even full shot glasses at that. When he felt like he absolutely needed a drink, he'd pour a shot of whiskey. His withdrawals, which were getting the better of him sometimes, were slowly subsiding. The headaches and the trembling hands were retreating and that made Bobby feel much better; like he was getting somewhere, gaining control back over the substances that he was abusing.

The Ritalin was becoming easier to tame. Bobby had managed to get it down to only one pill a day. That pill was taken usually around seven o'clock to keep him up through the night to stave off long bouts of sleep that would most likely give birth to some nightmares that would surely turn into howlers. When he did finally crash during the weekends, dreams did come, but nothing out of the ordinary, nothing scary.

The weekends had gotten better. The weekends used to be earmarked for Bobby to crash and burn and drink himself to sleep; no Ritalin during that Friday, Saturday, or Sunday. But things had changed. The name of that change was April. Nowadays, Bobby did not use the weekends to crash and burn. He used them to spend more time with April whom he was falling in love with more each day. She sparked the much-needed change in Bobby Downey.

"I want to change for her," Bobby told Ben one day in his office. He was sincere about that statement. April was the best thing to have come out of Freddy's death and his divorce and Bobby knew it.

Bobby still saw Freddy from time to time. Sometimes it was in the house, in his bedroom, in the kitchen, or in the living room conducting himself just like he did when he was alive and being a kid. Sometimes he and Freddy would interact with each other. He stopped being scared by his son some time ago and looked forward to seeing him whenever his mind decided it was to be so or if Freddy indeed was a ghost that was haunting him. Bobby never knew exactly what Freddy was.

It didn't matter to him if he was a hallucination or a ghost. Seeing Freddy was usually good. He had figured out that seeing Freddy was nothing to be afraid of; except for the dream of that day he died. That's what Bobby avoided at all costs. That's why Bobby took the pills to stay awake and keep his mind going. That's why he drank so much hoping to drink away the memory. There was no erasing that memory. It was etched on his mind forever.

Other good notes in Bobby's life were that he and April were still close, still getting to know one another, still in love. Bobby was slowly mending from the hurt and pain from when Dana walked out on him and left him to deal with the aftermath of their son. The days and nights without his wife still caught up to him from time to time but the hurt was waning. April was a pleasant balm for the burn on his heart when it came to what Dana had done to him.

April, never telling this to Bobby, had never seen a man so shattered in all of her life and often times wondered if he was ever going to get to a place where he could feel good again. She knew that he had made some improvements, could see it in his slow weight gain and could see it in his eyes. Those eyes still had thorns of pain that would perhaps never go away. April accepted that fact. She loved whatever remained of Bobby Downey.

2

Chris Schilling eventually moved into Steve Medlen's boyhood home in mid-February. It was the home where Steve stayed until he moved out for college and later visited with his own family when he was older. A dark cloud hovered over the home now as a new set of Medlens along with an outsider, Chris, occupied it. Ben watched as Chris turned his mother into something else, something drastically different, that was not anything like the woman he had known all his formative years. She was degenerating into a foul-mouthed, cigarette-smoking, alcohol-drinking, horrible-attitude woman that stopped caring for anyone but herself and her new boyfriend. The drastic transformation was over a short time and the speed at which the transformation happened was frightening. Ben compared his mother's complete and utter change to that of an insect's life cycle.

First was the egg. That was when she had met Chris when he came in with a prescription for painkillers in the pharmacy where she worked. The two were attracted to each other instantly for whatever reason. Ben never could see it because Chris looked like the poster child for white trash. The weeks after that initial contact, Chris would find any reason that he could to come in there to see her. It would be a cute story had it not been for Chris Schilling. He was a dick, a pill-popping son of a bitch who now trimmed trees for a living; another job added to the ten he already had in the last three years. There was just something about him that Bailey liked. Maybe it was the way he showed the older woman in her forties attention. He was younger by ten years and that made Bailey secretively feel better about herself. From that, her attraction only grew stronger because, for the first time since Steve, she felt wanted again.

The next stage in Bailey Medlen's drastic metamorphosis was the larva stage. Bailey and Chris' relationship began and the two of them talked and saw each other all the time as they got to know one another. She had hatched from the egg and was a larva at that point. She was changing slowly to what she was going to become, not what she used to be when Steve Medlen had married her a long time ago. Bailey's new identity was associated with her new younger man; a man that would go on to totally corrupt her and her value systems that she once held so dear.

Then came the pupa stage. The radical changes that Bailey had undergone began to display in such a way that it literally scared Ben to death. It was not until he heard her cuss him and smoke that he knew that her change, her metamorphosis, was complete. To further her change, to put more distance between the old Bailey Medlen to the new Bailey Medlen, she had gotten a tattoo on her arm. It was something of a heart with a twisted rose around it. It looked to Ben as something a woman of white trash stature would bear; probably Chris' idea because he was covered in them looking as if they were done in someone's kitchen on a drunken Friday night. Ben guessed that they were.

The adult stage in the metamorphosis was where his mother was at currently. She was something that Ben did not like, not one bit. She had mirrored her new boyfriend's mannerisms and attitudes toward life in general. They both cussed like sailors, smoked like chimneys, and were complete slobs around the house. The house used to be neat, clean, and organized, but since Chris moved in the house it was like a pig sty: dishes were piled up in the sink in the kitchen; the garbage can was overflowing, and dirty clothes were everywhere. Food from days gone by was left to harden and the smells from all that besieged the entire home downstairs and up. This was not his mother, not the Bailey Medlen he knew anyway, back in the days of old.

She was one of the cleanest people that he had ever known in his life; organized, too. She was the type of person that always said everything has a place and a place for everything. Not now; not since Chris Schilling moved in. All that went by the wayside. Her changes had gotten so bad that when Chris would decide that he was going to call out of work, Bailey would call out, too, and say that she had a migraine. The two of them would sleep past noon and then drink the rest of their "off day" from work.

Ben stayed in one of two places: at Abby's house where he stayed as long as he possibly could before her parents said it was time to go. As much as they liked Ben, they didn't want the notion that he could sleep over at their house any old time he liked. Harry Maddux was a traditional man, a good soul, but once he was angry you had better stay out of his way. Once the man's temper was lit, there was no stopping him. Ben always minded his P's and Q's around Harry. They liked each other but if something ever happened to Abby while she was with Ben, Ben knew that Harry would probably kill him. Abby was the apple of that man's eye.

Ben knew that Abby was concerned about his home which was the polar opposite of hers. She hated that Ben had to deal with the issues that he had at home and wished that there was a safe place where he could go.

"What about your Aunt Stacy?" Abby asked.

Ben shook his head as they sat on the front porch swing at her house that cold February night. "I thought about it. But she's got her own problems with her cancer now. She doesn't need my bullshit."

"I wish there was something that we could do. I don't like you living there with what's going on."

"I know... just ain't many options I have: my bedroom and hope for the best or down at the park sleeping like a hobo." Abby took his hand and held onto it firmly. "Other than that…just work with what I got."

It was in the middle of February on an idle Wednesday night when Ben came down the stairs to get some cookies out of the cabinet. Bailey, since Chris had moved in, had stopped buying groceries. She was just picking up what she and her new man liked and had forgotten all about her son. That was fine with him. He had been foraging in the kitchen and would take some of what they had. Most of it was junk food, which was rightly fine with Ben. He lived on that stuff anyways. If he wanted a really good dinner, Jessica Maddux always cooked a nice supper and he was always invited to eat there; which he did nearly every day of the week.

Ben was in the kitchen that night opening the cabinets in the dark, prowling around quietly to find something to feed his growling stomach. Chris' voice came from behind and caused him to jump with fright. Chris' voice was that of a backwoods redneck, bar-hopping country boy. And that country boy had a country boy job; cutting trees, which he only worked when the weather was good or when he felt like it which was mostly never. In other words, he was a bum, a loafer. Ben hated that voice; hated hearing it.

 "I'm just looking for something to eat," Ben said, hoping that the new man in the house would leave him be.

"Food ain't fucking free you know. We pay a lot for that shit. Maybe you need to start chipping in," he said there in the darkness, leaning up against the archway between the kitchen and the dining room.

Ben heard the switch of a lighter and turned to see Chris light his cigarette in the darkness. A red-orange glow pinpointed where the lanky flannel-wearing man was.

"Yeah well, I don't work so there's that," Ben said, trying not to sound nervous although his insides were quivering. For some reason, he was intimidated by this man, who was not bigger than him at all. At best they were the same size. However, Chris had the look of a person that liked to fight and got off on it.

Chris blew smoke into the air, "When I was your age I was out cutting grass, bushes, painting houses for cash. The old man made sure of that… made sure that I wasn't prowling around in the cabinets at night for shit that ain't his."

"Well, certainly helped you in your career as a…what is it?" Ben snapped his fingers trying to be as sarcastic as he could be, trying to be Bobby Downey. "Tree trimmer…that's it."

"Boy you got some balls on you, you know that?" Ben stood across the kitchen and looked at Chris through the darkness. He could see him a little, the outline of his frame and the cigarette glow.

"You better get to knowing the program around here. I'm in charge now. And I ain't about to take your mouth. This is your free warning. Next time you say something out of line, you're going to catch an ass whopping. And I ain't your fucking daddy. I'll do it and not think twice about it."

That was it. Ben was filled with blind rage and before his mind could shut down the rest of his body, Ben ran across the kitchen and tried to grab the son of a bitch that had just spoken of his dad. He was going to beat that prick within an inch of his life. Chris, who liked to fight whether he won or not, was too quick for the kid. He grabbed Ben in mid-stride and clutched him by the throat and slammed into the wall, hand squeezing his windpipe, cigarette pinched between his lips. It all happened so fast that Ben didn't realize what had happened.

Ben and Chris' noses touched and he could smell the stench of tobacco and whiskey that he and Bailey had been drinking that night.

"This is free, Boy. Like I said, next time it's an ass whopping. You got me?" Ben had his hands on Chris' hand that was around his throat and tried to pry it loose. It was no use.

Chris did not look strong, but he was stout; a lot more so than he thought when he rushed him. Ben did not want to back down, he did not want to show this prick that he had gotten the upper hand on him, but there was nothing he could do. He was too scared of him to be honest. And he hated himself for that; hated himself a lot. And since he showed Chris that he could not stand toe to toe with him, that would give the man a license to intimidate him even more. Ben was now powerless beyond that dark kitchen.

Chris finally let go of Ben and backed away from him, "Now get to bed and I don't want to see you down here prowling in this kitchen unless you're fucking buying stuff put in here." Ben stood there rubbing his throat, tears of hurt and rage welling up in his eyes.

He was trembling. The two of them stood in the darkness of the kitchen and looked at each other. There was an eerie silence as Ben could only see the outline of Chris's frame and that damn cigarette between his lips.

"Now go on!" Chris yelled and without even thinking of it, Ben turned tail and ran away and up the stairs and into his bedroom where he broke behind the door and locked it. Downstairs in the kitchen, Chris blew smoke and grinned, on the verge of laughing. "Pussy." Chris said in the darkness.

4

Ben sat in Bobby's office in silence. Bobby could see what he thought was faint bruising around Ben's neck but was going to wait him out and see if he wanted to talk about where that came from. Bobby didn't think it was from a fight at school because he would have heard about it of course. Bobby wondered from behind his desk if he and that man that was living at his house had mixed it up.

Before Ben came into his office, another student, a senior, Ellen Thomas, was sitting on Ben's chair. They were discussing colleges and her goals as a future lawyer. Bobby had only met with Ellen a few times during her career there at Central High as she was not one of his red file folder kids. She was really smart, an A-B student, active in a lot of clubs and man did she like to talk. Usually about nothing really, she just popped in to say hi to Bobby in between classes, and then once she got to talking about her future, grades, her boyfriend, and the prom she did not stop until Bobby found a pause and told her that he needed to make a call. He even went as far as picking up the phone receiver. That did the trick.

Afterward, just from listening to her, Bobby was exhausted and didn't feel much like talking. When Ben showed up, Bobby was all talked out, which he did not think was even possible. Some people can zap your energy by just talking too much. Ellen Thomas was one of them.

"So what's the deal with the bruising on your neck there? Some auto erotic asphyxiation going on?" Bobby asked, tired of waiting for Ben to address it.

Ben looked at him like a deer caught in the lights of an oncoming truck on the dark highway.

"It's nothing."

Bobby nodded his head and smiled, "Yeah, I don't believe that. Was this a suicide attempt?" Bobby was serious about that question.

Ben looked at him gravely and then scoffed, "No."

"Then what is it?"

Ben and Bobby locked eyes. Bobby saw what he thought were tears forming in them. Ben considered replying. Bobby could tell that the kid was trying to muster the courage to do it, to say whatever it was he had to say. Ben managed to open his mouth like a trout out of the water and then thought better of it and closed it.

"Somebody do that to you?" Bobby asked, now piercing Ben with his stare.

Ben looked around the office and tried to wrangle his emotions that were running all over the place. He didn't want to cry there in front of Bobby, but the more he tried to maintain his composure, the more he felt his grip loosen. He thought about getting up and walking out of the office but didn't. He knew that Bobby was on his side, the only adult that was. And he knew that he could tell him anything. So why was this so hard? Why was telling Bobby about Chris putting his hands on him and scaring him so badly that he cried himself to sleep in his bedroom so hard? Ben readied himself and was going to tell Bobby.

Then Bobby assumed with a question, "It was this Chris guy, wasn't it?"

Ben thought that for the first time that he had known him that Bobby sounded like a father. It was the way his voice lowered, the way it expressed concern. Ben only nodded and looked off to the side. Tears were there, but they were in a holding pattern in his eyes. Bobby leaned back in his chair and ran his fingers through his hair and exhaled loudly in disgust.

"What happened?" Ben looked back to Bobby.

It was then the tears came and he told him the story. By the time he was done telling it, Bobby was ready to punch something, he wore that emotion on his face. It was an intensity that Ben had never seen before in Bobby. Bobby was so angry that when his heart beat, his eyes jumped.

"You tell your mother?" Bobby asked.

"It wouldn't have mattered. Mom's changed so much that she would have told me that I was making it up or that I deserved it. Either way." Ben had dried his eyes on his shirt and cleared his throat. It felt good to cry, just to let it all out like he had up in his dad's old bedroom.

"This hasn't happened before has it?" Bobby asked.

Ben shook his head, "No. But now he knows I'm afraid of him. And he'll do it again. Maybe something worse next time." Ben spoke lowly, soberly, like an inmate on death row knowing that his execution was coming up sometime soon.

The two sat there in silence again. Bobby was soaking in what Ben had revealed to him and Ben was thinking about what the next time was going to entail when he and Chris would cross paths again; which was sure to happen. Chris liked to fight. Win or lose, he liked to fight.

Bobby didn't know exactly what to do in this situation. He wanted to find this Chris guy and beat the holy hell out of him. He wanted to beat this guy down so much that by the time it was over he couldn't lift his arms to throw any more punches. Bobby was not a fighter by no means, but when it came to things like what Ben, a kid, had told him, then he could manage.

"You know it's not safe there, right?" Bobby said, stating the obvious.

Ben laughed to himself, "Yeah, no kidding."
Bobby knew that the boy was hurt and scared. He'd lost his dad and now even though his mother was not dead, she was gone, too. Ben was virtually on his own. "What do you think is your next step here?"

Ben sat still and considered Bobby's question. He'd given that plenty of thought. "I don't know. Not much I can do right now. I tell you what I'd like to do…move away from there. I just can't stay in that house anymore."

Again the two of them sat there in silence and pondered what had just been spoken in that office. Ben looked at his wristwatch and noticed that the meeting was getting close to concluding. "So…enough about me. What's going on with you?"

Bobby looked at Ben incredulously, "Me? You got a crisis going on here…"

"I want to talk about something else before I go. What about you?"

Bobby looked at Ben, "I'm drawing back on my pill addiction. Drinking has cut down considerably. But I'm getting better. Getting more of a handle on things I guess…sleeping more."

"You can do it."

Bobby smiled politely, "I hope so."

"How're things with April…ur, Ms. Murry," Ben corrected himself.

"Things are good, man. Things are good. She's the best…got to be because I'm a handful."

"You guys make a good couple. Everyone in school thinks so. You think there's a future there with her?"

"I'm beginning to think so, yeah." Bobby smiled, thinking to himself about what life would be like married to a woman like April. He and Dana's marriage had become the victim of Freddy's death and that's why it ended. But Bobby and April's future, as far as he knew, did not have any monsters hiding in the closet just waiting to spring out at the last minute. There was not a dead child that they were dealing with separately. There was not a red Firebird that ruined everything; no Jim Thompson.

The only thing that Bobby could think of that could ruin his and April's future together was Bobby himself. He carried too much baggage and wondered at times when he and April were alone if that was going to be too much for her to bear. But April Murray had proven to be much stronger than she appeared to be. Thank God for that, Bobby often thought.

"That would be good. You deserve to be happy, you know?"

"Sometimes I don't think so."

"Why?" Ben quizzed.

"Because I have a hard time being happy when Freddy can't be… anything," It was Bobby now that was on the verge of tears. Since he stopped popping Ritalin like crazy and went with the prescribed amount, the once-daily pill, his emotions had gotten away from him quicker. Not rage or violence, but tears of painful memories from a time not too long ago. Bobby started nervously biting at his fingernails.

"I haven't been able to really move on since that day. Sometimes I do seem like I've moved away from it a little, just because time demands it. But it's like sometimes I'm stuck outside my house watching that red Firebird fly down the street and kill my son. I see it every time I look out my windows at home, or when I walk out to my driveway. My eyes always go to that part of the street. I know that the best thing to do is to move away like Dana eventually did, but moving would be like me leaving him behind. I'm not there yet. I don't know if I ever will be."

Bobby sat there and just looked down at his desk replaying what he just said in his mind. It was the truth. Ben knew exactly what Bobby was saying; what he meant, and how he felt.

"I know. But believe me, leaving doesn't help things. I'm still locked in my old house back in South Carolina. Hundreds of miles away and I'm still there most times. Mom forced a move and for what? What did it really accomplish?"

The bell rang and both guys in the office jumped at the sound as they did often during these meetings. Ben got up from the chair and looked at Bobby who sat looking as if he was in some sort of reflective form of thought. He looked far away in his eyes. And maybe he was. Maybe he was back to that day when his life fell apart. To Ben Medlen, Bobby looked haunted. Ben stood there and looked at Bobby and wondered if being an adult is that hard then why in the hell do I want to grow up?

"I'll see you later," Ben said. Bobby nodded to him and tried to smile.

What was wrong with Bobby at that moment was that the vision of Freddy disappearing underneath that red Firebird flashed into his mind. That was happening more so since he had dialed down his pill intake. His mind was slowing down more. And when it slowed, thoughts of Freddy came.

Chapter 20

1

March

March came in like a lion for Bobby. The month had promise and there were some real and true positives breaking Bobby Downey's way. April was one of those positives in his life; another positive was that he had stopped drinking entirely. His gradual withdrawal method had appeared to work as it concerned the bottle of wild Turkey that had become a staple within the cabinets of his kitchen. Now, Bobby was happy that he was clean from the clutches of the devil's drink.

With the pills, he was taking the proper amount to calm his issues with ADHD. Thoughts of his son came into his mind randomly now. The dreams of that day Freddy was run over out in their street came back into his dreamscapes slowly causing Bobby to wake with fright, pouring sweat, and disorientation.

Each time he dreamed of that day, the dreams felt more and more real. He thought about upping his pill intake again to keep him awake only snatching a couple of hours here and there to suppress the dreams like before, but Bobby had decided that it was best to work them out himself. The question was: when would they stop? Would they ever?

The anniversary of Freddy's death was in March and Bobby knew all too well that the day was coming. He feared it when he saw it on the calendar in his office. The date needn't be circled because it was a date that would forever be burned into his mind. It was a terrible memory that would never leave Bobby and he knew that. It might slack, and it might subside at times, but it was always there; taking residence in one of the many rooms in his mind where he kept things. In the room where Freddy's death lived, Bobby used pills and booze to keep it locked. That door, a locked door, never stayed locked really. Now that the booze and pills were of no concern for Bobby, the locked room where Freddy stayed always opened whenever it wanted, which was usually bedtime when Bobby was at his most relaxed.

With the day approaching the year anniversary of Freddy's death, Bobby did whatever he could to not think about it. It had been a year since that terrible day and with each day that it got closer to the date on the calendar, the more and more he wanted to go by the liquor store and buy a bottle of whiskey and drink to forget. Bobby nearly capitulated to the siren call of the bottle as that day got closer. He found himself sitting in his car outside Sid's Liquors. He intended to walk in there and buy a bottle of his favorite whiskey and take it home and drink it all. He opened the car door and walked across the parking lot and reached for the door. He stopped coldly.

He knew that this was a do-or-die moment. If he opened that glass door he would destroy all the good work he had done. But there was Freddy's death, the date on the calendar, that forced him there. Bobby opened the glass door and was about to go inside. Suddenly, he stopped and without thought, he let go of the door. He walked away back to his car. He drove out of the parking lot and never returned. Instead of drinking away the night, trying to forget what happened a year ago out on Maple Lane when a red Firebird came screaming down the street, Bobby sat in his recliner, the lights low, listening to some 80's new wave music on his stereo, looking at old scrapbooks of his family: Dana and Freddy; the good times as he remembered them.

It had been a very long time since he had whipped out the oversized scrapbooks; pictures of points in time that were frozen forever; pictures that showed how good things once were; pictures that showed him and Dana hugging and smiling; pictures of Freddy as a newborn at the hospital; pictures of Freddy's first birthday, and all the birthdays after that; all the Christmas Days and Halloweens; the first days of school; the little league baseball games; everything. The pictures made Bobby cry and laugh at the same time. Most of the pictures that were inside those scrapbooks he had plum forgotten about. Others he recalled very well as if they happened yesterday.

The night had turned into the next day. Bobby had spent the entire night looking at the pictures in all those books. He only paused to answer the telephone when April called. Instead of drinking away his son and his ex-wife, Bobby chose a different way; he chose to travel down memory lane and recount the happy times in those books. After he closed the final book that ultimately led to the final snapshots of them as a whole family, Bobby had a sappy notion to reach out to Dana and thank her for not taking the pictures with her when she left. Then he realized he didn't have her number. Hell, to come to think of it, he didn't even know where she lived anymore. Why didn't she want these, Bobby wondered.

When the day came that marked a year gone by since Freddy's death, Bobby held it together the best he could. That day hurt, much like the lucid dreams he had when he slept, of seeing that day transpire over and over. His mind was in a time loop. The only thing Bobby knew was that it was just going to have to cycle itself out. Eventually, it will get easier, Bobby told himself. That Sunday, a year after Freddy died, Bobby thought about going to visit the grave of his son.

He had not been there since the burial. Going there scared Bobby. Seeing the tombstone in his mind's eye marking his son's name made tears form in his eyes and he got all emotional. He got into the car and pulled out of the driveway heading to Freddy's final resting place. Bobby got as far as Keith Street heading for the cemetery before he turned around and headed back home. "I can't do this," Bobby said to no one. "I'll do it later…it's too soon."

2

March had also come in like a lion for Ben. He tiptoed through the house since his and Chris' altercation in the kitchen that night. He tried to stay off the man's radar and had done a pretty good job at doing that. There were times, however, that Chris would catch him alone and badger him on those days when he did not go to work and Ben was home after school. He tried to make it a point not to even come home until he knew his mom was home but in reality what kind of protection did that even offer? None.

Mostly, when Ben came home from school he would check to see if Chris' beat-up old Ford pickup truck was parked in the driveway. It usually was because that guy hardly went to work since moving in. On those days when Chris was home, Ben would just walk to Abby's house or stay down at the park. He hated what his life had turned into.

Several days into March, Ben had walked home from Abby's house only to find that Chris and his mother were smoking pot and drinking liquor in the living room. When he opened the door, he nearly got a contact high from the weed smoke. Chris had sunk Bailey even lower. She was now smoking weed. As they laughed at Ben, he walked through the foggy living room and up the stairs to his bedroom. The smoke had stuck to his clothes and he could smell the house all the way up to his sanctuary. He sat down on his bed and cried. Everything was spinning out of control and there was nothing that he could do about it but wait until he graduated high school the next May and move away, back to South Carolina. The question was: could he make it that long?

3

Bobby and April were at her house, on a Tuesday evening this was, when April decided that she was going to ask a question that she told herself that she was not going to bring up; at least not anytime soon. But there she was about to do it. Sitting there snuggled up on the couch watching a documentary on National Geographic on space exploration, April said, "Can I ask you something?"

"Sure. Fire away," Bobby replied, holding April with his right arm as she lay against him on the couch.

"Do you not want me to ever come to your house? I mean I didn't know if it was because that was yours and Dana's place or…what?" April asked. And now that she said it out loud, what she had wanted to ask for weeks and months, it sounded stupid. She wished that she could take it back but it was already out.

Bobby sat for a moment and thought before he replied. He took his arm away from April and she rose up and the two faced each other after Bobby repositioned himself on the couch. "It's complicated, I guess."

"How so? Talk to me," April told him.

Bobby looked at her and considered for a few seconds about getting into the subject of home. It was a subject he did not reveal much to April. It was just a hard subject for people to relate to. If they were planning on having a future together, which Bobby wanted and he knew April wanted as well, he was going to have to start pulling the curtain back some and allow her to take a look at the man.

"I can barely be there myself most times," Bobby began. "It's not a happy place, not like a home is supposed to be. Not like here. You know, your place here is relaxing. It's not filled with bad memories like mine. But I can't just up and leave like Dana did. I wish that I could sometimes. I think that would help, but I just…can't. I wish sometimes that I was as strong as

Dana. She knew…she knew what staying in that house would eventually do to her. Hell, maybe I knew…I think I might have mismanaged the entire situation.”

“I thought it might be me or something,” April said.

Bobby shook his head, “It’s not. I promise you that. See,” Bobby got up off the couch and ran his fingers through his hair, a nervous thing he did, and began to pace about the living room. He was about to expose himself, and all his problems. If they were going to have a future together, one that he very much wanted, he had to be completely open and honest with her. They had talked a lot since they met and fell in love, but he had never waded too deeply into the honesty pool with her.

He was guarded and April knew that. Bobby had walls built up and April had been trying to scale those walls for a long time. Bobby could tell that she was getting tired of never making it over. It was time for Bobby to lower them, lower the walls so April could see what was on the other side. All there was on the other side was a man that was barely hanging on mentally; a broken man.

“I don’t even know where to start with this.”

“Just start at the beginning,” April helped.

Bobby stood next to the bay living room window that looked out into the neighborhood as darkness covered the place. He was trying to find a starting point. Maybe the beginning like April said.

“I’ve told you about Freddy getting killed that day out in the street. But what I didn’t tell you was that I saw the car fly down the road and then I heard the screaming and the crash.”

April felt like she had been punched in the stomach by this revelation. She was speechless.

“Me and Dana had just finished having an afternoon sex romp up in our bedroom since Freddy was out of the house playing Wiffle ball out in the street; nothing unusual about that because that’s what all the neighborhood kids did. They don’t anymore. Not after what happened.

"I had gone downstairs and went out the back door to finish mowing the lawn. I took the mower to the front because the back was finished. I heard this car coming down the street. It was loud and fast. It blew by me so fast and it was heading toward the kids. It was a red Pontiac Firebird.

"I was frozen there in my front yard. I saw it heading to where the kids were playing because I could hear them yelling. I started to run over to the edge of the front yard where the sidewalk was. Freddy was standing there behind their version of second base. The others saw the car coming and screamed and darted away. But Freddy's back was turned to the car. I don't know if he didn't hear it or what, but by the time he turned around he was hit. He was underneath the wheels.

"I screamed and ran over to where Freddy was and by that time the car had crashed into a tree. I was too late to do anything."

April sat there with tears in her eyes. She was sorry that she had asked about his house now. This was more than she wanted to know. But it was about to get much worse. She was about to find out how messed up Bobby Downey, her boyfriend, was.

Bobby leaned up against the wall, hands in his jeans pockets, head looking down at the living room floor. "After that nothing was the same. Nothing…food tasted different… smells were different. I couldn't even laugh anymore because I felt that was a betrayal to Freddy somehow. Mine and Dana's marriage fell apart shortly after; wasn't anybody's fault. It just…happened, I guess.

"She got help processing Freddy. I didn't; thought that I could handle it on my own. She wasn't by no means over her son, I mean what mother could be? But she was moving on a bit. Better than I was for sure and I resented that, I guess. I resented it to the point that I felt that she was a traitor to our son. I understand why she did what she did now. Took me a while, you know, to figure it out. But I got it.

"Eventually, she couldn't stay in the house. There were just too many memories, you know? She wanted to leave. Move as far away as possible. And I don't blame her now. Back then I did. But I couldn't do it. I mean, that's where we all were, back when we were a family. She just told me that it was killing her seeing the rooms where Freddy used to walk in or play. She couldn't look out the windows into the backyard where he used to play and camp out with his friends. Dana hadn't been inside Freddy's bedroom since he died. She could never bring herself to go in there.

"But I think the kicker was that every time she walked out of our house, she automatically looked down the street where he was killed. It was a constant reminder to her…it is to me, too. She wanted me to come with her and I refused. I saw her moving away from our house as an act of treason. And I wasn't going to be with someone that could just walk away from what we had. I mean, Freddy's memory was alive there. Still is. And she was willing to just leave? I couldn't do it. It felt like I was turning my back on him somehow. Sounds crazy now, but back then that's how I felt.

"So, Dana left for good. I stayed behind to deal with the aftermath. I figured that I was the watchman at the lighthouse, you know? Me and Dana eventually get divorced. Not that I wanted to. But we were just too far apart on our differences. She abandoned the marriage…me… and our son's memory. I couldn't forgive that back then…but now? I have to. It wasn't her fault.

"I started having nightmares about Freddy and about that day shortly after we buried him. I started being afraid of sleep. So, I started taking methylphenidate…Ritalin to most people, to keep me up, to keep me going, keep me focused. But not just one or two pills like the doc prescribed. I was taking four to five a day harder days, six. Rare occasions seven or eight. I had multiple doctors and pharmacies feeding my addiction. It kept me from sleeping, kept me from focusing on him for the most part. But when I would feel myself crashing down after the pills wore off, those thoughts of my son and Dana came seeping in and I'd take more pills and start drinking. I was looking for anything to just take the memories away because they hurt so much. There are times that I just wanted to end it all because I never thought there was a way out, especially after Dana walked out. When she left, that took the last bit of hope…that I would be okay.

"I've been seeing and hearing Freddy in the house and outside. I don't know if he's a ghost or if it was the hallucinations from the drugs or my sleep problems. Maybe it was a mixture of everything. Since I've drawn things back considerably, I see and hear less of Freddy. But I still dream of being out there in the yard that day when he was killed down the street. "Eventually, Dana found out what I had been doing with the pills. She knew that I was hitting the bottle hard but the pills being mixed in were too much. Dana confronted me on it. I think that helped push her away, too. It was too much for her to bear. She was watching me kill myself slowly and I was. Nothing I could do at the time…I ended up pushing her away by not being available to her.

"I've never invited you to my house because it's a true house of horrors there. It's where all the pain is. And it's nice to leave it sometimes. I understand now why Dana left. Back then… I didn't. But nowadays…I do."

April sat there crying for Bobby, crying for his pain because she felt it radiating off him. She was sorry that she asked, very sorry. But at least the cat was out of the bag. No more secrets. Well, Bobby did have one he was putting off telling.

Bobby stood there looking at a speechless April Murray sitting on the couch. She was in deep thought by Bobby's tale of woe. She would look up at him a few times and try to open her mouth to say something but the words would not come out. They wouldn't come out because there were no words to articulate how sorry she was for him having to go through all of that. Finally, she managed, "You still drinking and doing the pills?"

Bobby, still leaning up on the far wall of the living room taking in the moment, shook his head and replied, "No. I um…stopped drinking finally. Cut my Ritalin consumption down to just one pill a day. So, I'm only taking the prescribed amount. Nothing more. I sleep more but I also have terrible nightmares. I'm just learning to deal with them as they come these days. There're days I want a drink, something to take the edge off…but I don't do it."

"I'm so sorry that I brought all this stuff up," April spoke, feeling bad that she opened a wound that he was trying to heal.

"It's okay…really. It was the elephant in the room…couldn't be avoided for much longer."

After Bobby and April sat and stood there for a long time in silence, both digesting the big reveal, April finally asked another question, "Anything else you want to talk about?"

Bobby stood, back against the wall, and dropped his head scanning his mind. There was, something else he had not told April. "Matter of fact there is," he began. "I'm out of a job after May."

April sat there and looked as if she was hit by a truck. Bobby could see the confusion on her face, "What?"

"Yeah, Glick is doing this budget cut thing where he's proposing to cut all the guidance counselors from the district. His plan is going to save like a million dollars a year or some such thing along with pushing out the teachers that are close to retirement; wants to consolidate classrooms making them bigger."

"What? He's just a principal he can't do that."

"You're right. But he did come from Nashville and he's got friends and high places and as well as Franklin's ear who has friends. From what I was told, the two of them are teaming up to get this done. Once it's finished and the vote is taken, which it will pass, all kinds of money will be saved and it will be a road map for the rest of the districts to save money. Glick is only at our school to get experience as an administrator and then he's gone. He ain't long-term. Franklin is looking to get a job with the state educational department and I think Glick wants his job or something like that. I don't know the actual mechanics of it. They're taking care of each other on this one because Glick has the strings to get Franklin to Nashville and Franklin can move Glick as the new super. That's the new rumor I heard last week."

"So are the displaced guidance counselors going to get those teachers they're planning on pushing out positions?" April quizzed.

Bobby shook his head, "Nope. Four teachers retiring at the end of the school year, and several others are close and they're planning on doing something to get them gone somehow. Once we're gone and the teachers, they plan on condensing those teacher's classes into existing ones, making class sizes much bigger."

"Why pay two teachers when you can pay one and make the class bigger?" April said absently, not to Bobby but more to herself.

"And Glick doesn't like me anyways. So, I'm out after May if the vote goes to budget cuts. But I'm sure that it will."

"So what are you going to do?" April asked.
"I don't know."

4

Ben was up in his bedroom doing his homework on the night when he and Chris came to blows in the house where his father grew up. Up to that point, things in the house were tense, only when Chris was there which was all the time since he moved in and quit his job as a tree trimmer. His mother was keeping him up and that was Chris' plan to begin with, Ben thought. He had corrupted his mother by taking her from this beautifully sweet and caring woman to a white trash county doppelganger. Ben hated Chris for that; hated him immensely.

If he could have, Ben would have taken a kitchen knife and slashed Chris' throat. He thought about that several times and told Abby about his desires. She didn't recoil at what Ben had expressed to her. She had seen the stress her boyfriend was under, and had seen the changes that Bailey Medlen had undergone in the short time she had known her. Abby knew of the verbal and physical abuse that Ben was going through. The two of them shared many tears out on her back porch.

On the night of the big brawl, Bailey was at work at the pharmacy. Chris was down in the living room watching boxing and drinking. When Ben had come home from Abby's through the front door, he noticed that his future stepfather sitting sprawled out on the couch watching TV with his legs propped up on the coffee table. By the looks of it, he'd already gone through a twelve-pack, and the empty cans were all over the place.

"In comes the pussy, everyone! Watch him come home from school!" Chris mocked as Ben walked through the living room not looking at him, just trying to get by him. "Did you hear me?!" Chris' voice boomed loudly from the couch.

It caused Ben to jump with fright. Chris tried to get up from the couch and get into the boy's face but he fell on the floor laughing. He was too drunk to even stand. Ben shook his head and walked up the stairs. This scene had been commonplace at the Medlen home these days. Apparently, his mother approved and did so by partaking in his debauchery with him.

Ben was up in his bedroom and had finished the last of his homework.

He was listening to music and thinking about the state of his current life when his stomach growled so much that he had to finally submit and get something to eat. He had put off going down into the kitchen because Chris was still drinking and he could hear him down there yelling at the TV. The one thing about Chris that Ben had figured out through many run-ins with him was that when he was drinking you didn't even want to be in the same house.

Chris had started something new in the house: he had started putting his hands on Bailey on those drunken nights. Lately, Ben had seen his mother with bruises and traces of blood under her nose. Sometimes he could hear his mother cry downstairs from Chris' rampages where he would afterward leave the house after breaking glass and busting lamps. A few times he had even put his fist through some walls. The holes were still there.

His leaving was never for good. Chris would always come home and apologize and Bailey would take him back. He promised to do better. He never did and never planned to. Ben knew that to be true. People like Chris only knew one thing: violence. And if Ben could somehow vanquish his fright of Chris, he would show him what violence was all about. He would beat that country-fried prick for all the times he cussed him; for turning his mother into something she was not. He would beat Chris for every bad thing he'd ever done in his wretched existence. Those thoughts were waking dreams he had from time to time and Ben knew that one day things would come to a head and it would be him vs Chris.

5

Ben came down on that night from the stairs and when he stepped off the last rung, Chris started running his mouth again; calling him his go-to word, pussy. Ben had heard that so much from him that he just ignored it. And then Ben could hear the clanging of empty beer cans as Chris managed to get to his feet without falling this time. Ben was at the fridge prowling for something to eat that would quiet the roaring in his stomach. Nothing. His mom had virtually nothing in terms of groceries. Ben began to open the cabinets and found a box of Cheese Nips. They were nearly empty and what was inside was stale. Someone had left the tabs open.

"What the fuck did I tell you about food in here boy?" Chris' voice boomed as he managed to walk into the kitchen. He leaned up against the archway like he did the first night he put his hands on Ben.

"Yeah, I heard you the first time," Ben replied feeling a little bit more courageous than before. He was growing more confident. Ben was still scared of the man a little, but not as much these days. Maybe it was because Ben was getting fed up with his mouth and him moving in and taking over. Ben was looking for a fight that night to be honest. He wanted to feel him out. He wanted to know that if those two started to tangle could he get in some good licks? Ben felt as if he could. He was not a fighter by no means, but Ben was tired of this prick; tired of it all.

Chris was having a hard time keeping his balance, even leaned up on the inside of the archway that was keeping him upright. "And?"

Ben turned around and was holding the box of Cheese Nip with his hand inside. "And nothing? You're not my boss…it's not your house."

Chris smiled, his eyes were bloodshot and glassy from all the drinking. He was looking for a fight, too, because that's what people like Chris Schilling did; look for fights.

"Been fucking that girlfriend of yours?" Now that was drawing the ire of Ben. He could feel his blood start to pump faster, his adrenaline coursing through his body leaving him to shake some. "Nah, probably not. Maybe I need to. You should bring her over one night and let her see what a man can do with it." Without even knowing it, Ben dropped the box of crackers and rushed across the kitchen, pouncing on Chris. He knocked the lanky framed drunk down and got on top of him. Ben started punching him. He got in some really good blows until Chris was able to flip him over on his back and it was Chris who was now on top.

Chris wadded his hand up in the collar of Ben's tee shirt and with his other hand, he started punching the kid in the face. The sound of his fist and Ben's face made a terrible dull thumping sound. Chris had rattled off five powerful punches before Ben was able to take his thumbs and push them into Chris' eyes. That did the trick. Chris flew backward and a bloodied and dizzy Ben scrambled to his feet and grabbed a rolling pin off the kitchen table and was ready to swing when Bailey came into the house through the front door.

She walked inside the dark living room that was only lit by the white screen of the TV, boxing was still playing. She walked through the sea of empty beer cans toward the kitchen. When she got to the kitchen where she saw Chris, who had gotten to his feet, and her son standing there holding a rolling pin, his face bleeding. "What's going on here?!"

"This punk ass bitch came after me. Little shit!" Chris said, using a nearby kitchen chair for stability. He was swimming in his head so much that he nearly fell.

"Ben?!" Bailey shouted looking at her son.

"What?! He started running his mouth!"

"I don't care! You're out of control!" Bailey shouted again.

"Me?! What about him?!"

"All you've done since I've got with him is be against us! The whole time! This is too much! You had better start showing him some respect because eventually, he's going to be your stepfather!"

Ben stood there and lowered the rolling pin. No matter how hard Chris had hit him that night, nothing hit him more than what his mom had just said. He had known that was where their relationship was trending towards, but it was a different thing hearing confirmation. That was an entirely different thing indeed.

"He ain't no dad of mine and never will be. I had one dad," Ben said lowly with conviction.

"Who couldn't even fuck your mom right. Ain't that right, babe? Go on, tell him how much more of a man I am than that dead fucking husband of yours." Ben tightened his grip on the rolling pin and lunged at Chris, hitting him in the jaw with it. Chris went sprawling onto the floor knocked out cold. Bailey screamed. That's all Ben remembered. The rest went dark.

6

The rest of the night Ben stayed at the park, in his stand-by place when he needed out of the house under the pines. The leaves on all the trees around the park were coming in since spring was in the air and as he sat there on his sleeping bag, his backpack was full of a change of clothes and his school books. His face throbbed and hurt when he tried to open his mouth.

Through the pain, he was proud of himself. He stood up to Chris and even knocked him out cold in the kitchen. He would have laughed about that but it hurt to even half smile.

He cried as rain began to fall through the canopy of intertwined leaves and pine needles above. He wanted his old life back. He wanted his dad back. His mom. He wanted his old bedroom back with the Ghostbusters movie poster on his bedroom door. He wanted his friends. He wanted that basketball court in the middle of his old hometown where he used to shoot basketball. He wanted it all back.

7

Ben and Bobby sat in the guidance counselor's office. Bobby had just been apprised of the fight that Ben and Chris had gotten into a week ago and all the things that came from Chris' mouth. And he told him that he was staying his nights at the park under the protection of the trees full time, not just a day here and there. Bobby sat there after Ben was finished recounting everything with weepy eyes. He could see that the kid was devastated and had been since his mother moved that guy into the home. Ben's face had bruises to back up the story.

"Aunt Stacy any better? Think you could stay with her?"

Ben sat there and shook his head, "She's still sick. I don't want to bring any of this to her house. She has enough going on right now."

Bobby looked down at his desk and looked at his blotter. In two months he'd be finished there at Central High and there was nothing that he could do about it. You can't fight city hall. He was tenured, which meant he would be very difficult to fire unless he was just terrible at his job, had bad reviews, etc. But budget cuts? Now that was a different set of circumstances altogether. Glick would find a legal way around Bobby's tenure status because he did not like him. Bobby saw no way out and had been thinking about this a lot more recently since his mind wasn't running on no sleep and was free of the over usage of Ritalin and whiskey. He was thinking a little clearer these days.

"You need out of that violent home, Ben. There're no two ways about it, you know? I could call social services but then they would put you in a foster home after they investigated and found that you were right. And that…that could be bad, too. I've seen some horror stories in my life regarding some of those places."

Ben chewed on his fingernails, nervous. "I know. But I ain't got nowhere else to go; can't really just ask Abby's parents to take me in. They're strict, man. I mean they like me and I hang out there a lot, but I couldn't ask them something like that. They'd end up talking to my mom and there's no telling what she would say to them."

"What does Abby say about all this?" Bobby asked, leaning back in his chair.

"We just been going over it and over it trying to figure out what I can do. All I know is that I can't stay there. It's hard not having a place to live. I just never thought I'd be homeless at my age."

Bobby saw tears in Ben's eyes forming. At that moment, Bobby's mind sprung into action.

Bobby knew what the solution was. And ethically it wasn't the right thing to do, maybe, but it was the human thing to do. What he was thinking could potentially cost him his job if anyone found out; for certain it would make waves. He was losing his job anyways so what did it really matter? When you got nothing to lose, you can't lose anything, right? "I know a place that you can stay."

Ben stopped chewing his nails and looked at Bobby. "Where?"

"My house. I uh…I've been staying with April…Ms. Murray, so much that I'm hardly ever there these days. You can bunk out there until we figure all this out."

Ben considered this for a few moments, "Won't you get into trouble with the school system or something?"

Bobby laughed, "Kid, if you only knew," Bobby leaned forward in his desk chair and propped his elbows upon his desk, and took a long good look at Ben Medlen. "I'm out of a job at the end of the school year."

Ben took the news like a boxer who had just been sucker punched. This was the only adult in his life that was concerned about him, who had listened to him, and he was telling him there in that office that he was going away? "Why?"

"Grown-up stuff, don't worry about it."

"What are you going to do?" Ben asked, biting his nails nervously again.

Bobby sat looking at Ben and smiled, "I have no idea. I just won't be here anymore." The two sat there and soaked that idea in for a bit.

"I thought that I'd tell you. It seems like we've been through a lot in this office and I wanted you to know that my time here isn't long."

Ben wanted to cry because it was like he was losing his best friend in the whole world. The fact of the matter was that he looked up to Bobby. He was a father figure to him. He was the closest thing to what his very own dad was. On the B-side, Bobby felt the same about Ben. Ben was like a Freddy copy for him. He saw this kid in some ways as his own son. The two were transferring what they had lost, all that they had ever known, into one another. And that was fine by the both of them. It helped them get through the roughest patches of their lives up to this point.

"So, when I said that you can live in my house, it's a real offer. I'll give you the keys. I won't be there. April wants me to move in with her. The subject has come up several times lately. I've just been kinda reluctant to do it because of Freddy. But since I've started drawing down my addictions, I'm starting to see things a little clearer…head is a little better."

"What if people find out that I'm living there? Won't that ruin your chances of being a teacher or counselor somewhere else? Is it unethical?"

"I don't know. Is it any more unethical than cutting a counselor out of a school just because money is tight? Don't worry about me, kiddo. I'll be fine. Something will turn up. Besides, it's time I leave that spook house anyways. It's bought and paid for. Nice place to raise a family. Quiet for the most part. Plus, you don't need to stay in a house that is ready to implode. It's a good deal. You can't continue to sleep at the park and you can't stay home either. Just tell your mom that you're staying with friends from now on if she even asks. So, are you still planning on moving back to South Carolina after you graduate?"

Ben sat there and was trying to process all the information he had been given in that meeting that was winding down. "I think so, yeah."

"What's there? I guess what I'm asking is, what are you going back to?"

Ben thought about this question for a few minutes. Why was he going back? He had no family there. His friends had stopped calling him and he had virtually stopped communicating with them. He had made new friends here at the school; a girlfriend even. He had no home to go back to because a new family was now there making new memories. So why was he planning to go back? To visit old ghosts?

"I'm not sure now…I've been thinking about that a little bit lately. I don't know if there's anything to go back to." Ben replied, realizing for the first time since being in Tennessee that the notion and love affair he had about going back home was just out of memory itself. There was nothing there. He had left and it was as if he wasn't even there at all. No landmarks, no markers, no nothing. He did not have a home now that he thought about it. He was a nomad.

"Think about my offer. Let me know. You'll need to get a job this summer to cover the expenses you know? But I'll cover the utilities for a while. I just…I just worry about you, Freddy." Ben nodded knowing that Bobby was unaware that he had called him Freddy. The bell rang ending their meeting.

"That could get you in some hot water, you know?" Sam said over the phone. Bobby had called to get some advice from his best friend; another set of eyes on the situation. He already knew what Sam was going to tell him but he wanted to walk it around the room a bit to gain some perspective. He would talk to April later who would echo the same things that Sam had pointed out.

"Yeah, but I ain't got to worry about a job soon. Hell, I'm out after school is over."

"Forget school, this could get you in police trouble…like arrested maybe."

"I'm not even living in the house. He will be," Bobby said.

"It won't matter, dude. Look at it on the face of it: you got a minor living at your house without the permission of the parent."

"Man, his mom is a joke, and that guy she is around may end up hurting him bad one day or worse…maybe even kill him. He doesn't get out of that house soon something bad might happen that nobody can come back from and he can't live down at the park. Kid has no options."

"Why are you so intent on helping this kid this much?" Sam asked.

Bobby sat there on the phone. He knew why. "Because," Bobby started, "he reminds me of Freddy. He's lost so much…he's a good kid. He just needs a break is all."

"And you're okay with it if something blows up in your face over this? I mean, this type of stuff could get you investigated if the wrong people got wind of it. It doesn't look right, Bobby. I know that you are just trying to help…"

"I'm trying to do the right thing here! Why is that so hard for you to understand?!"

"I understand it!" Sam yelled over the phone. "But you can't help them all! You just can't! Just do me a favor and call Child Protective Services and let them handle this. Okay? I don't think you need to be involved anymore than you already are."

After a few moments of silence, Bobby said, "Maybe you're right. I wasn't seeing this clearly; got too invested in a kid this time." Bobby didn't mean that. He was still going to let Ben live in his house but he did not want to hear Sam making good sense anymore. Bobby knew that Sam was only looking out for him, of course he was. But there was Ben who reminded him of Freddy who needed a break. It did not matter what came next, Bobby had already dug in his heels and was going to help Ben.

Chapter 21

1

April

Ben had been living at Bobby's house for a few weeks. It was a nice house. Nice rooms. Nice lawn and a nice quiet street. The best part was that it was not his home where Chris and his mother spiraled out of control and it was not the park where sleep, at best, was thin. What else was crazy was that Abby lived just a half mile down on the same street where the Downey family lived. Abby knew that Freddy Downey was run over while playing Wiffle ball. She didn't know Freddy personally but had seen him out in the street with the other neighborhood kids playing from time to time. Freddy's tragic story was told to her by Abby's parents when it happened.

Walking over to her house was a breeze now and he nor Abby told her parents about his living arrangements. Neighbors had seen Ben coming and going from the house via the bus or walking to and from Abby's place. The neighbors were friendly and waved each time they saw the boy, not knowing if Bobby had a nephew or what. What they did know was that it wasn't Freddy Downey. Those same neighbors wondered where Bobby was. They had not seen him in a while. They wondered where he was. He was a nice guy; too bad about his son though, and later his marriage. Mrs. Wilson, the neighborhood busybody, kept her eye on Ben. She knew that Bobby, her neighbor for years and years and who she shared a property line with, had been intermittently in his house lately and wondered who the kid was that was staying over there. It was strange to her and she wanted to know more about who this kid was and his relation to Bobby.

Ben, for those first few days, stayed mostly in the living room, kitchen, and in the bedroom that was supposed to one day be for another Downey family member. Of course, it never happened that way. Ben felt like a guest in that house even though Bobby had given him the lay of the land and told him to make himself at home. Ben was a little uneasy about doing that. It wasn't his home. His home, his real home, was in South Carolina where a new family lived. Ben hoped that the new family never had to go through what he had to. He was for sure that the house would be great to them much like it was to him until the end came.

2

Bailey had no idea that her son had even stopped coming home or for that matter living there. She always assumed that he was upstairs in his bedroom doing whatever it was that Bens did. It wasn't until the second week of April that she went up to his bedroom and opened the door to find everything neatly in its place except for his game console. Had she looked in his closet she would've seen that all his clothes were gone. Everything else looked normal. So, still having some mom left in her, the parts that had not been stripped away by Chris' profound influences, she wondered why she had not seen her son in what felt to be a long time.

What was worse was she just now noticed she had not seen him. Weeks had passed since Ben silently moved away without Bailey knowing it. She left the room closing his bedroom door behind her, went downstairs, sat on the couch and leaned over the coffee table, and sorted some crushed-up pills that she had swiped from her pharmacy. Chris would be in later to help her snort up the rest. Bailey Medlen, the once proud wife and mother was on a road to nowhere with a man that was to be her doom.

3

Ben was gone and would never be back to the original Medlen home. Once he was gone, he never looked back at the house that his father had grown up in as he walked away from it. The house that his father had grown up in had become a place of the broken-hearted and broken-spirited. Ben shed no tears for leaving, not like he did when they left his home in South Carolina. His mother had allowed Chris to come in and ruin everything; the house and his mother most importantly. He hated that man and wished nothing but the worse for him.

Ben had Bobby's whole house to himself and his mother had no idea where he was staying. She didn't care. Not anymore. Ben did do something that he had been told by Bobby to do once he was settled.

"You need to at least call your mom and tell her that you're okay."

"Why?"

"Because I said so, that's why," Bobby replied.

"Man, she doesn't…"

"Listen!" Bobby snapped. "Just make the damn phone call, okay! You don't have to tell her much. Just say that you're staying with a friend from school and that it's a bad environment there at home. Just let her know you're safe." Ben gritted his teeth because he did not want to even have to speak to his mother, but he listened to Bobby.

So, the next day, Ben made the phone call to Bailey's work and told her exactly what Bobby said to say. They got into a heated exchange over the phone but then it cooled. She understood Ben's stance and took Chris' side ultimately and told him not to come back until he was ready to apologize to him. Ben laughed and said that would never happen in a million years. Bailey hung up on him and that was the last time he ever spoke to his mother. That April, Ben had entered into a new chapter in his life: his mother was gone.

4

All of Bobby's stuff was still in the house. It was like a museum of who the Downey family was. Pictures hung on the walls, trinkets like snow globes sitting there on the mantle that read COLORADO and MAINE written in black capital lettering, telling visitors where the globes had come from. The Colorado trip was back five years ago and the vacation to Maine was the summer before Freddy was mowed down. The dust had collected on the glass making it look dull. Ben took the MAINE snow globe, which had a log cabin inside of it, and gave it a hearty shake. The white flitter swirled around the water making it look like snow was falling but only for a few seconds. Then it was over.

Ben, over the days, began to explore the house a little more. He examined all the rooms and the one room where he dared went into was the bedroom of Freddy Downey. That door had been shut and was surprised that a warning had not been affixed to it making sure that trespassers beware of not entering this bedroom. Just being inside it gave Ben the willies.

Bobby did not speak a whole lot about his dead son. He gave out bits here and there throughout their meetings over the school year but nothing revealing; nothing major, no likes and dislikes, no hobbies. He told Ben some stories here and there about Freddy, but Ben still did not know the kid. Maybe that was on purpose, he didn't know.

Ben, standing in front of the bedroom door of what used to be Freddy's, pushed it open as it yawned all the way, lightly touching the wall inside. He took a few steps inside and was now in the museum that was the Freddy Downey Memorial. Everything was neat and in place. Everything was exactly as he had probably left it on that day he went out to play Wiffle ball and was killed in the street. It was sad really and even though he had never met Freddy Downey, he got a sense of who he was and maybe who he was going to be by just being in that room.
Ben went deeper inside the bedroom and looked around, looking out the window that overlooked the backyard. It was a typical kid's bedroom, not much more unlike his own back in South Carolina, but younger in decor than his. Ben walked out leaving the bedroom door wide open forgetting to close it. After Ben was out of sight, the door slowly began to close and shut silently.

Chapter 22

1

May

The month of April had been lost to the past and May was up for grabs. The school board took a vote, just like Pete Samples said they would. The budget cuts were approved however, the plan to push out those teachers that were close to retirement failed…for now. It was going to be revisited next year. The schools' guidance counselors were out, that was for sure. All of them were very upset about their ousting but what alternative did they have? Nothing. There were four teachers around the district retiring at the end of May and those spots would be available for the displaced counselors to interview for. That was a provision that was included by one of the eldest board members, Jeff Givens, who said he would vote in favor of the cuts if they could find teaching positions within the district for four of the displaced guidance counselors. Of course, not all of the cut guidance counselors would get one of those jobs, but it was better than not having any shot at all.

Bobby Downey knew where he stood with Glick. They didn't like each other. Nothing was ever really said nor did they have any words with each other. Pretty much Bobby stayed out of his way. Glick did the same. But you can always tell when someone doesn't like you. It's a vibe you catch. Bobby caught that vibe with Glick. He knew with only four teaching jobs up for grabs that he would not get one. Other guidance counselors within the district at their respective schools had been with the school system longer than him; some of them were even younger, too, which caused Bobby to be at a disadvantage.

When the news came down on how the board voted from Pete Samples, Bobby was not shocked at all. He and April discussed his next options over dinner at her house that following evening and inventoried all his viable options. He had some good ones, but most, if not all, were going to require him to move. One of the more probable choices that Bobby had was over at the Miracle Lake Rehabilitation Center. He had a friend there who was in administration that had told him that if he ever wanted a job there he could make it happen. Bobby told April that he was going to give him a ring and see what he could do for him. "My days in school are pretty much over with," Bobby told her.

2

Ben had been staying at his new home thanks to Bobby. He had been living there a little over a month now and although the days had turned to weeks, he was still a prisoner to the past. He had lost his father and his mother as well. He had not talked to her in a long time, not since that phone call that Bobby ordered him to make to let her know that he was okay. Eventually, Ben phoned his Aunt Stacy, who sounded better from the cancer treatments she was undergoing. He told her that he was doing fine, all things considered. "I'm staying at my high school guidance counselor's house while he lives with his girlfriend."

"Well you know you have a place here if you need it," his aunt told him.

"I know…just you being sick I didn't want to be a bother. You got a lot going on."

Ben told her all about what was going on at his old home, at least his version of it. Stacy had already heard the other version from Bailey and wondered if any of it was true. Stacy had told Ben that Bailey did not sound good the times she talked to her and that she seemed a lot different these days. Ben explained in detail what was really going on over there. Then Stacy had some things to tell Ben.

His mother, from what Stacy had reported, was not doing good at all. She had lost her job at the pharmacy. She was caught stealing pain pills out of the pharmacy and her license was going to be pulled. She could even be facing jail time but it was too early to tell. Ben surmised that there was no doubt that his mom was stealing them and giving them to Chris so he could sell them or abuse them. He had gotten Bailey hooked on them as well. Ben had seen evidence of their drug problem downstairs in the living room when he lived there.

Stacy proceeded to tell Ben that she tossed Bailey and Chris out of that house. When Ben asked where they were staying, Stacy had no idea; "Homeless, probably," Stacy replied with a hint of guilt in her voice. Ben wanted to cry for his mother and the utter destruction of their once-happy nuclear family, but the tears didn't come right then. They would gush later in the guest bedroom where Ben slept right across from Freddy Downey's room. He was sad for his mom and wanted to reach out to her. But he knew deep down that she was too far gone now and staying away was the only way he didn't get pulled down with her. Besides, she would never leave Chris. They had come that far together and it stood to reason that they would fall together. When it came to people like Chris and Bailey, everything was eventual.

3

Bobby's days as a guidance counselor, a sounding board for those in trouble, and a go-to person within the school for those wayward kids, were numbered. None of the kids in school knew that after the twenty-fifth, he would be out for good. That only gave him a couple of small weeks to make a difference in a few of the kids in the red folder; if there was a difference that could be made. Bobby hoped to save at least one maybe.

Bobby and Melaine Stubbs were walking outside the school, alone on the perimeter of the school on the inside of the fence talking about how things were going. They had not met at all in nearly a month because she was absent from school on the days they were supposed to meet. It was a bright sunny morning and it was going to be a hot one you could tell; that mid-morning stroll that Bobby and Melaine were on was an indication of that when Bobby could feel his clothes sticking to him already.

"School's almost over," Bobby remarked, hands in his pockets keeping in slow stride with Melaine.

"Yeah, and then I'm out of this hellhole."

"Not much longer, kiddo. Grades look better. Looks like graduation with no summer school. That's a win."

Melaine flicked her pretty blonde hair out of her eyes, "Yeah not bad I guess."

"Hear I'm leaving after the twenty-fifth?" Bobby asked.

"No I didn't," Melaine sounded genuinely concerned. "Another school?"

Bobby shook his head, "Nah, they're giving me the ol' push out. I won't have a job in a couple of weeks. Budget cut thing.”

“That’s total bullshit. You’re awesome.”

“Not awesome enough.”

The two of them walked in silence for about twenty yards before Melaine said, “Well who’s going to keep up with the risky people like me? Had it not been for you, I don’t know what I’d done. You’re the only one that really cared around here.”

Bobby smiled. I was able to break that shell of hers after all. “I don’t know. Me and Ms. Murray have talked about that for a bit. Probably nobody. She’ll still be here though. She’ll look after who she can, I guess. But our school district decided that having counselors was a waste of money. They think that mental health is just a fad, I reckon.”

“Fuck’em, Mr. Downey. What do they know, huh? You’re the only one in school that we can talk to. All of us know that. Most of these teachers in here don’t care about us.”

“I know,” Bobby said, knowing that Melanie’s strong statement was the truth. “I’ve been kinda down about it since I was told. I mean, I poured my life into here you know?”

“Well, you’re a smart guy. And kind, and super funny. You won’t have a problem finding some other school to take you I’m sure, right?”

“Well, we’ll see, I guess… might just get out of the school system entirely. I don’t know yet… So, what’s in front of you now? After graduation?”

Melaine laughed a laugh of not knowing what the future might be. Most kids her age had no idea. Does anyone? “No clue, really. I guess get a job and maybe go from there. See what my options are.”

“No college?”

Melaine shrugged, “Maybe, I don’t know. I just want to get out of school for a bit and then decide what I want to do.”

“You still thinking about being an attorney?”

Melaine considered this before she replied, "Yeah, I'd like to be. But I don't know if I'm smart enough for that. Plus the years of school it'd take…"

Bobby interrupted, "You're plenty smart enough, kiddo. You just got dealt some terrible cards in life. My advice?"

"Okay?"

"Take a year or two off from school. Get out and get some experience in life under your belt. Positive life experience, not that shit you've been getting. Okay? Surround yourself with good people and cut the bad ones out. We are products of our environments, you know?"

Melaine smiled as they walked. She swatted her blonde hair away from her eyes, "Will do."

Bobby and Melaine stopped walking as they found themselves back at the front of the school entrance, where they started. "Well, this is it for us, Ms. Stubbs."

Melaine looked at Bobby as if she was going to cry. She had been seeing Bobby for a long time and told him things that she had never told anyone, not even her court-appointed counselor. There was just something easy with Bobby, a safety. She had always looked forward to seeing him during those meetings because he did something that no adult ever did with her: listen. Just sit and listen and never judged her no matter what she confessed to him. And some of it was bad. "Thanks for everything," Melaine hugged him tightly.

Bobby smiled and hugged her tightly back. And when he pulled away, she had tears in her eyes. "Good luck out there, Melaine. Don't settle. Cut your own path." The two of them stood there looking at each other for a moment. Bobby felt himself about to tear up, "Now get out of here and get to class, you're bothering me."

Melaine smiled and laughed, "See you around, Mr. Downey." Bobby watched her walk up the sidewalk and back into the school building, disappearing through the metal gray double doors. Something about today's walk with Melaine made Bobby think that maybe she would turn out okay. Just maybe.

4

A week before school was dismissed for the summer, Ben Medlen was outside cutting the grass in the front yard on a quiet Wednesday afternoon after school. The back, which was way bigger than the front lawn, was already finished. Ben had no problem with cutting the grass. It reminded him of cutting the grass back home in South Carolina at his old house. Steve would cut the back and Ben would cut the front: a father and son team. After they were finished they would sit in lawn chairs in the side yard drinking Coca-Cola's and looking at the nice newly mown lawn under a shade tree. God, it looked so pretty after we'd get finished, Ben could remember.

Each time he was outside mowing the grass, Mrs. Wilson, Bobby's nearest neighbor with who he shared a property line with, was always out there watching the kid. She had never seen the boy before and being a busybody, a notorious one at that, she got on the phone with some of the other residents on Maple Lane and asked them who the kid was mowing Bobby's yard.

"Because he apparently is staying there, too. He looks sixteen. Why does Bobby have a sixteen-year-old staying with him? Don't you think that's strange, a middle-aged man hanging out with a kid? You think it's a nephew or something? You think it's got to do with his own son being killed out here? I think we need to know who this kid is. I've seen him walking around the neighborhood some. I think he goes and visits the Maddux family. I've seen him, at least I think it's him, with their daughter. I wonder if her parents know about him staying in Bobby's house? I wonder if the school knows?" Mrs. Wilson was about to ignite a huge powder keg in Bobby's life as if he needed anything else to deal with.

Ben had finished mowing and released the lever on the push mower and it shut off. He wiped his forehead. He was about to go inside and cool off when the old lady who lived beside him came walking to the fence in a big floppy hat calling to him. Ben walked over to the waist-high wooden picket fence and met her. "I don't think we've met before."

"I'm Ben Medlen," he held out his grass-stained hand for Mrs. Wilson to take. She did, reluctantly, and gave a nearly non-existent pump.

"Where's Bobby these days? I see him sometimes but not lately."

"He's been staying at Ms. Murray's house. She's a teacher at our school."

"Why for?"

Ben looked around and began to calculate that this woman was a fact checker and neighborhood watchdog. "Because they're going out together. Eventually, I think they're getting married."

"And you're…what? A chore boy?" she asked.

Ben was about to stop answering her questions and go inside. But he was a polite kid. "No. I'm staying here for a bit. Bobby gave me a place to stay. He told me to keep an eye on the place since he wasn't going to be staying here."

"And your parents are good with that arrangement?"

"My dad is dead and my mother is on drugs. It was a bad situation at home and Bobby said that I could stay here until I got things figured out."

Mrs. Wilson, who looked to be eighty-plus and full of trouble from the best that Ben could tell, said, "You know that Downey boy got ran over and killed out here, right? Did Bobby tell you about that?" Ben nodded. "I don't think they were watching him. They used to let him go out in the street all the time. I told everybody around here that one of these days one of them kids is going to get killed. And look at what happened. I was sitting on my back porch when it happened. I can still hear it sometimes, that car slamming into that tree. Gives me chills." Mrs. Wilson droned on.

"Yeah, well. I gotta go get something to drink. It's been nice talking to you." Yeah right, Ben thought as he turned to head back into the house. Mrs. Wilson watched him as he went and wondered how the school would take the news of a student living in a teacher's house.
She didn't think it was right; not at all. She was going to make a call to the school and get to the bottom of this. "Maybe they need to know what's going on with one of their teachers," she told her cats once back inside her house. She looked up the phone number of the school in the phone book.

Chapter 23

1

The last week of school had arrived. Bobby sat on the bleachers in the empty gym with Stu Grissom. He was the other red file kid that he was talking to. He had already checked off Melaine and something inside him told him that she was going to be okay: just maybe. Talking with Stu, Bobby had a more concrete feeling about his future. Stu had turned things around, slow as they were, he had turned them around all the same. So far, it appeared, he was two for two; batting a thousand. "So, the new foster parents working out okay?"

Stu, sitting beside Bobby on the bleachers looking out across the empty gym nodded and smiled, "Yeah. They're good people. I like them. I wished that I'd met them a long time ago though. Thanks for getting me out of that situation with the old ones."

"Well, you got them now. I'm just glad they came open. Most foster places, the good ones, are full and the ones that aren't are like the one you came from."

"Yeah, I love it there. I hear that you're out the door in a little while."

Bobby looked over at Stu, "How did you hear that?"

"Melaine might've said something."

 Bobby nodded, "Yeah it seems that way."

"What are you going to do with the rest of your life? Crazy that I get to ask you that, ain't it?" The both of them laughed.

"You know, me and Ms. Murray have been talking about that and I think I'm either going to finish up my doctorate and open my own practice or go work at this rehab clinic. I've got some options that we're talking about."

"Right on, man. You're good at this kind of stuff. Better than most I've dealt with."

"Thanks. Sometimes I wished that I could save all you guys."

"Not possible, bro. Some of us are too damaged by the time you see us."

"Yeah, I know. So…University of Tennessee, huh?"

"Yup. Moving to Knoxville in July and get settled in. I already got my paperwork and such taken care of. Loans are put through…going to be staying at a dorm. I'm all set. At least, I hope I am."

"Good. Glad to hear it."

"Listen, I couldn't have done all of this if not for you. Thanks, man." Stu held out his hand and the two shook. "Thanks for always listening to me talk."

"Glad I could help."

"I've never had an adult listen like you did. And just having that helped. A lot."

Bobby sat there on the bleachers and felt good about the red file folder for the first time in his career. "It was my pleasure, Stu. Still interested in the FBI?"

Stu smiled and shook his head, "Nah. Who wants to work for the fed?" They both laughed. "I was thinking about counseling. I want to be like you and help kids like me. Pay it forward."

Bobby's heart warmed. Stu was going to be okay.

2

Bobby was walking to his office from his meeting with Stu Grissom when over the intercom Glick got everyone's attention: "Mr. Downey, come to the office, please. Mr. Downey, to the office please." It was the rough Southern voice of Glick. Not to worry, he and Glick wouldn't have to see each other not much longer. Soon he would pack up his office in a few boxes and move along into the vast unknown like he was never there. But there was one thing that was a reassuring constant in his life, something positive: that was April Murray, the woman he was going to ask to marry later that night. He had it planned out.

They were going star gazing, astrology was a hobby of April's and there was a place for doing such things out on the outskirts of Claxton that everyone knew called Big Hill; no houses or street lights for miles and miles. "Light pollution," April called it. People could see the stars and the constellations without any trouble at all. It was her favorite place in the world and it had become Bobby's as well. He was going to propose to her at Big Hill later on.

But first, he had to see what in the hell Glick wanted. Probably to rub salt in the wound, Bobby thought. Maybe he wanted to dismiss him early. Either way was fine with Bobby as the gravity of knowing that he was walking the halls of Central High for the final times hit him and hit him hard. So much in fact that he stopped and stood there for a moment and took it all in: the low distant chatter or people; the smell of whatever the custodians used to mop and wax the halls with; the cool air conditioning; the flyers that hung on the walls; the announcements. He realized walking back from the gym after talking with Stu he was going to miss everything.

3

Bobby walked into Glick's office and there he was sitting behind his desk with a look of grimness about him. Standing beside his desk was a man in a cheap black suit. "Could you take a seat, Mr. Downey? Detective Lang has some questions for you," Mr. Glick directed in his Southern voice.

Bobby slowly sat down and looked at Glick and to this detective Lang. "What's going on?"

"Mr. Downey, we got a call about you having a minor that goes to this school staying at your house. Know anything about that?"

"Yeah." Bobby was stunned, his mind was not working. It was as if all thoughts had mired in the mud. "Is that against the law or something?"

"Well, it is if there's a relationship there," Det. Lang replied.
Bobby looked at Glick who did not look like he was happy about this turn of events. He almost looked as horrified as Bobby felt. Was that even possible?

"You mean like a sexual relationship?" Bobby felt awful even saying it out loud. That was the craziest thing by far he had ever said in his life.

"Well, that's what we need to discuss. There's also the indication that there's been another student coming to your house, a sixteen-year-old girl that goes to this school as well…any truth to that?" Detective Lang asked.

Bobby was trying to answer the detective's question but his mind was still stuck in the mud. This was all coming at him from out of nowhere. He had no idea what was going on or how this even started. It honestly felt as if he was having one of those nightmares. But this wasn't Maple Lane and he wasn't watching his son get mowed down playing Wiffle ball.

"No. Of course not."

"I'd like for you to come down to the station for some more questions regarding this, Mr. Downey. Would that be all right? That way we can maybe get to the bottom of this thing."

"Am I under arrest or something?" Bobby asked bewildered.

"Not right now. We just want to get to the bottom of this thing," Detective Lang said.

Bobby nodded and rose to his feet, "Can I drive myself?"

"You can ride in the back of my car. Again, you're not under arrest. I just want to ask some more questions is all and see if we can clear all this up." Bobby looked at Glick and saw something that he'd never seen in the man's eyes before: fear. What was he afraid of? Afraid of one of his own having been sexually active with students in his school?

A bewildered Bobby Downey and the thick older detective walked out of the office and down the halls. Kids were walking every which a way and Bobby and the detective were trying their best to weave through the traffic. They made it outside and to his car which was parked directly out front across from the heavy gray metal double doors where the buses usually lined up for the day. Detective Lang opened the passenger-side back door and invited Bobby in. He got inside and the door slammed shut. A few students saw what was going on but really didn't think much about it.

Chapter 24

1

Sitting in a medium-sized room where Bobby guessed interrogations were performed, he and Detective Lang sat at a table across from each other. They had been in this room for what Bobby could make out for forty minutes, maybe longer. The detective was jotting stuff down that Bobby had told him, and asked his questions, some of them outlandish. "So nothing going on out of the ordinary, Mr. Downey?"

"No, like I told you, Ben Medlen is staying at my house because his mother is on drugs and her boyfriend has been picking fights with him. I've been staying at April Murray's house because I plan on marrying her; asking her tonight, matter of fact. And since I don't live there anymore, I just thought it was a good idea for Ben to have a safe place to stay until he can get things figured out. He spoke to his aunt about it and told her what the situation was all around."

"This isn't normal practice for teachers is it?" Det. Lang asked again, going back in circles with his questions. Bobby had noticed that he was good at his job, asking the same questions in different wordings, hoping to trip Bobby up. It was his job. But the truth was the truth and Bobby answered them, all the same, each time.

"I'm not a teacher. Like I said earlier, I'm a counselor at the school… guidance counselor. And no, it's not normal practice for teachers to give a house to a kid, but…I'm trying to help him through all of this. Me and April both are. He came to Tennessee because his mother moved him here after his dad died last year. He's been a fish out of water ever since."

"And you've been what…a trusted adult friend?"

Bobby knew where the detective was trying to drive the narrative, "Someone who is professionally trained to help. He has no one out there. For God's sake, he was sleeping at the park some nights because that guy his mother is with tuned him up a couple of times. You ought to be looking into that."

"What about this young girl? There's been an accusation that there's been a young girl staying with you at the house with Ben."

"I have no idea where you got that one. I don't have a young girl living there or visiting there to my knowledge, detective. You can ask Ben if his girlfriend, Abby, has been coming there, but I don't know anything about it because I don't live there. I stay with April. You can ask her if you want."

"So you don't know what's going on there then? Would have no clue what Ben might be up to?" he scribbled on his legal pad, flipping the page over to write on a new sheet of yellow-blue lined paper.

"No. Ben has a girlfriend named Abby Maddux. She lives down the street I think; possible that she has been coming over to hang out with him. I don't know. I'm never there."

"Possible, I guess. So where do you think all this came from? I mean, things like this don't just come out of thin air do they?"

"No, they don't. But sometimes people lie and make assumptions without knowing what's really going on. Some people just like to watch the world burn," Bobby said.

"They do," Detective Lang replied, leaning back in his chair and tossing the ink pen down onto the pad. "I want you to know that I think you're legit. Okay? I do. We're going to speak with Ben as well later on, and then follow up with this girl and her parents."

"Please do, because I'm not there at that house anymore. I moved in with April a while back. Talk to her. It's gotten hard to stay at that house since my son was killed out in the middle of the street last year. I just…it was time to get away from there."

Detective Lang nodded, "I know all about that one. Sorry about your loss."

"Yeah. Me, too."

"Well, I think you check out, Mr. Downey. I do. I think this is a big misunderstanding is all. That's between you and me. Something like this involving a person at the school and a student we have to investigate it, you know? The school will, too, I'd imagine. But you should've probably gotten with social services if his house was this bad."

"Probably so. My fault on that one. But you also know how the system is, too. I see those kids every day that the system fails. I didn't want it to fail Ben. He's been through enough as is."

Det. Lang nodded his head in agreement, "See it every time. Sometimes they don't pull these kids out until it's too late and we're called out to clean up the mess. I've seen more than I want to, that's for sure."

"Look, I was just helping Ben out of a tough situation. He doesn't have a mom anymore because she's on drugs and she's with some guy who's on them, too. His aunt kicked them out of that house and now who knows where they're at. Ben doesn't need to be in that situation. I'll be his foster parent or whatever I need to do to make sure he's okay until he's eighteen and out of school. At this point, he's my ward."

Detective Lang sat there and looked at Bobby for a moment and was convinced even more, "Let's get you back."

2

Detective Lang had Glick call Ben Medlen to the principal's office. And when he entered, he was like Bobby, bewildered, his mind stuck in the mud at Detective Lang's questions. But his mind was better at rebounding than Bobby's. Ben settled in the chair across from Glick's desk, an office he'd never been in before, and answered the detective's questions. Ben was sure that it had to be that old woman, that old crow of a woman, who had started this inferno of accusations and aspersions about Bobby. He was offended and angry that someone could be so cruel and calculating.

"So the relationship that you and Mr. Downey have is just a friendship or…"

"He's my counselor, sir. My dad died last year and my mother moved us up here. I started seeing Mr. Downey and we meet in his office for a counseling session once a week. Sometimes when I need to talk…he always makes time; been doing that for a while now. He's helped me a bunch."

"And what about this house? That's crazy that a counselor just up and gives a kid a house to stay in, isn't it?" Detective Lang asked. He was trying to punch holes in the story, just to make sure that his gut feeling about this was true about Bobby. He didn't believe that there was anything out of the ordinary going on here. But he still wanted to explore everything just to make sure, just to make it a true inquiry.

"Yeah, he just told me to stay there because he wasn't living in it anymore because he and Ms. Murray, a teacher here, are living together at her house. Mom's gotten into drugs really bad, especially when she met this Chris guy. It just got bad living there and since I don't have anyone to help, I was staying at the park at night to sleep. My aunt…she's been sick so I didn't ask her to stay there. She doesn't need to worry about me. I'd spent the days over at Abby's house, that's my girlfriend. I told Mr. Downey what was going on and he offered me his house. He said that he would pay for the lights and water and such but I needed to look for a job and take over those duties; which I am this summer. This gives me a safe place to stay until I figure out what's next after I graduate next year," Ben explained, trying to keep his nerves down.

"So, Mr. Downey has never asked for any sexual favors or…"

"Hell no!" Ben was sickened and offended by this. "Mr. Downey is an honest man…a good man. He's like a dad to me. My dad was like Mr. Downey. I think that's why I gravitate so much toward him."

"Has your girlfriend ever come over to visit you while Mr. Downey was at the house?"

"No. Abby sneaks out of her house when her parents go to bed. We hang out and make out on the couch in the living room. Just typical teenage stuff, you know? Mr. Downey would probably kill me if he knew that Abby was coming over some nights…her parents too."

Detective Lang, who was sitting on the corner of Glick's desk, legs dangling off the edge, looked at the principal and then back at Ben, "Thanks, Ben. I appreciate you answering my questions. If I have anything else I'll contact you."

"Is Mr. Downey in some kind of trouble? Because I didn't mean to get him into anything. He was just trying to help me out. I got nowhere else to really go. Aunt Stacy has got cancer and I don't want to go there and watch her die…"

"I think it's going to be fine, son," Det. Lang replied. Ben smiled halfheartedly and got up from the chair and walked out of the office closing the door behind him.

"You think it's going to be fine or do I have a scandal at my school?" Glick asked.

Detective Lang got up off the desk and stood up, "I think everything just got blown out of proportion by someone that didn't have their facts straight. What do you think of Bobby Downey?"

Glick leaned back in his chair and adjusted his glasses on his face. "Well, he seems like a good fella. We don't jive really, but maybe that's more me than him. People around here like him an awful lot. I kinda do, too, I reckon…if I'm being honest."

"Why is that more you than him?"

Glick paused for a brief moment before he answered. He was in thought. "Because he's the type of fella that I always wanted to be. I just ain't got what he's got in here," Mr. Glick said, patting his chest.

Detective Lang clicked his tongue and rapped on his desk twice, "Well, I'm out of your hair for the day. I'm going to file all of this away and go home. There's nothing here. Worse thing is that him being a counselor he should have known the protocols and called social services and let them investigate. But that's another conversation since the mom is MIA. I'll come back and talk with Abby Maddux. But I think everyone is fine. Sleep well, Mr. Glick." Detective Lang wished the principal well and left, leaving Glick to sit there and think about things for a bit.

He leaned up at his desk and took a pen out of his shirt pocket and wrote himself a note on a small yellow Post-It note, pasting it on his computer so he could see it first thing tomorrow morning. He got up and left his office for the day, shutting off the light and closing the door.

The note that he scribbled himself was a reminder of something he was going to do. A deed.

3

After school, Bobby and April sat at Pete's Burgers, a local dive where it had a feel of the 1950s about it. Bobby and April sat in a booth, the same booth every time that they came as they were regulars there. They didn't even have to order and the waitress, Flo, never bothered because it was always two cheeseburgers, fries, and two chocolate shakes. They came once a week.

Bobby had not told April about what happened until school was out. When he told her she was shocked and then angry. He had to calm her down. By the time she was calm, she had eaten all of her burger and wasn't even aware that she had. Bobby just watched her go. "Is everything going to be okay?" April eventually asked.

Bobby nodded, "Yeah I think so. The worst thing that I did was probably not get child protective services involved. But oh well, I can live with that. But I'm good. It's not like I got to worry about losing my job."

"Who do you think even said anything about Ben living there?"

"Probably Mrs. Wilson to be honest. She's always in people's business there in that neighborhood. I remember she got into Dana's face before she left telling her that if we were watching Freddy he'd be alive. I had to hold Dana back from hitting her. She's just a trouble-making old bitch is all."

Bobby changed the subject and asked if they were still on for the Big Hill tonight. April smiled and said of course they were. He was going to ask her to marry him but of course, she was totally unaware of his intentions. He got butterflies just thinking about it sitting there in that booth. He had the ring bought a few weeks ago and was thinking of ways to ask her. And then she asked if he wanted to go stargazing. The ring was at home in his top dresser drawer for safekeeping. He thought about keeping it at her house but was afraid that he would lose it or that she would find it. No chance of that happening there at his old house. He just had to swing by before they left for Big Hill and grab it.

4

Ben had called Bobby when they arrived at April's house. They compared notes and discussed their interviews with the detective. They had all agreed, April included as well as Abby later on to Ben, that someone just wanted to cause trouble. Trouble was indeed caused, but thankfully the detective in charge of handling the investigation, which wasn't much of one, believed all those involved. There was no evidence telling him otherwise. Case closed. Ben told Bobby about Mrs. Wilson asking questions at the fence the other day and Bobby knew about her reputation for sticking her nose in other people's business. He had dealt with her in the past and did not like the old woman much at all. He once told Dana that the best thing that Mrs. Wilson could ever do in her wretched life was to die a slow death.

When Freddy was killed, Mrs. Wilson had the audacity to tell Bobby and Dana one day out in their yard that they should have been watching their kid because if they had he would not have been run over. She went on to say that they were terrible parents who should be brought up on child neglect charges. Bobby gave her a good cussing and Dana tried to climb over the fence to whack her a good one. But Mrs. Wilson escaped back to her lawn and her house. That was the last time that Bobby had ever talked to the old woman. She knew to steer clear of him.

5

The night was closing in on the town of Claxton. Inside the Neon Tiger, a local tavern, several drinkers sat at the bar mostly alone thinking to themselves and staring down at their drinks. It was run by Miles Jackson, a tough ex-biker from the rough and tumble seventies. That evening, Miles was sitting at the end of the bar per usual reading Field and Stream while the Atlanta Braves played on TV. It was a quiet evening in the bar, just the way Miles liked it.

Wes Jenkins, a regular at the Neon Tiger, sat smoking a cigarette drinking at the bar watching the baseball game. He had been talking to anyone sitting close to him about his job. Bitching about it was more like it. Wes was a bulldozer operator with Smith Excavating there in Claxton and had been with the company, or outfit which Wes frequently called them, for nearly fifteen years. "They don't pay me worth a damn, you know it?" Wes would always say in there when he got a few in him to anybody that would listen to him. He was not a mean drinker. Miles never had any problems out of him at all. He was the ninety-nine percent that behaved while in there. Wes never got loud, never put a quarter in the juke and danced. He just talked about work, pussy, sports, and politics.

Before the Braves game went into the fourth inning, Wes was feeling more tired than usual. It was due to the overtime that he was putting in on the bulldozer. They had been hired to grade off the entire sixty acres of McAllister Farm for a planned subdivision. With the days being longer, that meant the work hours were longer, too. It was not much of a stretch for Wes and the rest of the operators to clock in with twelve to fifteen-hour days. Wes had not been sleeping much and was feeling that tiredness slam him pretty good all of the sudden. Before he knew it he felt his eyes get heavy and all he wanted to do was just rest them for a few minutes. He thought about just resting his eyes in the bar for a bit; just catch a few winks.

Deciding that he had better get home, Wes slowly got off his stool and stood there weaving a bit. He wasn't drunk, just three beers and a half of another one; far less than his usual on Friday nights when he could drink a twelve-pack and have to be taken home. Miles always made sure those he felt had too much got home safely. Wes was just more relaxed than usual and tired…God, he was so tired.

"You need a ride, Wes?" Miles asked, noticing his demeanor.

"Nah, I'm good Miles. Nothing that a good night's sleep can't fix. Just fucking wore out is all. I'll see you later."

He got himself straightened up, tipped a wave to Miles who tipped a wave back, and across the bar he walked out of the door. It was the last time that anyone would ever see Wes alive. When the news came the next day, Miles told people that Wes did not leave the bar drunk that night. "I know when my patrons are plastered, especially Wes. He just seemed more tired than usual."

6

As Wes sat in his black Pontiac Firebird at the Neon Tiger, trying to stay awake and wondering if he should just take a quick nap, Bobby Downy arrived at his old house that evening. He walked across the lawn, up the walkway, and up the front porch he went. He opened the front door and saw Ben sitting there in the living room watching the same Braves game that was on at the Neon Tiger.

"You always keep my door unlocked? I could've been a burglar or something.”

“Yeah, but you weren’t,” Ben replied in that snarky playful tone he adopted from Bobby.
Bobby walked over and sat down in a chair, “You okay?”

Ben looked around confused, “Yeah, I guess so. What do you mean?”

“With the detective stuff?” Bobby replied.

“Yeah, totally. Just someone trying to start trouble is all. Abby’s mom and dad are pretty upset though.”

Bobby nodded, “As well I thought they would be.”

“I don’t think she’ll be allowed back over here for a bit. Or me over there for a while.”

“Understandable. I’d probably be the same way. In fact, I know I would. Punishment fits the crime.”

“They called that detective that talked to all of us and he told them there was nothing there. I think her dad wants to talk to you though,” Ben said.

“I’m sure. But I’ll go over there tomorrow. I’ll call over there first thing in the morning and ask to speak to them in person; right thing to do.”

“So what brings you by tonight?”

Bobby looked around his living room in shock at Ben’s question, “I still own this place.”

“I know that, but why are you here? You hardly ever come here.”

“I have to get something.” Bobby got up from his chair and went to his bedroom. A few minutes later, he reappeared with something in his hand. It was a small white box. “Got the ring awhile back…going to ask her to marry me up on Big Hill tonight.”

Ben took the ring box and opened it to inspect the diamond. It glistened in the lights of the living room. “That’s awesome! Good going man! I guess this'll do," he said, handing it back to Bobby.

"It'll have to. Set me back a couple of grand."

"So, you're doing it tonight, huh?"

"Yup. I'm leaving here and going over to her house. She wants to take me stargazing and then when the moment is right, I'm going to pop the question."

"Congrats, man. I'm really happy for you," Ben said from his seat on the couch looking up at Bobby.

"Well, I'm outta here. Lock up behind me. I'll be by tomorrow after I go see Abby's parents. Have a good night."

Ben tipped a wave, "Good luck!" Bobby walked out of the house and closed the front door for the very last time. It was the last time Ben would see Bobby Downey alive.

7

Bobby was driving in the direction of April's house that evening. Darkness was all around. The streetlights were on in straight-line patterns lighting the way for the nighttime travelers. He was about halfway to April's house when something came to his mind. He was actually going to ask April to marry him. The mere thought of that caused him to smile as he slowed to stop at a red light at the intersection of Elm and Hurst. The traffic light at the intersection was notorious for its long red light holds. So much so, that many complaints were made at many town hall meetings. Nothing was ever settled. The city's powers that be didn't think it was really worth their time to adjust the red light's hold time. Sometimes at night when it wasn't busy, people were known to just look around the intersection, see that it was clear, and drive on through the light. It happened more in the wee hours of the morning than it did around nine o'clock as Bobby sat there thinking about April.

8

Wes Jenkins was heading home and coming down the hill from the Neon Tiger. He had the window down so the air could keep him awake. It

272

worked somewhat. He tried like hell to keep his eyes open while driving. Sometimes his eyelids fell and he snapped them quickly back open as he felt his car drift to the right side. He turned his radio on. CCR's, "Have You Ever Seen The Rain", had just started. It was one of Wes' favorite songs. It reminded him of his youth. Suddenly, he felt energetic again. He was only three miles from home. "Three miles ain't nothing, Wes," he told himself. As he came down the hill from Elm Street, Wes could see the intersection at Elm and Hurst. He hated that red light because it always held cars for way too long. He knew that if he got caught by the red light his eyes might fall again and may not open. Coming down the hill he saw the green light. As he got closer, Wes prepared himself to get past the light even if it changed to red.

9

The traffic light finally turned over to green after keeping Bobby captive for at least three minutes. Bobby pressed the gas and snuck a quick peek at his passenger's seat. In it sat the white ring box. He got butterflies as he looked at it as he began to cross the intersection. He never saw what hit him. It happened so fast. His neck snapped to the left side violently, hitting the driver's side window and cracking it into a huge spider web. Bobby was dead before his car was flung into the bait and tackle shop that stood on the corner of the intersection.

10

Having a feeling that he was going to get caught by the light, Wes stepped on the gas a little harder. Doing sixty down the hill was way too fast, especially driving towards an intersection that had seen its share of accidents over the decades. The traffic light flipped to yellow. Instead of slowing down, Wes sped up even more. "Ain't going to catch me!" He snuck a peak in his rearview mirror to make sure there were no cops around to witness his running of the red light.

Just then, the yellow turned to red. "Too bad." Wes came off the hill flying and was not going to be stopped by some long-ass red light. He was way too tired to sit and didn't think his eyes would stay open just idling at an intersection. He had momentum in that speeding car and it was keeping his eyes open; home was not that far away.

Before he could do anything about it, Bobby's car came into view as it came across the intersection getting the green to go on his side. Wes did not have enough reaction time to hit the brakes. His tiredness had altered his reaction time. He didn't have time to scream when the front of his black Firebird T-boned Bobby Downey's driver's side. The sheer force of the hit sent Bobby's car in a heap of metal and plastic across the intersection and into a small bait and tackle building.

Wes' car managed to crash into a tree that had stood for decades on the Elm side of the intersection some thirty feet away. Wes, just like the man inside the car he hit, died instantly when the front of his car bounced off Bobby's car and somehow ran hood-first into the maple at what troopers estimated around forty, after the initial hit on Bobby's car. Wes, not wearing a seatbelt, was slung through the windshield, headfirst into the tree.

11

Inside Glick's office, the yellow Post-It note that was affixed to his computer, a reminder of what to do the following morning, was left stuck there as news came down about Bobby Downey's death. Glick didn't make it into his office that next day. He was too busy with students and faculty, talking about the tragedy of one of their own. On that piece of sticky, yellow paper square were the words scribbled in ink: Call Franklin about recommending Bobby Downey for a teaching position for next year. Too good to lose.

Author's Note

This story was one of the more emotional ones that I had ever written in my career. The themes are of death and loss; how we process it all when it comes knocking on our doors. These themes are something that I think we've all had to deal with at some point or another in our lives. If you haven't yet, then you are one of the lucky ones. I think stories where the characters are just like us, dealing with things we've had to face make the reader, and in this case, the author, closer to the characters in a book. I certainly grew closer to Bobby and Ben in this story over the time I wrote it. I felt their struggles and pains. Hopefully, you did as well, provided that I did my job correctly.

There's also another theme within the story that gets lost: hope. Hope is ever-present, and when all is lost, what else is there but hope? Hope is the weapon that we use against the pain and loss, a bright light in the darkness. Hope is the notion that we cling to that things will get better. Hope, as some say, is eternal. When I was writing this novel, even though I knew how it was going to go and eventually end, I found myself rooting for Bobby and Ben, hoping they would find their own personal hope; that maybe they could overcome their personal losses and find something to run to, something that would rebuild them, not as they once was, but as something else, something better perhaps.

Maple Lane is my attempt to say that sometimes life can be really good, not a cloud in the sky, everything is aces, and then right when you least expect it, something comes and changes everything, turning your once safe and beautiful world upside down fundamentally. Maple Lane asks, how do you deal with the losses you take? How do you keep going when there's nothing left? Who do we put our backs up against when everything we've ever known is gone? More importantly, how do we find the courage to keep living? To smile? To laugh like we once did?

Death and change are two agents that will never go away. But another agent is working on the other side…hope. Never lose it because once you do, the darkness will consume you.

I would like to thank you, the reader, for coming with me once again. We've got more roads to travel, you and I.

See you in time!

—Matthew McConkey, February 15th, 2023

THE AUTHOR

Maple Lane is Matthew McConkey's second published novel. He is also the author of two additional novels, *Summerland* and *Home Again*, and two collections of short fiction, *Everything Fades in Time* and *Scarecrows and Shadows*. He lives in Tennessee.